I0730516

RYANN FLETCHER

Clocktower Elegy

Copyright © 2025 by Ryann Fletcher

All rights reserved. No part of this publication may be reproduced, stored or transmitted in any form or by any means, electronic, mechanical, photocopying, recording, scanning, or otherwise without written permission from the publisher. It is illegal to copy this book, post it to a website, or distribute it by any other means without permission.

This novel is entirely a work of fiction. The names, characters and incidents portrayed in it are the work of the author's imagination. Any resemblance to actual persons, living or dead, events or localities is entirely coincidental.

Original cover art by Indy @Strooooble

First edition

ISBN: 978-1-7393585-7-0

*This book was professionally typeset on Reedsy.
Find out more at reedsy.com*

*To every woman who was forced to get revenge when being nice
didn't work:*

may this book be your alibi.

Contents

Chapter One

Bright sunlight, humid and oppressive, beat down through the windows of a house on the upper west side, drawing a bead of sweat from her forehead that she magnanimously allowed to slide over sharp cheekbones, falling to drip down onto her collar. Summer in Verdance had arrived, and while heat was a vacation from the freezing temperatures of winter, in the city, it was out of the icebox, into the frying pan.

"Ginnie?" Arthur prompted, his stare boring into her the same way it had for the past six shadows-damned months. "Did you hear what I just said?"

"Yeah," Virginia lied, popping the joints in her fingers just to feel the light pain of relief. "Homicide."

"I never said it was homicide. We haven't confirmed either way." He leaned in closer, so much so that she had to resist the overwhelming urge to jerk away from him. "Did you know that it's homicide because of your seeing?" he whispered.

She took three steps backwards, nearly colliding with the coroner. "Sorry," she muttered, straightening to adjust the twisted strap of her left suspender. "No, Arthur, that's not why. I have eyes, don't I? It's obvious that he didn't do this himself. There's no way that distributor overdosed. He'd know what human limits were better than anyone, even with this new potent stuff cropping up in the city."

"That was my thought, too." Arthur waved several detectives into the room, watching as they observed the body. Approximately six-foot-one, broad shouldered, built like a brick shithouse, it was Merv Knuckles, a known member of the Kraken crew who'd worked his way up from being an enforcer. He was on his back, purple-tinged eyes wide as he stared up at the ceiling, the bleached bed sheets pulled up to his shoulders and topped with a light grey feather quilt. "If we can't get a lid on this, the feds are going to be all over it." He turned, pointing the photographer towards one of the evidence flags. "They're looking for any reason to get overly involved with our cases. That new anti-terrorism Nether law means they have all kinds of jurisdictional seniority over the VCPD that they didn't before."

"I'm not with the VCPD, so I fail to see how this is my problem," Virginia retorted. She tilted her head, examining the scene. "No signs of forced entry," she said. "No signs of a struggle, either."

"Everything points to an accidental overdose, Ginnie," he replied. "Except for the fact that he would have known."

"Suicide?" she asked. "Although, I can't imagine kicking my own bucket if I was running half the city's Nether rings, and living in a place as nice as this one." She gently tugged the blanket down after the photographer had finished, turning over the victim's hand. "No visible defensive wounds, as far as I can see." She pulled it down further, grimacing. "Naked."

Arthur picked at the badge on his arm, the tiny metallic clasps inaudible against the din of the investigation. "I need your help." He sighed and pulled out his notebook, the cover bent and worn at the edges.

"Just say whatever it is you have to say, Arthur, I don't have all shadows-damned day." Virginia folded the blanket down over the bed sheet, leaving the corpse for the coroner. "Out with it, Dixon."

"You haven't been at headquarters much recently."

"And?"

He watched her, moving aside for the additional detectives to exit. "And as a consultant, I would have thought you would consult more." He straightened after they left, the weight of his position already taking a toll in the lightly greying five o'clock shadow that fanned out across his jawline. "Especially after learning what you did at that compound." He turned, staring, the same way he'd been staring at her for months, as if he expected her to look any different than she always had.

Virginia's jaw clamped, her teeth grinding with the indecision. She hadn't told Arthur that she'd been unable to access those abilities again after the raid, and she didn't want to, either. She didn't want to discuss it at all. "I've been busy with clients."

"More missing mythics? Because you know, they really should be reported to the VCPD for—"

"No," she interrupted. "Minor financial crimes. An inheritance, some fraud, a huckster here or there. You know, the kind of stuff the VCPD can't be bothered with."

"That hardly sounds like a full schedule, Ginnie," he replied. "And if I know you, then those cases aren't scratching that itch."

"It's better than almost dying twice in ten days," she shot

back. He was right, but she'd never admit it. Virginia dusted along the metal bed frame, hoping for usable prints, but finding none. "It's perfectly respectable work."

"I just thought you'd be reaching for more challenging cases." Arthur was testing her, and they both knew it. Instead of pushing further, he gestured towards the snag in the carpet amid flattened fibers. "What do you think?" he asked.

"I think that no matter what you find here, the feds are going to stick their paws into it." Virginia pushed past the door and down the steps, Arthur in close, irritating pursuit. She was hunting for any sign that the victim had fought back. "Whoever dragged him up the stairs, it was someone strong."

He nodded, still watching. "Nothing for sure?"

"He was probably dead already," she replied. "Either that, or unconscious. It's plausible, given how much Nether must have been in his system." Virginia inspected three nearly invisible droplets gathered on the stairs, likely old stains. They definitely weren't blood. "Assuming it's a crew hit, do you have any leads?"

"None," he replied, shaking his head. "None of the usual suspects are talking."

"No connections?"

"None that we can find." Arthur stood just over her shoulder, examining the droplets. "But I thought that you might see something that we hadn't."

Virginia turned, brushing him off. "You don't have to hover, you know."

"It would just be very advantageous if we—"

"There's that word again, *we*." She ducked under his arm and moved several framed pieces of artwork aside, looking for a hidden safe. "There is no *we*." She rifled through the drawer before slamming it closed again. "No hidden valuables. Pity."

"It would just go into evidence, anyway."

"Obviously, Arthur." She allowed herself a private roll of her eyes before she turned back to face him. "Could there have been any witnesses? Neighbors, maybe? Or a gardener?"

"I asked around, but nothing. The bedroom window is blocked by the scaffolding of the neighbor building an extension next door. Shouldn't have been allowed, but Eugenia Patten on the council signed off on it." Arthur followed her into the back room, leaning against the door frame with one shoulder. "It's a shame we couldn't put her away for taking all those back-hander bribes."

"She's got enough lawyers to get out of anything," Virginia retorted. She was growing tired of his shadow, preferring to work alone given the opportunity. She reached out, brushing her fingertips against a desk drawer's handle, but nothing came. "I'm not surprised you didn't nab her."

"Do you sense anything?" he asked.

"I don't know, do *you*?" she shot back. "You're the sheriff, maybe you could deduce something for once."

"And you're a—" he stopped himself, moving closer in the room and reducing his voice to a whisper. "A seer, Ginnie."

"It doesn't work like that." She avoided him again, crossing the corridor into the kitchen. The marble countertops were spotless, no doubt scrubbed by an underpaid cleaner. "Sends a message, doesn't it? Killing him at home?"

"I was ruminating on that, too."

"Turf war?" Virginia asked, leaning against the smooth, unmarred surface. "Competitor moving into the area?"

"Not impossible," Arthur agreed. "It would be helpful to get a clearer reading."

"It's difficult when you're following me around." She dodged him again, circling the wood island in the center of the kitchen to prod at several untouched, sharpened kitchen knives. "If I could just call it up like that, I would."

"Can't you?" he asked.

Virginia barely repressed a sigh and a snide remark. "Obviously not. If I could, don't you think I would have known a little sooner?"

He peered out the kitchen door, waving an officer down the corridor towards the back entrance. "Have you used it at all since the raid?"

The question hung in the air thicker than the encroaching scent of death and decay. "I have to get to an appointment," she replied, choosing to ignore it entirely. "I'm already running late and midday traffic downtown is a shadows-damned nightmare."

"Ginnie."

"Arthur."

He hesitated, running a hand over his bald head, shiny with the glisten of sweat. "You haven't, have you?"

"It doesn't matter. Maybe it was one too many hits to the skull. Maybe I imagined the whole thing," she sniped. "I told you, I have to get to the office. *My* office."

"Jo said it was pretty stark, what happened then. Ursa's apartment, then Fiske's compound." Arthur exhaled unevenly, unsure. "Whatever this is, seeing or... or something else, you should try to figure it out. I'm worried about you, Ginnie."

The words sparked through her chest like lightning, destructive and devastating. She drew in a breath and held it, trying to convince herself that punching him in the jaw wasn't in her best interest, and neither was sprinting away from the scene. "I'm pretty sure you lost that privilege a long time ago."

"Wasn't it you who said we were friends once? Why not try to get back there?" he asked gently, *too* gently, giving her a look of pity that roiled in her gut.

"Now isn't the time for this," she replied gruffly, pushing past him into the immaculate living room. "I have work to do, and so do you."

He grabbed her gently by the elbow, pulling her closer so that he could whisper. "Ginnie, the feds picked up three ex-Ruby Thorn enforcers last week, and they're singing louder than canaries in a coal mine about an inferno witch causing a lot of damage last winter."

"Shit," Virginia grumbled, allowing him to stop her. "Did they know Jolie's name?"

"They knew enough to have feds asking me why I didn't follow up on tips about an unregistered inferno witch, maybe a fire demon around last winter." Arthur gave her a sideways glance, half squinted in the overbearing sunlight filtering through the large bay window. "They heard enough to be asking questions, and they're not going to stop until they find her. Those goons would give her up in a heartbeat if it meant a reduced sentence for themselves. I have to tell the feds something at some point, and I think it would be better if she wasn't in the city."

"I'll think about it." She picked up an expensive, empty vase, blown glass and shimmering. It probably cost more than her yearly salary. "I have to go."

Arthur didn't reach for her again, knowing better than to make her stay. "I thought we could grab coffee with Captain Lindell, really dig into the meat of these deaths," he offered, adjusting the silver belt buckle that matched the badge on his arm.

"I don't need coffee to pass off my notes." Virginia stepped through the front door, squinting at the assault of the afternoon sun. "I've got too many cases on my docket for that."

"You know, I had hoped that by working together on the Fiske thing, you two would at least grow into a professional respect." He eyed her again, and she was so tired of being so exposed, so seen, especially by him.

"Take it up with her."

"Did you an Lindell have another argument?" Arthur was at her shoulder now, asking her in a muted, overly calm tone.

Virginia barked out a laugh. "No."

"I just wondered, seeing as you've been avoiding the station."

"I already told you, I've been busy." She waved at the up-and-coming north side neighborhood, one more sign of just how much Verdance was changing. "You should make yourself busy with this overdose, or homicide, whatever it is." She shrugged dismissively. "I'd be making it my top priority, if it was me."

"Sheriff Dixon, the coroner needed to speak to you," one of the detectives said. She flashed a smile at Virginia, who decided to pretend that hadn't happened.

"Sure," he replied with a curt nod. "Ginnie, I'll give you a call at the office if anything jumps."

"Call the apartment if it's past five. Jolie will at least

be there, she can take a message." Virginia strode away, regretting having picked up the phone that morning. Another mysterious death, feds, and shadows-damned Arthur to deal with. The only thing that would make it worse was having to deal with Shirin, too.

"Vane!"

Virginia groaned and kept walking. If she was quick, she'd make it to her car with plausible deniability that she'd heard anything in the first place. Her fingers were on the handle, almost an escape, when Lindell caught up with her.

"Hey," Lindell said, pressing a hand against the car door. "Didn't you hear me?"

"I have a lot on my mind."

"If I'd have known you'd be here, I would have—"

"Would have what?" Virginia interrupted. "Called the feds to let them know they'd have jurisdiction?"

Shirin pressed harder against the door, her bicep flexing beneath the crisp white of her uniform shirt. "No, I would have shortened my shift to make sure I didn't miss you. You've been a hard woman to get hold of."

"You need to relax," Virginia hissed, wrenching the car door open anyways, the hinge creaking with protest. "Arthur already suspects something is going on."

"Why, did he say something?"

"Yes." Virginia climbed into the car, shoving the key into the ignition. "And this isn't a conversation I want to have at a crime scene." She settled into the seat, ready to drive the moment she had the opportunity. "My guess is a homicide, he pissed off the wrong undesirable." She nodded towards the bakery as her car's engine rumbled quietly. "Look for yourself."

"Not just a plain old overdose, then?"

"Did you really think we'd get that lucky?"

Shirin studied her, forearms rested against the door despite the heat and the black metal of the car. "No, I suppose not, but it's not as if overdoses are uncommon these days."

"It's homicide, Shirin. A crew hit job, one more for the books. Tell the family to contact his life insurance company, and let's call it a day." Virginia slid the car into gear, easing forward enough to get Shirin to release her grip on the door. "I'll see you around."

She pulled off the driveway and back onto the road, the suspension or something else rattling underneath. She turned left, towards her apartment. It was almost lunch time, and she hadn't left anything for the kid to eat.

***

Her keys landed on the side table with a loud metallic clank, and she was passingly aware that one of those days, she'd wind up scratching the wood if she kept doing that. "Hey," she called across the room.

"I thought you were going to the office after," Jolie replied, unfolding her legs from beneath her and stretching her long, willowy arms over her head. "I would have made lunch."

"With what? Not much in the cabinet."

"Few cans of tuna left." Jolie nodded towards the half-empty can sitting on the counter. "There's one slice of bread left, if you want it." She turned down the radio, which had been playing a light jazzy number, something inoffensive and bland. "I don't think Emmy would mind sharing."

"I still can't believe you named that cat," Virginia grumbled, ignoring the tuna and the bread to reach for the kettle. "What is Emmy short for, anyway?"

"Emerald, for his eyes." Jolie set the can aside for the cat. "Like yours!"

"Do you mind?" Virginia asked, nodding at the dented silver of the percolator.

Jolie grinned and shot a small flame across the room, drawing a shrill whistle from the kettle almost instantaneously. "I'm getting good, right?"

"Yeah, it's been almost three days since you practically burnt the place down." Virginia steeped the coffee, inhaling deeply as the liquid turned from a crystal clear to a deep, moody brown, nearly black in color. "It was another overdose," she said casually, but felt the girl stiffen even from across the room.

"Oh?"

"Yeah, a place on the other side of the river."

"Do you think it was another homicide?"

Virginia nodded, slipping three sugar cubes into her coffee along with the last of the milk from the small ice box. "There's no way a Nether distributor wouldn't know what a fatal dose is. Besides, the scene felt too clean, not chaotic like an overdose would."

The radio hissed in quiet static just long enough for Jolie to reach over and smack the top of the box, renewing its vigor for mediocre jazz. Inhaling deeply, Virginia savored the scent of the coffee, her second that day but her first that afternoon. The first one was never as good, too bitter with impatient brewing. She blew on the steam, resenting the heat radiating into her palms in the summer weather, but craving its stability just the same. "Any news on the apartment across the hall?" she asked casually.

"No," Jolie said simply. She folded her legs beneath her again, hugging her arms around her knees.

"What's the matter?"

"Nothing."

"Alright." Virginia wasn't one to pry. Not when she'd spent years trying to keep people out of her business, instead of wrapped up within it. "What do you want for dinner later? I'll pick something up on my way back from the office."

"I don't mind."

"Noodles?"

Jolie shrugged in response, and Virginia stood curiously rooted to the spot in the kitchen. It was obvious that the kid was upset, but what was she supposed to do about it? "We could get something else, if you're sick of noodles," she offered.

"Noodles are fine."

"Okay." Virginia sipped her coffee, suddenly wishing she'd had a cigarette instead. At least that took the edge off more than the caffeine did. "I have that case to work, that minor financial fraud thing. You know, with the family."

"Heinrich Harrow," Jolie supplied. "Still no word?"

"No, and I'm starting to wonder if he's even in the city anymore." Virginia gestured to the wall, where all of her cold cases were hung, all of them testaments to her failures as an investigator. "Might be another one for the wall of shame."

Jolie followed her stare, her eyes settling on the one that haunted Virginia most, a young woman with pin-straight brown hair pinned back over the top of her head, and a huge smile aimed at someone just out of frame. "I think you'll figure it out. Heinrich Harrow can't be smarter than you. I mean, he was brainless enough to leave a paper trail so wide, even his niece found the evidence without looking too hard."

"He doesn't have to be smarter than me, I just have to miss the right clues. Sometimes it's a footprint obscured by a snow storm, sometimes it's a well hidden affair, occasionally I just missed something." Virginia crossed the room with her coffee in hand, reaching out to smooth the edges of the yellowed photograph. "She wasn't smarter than me, just unlucky."

"Is she dead?" Jolie asked, and Virginia appreciated the blunt stab of the question.

"Yes. For a long time, now."

"Who was she?"

Virginia tensed, her breath catching in her throat again as certain memories sprang to the surface, unbidden. "No one. Just another cold case."

"Doesn't seem like no one."

"She's been gone a long time." Virginia drained her mug, steadying her breaths before she turned around. "It doesn't matter. These old cases are just an intellectual exercise."

Jolie eyed her suspiciously, but didn't argue. She didn't ask so many intrusive questions, didn't poke and prod, and to her credit, she made a mean pancake. "Can I go with you to the office?" she asked quietly, as if she expected Virginia to say no.

"I didn't think you'd want to. It gets pretty dull."

"I can file things for you," Jolie offered. "Or dust, or—"

"You had me at filing," Virginia interrupted. "I don't think a damn thing has been filed there in at least ten years. Besides, then we can both pick what to get for dinner." She dumped the rest of the coffee down the kitchen sink, almost mourning it but celebrating her mouth's temporary vacation from the heat. She wasn't going to fight the kid tagging along, not when Arthur was worried enough to be sending squad units to keep an eye on the building.

Virginia slid into her shoes once more, twirling her ring of keys around an index finger as she waited for Jolie to pin her hair back into a frizzy, wild bun. She had a bad feeling about these homicides, one that glowed like an ember in her gut, and the first since she'd gotten the shit kicked out of her at Fiske's compound.

Chapter Two

Almost a week passed with nothing more than incremental, meaningless progress. The Heinrich Harrow case remained unsolved, and Virginia had been dodging calls from Arthur for days, trying to drag her into more VCPD consultancy than she cared to deal with.

Virginia flipped through the Harrow case file once again before slapping it closed on her desk, punctuated with a heavy, frustrated sigh. "Do you know where that other case wound up?" she asked, shoving it across the scratched wood. "I'm tired of looking at this."

"Of course," Jolie replied, pulling it from a file cabinet against the wall, the nickel handles rusting where they met the metal. She set it on the desk and flopped into the chair opposite, her feet propped up on the edge of the desk.

"I have to say, having things organized is a nice change," Virginia admitted, reaching for the manila file. "I can't believe how much you've managed to get done with just that old cabinet you rescued from the curbside."

"I like to keep busy." Jo lowered her feet to the ground, glancing at the percolator on the table across. "Coffee?" she asked.

"Yeah, fill it up," Virginia replied, nudging her mug towards the edge of the desk. "Be careful, or I'll start to get used to this." She glanced at Jolie, dressed in Virginia's oversized hand-me-downs. "The practice isn't making enough to pay you."

"Free room and board seems payment enough." Jolie heated the percolator instantly, almost igniting a deep forest green sweater sleeve as it hung down past her fingers. "Assuming you're not kicking me out yet."

"No, not yet." Virginia drummed her fingers against the file, still unsure of how to proceed with the girl. She couldn't just turn her out onto the streets, not after everything with Fiske, and certainly not with the feds sniffing around. The shelters would throw the kid back onto the streets the moment they realized she was a mythic, claiming it was for protection of the others, but really, it was just their own prejudices and fear. "Keep making decent coffee, and I'll forget you've been sleeping on the sofa for six months."

"Done," Jolie said, sliding the mug back across the desk. "We're almost out of beans, though."

"Alright, we'll pick some up later."

The door eased open, a polite gesture that the hinges were unfamiliar with. Even so, the frosted glass pane rattled as the latch released with a turn of the door knob, emblazoned with a large letter V.

"Ms. Harrow," Virginia said, standing up. "Is everything alright?" She nodded towards the kettle. "Coffee? It's fresh."

"No, Ms. Vane, I don't want coffee," the young woman said, closing the door behind her, wiping a bead of sweat from her forehead before it dripped down onto her pink floral dress, emblazoned with hundreds of tiny buds. "I need you to find my uncle. Need I remind you that he took off with every last red cent my family had?"

"I told you that I would call you when I had a promising lead," Virginia answered evenly. "Unfortunately, every lead has wound up in a dead end." She nodded towards the chair. "Please, sit."

Nina Harrow shook her head. "No, ma'am, I don't wish to sit. Are you even working on my uncle's case?" She gestured to the top file with a scowl. "That's not his file, is it?"

"No, but—"

"Ms. Vane, I understand from others that you're good at your job, so I am personally mystified as to how three weeks have passed since I last heard from you. Not to mention, I called your office here several times yesterday to no avail." Nina tugged the fabric of her dress away from her skin, no doubt as miserable as Virginia was in the Verdance humidity. "Of course I felt like I should visit you in person to make sure you haven't run off with what little was left after my uncle took us all for fools."

Virginia swallowed back a grimace. In dodging calls from the VCPD, she'd inadvertently been dodging calls from clients with active cases, too. "I apologize, Ms. Harrow, we were out in the field yesterday," she lied.

"Looking for my uncle?"

"Your uncle isn't my only case, I'm afraid."

"Please, Ms. Vane," Nina Harrow pleaded, tugging at the short sleeves of her dress, distorting the flowers with every yank of the fabric. "My family won't make rent next month if you don't find him. My parents are old, they can't work like they used to." She looked away, past Virginia out to the street. "I don't make enough at the dress shop to support them, and my brother ran off to the coast with some girl he met down on the docks."

Virginia chewed the inside of her cheek, searching for answers she didn't have. "The paper trail he left here in Verdance was significant, but the case came to me too late to do anything much with that evidence. Your uncle was long gone from the casinos and the clubs before I got there, and no one remembered him much. They said he was quiet and inoffensive, which rarely turns the heads of a bouncer." She shuffled the files, bringing Heinrich Harrow's to the forefront once more. "Is there anywhere else he would go? Anywhere else he might be?" she asked.

"No," Nina answered, shaking her head. "As far as any of us know, he rarely even left the city."

"No old flames, no contacts in another city? Nothing?" Virginia pushed the file towards the young woman, motioning for Jolie to pour another coffee for their client. "As you can see, he's gone dark. Those accounts have been drained, they are empty. None of his usual haunts have seen him. Ms. Harrow, either your uncle has skipped town, or he's laying in a ditch somewhere."

"I've already checked the morgue. Shadows know finding him there would be the easiest and best solution. We could reclaim whatever was left of what he'd stolen, and then he's welcome to rot in hell for what he's done." Nina Harrow released the grip on her dress, clenching her fists at her sides. "After everything we did for him, I just don't understand how he could repay my parents' kindness like this."

"People can surprise you," Virginia said, pushing away memories of her own betrayals. "I'm sorry to press, Ms.

Harrow, but you're sure there's nowhere else he might be?"

"There was a place a few hours south of here, but he hasn't been there in years."

"Where?"

Nina Harrow sighed quietly, taking the steaming mug from Jolie. "Birch Hollow."

Red-hot sunlight streamed through the gaps in the blinds, landing on Virginia's skin like boiling water. She resisted the urge to flinch, both from the name of the town and from the hot glow. "I've never been," she lied. "How far south?"

"About one-hundred and sixty miles south down the interstate," Nina Harrow answered. "It's a small place, a group of a few towns. Not much there other than corn fields and despair. I doubt he'd wind up there, everyone he knew from then is dead now."

Virginia rapped her knuckles against the desk, whacking bone against the wood. *Tap, Tap, tap.* The rhythm of it was soothing in a way, but the questioning glance from Jolie across the room made Virginia stop the motion, forcing her hands into her lap. "I don't want to rule anything out prematurely, but I'm afraid my services don't extend that far from Verdance."

"Why not?" Jolie asked, but Virginia silenced her with a stern glare. "Oh, right," she said, covering, "there are plenty of other cases that need seeing to."

"Yes, I've been very busy these past months," Virginia added, another lie to add to the pile she'd been curating from the moment Nina Harrow opened the office door. "If your uncle is in Birch Hollow, then I'm afraid you'll have to find a local investigator there to flush him out from wherever he's hiding."

"Do you really think he's down there?" Nina asked.

Virginia shrugged casually, desperately trying to ignore the slow creep of dread that was inching up her spine, one awful vertebrae at a time. "I wouldn't presume to rule anything out. One thing is for sure, Ms. Harrow. If he's in Verdance, he has help keeping a low profile. Is there anyone here he'd turn to?"

Nina shook her head again. "No. He's burned just about every bridge in Verdance, as far as that's concerned." She set the mug on the desk, leaning forward until the fabric of her dress brushed against the wood. "Please, Ms. Vane, my family can't afford another investigator. If he's in Birch Hollow, then—"

"If your Uncle Heinrich is in Birch Hollow, you might be best off driving down there to find him yourself," Virginia interrupted. "As I've explained, my services do not extend far outside Verdance." She turned to the blinds, fussing with them to eliminate the warmth cascading through the slats. "I am sorry, Ms. Harrow. If I find more information here in Verdance, I will surely let you know as soon as possible."

Nina stood, her delicate features set into an ugly scowl. "They said you were the best, you know." She slung her purse over her shoulder, staring across the desk. "I guess they were wrong."

"As I said, I am sorry," Virginia repeated, recoiling from the sting of her words. "I don't know many private investigators who would drive south for hours to find someone, not without some sort of additional compensation." She held a hand up, preemptively silencing Nina. "And there is no compensation enough for me to agree to that."

"You've been a disappointment, Ms. Vane," Nina Harrow

said, her hand on the door knob. "Good riddance."

The glass pane rattled noisily as the door slammed, and Virginia braced her palms against the desk, trying to ignore the impulse to sweep the files from her desk in a petty rage. She seethed, exhaling through her nose. If she sent the pages flying, it would just mean more work for Jolie. "Well," she said finally. "I guess we should break for dinner."

"No compensation enough?" Jolie asked, pressing the very issue that she shouldn't.

Virginia looked over at her, the tiny slip of a thing swimming in the ill-fitting clothes. "No."

"Why not?"

"Because driving south in this heat sounds like a one-way ticket to hell," Virginia answered. "What do you want to eat?"

"Don't you want to solve the case?" Jolie pushed. "What if Heinrich Harrow is hiding out down there?"

Virginia stacked the files neatly, handing them over to be filed in the cabinet. "Birch Hollow is a crappy little one-horse town, and you couldn't pay me enough to look it in the face again."

"Again? So you've been there?"

"No."

"But you just said—"

"What do you want to eat?" Virginia asked again, desperate to change the subject. "There are a few places on the way back home—back to the apartment, I mean—we could stop any place you want. There's the noodle place, but there's also flat breads, or the place with that spicy rice you liked so much."

Jolie opened her mouth to argue, but took the files instead, nodding. "Maybe the spicy rice. Haven't had that in a while," she said.

"Spicy rice it is."

The filing cabinet creaked in protest as the drawers were pulled out and then closed, screeching as metal ground against metal. Jolie leaned against it, rolling up her sleeves for the fourteenth time that day. "I'm sorry, I didn't mean to pry."

"Birch Hollow is a dump, Firefly. You don't want to go there." Virginia rolled up her own sleeves, desperate for the feeling of cool air against her stifled skin. The blinds blocked sun, but any semblance of breeze, too. "And I doubt Heinrich Harrow is there. Chances are he's still here in Verdance, hiding out in some Nether den." She didn't quite believe it herself, in no small part because Harrow had never shown any interest in Nether, according to his family, and because his paper trail stopped stone dead two weeks prior. If he was still in Verdance, he was likely dragging along the bottom of the lake. "So, what do you want to do after dinner?"

Before Jolie could answer, the phone rang.

They both stared at it for a moment as the bell clanged angrily, adding more unease to an already frustrated tension in the room.

"Should I answer it?" Jolie asked.

Virginia started to shake her head, but stopped herself. Nina Harrow had tried calling but wasn't able to get through, and it had led to an upsetting confrontation. Arthur might not be on the end of the phone, it could be a client. "I'll answer it," Virginia said, letting it ring thrice more before she lifted the receiver.

"Virginia?"

"Shirin." It hadn't been Arthur, but Shirin was somehow worse. "What do you need?"

"I've been trying to catch you, but you weren't at home."

"You went to my apartment?" Virginia asked.

The line crunched with static for half a heartbeat. "You weren't picking up the phone, what was I supposed to do? Headquarters is fresh out of carrier pigeons," Shirin explained. "There's been another murder."

"So much for a quiet afternoon," Virginia replied. "Where?"

"Illegal casino in the basement of that little restaurant—"

"By the lake," Virginia confirmed, not needing the rest of the answer. "Leads?"

Shirin exhaled softly, but it was loud enough to cloud the line for just a moment. "It's one of Fiske's." She hissed out a sigh, holding the receiver away from her mouth this time.

"You should get here. The sheriff wants to speak to you."

"You're there now?"

"Yes," Lindell said. "I'm calling from a phone box a quarter of a mile up the road. Your specific expertise would be advantageous, Virginia. Avoiding this case would be a mistake for your investigation practice."

Virginia fought the urge to argue and to refuse. Leads for Harrow were thin on the ground, and so was work the past couple of months. "I'll be right there." Jolie stared from across the room, eyes innocent and questioning. She didn't need to see any more than she already had in her short life. Virginia sighed. "I'm coming alone."

Chapter Three

The drive out to the lake was a frustrating one, thick with early evening traffic in the wrong direction, cars lined up all along the shoreline, their exhaust rising into the sky in thick, diesel-laden clouds. Virginia tapped her fingers against the steering wheel, willing the jokers in front of her to find the shadows-damned gas pedal.

Around the bend of the lake, a more diminutive skyline reached towards the clouds, built of apartment buildings, and then pharmacies and schools, and then, finally, right where the city's streets began to spread into wider, more suburban lanes, a group of restaurants and shops that catered to the wealthy. The Carlyle's brick exterior was painted pink, the columns supporting the roof matched in hue. She'd never been inside, not with the prices they were charging.

Squad units were swarming the scene, parked up across the patches of parched, dying grass that crunched under Virginia's shoes, releasing puffs of dust with every step.

The restaurant was flanked by two upscale boutiques, the kind with mannequins sporting ugly high fashion in the windows. Officers ducked under the cordon tape, taking photos and making notes. Virginia nodded at the coroner as she made notes on her clipboard.

"Ginnie, good, you're here," Arthur said, waving her over to the barrier. "I was worried we wouldn't be able to catch you."

"You caught me, alright," she said. "Are you two aware that I have cases outside of whatever you want me to do for you? Need I remind the VCPD that I am a consultant only, and a poorly paid one at that?"

"I wouldn't say that you're poorly paid."

"My bank balance begs to differ." Virginia shifted her weight, leaning to glance into the building. It was dripping with crystal chandeliers, and beset on all sides by thick hand-woven rugs. "Who's the vic?"

"Waiting on positive identification, nothing found on the body." Arthur nodded towards the ambulance parked parallel to the sidewalk and then shook his head. "But you'll probably recognize him as—"

"One of Fiske's," Virginia supplied. "Lindell said. Which?"

"Looks to me like it's Bobby Marcus."

Virginia sucked her teeth as she clawed through her memory. "Doesn't he own this place?"

"Not officially."

"No leads?"

He shook his head again. "Nothing."

"Is the coroner finished in there?" Virginia asked. "I could take a look around." She wasn't squeamish by any means, but there was something particularly horrifying about the scent of decaying flesh that was already lilting on the breeze as it blew through the building.

"She's through, yes." Arthur lifted his face to the sky, a cloud darkening the sky as it hung heavy over the lake, blocking the worst of the sun. "I was hoping you might be able to see something the rest of us haven't."

"*See* something," Virginia repeated. "Right." She stifled the growl that lay dormant in her throat and stepped over the threshold, immediately swallowing back bile at the smell of rotting flesh. "Shadows," she whispered, her eyes watering. "You'd think it wouldn't be this bad, given he can't have been here long."

The stench was thick in the air, and pulled a gag from Arthur's throat. He tugged a pristine white handkerchief from his pocket and held it over his face, wincing. "The heat," he said between empty retches. "We'll take a quick look and get out of here. Those clouds look threatening, and I don't want to get caught in any more traffic this week. Mona will have my head on a silver platter."

Virginia tossed him a sideways glare as she sidestepped around the florid front desk, embossed with gold lettering. "I'd hate for that to happen," she mused dryly.

"What do you make of this?" he asked, leaning his head out an open window for fresh air. "Nether again, but I don't think we can call this one a suicide."

"Why's that?" Virginia asked, heading straight for the hidden staircase in the kitchen where officers were swarming.

She descended the stairs, the carpeted wood soft and quiet. Three detectives were crowded around a small round table until she approached with Arthur, scattering them. "Shadows fucked," she whispered. "No wonder you called me."

The corpse was posed in the chair, sitting at the table as though he were gambling, face twisted into a terrified expression.

"No denying it, I'm afraid," Arthur replied. He shook his head, a frustrated rumble in his throat. "Shadows fucked, indeed."

The corpse was wearing a high-end suit, probably made by a tailor uptown, bare feet on the rug. Charcoal grey and double-breasted, the lapels crisply pressed and the shirt beneath showing off ruby cufflinks at the wrist. "Photographers already been?" she asked, despite seeing the yellow numbered flags on the ground. Protocol was protocol.

"Yes."

She eased around the back of the chair, gingerly pulling the blazer away from the body. "No immediate signs of trauma," she said. "No gun shot or stab wounds." The green felt table had mahogany legs that matched the rest of the basement interior, and a royal flush laid out in front of him. "I'm guessing he liked to play poker," she said.

"Loan sharks, I'm guessing," Arthur offered. "Might be that they're making the rounds."

She shook her head, brow furrowed. "No, this feels different. Sharks like to make a statement, sure, but those statements are usually clumsy. Not many with a flair for the theatrical, and the drama of this staging is very intentional."

"What else, then?"

She ran a hand over the table, willing something to come to her, but nothing did. "Rival crew, maybe. Possibly a return hit for our friend Merv Knuckles." His hat was tipped low over one side of his face, but not low enough to obscure the obvious tinges of purple-pink that ringed his wide-open eyes. "Feds are going to be all over this if you're not careful."

"The feds are already coming, Ginnie," he warned. "I'd be surprised if they weren't already assembling a team to drive out from the capital to go all in on this Nether stuff. It isn't going to help that those two in lockup have lots to say about the fires last winter, that's only going to make them dig further into old cases."

She exhaled sharply, blowing a cloud of dust apart just as several fat rain drops landed on the windowsill, sending a delicate splash to settle against the brick. "You know, Arthur, if you could get a handle on this city, maybe I wouldn't be having to run all over the shadows-damned place trying to clean up these messes. I have my own job, you know."

"I'm doing you a favor in keeping that girl's name off the paperwork and away from the press. I'd have hoped you'd remember that." He gagged again, pulling his shirt collar up over his nose and mouth.

Virginia rolled her eyes, pushing through a swinging door that led behind the basement's bar. "Doing *me* a favor?" she retorted, making note of the untouched cash register, still stuffed full with bills. "Seems to me she was the key to all of that and you know it. Where would your ass be, if the city council knew you went rogue that night? Not sitting in that sheriff's chair, I can tell you that much."

"Ginnie—" he protested.

"You can't stay out of trouble in this city for five minutes, can you?" she interrupted, poking at a gilded trunk beneath the counter which held the illegal casino's chips. "We'll see what the coroner says, but my guess is that the victim isn't long dead, even with that smell." She bent, pressing an outstretched hand to rest against the glittering metal and wood, willing something to come. Nothing did. She stood again, kicking the trunk. A panel came loose and splintered onto the carpeted floor, spilling piles of painted wooden chips stamped with the Ruby Thorns crest. "Definitely one of Fiske's."

The sound of rain against the concrete upstairs drifted down the stairs in quiet gasps, the patter unmistakable. "I don't know what else you want me to say, Arthur."

"You always have more to say. Usually, it's all I can do to get you to shut up," he said, nudging her in the shoulder.

She shook him off, hearing the joke in it but the irritation remained nonetheless. "I don't think it's a good idea for you to head down that road," she growled. "Besides, I'm sure Shirin—Captain Lindell will have her own theories as to what happened here."

Arthur raised an eyebrow at her, taking the handkerchief away from his face just long enough to sneeze, disturbing the air current. "Yes, I'm sure she will," he agreed. "And last we spoke, she and I were on the same page as far as Jo is concerned."

"Any other casinos out this way?" Virginia asked, ignoring his comment. "Maybe one owned by the Krakens?"

"Maybe," he answered. "It's hard to tell. It's not like they advertise in the papers, and their grunts are unlikely to squeal even if we pick one up."

"Witnesses?"

"By all accounts, it was after hours, and all the other places around here would have been locked up for the night."

"Right." Virginia tugged the small notebook from her pocket, making notes in the margins, sketching a rudimentary map with the stub of a pencil she'd left tucked behind her ear. "I'll need to look at a better map, but so far these killings are all over the place. No themes, no specific neighborhoods. Doesn't seem to follow the patterns of a turf war."

"Therein lies the problem," Arthur said, sidestepping the table to point at her map. "Lindell and I can't make heads or tails of it. From what we can tell, it seems completely random."

"I doubt that." Virginia stuffed the notebook back into her pocket and dreaded walking back to her car in rain that heavy. She'd be drenched by the time she got home.

Thunder rumbled eagerly in the distance, and the reflection of another flash of lightning danced across the stairs. The streets were wet, and departing squad units had to navigate the miniature floods gathering where the storm drains couldn't keep up. "Nice restaurant," Arthur mused aloud.

"For a place practically out in the suburbs, sure." Virginia climbed the stairs behind him, noting the absence of any signs of struggle. "At least the crews are keeping it in the family so far."

"No one seems to mind too much when they take each other out." Arthur stopped in the doorway, glancing back towards the kitchen area, out past the matching pairs of chairs, the tables all covered in starched white tablecloths. "Ginnie, I am trying to impress upon you the severity of this situation."

"I'm aware." Thunder cracked overhead, and while Arthur flinched, Virginia didn't. Wind blew across the lake, drawing waves to break against each other and boats to list from side to side in their moorings. She stretched her fingers out for the brass door knob leading to the back office. Tentatively, skin brushed against metal, and she tried to open herself to whatever she was, but still, nothing came. "I'm sorry I can't be more help."

"What are you two doing?" Lindell asked as she stepped inside the restaurant. "If you haven't noticed, there's one hell of a storm outside."

At the edge of the horizon, a clear patch of sky peeked through, showing off the remains of a spectacular sunset, with streaks of red and gold vying for dominance. "It will clear soon," Virginia said. "These summer squalls never last long."

"What are you, an almanac?" Lindell caught up to them, shaking the rain from her cap before putting it back on her head.

Virginia sidestepped Lindell, pointing at the clearing sky. "See? It's already stopped on the other side of the lake."

"Maybe we should talk about this case at your office to-morrow," Lindell offered, her brow lightly furrowed. "Clear a few things up."

"I'm busy."

"Busy with what? The Heinrich Harrow case?" Lindell shot back, clearly smug that she knew something Virginia didn't. "His niece called headquarters today, complaining that a conwoman private eye was welching on a deal." She smiled, but there was something distinctly unfriendly about it. "I assumed that had something to do with you."

"Nina Harrow thinks I should drive three hours south on the interstate to a little hole in the wall town called Birch Hollow on the off chance her lazy, philandering uncle might be hiding out there, and without any extra fee." Virginia shrugged aggressively at Lindell, pointedly, trying to prove a point. "Would you take that deal, Shirin?"

"Birch Hollow?" Arthur asked. "You have a case in Birch Hollow, Ginnie?"

Virginia shot him a look, her arms folded over her chest. "No. I do not."

"I know how you are with an unsolved case, and Birch Hollow—"

"Is somewhere the rest of the world forgot," Virginia finished. "It's not worth my time. Chances are, her uncle is right here, ankle deep in lake sand." She pointed out at the water, now calm with the passing of the storm. Where the sky was visible, it was completely clear, no hint that a storm had even occurred. Nothing more than sunset and skyline and the evening promise of another heat wave the next morning. Already, the humidity was stifling. "He was big into gambling and blew through the family's assets. My guess is that he cozied up to the wrong loan shark."

"I could run some names for you," Lindell said easily, taking up residence against the antique fireplace's hearth, the soot smudging against her pristine blazer. "If you want."

"No, thank you Captain Lindell, but I can manage my case load on my own."

"I'm just trying to help, Ms. Vane."

Virginia huffed out a breath. "Careful, I wouldn't want you to get dirt on your perfect uniform, Captain." She stepped back around the desk, reaching for a drawer handle as she did, but again, nothing came. "I have no intentions of putting myself in the poorhouse to solve a case like this one. The man is dead, I'd be shocked to learn otherwise." She stepped out into the twilight air, rancid with stench and the weight of the humidity. Heinrich Harrow may well be in Birch Hollow, but she had no intentions of finding out.

"If you realize you need help, give me a call," Lindell said, tossing a wave to Arthur. "Sheriff Dixon, I'll work up the report for this and have it on your desk in the morning. No doubt the feds will already have landed by then." She tilted her head towards Virginia and opened her mouth, but whatever it was she was about to say, she thought better of it.

"See you in the morning, Captain," Arthur replied, and his voice was raspy from exhaustion or the strain of breathing through a handkerchief, or both. He followed Virginia outside, waving off the remaining squad units. Most of them had left when the storm started. "Ginnie..." he started, letting the name whisper into nothingness.

Virginia lit a cigarette, the need for it overcoming her desire to not let Arthur see her smoke. He'd always been annoying about it, ever since he'd quit. "Want one?" she asked, holding out the tarnished silver case.

To her surprise, he took one, and then lit it with a flip lighter from his pocket. "Thanks."

"Since when do you smoke again?"

He laughed darkly, blowing a plume out into the encroaching darkness. "Since moving back to fucking Verdance."

"Does your wife know?"

"What do you think?" he challenged. "No, Mona doesn't know. Shadows, Ginnie, I've even stooped so low as to have a spare shirt in the car so she won't smell it on me."

Virginia exhaled a laugh through her nose, already halfway through the smoke. "Good luck keeping up those appearances. She's going to find out. And when she does..."

"When she does, I'm a goner," Arthur said. "Until then, I will thank you for your discretion."

"Does Lindell know?"

Arthur shrugged. "I don't know. Maybe, maybe not."

She parted her lips for the delicate spirals of smoke that twisted upwards into a cloudless night, and exhaled with a fierce hiss, frustrated by their delicacy. The taste of ash burned on her tongue, a welcome displeasure, a strange comfort from the ember lit between her fingers. "I'm not going, Arthur," she said again. "There's nothing for me there."

"Ginnie," he started, rubbing at his head. "There's no way around it. You can't figure it on your own. It's been months, and nothing."

"So? Maybe it was a fluke."

"If you would just talk to her, then maybe you could get your head around being a—well, around whatever this is." Arthur shoved his hands into his pockets, the same way he always did when he didn't quite know what to say. "It's important that you get a handle on this. I worry about you."

Virginia rolled her eyes, stubbing out the cigarette against the damp brick. "That's my business, not yours. I got along just fine for forty-eight years without whatever that was, I'm perfectly fine if it never happens again." She took another cigarette from the case and struck a match, taking three tries before it lit. "Better than fine. Great. Excellent, even."

"You'd throw away that potential?" he asked.

"Don't talk to me about throwing away potential. You could have traveled the world doing what you loved. But you were scared, so you joined the force instead," she replied.

He shuffled his shoes in the dirt. "And look at us now."

"Yeah," she grumbled bitterly, "Look at us now."

Arthur took two awkward steps across the alley, as though he thought she would attack him, and not inhale another lungful of smoke. He cleared his throat gently, looking out the corner of his eye at her, dark pupils shining in the night's glare from the water. "I always did wonder, you know."

"About?" she asked, even though she wasn't particularly interested in the answer.

"If there was something different about you."

"There's nothing different about me, Arthur."

"You solved cases that had been cold in the ground for months. For years!" He shook his head, shuffling the sole of his shoe against some loose gravel. "I could never do what you did, and it ate at me." He tilted his head. "It still does."

"Did you ever think that maybe I was just a better detective?" she snapped. "Maybe I just worked harder, and longer, and maybe I'm just smarter than you and it has nothing to do with being a—of—" she stopped short, still unable to say it out loud.

Arthur sighed. "Ginnie, let's not turn this into a pissing contest."

"I'd win."

"Go see your mother," he pressed.

"I'd rather die."

"You can't afford for this Nina Harrow woman to be gossiping about your practice behind your back, and with these two in lockup it's best that Jolie is out of sight." He leaned to the side, nudging her shoulder with his own. "Good opportunity to go home for a while."

"Why don't you go? My mother always liked you better than me, anyhow." Virginia took a long drag, waiting for him to argue, but he didn't. "I'll drive Jolie out to the coast."

"The coast doesn't have answers, Ginnie."

"Neither does my mother." She sent ash out in a fine spray from the end of her cigarette with a sharp flick. "She'd probably have me locked up just for asking about this. Shadows forbid anyone she knows hears she's related to a mythic."

Arthur shrugged again, the hem of his untucked shirt dripping with the remains of the rain shower. "Maybe she's mellowed in her old age."

"Her?" Virginia barked out a laugh. "Never. She'll be picking fights just to spit in someone's eye long after she should have been in a grave."

"Harsh."

"Please, she's more bile than blood, and you know it." Virginia took one last drag, savoring the burning, ashy taste at the back of her throat. "The feds are really coming, aren't they?"

"Yep."

"Fine. I'll go to Birch Hollow." Virginia dropped the butt onto the ground, burying it under the dirt with the toe of her shoe. "But I'm going to hate every moment that I'm there."

Chapter Four

Corn rustled angrily in the reticent breeze, audible even over the sound of the car's protesting efforts. Birch Hollow, ten miles.

Heat through the windshield reverberated against the torn fabric interior, the weight of it sitting against her chest like an impending coronary.

Home.

Unlike other four letter words, she tried to avoid it as much as possible, the syllable tasting like a bitter poison against her tongue.

The engine had been making a troubling thunk since the junction a hundred miles back. A problem for another day, if she was lucky. Something to be dealt with immediately, if she was luckier. No one could argue with a broken-down car, not even her mother, although she would doubtless try.

Blame would follow, regardless.

The scent of overripe crops slithered in through the gaps in the windows, too sweet, cloying, like drowning in molasses.

Nine miles to Birch Hollow.

The tires rumbled over poorly maintained roads, and she'd long since stopped trying to avoid the potholes because a blown tire and hours spent walking back in the other directions were immeasurably preferable to the mundane nightmare that lay ahead.

Waiting.

The pristine estate would be ascending out of the fields, spiked wrought iron gates reaching towards the unsettlingly endless sky and the red brick baking in the sun. Virginia wondered if anything had changed since the last time she'd been there. She wondered if her name was still carved in the back of her childhood closet, the letters messy and uneven. Even the thought that it was still there, waiting patiently for her to rediscover, landed a weight in her stomach that she couldn't dislodge.

"Not long now," Jolie said, leaning forward onto the dashboard. "Only eight miles left." She stretched her arms over her head with an exaggerated yawn, blinking against the harsh sunlight reflecting off the faded pavement.

"Yeah," Virginia replied. "Not long."

"Where are we staying while we look for Heinrich Harrow?" Jolie asked.

True to form, Virginia hadn't even mentioned the issue of her mother. After she'd left the restaurant and casino, she returned home and passingly informed Jolie that she'd decided to track down Heinrich, after all. No words passed her lips about federal agents looking for an inferno witch or a fire demon, no words about her mother, and certainly none about her own past. "My mother lives here," she said simply.

Jolie nodded, knowing enough, mercifully, to not ask more questions on the matter. "Lots of corn out here," she said instead.

"Plenty of it," Virginia agreed. "Miles and miles of nothing but this." She rubbed her eyes, desperate to stave off the boredom dragging at her eyelids. Driving south in the state was always a trial, and never something to enjoy, whether she was involving Birch Hollow or not.

It had been nigh on twenty years since she'd been back. She hadn't set foot on Birch Hollow ground since her mostly-absent father had gone missing, presumed dead. There had been a poorly attended funeral. He'd spent his life making more enemies than friends, and it showed in the empty pews and the short, abbreviated service.

"If you like farms, it's the place to be," Virginia added after a moment of comfortable silence, breaching it before they got too familiar with the soft embrace of quiet. They wouldn't get much of it once they arrived at their destination.

"I don't know if I've ever thought that much about farms," Jolie admitted. "But it's nice to be out of the city, I guess."

"You'll be bored of the landscapes here in about ten minutes." Virginia sighed heavily as they passed another mile marker. Five miles to Birch Hollow. "I was bored of them from birth."

"Did you grow up here?" Jolie asked, tentative, pushed back in her seat like she was bracing for impact.

"Unfortunately," Virginia answered, and because she was desperate for any kind of distraction, she added, "So did Sheriff Dixon."

"Oh. Did you know each other?"

"We were best friends." Virginia flicked on the turn signal at an empty, desolate crossroads, the dread germinating fresh shoots of weight in her lungs. "It was a long time ago."

Jolie's face was questioning, but she didn't ask, and for that, Virginia was grateful. The girl stared out the window at the endless, tessellating stalks of corn, standing straight and tall in the still air. Miles and miles of nothing but corn, already waist-high and ahead of schedule. As long as the heat didn't turn to drought, it would be a healthy harvest in the autumn.

"Where do you think Heinrich Harrow is hiding?" Jolie finally asked, when they crossed the two-mile marker. "Friends? Does he have family down here?"

"An old lover, I'm guessing," Virginia replied. "You're too young to know it now, but these things tend to rise up out of the woodwork more than once as you get older." The memory of Astrid's most recent betrayal still burned fresh in Virginia's chest, and unconsciously, her knuckles tightened around the steering wheel. "He'll have come down here to let things in Verdance calm down, in hopes that whatever investigator his family hired would stop looking."

"Not you, though," Jolie said, and there was an unfamiliar glint of pride in it that Virginia flinched from.

"Seemed like a good time to get out of Verdance," Virginia said airily. "The city is stifling in this weather. Besides, Nina Harrow is more than willing to cause problems, so it's easier to just do what she wants."

"Problems?"

"She called the VCPD to tell them her investigator was trying to scam her out of a deposit. It doesn't matter that no other PI in Verdance would do this, either, she was happy to spill her guts to Captain Lindell anyway."

Jolie shifted in her seat, her forearms braced against the dash as she lay her head there, watching the fields as they passed in a noisy, clunking blur. "Did Captain Lindell tell you to come down here?"

"Not in so many words, no." Virginia's shoulders tightened as they passed the faded, chipped sign: *Welcome to Birch Hollow, Home of the Corn Festival.* She'd passed that same sign countless times in her youth, but after two decades of absence, the sight of it was like taking a wooden stake to the chest. "Captain Lindell has other concerns."

"Like the murders back in Verdance?" Jolie asked, picking at her cuticles.

The car rumbled over a patch of unpaved road, and Virginia cringed at the raucous rattling beneath the hood. "Among other things," she answered. "Nothing for you to worry about." The wheels came to a rest at a stop sign, and the engine idled noisily, and she waited.

Jolie rolled her window down further with the hand crank, leaning out of the car, her bright, curly hair a shocking bronze in the summer sun. "Did you forget the way?" she asked with a giggle. "Should I get the map?"

"I didn't forget." Virginia's hand rested on the gear shift, still unmoving. "I was listening to the engine. I don't know that this car will make it back to Verdance without repairs. Something is knocking around in there." She'd hoped the car would have broken down a long way back up the interstate, far from Birch Hollow and far from those particular responsibilities. Jolie would have been just as safe in some roadside motel, and arguably, safer. Shadows only knew what would be said when they pulled up to Virginia's mother's house.

"Is there a mechanic in this town?"

"Probably, there used to be. It's been a while since I've been here."

Jolie pulled her head back into the car, settling back down

into the passenger seat. "Why did you leave?"

"I'm not cut out to be a farmer," Virginia replied. "And out here, you're either a farmer, or you're nobody."

"Is your mother a farmer?"

Virginia sighed. "No. She's...." Shifting the car into drive again, more tightness closed around her chest. "Stay in the car until I talk to her."

"Are we almost there?"

"Yeah. Around the corner." The tires rumbled over brick, the car's metal frame reverberating with the unintentional rhythm. Virginia clenched, hoping to relieve the tension between her shoulder blades, but the muscles refused to release. The house, her mother's house, stood there, the same as it always had. It was the same as it had always been, the glass polished, the porch swept free of any errant leaves, and the sight knotted guilt in Virginia's gut harsher than a punch.

She put the car into park, cutting the engine. Despite knowing she had to get out of the car, she found herself still sitting in the driver's seat, her hands squeezed around the wheel so tightly that a vein bulged slightly in her forearm.

"Is this it?" Jolie prompted, her hand poised over the door handle.

"This is it," Virginia confirmed, not even protesting when the girl jumped out of the car, already taking in her sur-roundings. If she wasn't careful, Jolie would wind up a broke investigator, too. "Wait," she finally interrupted, taking the keys from the ignition. She closed the car door behind her, leaning against it until the latch caught even though it was very unlikely her mother didn't already know they were there. "Wait," she said again, quieter this time as she caught up to

Jolie. "Let me go first. She's—I haven't been home in a long time."

Virginia removed her shoulder holster, not wanting to unnecessarily escalate any confrontations given her mother's disgust about her chosen career. She tucked her gun into the glove compartment, but held the silver knuckles in her palm for a moment before pocketing them. She held her hands aloft as she walked around to the front of the house, already unpacking the many regrets she had.

There her mother was, twenty years older at least, maybe four inches shorter, it seemed. Her ankles were crossed in a demure pose, her posture perfect as always. She was reading a small, leather-bound book, but beyond the light glare of the metallic, embossed cover, the title wasn't legible at that distance.

Virginia stopped just short of the steps, not quite ready to breach the threshold of the house. She cleared her throat lightly, already craving another cigarette, but she'd hidden her case back in the car.

"Ginnie?" her mother asked, setting the book aside. "Is that you?"

"It's me," Virginia answered.

Her mother stared down coldly from the porch. "If it isn't the prodigal daughter," she replied. She had the high ground, and knew it. "What must you need from me that you've finally come home?"

Virginia's jaw tensed, stopping her from replying just long enough for her mother's stare to land on Jolie.

"You're a bit old for a shotgun wedding, Ginnie," her mother said. "Although it looks like I'm about fifteen years too late for that announcement. I'd ask if she's Arthur's, but he'd never run out on a real family." She stood, the intricately wound chair scraping lightly against the porch. "So whose is she? I imagine that's why you and Arthur split."

"Her name is Jolie, and she's not mine," Virginia finally managed to growl. "She's here on work experience."

Her mother smirked, raising herself to her full, abbreviated height. "I should have known. She doesn't have your frame." Beckoning for Jolie to follow, she pulled open the screen door, holding open the painted white wood, waiting for them to enter.

The steps may as well have been an unscalable mountain, despite their shallow rise. Virginia shuffled up one stair at a time, every muscle in her body screaming at her to run.

"I have to say, I don't know what a darling thing like you is doing following Ginnie around. No real future on the force, and I told her that from the start. But oh, no, she didn't want to hear it from me. Not from her *mother* of all people." Her mother's stare traced over Virginia's face, landing on her scars. "What happened to you?" she asked, a tuft of taffeta getting caught in the gold hinge and tearing a hole in the hem. She didn't seem to notice, despite her immaculate way of dressing. She reached out for Virginia with soft, unweathered hands.

Virginia pulled back from the unwanted grasp, the unfamiliarity of the gesture and the expression on her mother's face too much to handle ten seconds after arriving back home. If she didn't know any better, she might have assumed her mother was concerned, but previous experience suggested the opposite. "Nothing."

"What have you done to yourself?" Her mother's tone had shifted back to the familiar cold, harsh tone she was used to.

"Nothing," Virginia repeated, turning her face away. "Long time ago."

Jolie tossed an apologetic glance at Virginia before following her mother into the house. "You know, Mrs., uh..." she trailed off.

"Cabot."

"Mrs. Cabot, right—Virginia is actually very good at what she does."

Virginia was left standing alone on the porch, somehow unable to bring herself to open the shadows-damned screen door and go inside. It wasn't as if the entire place would collapse in on itself the moment she set foot over the threshold, and yet there she stood, fingers curled around the handle, unmoving.

"I know your father was a lazy louse, but even he managed to open a door by himself," her mother called from the kitchen, her laughter hollow.

"He's lucky enough to be dead already," Virginia muttered, yanking open the door with a fierce twist of her wrist.

The house held too many unwanted reminders of memories she had long since tried to forget, the vestiges of memorial specters haunting every corner of every room. The starched curtains hung over the windows, their rods embellished on either end with florid iron swirls that twisted into each other.

"Do you want some lemonade?" Jolie asked, holding out a glass, the ice cubes clinking with temptation in the glass.

"Ginnie doesn't like lemonade," Virginia's mother answered. "Never has." She sat down in her easy chair, gesturing towards the sofa. "So. There must be some reason you're here now, and not twenty years ago when I asked you to come see me. Or fifteen, or ten." Her mother took a long sip of her lemonade. "Or five."

"I've been busy," Virginia replied.

"I have no doubt that your time has been occupied." Her mother crossed her ankles, tilting her chin upwards. "It can't be enough for a decent lifestyle, no?"

Virginia bristled. "It's decent enough." Her mother arched one perfect eyebrow in question. "It's not money I want, Mom," Virginia retorted, answering what hadn't been asked. "I had some questions about things."

"You've got questions? *I've* got questions, Ginnie," her mother said. "The first of which is didn't I teach you to never show up empty-handed as a guest?" She laughed, waving it off. "I'm only joking, of course. Still, it is nearing supper time." She tilted her head at Virginia, her shorter stature somehow still just as intimidating as it always had been. "You could be a dear and run into town for me, couldn't you?" Her mother reached over, patting Virginia's arm. "It's good to see you, Ginnie. You've been missed."

There was an ache growing in Virginia's chest, and whether it was guilt or nostalgia, it hurt all the same. It was one of the many reasons she could never stand to be home. "Sure, Mom. What do you need?"

"Just pick up some chicken, Ginnie, no need to put on airs. I imagine this young lady would appreciate a good meal, given how she looks three breaths away from fainting."

"Jolie is fine, Mom," Virginia protested, sensing Jolie's hesitation at where the conversation had turned. "Same place as before?"

Her mother sipped from the glass, condensation already soaking the outside and dripping down onto her matching skirt suit. "Same place. You know as well as I do that Birch

Hollow rarely changes.”

“Right.” Virginia aimed for the door, a little part of her thrilled that she was escaping so soon. “Jolie?”

“Right behind you,” Jolie answered after rinsing her glass in the sink. Somehow, without being told, the kid knew how to keep things level. It wouldn’t be enough, of course, but even five minutes without an explosion was a feat to behold.

“You okay with chicken?” Virginia asked, striding to the car with long lengths, her steps almost comically wide. “There’s a couple of other things in town, but not much. A burger place, and a little shack near the river with a catch of the day type thing.”

Jolie climbed into the car, tucking a stray hair back into its large, unkempt bun. “Chicken is fine,” she confirmed. “Maybe we can ask around about Heinrich Harrow while we’re in town.”

“He won’t be in town,” Virginia replied, starting the car. The engine protested, but coughed into life after a few tries. “Bastard thing,” she grumbled, smacking the dashboard. “No, Harrow will be out at the town limits, most likely. Growing up there were always old barns out that way, some of them got turned into Nether dens, others into illegal casinos and betting shops.”

“Do you think it’s Nether?” Jolie asked.

The tires met pavement at the end of the brick driveway, and Virginia turned left, towards town. “It could be. His niece swears he never touched the stuff, but it only takes once.” She glanced at Jolie, hunting for a sign she’d been hurt by what Virginia had said. “Sorry. I just mean—”

“It’s alright. I can see how people would get hooked on it. Even half dead I still felt the power of it.” She cranked the window down, and they both sighed in the cooling breeze of the impending evening. They'd driven most of the day, and the sunset was illuminating the corn with an orange glow, almost as if it was on fire. Jolie stuck her arm out the window, playing with the wind resistance as they drove. "Anya said I might have died if they hadn't given it to me before leaving me on that roof."

"Yeah."

"I don't like feeling out of control." Jolie glanced back at her, pulling her head back inside the car. "Bad things happen."

"Like the library?" Virginia asked, keeping her eyes fixed on the road but keeping watch on Jolie in her periphery. The girl shrank back into the car's seat, turning away.

"Yeah," Jolie replied. "Like the library."

"I wouldn't get too bent out of shape about that. Zin is more concerned about the city coughing up for the repairs than how the hole got there in the first place." The truck rumbled over uneven pavement, just before the center of town became visible around the corner of one more shadows-damned cornfield. "You hungry?" she asked.

Jolie nodded. "Sure."

"This place has the best fried chicken you'll ever eat." Virginia put the car into park, opening her door with a creak. "Tomorrow we'll head out to the town limits. The sooner we track down Heinrich Harrow, the better." She didn't mention any of the rest of it. Jolie was only eighteen, and had better things to be worrying about than Virginia's interpersonal issues, or issues around her questionable status as a mythic, either.

Cracked sidewalk paved the way to the door of the restaurant, dandelions pushing up through the concrete like it was merely a suggestion, their puffy white balls empty, long since dispersed. Long-closed shops lined the path, with rusty door knobs and boarded up windows. One door remained open, the handle polished brass and delicate house plants in the display, their foliage thick and inviting.

The shop's bell jingled, and a familiar voice called out, "Jo! What are you doing here?"

"Anya!" Jo replied, rushing up the steps for a hug. "I didn't expect to see you here."

"You either," Anya replied with a hearty laugh. "And you're with Virginia, too." She waved, releasing Jolie from her affectionate grip.

Virginia fussed with her hair, knowing she must look a state from driving with the windows down. "What in shadows are you doing all the way down here?" she asked casually, straightening the sleeves of her linen button-down shirt. "I thought I was the only person who had the misfortune of knowing where this place was."

"Hmm," Anya began, a coy smile playing on her lips. "Remember about six months ago when I warned you against involving the VCPD in my work?"

"Vaguely," Virginia retorted, not liking where the conversation was headed.

"Do you also remember when you did it anyway, and our mutual friend Captain Lindell tossed my shop, confiscating a number of rare, difficult to replace reagents?" Anya held out a wide wicker basket, stuffed to the brim with leafy plants. "This is what I meant by difficult to replace. My usual importer in Verdance got picked up not long before that, so I had to drag myself all the way down here to meet with someone else."

"Wolfsbane," Virginia commented. "Since when is that illegal?

"Since eighteen months ago," Anya replied. "Impressive that you can spot it on sight. Not many can."

Virginia shrugged easily, feeling sweat gather at the base of her neck and drip down her spine. "Seamus has been my sparring coach for years. You pick things up, now and then."

"Well, between you and me, we've got one hell of a full moon headed our way in a few weeks. A blue moon, they say, and I just know I'll have a pack of baby werewolves in my shop the week after, desperate for something to take the edge off." Anya shifted the weight of the basket to her other arm, wiping a bead of sweat from her brow. "Feels like it's always worse this time of year. I don't know, maybe it's the heat."

"Yeah, maybe," Virginia agreed, still off-balance from seeing Anya in Birch Hollow in the first place. "Heat does strange things to people. And mythics, apparently."

Anya laughed, throwing her head back with such gusto that her silvery braid bobbed along behind her. "This is only half of it. I have another load to collect before..." she trailed off, struggling with the basket to check her delicate wrist watch glinting in the twilight glow. "Oh, shadows," she cursed. "I'll never make it back and forth before he closes. I'd hoped to be onto the next thing tomorrow."

"What's the next thing?" Jolie asked eagerly, holding out her arms to take the basket from Anya. "More ingredients?"

"Something I can only collect at midnight, I'm afraid," Anya replied. "I have more to replenish than just plants."

"And what's that?" Virginia prompted. "I hope it's not

dangerous."

Anya shrugged. "I guess that depends if you think banshees are dangerous or not. To some, perhaps, but they've never frightened me."

"I could help," Jolie offered, perking up after the brief conversation about the library. "If Virginia doesn't mind."

"I don't mind," Virginia said, even though she would miss Jolie's presence when she had to drive back to her mother's house. "But don't you want to eat first?"

"I have some prime sandwiches in the car," Anya offered, rubbing the red marks out of her arm where the basket had rested. "I got them from that good deli before I drove down. If I'd have known, maybe we could have come down together." She tilted her head. "We've covered why I'm here, but why are you here?"

"Case," Virginia answered simply.

Anya nodded. "Of course. I guess I didn't think you'd come out this far."

"I don't, usually." The smell of hot grease wafted down the fissured street, and Virginia turned towards the restaurant. "You two should get a move on, if you're going to finish before that shop closes." A tall, slender botanist stood lurking in the window, staring out at them with a potted orchid in his hands. "He doesn't seem like the patient type."

"I can bring her back tomorrow morning," Anya said, waving at the botanist. "Where are you staying?"

"Just come back to town, I'll be here," Virginia replied. "It's not as if you won't be able to find me. This place as about as much going on as a market in the middle of the night."

"Be careful, Virginia," Anya said, heading back up the steps into the shop. "A lot goes on at night, even here in Birch Hollow."

Chapter Five

Virginia pushed through the screen door, letting it slam behind her with a sharp snap. The chicken was already starting to get cold, as the drive back had been perilous in the dark, all the way out there with no street lights. She'd forgotten how to drive in that kind of darkness. Maybe she'd intended to.

"I'm back, Mom," she called, setting the brown paper bags on the table, varnish chipping at the edges but perfectly clean otherwise. "Mom?"

"I'm here, keep your skirt on," her mother muttered, shuffling into the room. "Though I guess you never were one for skirts." She looked up at Virginia, questioning. "Where's the girl?"

"We ran into a friend in town, she wanted to help with something." Virginia began to unpack the bags, setting each paper container out onto marble trivets, a foregone effort to protect the wood. "I'll pick her up in town tomorrow."

"Who's this friend?"

"Just someone from the city. Owns an apothecary, helped us out of a jam last winter."

Her mother started to unfold the lids of each container,

releasing the last of the steam into the already humid air. "What kind of jam? You're not in trouble, are you Ginnie?"

"Not anymore."

"Police business?"

Virginia bit her tongue, trying to buy herself some time. "Yeah, police business," she replied. Her mother didn't know she'd been discharged from the VCPD, and it didn't feel like the right time to let that story loose. It would only lead to dozens more questions, interrogation style. "Some crew was trying to get hold of Jolie."

"What is she?" her mother asked. "She must be something special to attract that kind of attention."

"She's—" Virginia stopped short, not wanting to tell the poor kid's story for her. "You'll have to ask her."

"I wouldn't *say* anything, Ginnie. I have some tact."

"It's just not my place. If she wants to tell you, she can." Virginia pulled two plates and matching utensils from the same cabinets and drawers they'd always been in, and a part of her resented that she remembered without even trying. The ghost of the house lived in her like a parasite, and it always had. "I have a case down here I'm following up on, some financial fraud. A man stole everything from his family and took off."

"That hardly seems like it's worth the department's time when there are crews running rampant all over the city," her mother chided. "Who's the chief of police up there now?" she asked. "Maybe they need a stern talking to about priorities."

"It's Arthur, actually," Virginia said, purposefully not looking at her mother when she said it. She wasn't sure she could bear whatever would come next.

"Arthur! Well, I never. He's certainly moved up in the

world, hasn't he?" Her mother frowned at the paper bag, poking at its emptiness. "Is that all?"

"They were out of those honey butter biscuits you like," Virginia replied with a shrug. "Sorry."

"Oh well, I suppose I wasn't hungry anyway."

"You should eat, Mom." Virginia nudged a box of chicken towards her, sliding it across the wood.

"What happened with Arthur?" her mother asked. "You two were always so close, I rarely saw one of you without the other. I wanted you to come out here when I heard that you'd parted ways—his parents phoned me, you understand." Her stare fell on Virginia's scars once more. "I can only imagine the mess you've gotten yourself into."

"That wasn't part of it," Virginia insisted. "Anyway, that's not why I'm here." She doled herself several pieces of fried chicken, piling a heaping portion of cole slaw next to it. She hadn't missed Birch Hollow, not even a little bit, but she had missed the chicken. "I needed to ask you about some family history."

"What's the matter, are you sick?"

Virginia glanced at her. "No, I'm not sick."

"If you're sick, I know the best little tincture that I got from the fellow in town." Her mother started rummaging through the cabinets, the chicken on the table abandoned. "It will certainly soothe what ails you, but you can only take it in small doses."

"I'm not sick, Mom." Virginia poked at her coleslaw before setting her fork down against the plate. "I wanted to ask if there is history of mythics in our family."

"Mythics!" her mother said with a gasp, closing a cabinet door a little too hard to have been accidental. "What do you need to know about that?"

"It's important, Mom."

"No, we don't have any mythics in our family, thank God." Her mother pulled a gold cross necklace from inside her house dress, kissing it briefly. "You should be grateful that none of us, not even your awful cousins, were afflicted by the Rupture."

"The Rupture didn't create mythics, Mom, it just revealed them."

Her mother set a fork into the sink with a louder clatter than was necessary. "I'm aware, Ginnie."

"I'm not trying to talk down to you, I'm just explaining." Virginia took a bite of the chicken, but the mood had soured more than just the temperament in the room. She set it down, pushing the plate away from her. "I just need to know."

"Not on my side, that's for certain," her mother answered. "And as far as I know, your father didn't either, although that man had plenty of secrets." She filled the sink with hot, soapy water, setting the dishes down beneath the bubbles. "For all I know he was both a shifter and a witch. He kept his own company faithfully, but no one else's." She turned, raising an eyebrow at Virginia. "Though you have always taken after his side more. It's why you have his green eyes and his pointed chin, his stocky shoulders. I prayed you'd grow out of it, but..." she trailed off for a moment. "You didn't."

Outside, the cicadas roared, the sound humming through the trees in waves, a strange, foreign comfort after so many summers in the city. Virginia picked at the chicken again, now cold and unappetizing. "Don't worry, we'll be out of your hair soon enough," she said.

"Ginnie..." her mother started, sitting across from her at the table. "I've missed you, all these years. I know things haven't always been the greatest between us, but I did always hope you'd come back to me." Her mother reached across the white table runner, patting Virginia's arm with more motherly affection than she'd shown in at least three and a half decades. "I wish it hadn't taken so long."

Virginia shifted uncomfortably in the chair, the cushion sinking down to the frame. "It's complicated, Mom."

"I certainly understand complication. I may be old, but I was your age too, once." Her mother sighed wistfully, releasing Virginia's arm to pick at the abandoned chicken with a frown. "It's never as good cold, is it?"

"No," Virginia agreed.

"Why ask about mythics, then?"

"It's a long story."

Her mother gave her a sideways glance, her eyes sparkling with something dangerous. "I love stories." She picked another chunk from a leg of chicken, depositing the cleaned bone back into the box. "Did something happen?"

Virginia's lungs seared with the words caught in her throat. The indecision of how much to share was always a stumbling block in Birch Hollow. "I don't know if I want to talk about it," she answered, honest with her mother for the first time in many years. "I would prefer we didn't."

"I'm your mother," she scoffed, taking the remaining chicken to the icebox. "What could you have to say that I don't have the right to know? If there's something wrong, you need to tell me." She glanced back at Virginia as she closed the icebox door, leaning against the counters to wipe her hands on the half apron tied around her waist to protect her dress. "So, what happened?"

Another wave of cicada noise drowned out the rest of the outside noises, deafening the house to anything else. "Arthur thinks I'm a seer," Virginia said finally, regretting the words as soon as they left her mouth.

Her mother was quiet for a long, frustrated moment. "A seer," she said quietly, and tacked a chuckle onto the end of her words. "Surely you would have known by now if you were. If you were a seer, Ginnie, you could have solved that Juliette Ashling case back when you were young."

The name rang in Virginia's ears louder than the cicadas, and her stomach churned with such vigor, she thought for a moment that she might have to revisit what little dinner she'd had. "I told him that I'm not, but he's insistent. I drove down to chase up a lead, so I figured I would stop by and ask."

"I didn't think the VCPD would have jurisdiction this far south," her mother mused.

"Special case," Virginia lied, sliding right back into the comfort of familial perjury. "So you don't know anything? No seers in the family? Everyone knows that it's hereditary, so if you aren't, and my father wasn't, then Arthur is off his rocker again."

Her mother nodded slowly, straightening the edges of the lace runner. "Well, you know what they say about seers," she said, not really answering the question.

"No," Virginia replied. "What do they say?"

"They can see everything except what's in front of them." Her mother gave her a strange look built half of pity and half of suspicion, a strange and unsettling combination. When the phone rang, she answered it, talking softly into the receiver as she always had. Virginia strained to hear what she was saying, only picking up every third word until she hung up a few moments later.

"Who was that?" Virginia asked.

"Do you remember Mrs. Speer from church?"

"Vaguely." She and Juliette used to steal Mrs. Speer's strawberries in the summer, sneaking through the trees and giggling as they ran back to the woods with their stolen prize.

"She's a bit worried about her son, that's all. She struggles now that her husband has passed on." Her mother straightened the phone on the side table, lining up the edges. "Between you and I, her son has plenty of problems."

"Did you say she lost some money?" Virginia asked. She didn't remember much about the Speers, just where they lived and that they had two sons, one older than her, and one younger.

Her mother's brow furrowed, irritated that Virginia had eavesdropped, no doubt. "Yes, her son lost some money to a con man in town. James Folst, I think she said." She fixed her collar as she checked her reflection in the dark window, frowning at it. "From what I hear, he's taken money from several folks in town."

"Is he still in town?"

"Oh, I don't know, Ginnie. I've only laid eyes on the man once, and that was at a distance. He drives a flashy car, cherry red with white rims. Nicest car in town by far." Her mother tightened her apron strings and let the loose ties fall back to her sides. "He's not been in town very long, but oh, the damage he's already wrought."

"What about the old gambling barns at the edge of town?" Virginia prompted. "Are those still around?" She played with the knuckles in her pocket, fingers toying with the edges. It was Harrow, it had to be. The town was small, unlikely to attract more than one creative thief.

Her mother turned to brush invisible crumbs from the counter. "Ginnie, those places are up to no good, always have been. I don't want you involving yourself in this, there are enough skeletons in this town's closet where you're concerned."

"That's a yes, then," Virginia replied, standing and rolling her sleeves back down, buttoning the cuffs at her wrists. She bristled, but tried to hide it. "And the old bar on main street, is that still a haunt for undesirables?" she asked. If it wasn't Heinrich Harrow, it had to be someone he was working with. Birds of a feather tended to descend on rural towns in unison, sometimes a tandem unit to squeeze as much as they could from unsuspecting victims. "Don't wait up."

Chapter Six

Club Cloud was a dingy hole in the wall where the exterior bricks had been crumbling for decades. The neon sign above the door flickered, the second letter c flashing in and out of existence. Club Cloud. Club Loud.

Virginia watched from the dark comfort of her car as drunk patrons stumbled out into the street. According to her wrist watch, the last call bell had already sounded. Hopefully, she wasn't too late. It was obvious that her mother was hiding something, and she wanted to know what.

She sighed, frustrated at the stuffiness of the car, but not wanting to attract too much attention by rolling the window down any further than it already was. Birch Hollow was no Verdance, and the club she was staring at was a far cry from the Sphinx. Even given how things had ended with Astrid the last time she'd seen her, she'd prefer that confrontation to being in the middle of nowhere, having to deal with her mother again.

"And stay out!" the club owner shouted, tossing a patron out on his ear. Virginia didn't recognize the owner, but she'd never frequented Club Cloud much anyway. It was a place for gambling and dirty deals, and she tried hard to stay away from both. Well, she had in her youth, at least.

The patron he'd tossed out was wearing a light blue cap, picking himself up off the sidewalk. "Yeah, and fuck you too!" he shouted through the closed door, and there were sounds of raucous laughter from within. It wasn't Heinrich Harrow, he was much taller, sinewy instead of broad, and had dark facial hair that obscured the bottom half of his face. He checked his pockets, fishing out a tan leather wallet and a set of gold keys, ostentatious even in the darkness of the abbreviated main street.

He unlocked the candy apple red car, and she leaned forward over the steering wheel. James Folst. It was perfectly detailed without even a speck of dust, which was some sort of automotive miracle given the amount of gravel roads that far from the interstate. He slammed the door behind himself, starting the car and peeling off for the edge of town.

Twisting the keys in her own ignition, Virginia followed, but at a distance. It was harder to remain unseen when there weren't any other cars on the road. There was a tractor turning left at an intersection, but that was it. The car rumbled along, and Virginia silently cursed it for that damnable rattle in the engine. They were heading for the town limits, exactly where she'd expected Heinrich Harrow to be hiding out.

"Birds of a feather," she muttered to herself. Maybe she'd somehow manage to nab both of them in one night. Both jailbirds with one stone, and then she and Jolie could be headed out of town and out to the coast first thing in the morning. It was a short-lived dream, however, because the fraudster turned down a dirt road, away from the edge of town.

It wasn't even so much a road as a deer trail, just tracks in dirt as they wound through a sparse patch of trees. Virginia cut the engine, worried that if she turned down that path, she'd never get the car back out. It was possible she'd been spotted, and it was a trap.

They were on the far side of town, about a mile short of where the old barns stood at the edges of fields, looking calm and serene on the outside, but harboring plenty of illegality within. It wasn't impossible that he was stashing his fancy car to hike the rest of the way, but it would be unusual. There was no need, not when three of the four cops in Birch Hollow frequented those venues at least a few nights a week. An open secret for a town that hid hundreds more.

She picked her way past thorny vines and brambles, cursing under her breath when one snagged at the fabric of her shirt, creating a pull in the weave. He was already fading into the dust ahead, still driving when she had stopped.

Regretting her decision, she looked back at her car but it was too late to change her mind. She pressed on through the trees, moonlight flickering down through leafy branches to dance on the path under her feet. His car had left deep ruts in the loose dirt. She could only imagine how treacherous the path must have been in spring, sunken with mud and half-melted snow.

Ahead, the car's engine stopped. Virginia froze, her hand halfway to the trunk of a tree to balance herself as she stepped over the large, exposed roots clustered at the base.

"Damned backwoods rift-hole," he grumbled, slamming the door. "Can't wait to make it back to the city."

Virginia hovered on the path, waiting for him to move. Though she was suddenly very glad that she hadn't stayed in the car, she also didn't want to risk him walking back that way and discovering her. He turned towards her, squinting into the darkness, and the silver knuckles in her pocket slipped easily over her fingers, an automatic, unthinking gesture that had saved her life at least a few times.

He grunted, the sound echoing back along the dust and dirt. He kept on walking in the same direction he'd been headed, disappearing into the thicket of trees. She followed, eager for the opportunity to gain some ground on him, but still aware that it was all too easy to get caught, and she wasn't on home turf, not really. She'd spent too much time scraping Birch Hollow out of her, burning whatever was left so she wasn't tempted to miss it.

The path grew darker the further she went into the woods, these trees much taller and denser than the ones at the start of the path. The light from the moon struggled to penetrate the canopy there, cloaking her in such a black night she could barely feel her way along the dirt and the dust.

Up ahead of her, he swore angrily, and there was the sound of a rock clattering along sandy soil. "Fucking middle-of-nowhere place," he muttered, but it was quiet enough that the barely present wind carried his voice easily. "Never coming out here again. It's going to take years to get this friggin' soil out of the car."

He emerged into a clearing, and the porch light of a small house, more of a cabin, really, lit up. It was the Speer homestead, looking much like it had decades previous. The orangey glow laid upon dead grass, yellow and crispy. High summer was never kind to lawns. "I'm here, finally," he called, climbing the three steps onto the porch.

The interior door opened, but whoever was in there stayed

hidden behind the door. Curious for someone to be so afraid of detection when no one was watching, but those addicted to Nether were rarely sensible in their aims. James Folst pulled open the screen door of his own accord, disappearing inside.

She watched from the tree line, but even stranger for the weather, the house was all sealed tight. The windows were all closed, as was the interior door, so there was no sound from within. Instead, she was enveloped in the blanket of insect noise, nothing but cicadas and crickets screeching their incessant drone, and somewhere in the distance, coyotes yipped in unison.

The lights in the house were on, every single one of them, from what Virginia could tell. Every window covered with a lace panel thin enough to see silhouettes through the delicacy, but she hadn't seen one yet. Whoever was in there was either lingering by the door, or there was a basement they'd disappeared into. They weren't uncommon in the Midwest, not with all of the tornadoes that continued to rip apart town after town, year on year, season after season.

It could have been ten minutes or an hour, it was hard to tell in the darkness. There wasn't enough light beyond the tree line to read her wrist watch, despite her futile attempts to catch a dull reflection from the house. Whoever that man was, and whatever he was up to, being inside a house was hardly a crime—but what would Mrs. Speer be doing letting in the man who conned her?

Virginia straightened, rubbing at the throb in her lower back. Perhaps it was the son. Or perhaps Mrs. Speer was hoping for reconciliation, repayment, or reparations for what the man had done.

She waited longer, so long that the ache in her muscles

began to stab at her angrily, insisting she give up the chase and return home. He likely wouldn't leave until morning, given the lateness of the hour.

Just as she was about to turn back up the path, there was a loud crack, and a muzzle flash so bright it pierced through the lacy curtains. There was another immediately after.

Virginia reached for her holster, alarmed that it wasn't there, and cursed herself for leaving it on the passenger seat of her car. She waited, hesitating, but for what, she wasn't sure. No voices escaped the vacuum of the small house. No sound had, except what she was sure was a gunshot.

She waited for him to reemerge, to wring blood from his ill-fitting checkered suit and climb back into his car, but he didn't. Something sick and gnawing landed in her gut, and despite her internal protestations, she crept closer to the house. There were no guards there, in fact, she would have been surprised if there was anyone within half a mile of the place.

Curiously, the porch stairs did not creak under her weight, even though she'd anticipated it. They were solid maple, from the looks of them, and recently varnished. The screen door was brand new, the paint still glossy and unmarred by either water spots or dust. She reached out for the handle but pulled her hand back, afraid she would alert whoever was still within.

The silver knuckles snug around her fingers, she side-stepped the front door to crouch under the window. There were no shadows, no sign that anyone was still in there at all. Virginia peered over the sill, grateful that the flower box was empty. Through the haze of the lace, there the man lay in a puddle of his own blood, which was oozing slowly across the wood, dripping down between varnished floorboards.

She ducked down to breathe, and once her lungs had recovered from the strain, rose up over the sill once again. It was certainly him, a scarlet stain starting to toil its way across his lapel. He'd been shot in the head, that much was obvious. His eyes were still wide in surprise, his mouth forming a word he'd never had the opportunity to say.

Someone was in there, and they were armed.

Virginia knew better than to bring a pair of knuckles to a gun fight, and was silently cursing herself to hell and back, wishing she could throw herself directly into the rift that the shadows had poured from for leaving her gun in the car. She slunk back into the shadowy safety of the tree line, heading for her car.

She'd have to call the Birch Hollow police, feckless fools that they were. Virginia knew better than to try dealing with it on her own. It wasn't her jurisdiction.

Nowhere was.

***

Officer Carsh was the first to arrive on the scene, lazily climbing his way out of the car, his spindly legs long and spider-like. "Well, if it isn't Ginnie Cabot," he droned in the same monotone he'd always had. "I didn't expect to see you around these parts again."

"Didn't intend to be here," Virginia said, deciding she wouldn't correct him. She'd already had enough run-ins with him, she didn't want to spark any more questions than she inevitably already had. "It's a long story."

The red and blue of the squad unit's lights flashed over the scene, the odd glow illuminating the thick canopy in quick strobes. The officer turned towards the house, adjusting his cap to sit higher on his brow. "What did you say you were doing out here?" he asked.

Virginia swallowed hard. "I didn't," she replied.

"It's a bit remote to have been a coincidence," he said, toying with his radio, turning it around in his hands. "And it's a bit late for a walk."

"I told you, it's a long story."

He sighed, ambling towards the porch. "I have to say, Ginnie, I didn't miss you sniffing around in things that don't concern you," he grumbled. "Town's been much quieter since you left."

She bit her tongue until the pain cleared her thoughts, the clamp of her jaw the only thing keeping her from losing whatever was left of her composure. Her skin prickled with midnight sweat, the run to the car, then rushing into town to the small police station, then all but sprinting back had been a trial in the night's humidity.

"Police," Officer Carsh called through the door, rapping sharply against the metal screen door. He tugged at it, finding it open, and so then knocked on the interior door, shouting out again. "We have a few questions for you."

There was no reply, of course. Virginia hadn't expected there would be, not when so many escapable moments had passed since the shot had rang out over the din of the summer's insects.

The officer glanced back at Virginia with a skeptical frown, the same one he'd had all those years ago. He was indistinguishable from his younger self, down to the even, measured gait he walked with. "I don't think anyone's home," he said.

"I'll come back in the morning."

"I think you should look through the window," Virginia replied, nodding to the left towards the sill.

He rolled his eyes but listened to her for once, and gave a theatrical gasp. "Well, what do you know," he said. "A whole lotta nothing."

"I'm sorry, a dead body is nothing now?" Virginia challenged, climbing the steps herself. "Honestly, some things in this place never cease to—" she stopped short, shock grasping her at the throat. "Where did he go?"

"Ginnie..." he trailed off, picking at the gold badge on his chest. "Does your mother know you're in town?"

"Yes."

"Maybe I should drive you back there. Maybe she can get you admitted at the county hospital tomorrow, or—"

"I'm not ill!" she protested, backing off the porch. "I was here, I heard two shots, there was a corpse just under those lace curtains. I saw it!"

Officer Carsh's face twisted into grotesque pity, reaching for her wrist. "This isn't the first time you've had these problems, Ginnie," he said gently. "You were warned back then to leave things alone. We all thought you'd gone off to the city and gotten better. Shadows, you joined the VCPD and we were all so proud of you."

"Don't touch me," Virginia said, yanking her wrist away. Blood was pounding in her ears and bile rose in her throat, greasy and present. "That was different, and you know it."

"It's not so different from where I'm standing." Officer Carsh sighed, peering through the window again, and in the glow from the cabin, the deepened lines on his face were more apparent. "There are no cars here, Ginnie. No people, no corpses. What am I supposed to think about that when you're dragging me out of bed in the middle of the night?" he asked. "I'm going to need you to give me a good reason as to why you were out here creeping around, and if it has anything to do with the Ashling girl, then—"

"No," Virginia interrupted, unable to dive down into that particular warren. It had been too long and too sharp to risk revisiting it. "It doesn't have anything to do with her." She raked a hand through her hair, her fingers coming away sweaty. "I was out for a walk, and wondered where this path led. I didn't remember it from before."

"I find that hard to believe, Ginnie," Officer Carsh replied. "Seems to me it would be best for everyone if I dropped you in the tank for the night, okay? Then tomorrow you can get on back to the city. I'd hate for your mother to see you like this."

Virginia shook her head. "No, I'm not intoxicated." She grabbed the flashlight off the holster at his hip, shining the bright light into her own face. "See? No signs of anything that would impair me. I am telling you that in the time it took me to get back to my own vehicle, get into town, rouse you, which took forever, by the way, and get back, someone cleared the body and moved his car."

"That's very far-fetched," he said. "Listen, it's late. I'll take you to the station, and you can call your mother in the morning to pick you up. I wouldn't want to wake her." His stare bored into her, looking for something that wasn't there, and never had been. "Your mother is getting on in years, you know."

"Yeah, I'm aware of how the passage of time works." Virginia turned back up the path, her hands shaking, and her lungs forgetting how to inflate. She just had to make it to the car. If she could make it to the car, then the whole nightmare could be over. She'd collect Jolie first thing in the morning and never look back.

"If you get home tonight and get gone tomorrow, we can just forget this ever happened," Officer Carsh said, following her. "Otherwise, I have to arrest you for trespassing."

"It's not trespassing if it's unmarked," she shot back.

He caught up to her, grabbing her by the elbow. "Look," he said, pointing at a sign half hidden in the foliage where the path forked out onto the road. "It *is* marked."

Virginia swore under her breath, knowing she wouldn't be able to shake him, not after that. She held her wrists out, ignoring the stray grey curl hanging in front of her eye. "Fine, Carsh. But I want a lawyer, and I'm choosing who we call."

"Ginnie—" he started, holstering the flashlight again. "I don't think we need to get too excited about all this, as long as you agree to cooperate."

"I want my call the moment we hit the station," she said. "I know my rights."

"Well, yeah, I'd expect you to." He gestured towards the squad unit, parked up right next to her car. "I won't cuff you if you go politely."

She swallowed back the urge to be impolite, to force his hand, to wind up in cuffs again, this time in Birch Hollow. Virginia nodded. "Fine." She climbed into the back of the car, leaning her head against the warm glass of the window. Things were unraveling, just as she'd feared they would.

Chapter Seven

It had been a good while since she'd actually spent a night in jail. The heat was stagnant and oppressive, rising up off the floor and hanging in the air. Breathing felt like drowning, but then, that was always how Birch Hollow had felt. It was suffocation from the town limits all the way back to the highway.

"Morning, Sunshine," Anya said, appearing like a vision from around the corner.

Virginia sat up, trying to smooth the wrinkles of her shirt in a feeble attempt to look respectable. "How did you find out I was here?" she asked.

"Sheriff Dixon," Jolie replied, following behind. "You didn't show up this morning, and your car wasn't at your mother's place. Anya called VCPD headquarters and asked Captain Lindell to run a check."

"Yeah, Officer Carsh wasn't interested in letting me go once he figured out I was calling in favors from Verdance." Virginia sighed, standing and tucking her shirt back in. "They have a real chip on their shoulders about the city down here." She didn't mention that Carsh thought she still worked for the VCPD, or why she'd been picked up in the first place.

"I tried to pay bail, but it sounds like they're more interested in getting you out of town," Anya explained, waiting at the iron bars. "What did you do?"

"Long story," Virginia replied. "Old grudges tend to stick around."

Anya snorted an indelicate laugh. "I'm shocked, Virginia."

"Are you getting me out of here or not?"

Officer Carsh ambled in, deep circles under his eyes. The decades had taken their toll on him. He was only seven years older than Virginia was, but age weighed heavily on his skin. "Hold your horses, Ginnie, give me a minute." He thrust a large silver key into the cell's lock, sliding open the door. "How long are you in town for?" he asked. It was phrased as a polite question, but the subtext was obvious in the context of the previous night.

"I don't know," Virginia replied, not particularly eager to assuage his fears. "As you said, my mother is getting on in years."

"Perhaps she'd be happier in Verdance?" he suggested, clipping the large ring of keys back onto his belt. "I know a few folks who've had their eye on her place for a while. Wouldn't be a hard sell, I don't think."

"Drop it, Eugene," she snapped, leaving the cell behind her. "I'll go when I'm damn well good and ready."

"You can't just show up here and start causing problems," Officer Carsh replied, hands on his narrow hips. "Birch Hollow is a fine town, and we'd like to keep it that way."

"Yeah, by brushing everything under the rug," Virginia shot back, emboldened by her freedom. "Send the fine to my mother's house."

Officer Carsh lingered in the doorway, even as she pushed

past him. "Ginnie, I have to warn you that I can't cover for you with this trespassing charge. If you don't leave town today, you'll be facing charges and a likely court date. Someone should tell your mother what you've been up to. I'm sure she'd be concerned."

"Yeah," Virginia replied. "Real concerned." She hovered at the door to the street, her fingers lingering on the handle. "Do you know of a Heinrich Harrow?" she asked. "Reports are that he's hiding out here. I would assume you don't want him causing problems, either." She didn't mention James Folst's corpse again, wary that Carsh really would have her dragged to the hospital.

"Never heard of him," Officer Carsh replied coldly. "Never seen hide nor hair of him around these parts. Maybe you should check those reports again, Ginnie."

"Or you could open your eyes," she retorted. "But then, this department has never been very good at that."

Anya's brow furrowed, and she herded Jolie closer to the door. "Let's go pick up your car," she said to Virginia, tugging at her rolled up sleeve. "Pick up some pastries or something."

Virginia straightened her lapels with a resigned sigh. "Yeah, fine," she grumbled.

"Stay out of trouble, Ginnie," Officer Carsh warned. "It's a small town. You never know who's watching."

"Not you, clearly," she muttered. Outside, the morning sun was already hot, sizzling the remains of dew on the crispy grass. "Thank you for the rescue," she said, and meant it. "I think he'd have let me sit in there until this afternoon, otherwise."

"So what did you do?" Anya asked, once they were out of

earshot of the police station. "Casual vandalism?"

"Unintended trespassing," Virginia answered with a roll of her eyes. "Went out for a walk, that's all." Whatever was going on out there, Anya and Jolie didn't need to wind up mixed up in it. "They have plenty of problems here, and it seems like most of them are with me."

Anya arched an eyebrow, but didn't say anything more about it. "We hiked out past the fields last night," she said casually. "I should be set for at least half a year, barring the possibility that Captain Lindell will toss my shop again."

"Are you ever going to let me live that down?" Virginia asked sullenly.

"Probably not," Anya answered, but handed Virginia a dark blue reagents pouch. "And Jo found some moon blossoms."

Virginia flipped back the straps, peering inside. There were around twenty small white blooms, already tied at the stems with hemp for drying. "I'm assuming that's impressive. What are they for?"

"Illusion magic." Anya took the pouch back, slinging it diagonally over her shoulders. "I used up the rest when we rescued Jo."

Jolie bent, picking a dandelion and blowing at the puff with a soft, girlish giggle. "I wish I'd seen it," she said. "But I was too busy dying on the roof."

"You'll have to try harder next time," Virginia said, but even the vague, hypothetical thought of Jolie being in danger set razors in her stomach, slicing away at her gut one flash at a time. "The bakery at the end of the street is our best bet for breakfast. None of the restaurants open until mid-afternoon."

"Won't your mother be worried?" Jolie asked.

"Yes, about that," Anya said. "I thought you were follow-ing up on a lead."

Virginia ground her teeth, savoring the sharp pain in her jaw. "I am." She toyed with her sleeve, rolling it down and back up again to straighten the cuff. "It's just a coincidence that I grew up here. Trust me, being here is hardly by choice." She fixed the other sleeve, grateful for something to focus on, some movement to fill the silence until she was ready to divulge more. "And she might be worried, yes Jolie," she relented. "But she'll be fine."

"Are you going to tell her what happened?" Jolie asked.

Virginia grimaced, turning up the sidewalk to the bakery's door. "I'd be very surprised if she didn't know already. Word travels fast in a place like this."

"Seems to me that while growing up in Verdance is a test of stamina and charisma, it at least offered me some anonymity," Anya said. "Until the Rupture, anyway."

"People here were whispering long before that," Virginia corrected. "They might not have known exactly what was going on, but they were certainly able to discern that things were happening just out sight of their periphery." She shrugged, almost petulant. "Half the place was accusing the other half of being involved in some sort of strange cult. Turns out, there was just a pack of werewolves and the like here, hiding from the city. Most have long since moved on."

The bakery was mercifully dark, the only light being the outside filtering through a rain-stained front window. "Are you coming?" Virginia called back through the open door.

"Oh shadows, are those cinnamon buns?" Jolie asked excitedly, breezing past Virginia to press her nose against the display glass, marveling at the options. "Look! Cinnamon buns!" she exclaimed.

"Get half a dozen," Virginia said, handing the girl a wad of cash. "Mom will eat at least two, but only when we're not looking."

Anya fumbled with the pouch, clasping and releasing the latch with a soft metallic pop every time she did it. "I hope you're including me in those calculations."

"Quinn, after bailing my ass out this morning, I'll buy you half the damned shop if you want it." Virginia pressed a hand against the wall for balance, and the fear of her seeing boiled relentlessly in her stomach, but nothing came. Perhaps she'd lost her touch.

"I didn't bail you out," Anya corrected. "I only nudged them."

"What did Arthur—er, Sheriff Dixon say?" Virginia asked.

"I only spoke to Captain Lindell." Anya tossed out a sideways glance, but Virginia ignored it. A frown settled on Anya's face, and she grew stony. "She was more than happy to leap into action on your behalf."

Virginia dug her hand into her pocket, searching for the cigarette case. How long had it been since she'd had one? "How magnanimous," she droned. "A paragon of virtue."

"What are you looking for?" Anya asked.

"Cigs," Virginia answered simply. "Haven't had once since the drive back last night." She cursed, turning out her pockets and only finding lint, a rubber band, two thumb tacks, and a crumpled receipt from when she'd gotten gas on the way down. There was no cigarette case. She dove into her pockets again, willing it to appear, but it didn't. "Shadows be damned," she hissed, already at the windows, looking for the opening hours of the gas station across the street, but not finding it. The matchbook was gone, too. "Bastard Carsh must have kept them."

"We can go back," Anya offered with a wide and genuine smile. "You could even get me to ask. I don't think he hates me as much as he hates you."

Virginia snorted a laugh. "I don't think that man hates anyone more than me, to be honest." Still, the loss of it burned like fire through a photograph, and she craved the familiar weight of the silver in her hands. "No gun, no cigs, no suspect." She leaned against the wall, letting it brace her head. "Perfect."

"I got a dozen," Jolie said, returning from the counter with a large powder-pink box. "I wanted to make sure everyone had enough." She shifted the weight of the pastries from one hand to the other, an excited bounce in her step.

"I'll take a cinnamon bun, Jo," Anya said brightly, reaching for the box.

"Eating inside is for customers only," the baker said, standing with his hands on his hips.

"We *are* customers," Anya protested, nodding at the box.

"Eating inside is for *real* customers," the baker reiterated, leaning over the fingerprinted glass counter. "Not tourists." He glanced at Virginia, tilting his head like he recognized her, and maybe he did. He'd run the place since she was a child. "Hey, are you—"

"There's a retaining wall just around the side," Virginia interjected, striding for the door before all the air was sucked out of her lungs by the vacuum of the past. "We can eat there." She pushed through the door into the growing heat, the wave of it hitting her all at once, immediately drawing a prickle of sweat beneath her arms.

"Are you okay?" Jolie asked, jogging with the box to catch up. "I'm sorry you were stuck in the station overnight."

"Don't worry about it." Virginia forced a smile, but knew from the concern on Jolie's face that it hadn't been very convincing. "I'm sorry I wasn't there to collect you this morning."

"It's not like you had a choice." Jolie swatted a small bee away from the box with a frown. "Damn, it's hot."

Virginia nodded in agreement, and then laughed lightly. "Too hot, said the fire demon." she said. "Quinn, are you ready for downstate heat?"

"I've had hotter than this," Anya replied, slipping a pastry out of the box as they walked. "Much, much hotter."

"Alright, no need to be gratuitous," Virginia chided, trying to convince both of them that the night spent in a cell hadn't impacted her. She joined Anya on the retaining wall, the cinderblocks as rough as she remembered, and already scuffing the backs of her brogues. "These are just as good as they used to be," she mused, despite the fact that the sugar was turning to ash in her mouth. *Juliette, Juliette.* The name pounded through her consciousness with every heart beat, pulling closer to the surface. They'd gotten cinnamon rolls from that bakery every Saturday when they were kids.

"Any leads on that case?" Anya asked politely, licking the sugar glaze from her fingers. "Are you going to drag this guy back to Verdance?"

"No jurisdiction," Virginia explained. "But if I find him, I can let his niece know where she can find him, if she desires her pound of flesh. No doubt Heinrich Harrow has already blown through whatever he stole."

"I can't say I'm sorry for the company." Anya brushed the

remaining crumbs from her palms and dress, letting them float to the ground like maple seeds. "I didn't expect to bump into either of you here. Jo was quite the apprentice last night, too."

"Oh?" Virginia prompted, grateful that the conversation was shifting in another direction.

Jolie took a large bite of her roll as she nodded. "Turns out I have a knack for plant identification," she said between bites. "Who knew?"

"It doesn't surprise me, you've read every damn book in the apartment at least three times over. Zin is going to throw me into the lake if I don't get those borrowed copies back. Librarians are scarier than any mythic, if you ask me." Virginia's treat was left half-eaten, the rest of it too much of a burden for her stomach to handle. She folded it into a napkin and slid it back into the box. "I'll finish mine later," she lied. What she really wanted was a cigarette and a very large shot of gin. "Anya, what's on your docket today?" she asked, eager to keep the conversation away from the corpse, the arrest, Juliette, her mother, and the fact that the car was still sitting near the path, sitting just off the side of the road. "Anything exciting?"

"I have a few more things to gather, but it's a few miles up the road in Murph Township. Do you know it?" she asked, reaching for a second cinnamon bun.

"I know it," Virginia responded. "It's small. Smaller than here, even. Stay away from the clocktower."

"What?" Anya asked with a laugh, coughing on the sugar she'd inhaled. "Why?"

Virginia shielded her eyes from the sun, resenting the oppression of the heat. "Bees," she answered simply. "Lots of them. They like the orchids and the lilies that bloom near there."

Anya took another bite, chewing thoughtfully. "Duly noted. And are you going to get yourself arrested again taking a walk late at night?"

"That depends," Virginia said. "Hopefully not. I'm sure Arthur and Shirin didn't appreciate my middle of the night calls."

"Why not call your mother?" Anya asked.

Virginia shot her a sideways glance. "She's old. I didn't want to scare her. I was fine, anyway. Carsh just wanted to throw his weight around. He doesn't get many opportunities here, as you can probably imagine."

"Come on," Anya said, pushing herself off the retaining wall. "I'll give you a ride back to your car."

"Don't worry about me, I'll walk over later." Virginia stifled a yawn, swallowing it back into her mostly empty stomach. She reached into her pocket, finding the knuckles and the comfort they held. Her holster, however, was still missing. Her gun was still in the car, near the woods, unguarded, and possibly already stolen, depending on the town's ratio of lowlife scum. "Actually, that would be great," she corrected. "I don't have my gun."

"Do you think you'll be needing it?" Anya asked, the corners of her lips gently upturned into a half smile. "Although, who knows in a place like this." She gestured across the street to a pristine, shining car, the metallic paint crisp in the sunlight. "Your chariot awaits."

Virginia followed her back up the sidewalk, crossing the empty street, stepping over the deep crevices in the concrete where weeds sprouted. "I didn't think you had a car."

Anya snorted. "It's Seamus' car."

Indeed it was, the license plate at the back framed in brass. "I didn't know you two were on car-borrowing terms. I didn't know you even had any contact after the thing with Fiske," Virginia said, almost burning her hand on the car door. Black paint was murder in the summer sun. Jolie was already in the back seat, her borrowed travel bag sitting at her feet.

"He owed me a favor," Anya explained. "And besides, he's up north with his brothers for the solstice, so he wasn't using it."

Chapter Eight

An overbearing, cloudless sky loomed overhead, bright with hot sunshine and speckled with far-off birds, flying away to far preferable destinations. The car stopped, the engine cut, leaving the trio with nothing more than the sound of vague buzzing near the base of the tree trunks lining the path. It looked almost inviting in daytime, a stark contrast to its threatening, cloistered darkness.

"Thanks," Virginia said, reaching for the handle. "When do you head back?"

Anya shrugged. "When I'm done, I guess." She twirled a strand of long, silvery hair around her finger. "I could stay, if you want."

"I think we're all set, but thank you," Virginia replied, shaking her head. She didn't need any more complications than had already arisen. "I appreciate the ride."

"Would have been a long walk in this heat," Jolie mused, jumping out of the car and slinging her pack over her shoulder. She tossed it into Virginia's car with a soft thud, leaning against the passenger side door. Her green, borrowed shirt was hanging off her, hiding the sharp angles beneath.

Anya grabbed Virginia's wrist, gently holding her in place.

"I mean it, if you need me, I'll stay."

"I just want to find this guy and get the hell out of here," Virginia replied, startled at the contact. She didn't pry Anya's fingers off of her wrist, despite the immediate and unconscious impulse to do so. "Birch Hollow isn't my favorite place."

"What really happened here last night?" Anya pressed, her crystalline aqua gaze boring into Virginia before she turned to steal a glance at Jolie. "Are you alright?"

Virginia reached for the handle again, this time popping the door's latch. "Yeah. I told you, I'm fine. Just want to get done and get gone, you know?" She hesitated, one foot outside the car and one waiting, unsure if she should share the truth with Anya Quinn or not. She leaned over, her lips next to Anya's ear. "There was a murder. I saw the vic, but by the time the cops got out here, there was nothing. They nabbed me for trespassing."

Anya raised her eyebrows, fingers tightening on the steering wheel. "You always manage to find the live wires, don't you, Virginia?"

"What's going on?" Jolie asked, pushing off the other vehicle to poke her head in through Anya's window. "Why are you both in here whispering?"

"Anya is going to hang around town for a few days," Virginia said. "We were just discussing some plans to grab dinner." She wasn't quite sure why she was hiding the truth from Jolie—after all, she'd seen more than her fair share of violence already, even at her young age. But then, maybe that *was* the reason that Virginia wanted to protect her. She licked the sweat from her lips, the taste of salt pleasant on her tongue but only served to increase her thirst. "Anya, can you wait a few minutes? I think I dropped something up near that cabin."

"You want to risk another trespassing charge?" Anya asked with half a smile.

"I was the one who called myself in," Virginia explained, hoisting herself out of the car. "So as long as you don't have a police radio hiding in your glove compartment, and some understandable desire to punish me more for the Lindell thing, I think I'm safe."

"You'd deserve it, if I did." Anya pulled her small satchel from behind her seat, dangling it in the air by the strap. "Finding all these reagents is an arduous task." She laid it on Virginia's vacated seat with a theatrical flourish. "But I can't say I was disappointed to find you—both—here."

Virginia ran her hands over the muddy metal, unsure how to interpret Anya's words. "If I'd known you were driving down, we could have shared a car and headed to the beach instead." She tucked a lock of hair behind her ear, trying not to notice her reflection in the window's glass. "Sea breezes would be a hell of a lot nicer than the dust from all this shadows-damned corn around here."

"Maybe we can solve this case and hit the beach," Anya said, her tone only half humorous. "I won't tell Sheriff Dixon if you won't."

"Arthur certainly has some strange ideas about what he can and can't dictate," Virginia grumbled, slamming the car door with exactly the right amount of aggression. "I'll just be a minute."

The trees rustled above her, a delicate but welcome breeze whispering through the thick foliage. The shade was a welcome change from the wide open concrete of the town center, paved over years before Virginia was even born. She scowled down at her shoes, covered in dust, the grit settling in her socks in a way that nearly catapulted her back to her own childhood.

Resting easily within the woods, the cabin was still there, the same as it had been the night before. Nothing had changed since she'd been arrested. Her footprints remained intact in the loose dirt, and Officer Carsh's, larger, deeper, lay alongside. She looked for others, hoping to see telltale tracks from the murderer, but found none.

Virginia stood at the base of the short path that led to the porch, watching for movement within. If there had been anyone in there the night before, Carsh would have taken them to the station to get a statement, but not until after she had been released. He was desperate to obfuscate the case, just like he had with Juliette.

She approached slowly, quietly, easing up each step of the porch and creeping around to the side where the window was.

"I thought you said you forgot something," Jolie said, a hand on her hip. She held Virginia's holster aloft, gun present and intact. "But this was still on the seat of your car."

"I forgot something else," Virginia lied. "And I told you to stay there."

Jolie stared.

"Okay, I didn't forget anything, but I just had to check something."

Jolie stepped closer, peering over the gentle elevation of the porch. "What are you checking?"

"Just wait there. I'll only be a minute." Virginia ignored the quiet, disgruntled sigh that passed Jolie's lips, and peered through the window for the third time in twelve hours. Still, there was nothing there, no speck of blood splashed against the dainty lace curtains, no sign that there had ever been a corpse. She shook her head, willing something to dislodge or change. Maybe she was starting to really lose it. Maybe Carsh was right, and she should just get the hell out of Birch Hollow while she still could, before whatever malignant, creeping tendrils wrapped themselves around her.

"Shadows," Anya swore, tripping through the thicket and coming out on the other side of the path, yanking her coral peach skirts free from a patch of brambles. She straightened, her brow furrowed. "Virginia, get away from there," she said quietly.

"Why?" Virginia pressed, remaining in place. "I was just checking—"

"Illusion magic, and a hell of a lot of it," Anya replied, already reaching for the satchel hanging at her waist. "Shadows only know what it could be hiding."

"Can you clear it?" Jolie asked, hooking the holster around her own shoulder. The sight of the baggy straps hanging loose and the gun nestled under the girl's arm turned Virginia's stomach, and she was forced to resist the impulse to stalk down off the porch and tear it off of her.

Anya popped the cork of a small vial, the contents holding their own faint glow, even in the searing sunlight that beamed down through heavy branches. "Maybe." She climbed the porch steps softly, slowly, the bottle in one hand, the other reaching for Virginia. "You should move. I don't know what this is. It's like nothing I've ever seen before."

"I'm fine," Virginia replied, slipping the silver over her knuckles and bracing her stance for impact or assault.

"You can't punch magic to death, you know that, right?"

Anya said, her tone barbed with fear. "Move."

"Can't punch magic, no, but I can just as easily punch whoever put it there," Virginia shot back.

Anya closed her eyes, chin lifted. "They're long gone. Something like this leaves a trail a mile wide, and there's nothing." Anya bent, swiping her fingers against the dusty boards of the porch. "No sign of anyone, no clues where they might have gone." She straightened, holding the tincture at arm's length. "If nothing else, the fumes from this aren't very pleasant. At least stand behind me," she instructed, her stare boring into Virginia with such force that it was undefeatable.

"Fine," Virginia growled, stepping behind Anya. It wasn't in her nature to cower behind anyone. She'd always excelled at taking any and all hits head-on, absorbing the brunt of it herself. No one else could be trusted to do the same for her.

Anya lifted the vial above her head before throwing it down against the porch, the glass shattering into tiny, glittering shards as the liquid sank into the wood with a quiet, inoffensive glow.

"What now?" Jolie called, still waiting by the tree line, one hand on the holster.

"We wait," Anya replied.

The planks eagerly drank in the fluid, allowing it to congregate within the grain, carrying it across the porch, shooting under their feet. Cold seeped up through the soles of Virginia's shoes, and she stepped off of the glowing planks, following Anya's lead. Pools of crisp bluish light collected in the knots of the pine for mere moments before the mixture sought out the source of the magic.

"It's like it's looking for something," Virginia said.

"And it's found it," Anya replied, nodding at the window. A hazy blue light collected around the corners of the sill, finding its way beneath the glass.

Virginia thought she knew what she'd find when she returned to the window. A corpse, the dead body of James Folst. What she did not expect to see was the lifeless form of one Heinrich Harrow.

Blood pooled under his skull, half an eye socket missing and the rest purple-pink with Nether use. A stack of bills was stuffed into his mouth, fanned out as though he was a fancy money clip. His jacket was missing, leaving bare suspenders against his stained white shirt. It was probably out of sight, along with his shoes, left by the door out of polite habit.

"Fucked shadows," she whispered, bracing herself against the porch's railing behind her.

Anya took in the scene with a frown, no doubt waiting for more magic to fall away. "Someone you know?"

"Not really. His niece is a client, he made off with the family fortune and came down here, for some reason." Virginia tightened her grip around the knuckles, unsettled by the scene. "I saw a corpse last night, but it wasn't him. It was some con man who's been defrauding people in town."

"This is layered magic," Anya explained. "Your fellow here was using an illusion spell to conceal himself, to front as someone else, no doubt to escape detection. Then, whoever decided to punch his ticket used more powerful spells to hide the body." She tore her eyes away from the window, apparently satisfied that the tincture had done its work. "Someone knew you were here last night, Virginia. Someone who knew you'd call the cops."

"How long had that man been in town?" Jolie asked, now

standing at the steps of the porch.

"Not long," Virginia answered. "I had thought maybe it was Harrow under an assumed name, before I saw him. I guess I was right nonetheless." She took a photo of Harrow from her pocket, holding it up to the window. "It's definitely him, that's for sure."

"Someone else is certainly involved," Anya said, swiping a finger through the inert tincture remaining at the edges of the window. "Maybe you could see something, now that the illusion cleared? I can't guarantee how long it will be cleared, it depends if someone comes back to revive the spell or not."

"I can't see anything," Virginia said, descending the porch's steps and taking the holster from Jolie, strapping it around herself instead. "I need to..." she trailed off. "I'd rather not report it to Officer Carsh. Rift only knows how that will go, given that last time landed me in a cell."

"We need to tell Nina Harrow that we found him, though," Jolie protested, leaning against the handrail, tying her unruly hair into a fluffy bun on the top of her head. "She'd want to know. Didn't you say she was trying to report you to the VCPD for not finishing the case?"

"I'm not so worried about that," Virginia said. "There's no law against refusing extra work outside the contract scope. Still... she's going to need to know sooner or later." She stole a glance back at the window, now dingy with water stains from some summer storm. The illusion had fixed that, too. "I guess we'll have to aim for later."

Anya exited the porch as well, one hand still on her satchel as though it could protect her from whatever magic there was left inside the cabin. "You need to find out what else Heinrich Harrow was up to," she said. "There was something unfamiliar about that magic, Virginia. I don't like it."

"Unfamiliar how?" Virginia asked, starting the journey back up the deer path to the cars at the side of the road. "Maybe it's just a branch of illusion magic you're not aware of."

"I don't mean to inflate my own ego, but I seriously doubt that," Anya said. "My aunt was extremely thorough in my training, and I've studied far more in adulthood. I can sense most things at twenty paces, know what it is and where the caster went. With this, it's like it wasn't even cast by a witch."

Jolie kicked a small pebble off the trail, and it bounced into the trees, where it disturbed a line of ants marching in the hot summer sun. "By who, then? Who else could have cast an illusion like that?"

"I'm not sure I want to know," Anya admitted. "Well, I mean, I do want to know, but it's an answer that might only lead to more questions." She frowned, pulling her skirt free from another bramble. "I was going to head back later today, but seeing this, maybe I should stick around."

"I'm sure I can handle it," Virginia reassured her, climbing into the driver's side seat of her car. "If you need to head back to Verdance, then go. We'll be alright." She thrust the keys into the ignition and turned, but the only result was a horrible thunking sound and a plume of black smoke that began to crawl out from beneath the hood of the car. "Perfect," Virginia growled, smacking her palm against the steering wheel. "Of course you'd get me all the way down here, only to die when I'm ready to get the hell out of this town before another body turns up."

"Looks like I'm definitely staying now," Anya said, holding open the door of the other car. "Get in, I'll take you to your mother's place."

"Jolie and I can walk," Virginia said, grabbing the cigarette case from her glove box. The moment her fingers brushed against the tarnished silver, the craving flared up in every vein, desperate for a hit of her preferred poison.

"It's about a million degrees, or about to be," Anya protested. "Come on, I bet she can't be that bad."

Virginia chewed her lip, wondering how bad it could really be if she chanced it, just that once. It had been twenty years, after all. Maybe things could be different, if she just tried a bit harder with her mother. "It's not that warm," she protested. "Jolie is a fire demon. She loves this."

"I wouldn't say that I love the humidity," Jolie grumbled, wiping sweat from her brow. "I prefer more of a dry heat."

"Good, the next time we head out of town on a job, I'll make sure it's a desert," Virginia said. "Maybe we'll get lucky and get jumped by a bunch of shifters instead of some overpowered illusion witch. Or, hell, we can head to the rift itself and have a good look inside, see what all the fuss is about."

Anya laughed, throwing her head back with it. "Come on, Vane, no one wants to go there. I heard that it's been abandoned for at least a decade now."

"That's what they want you to think, so no one wonders where all the damned Nether is coming from," Virginia shot back, but then inhaled and sighed. "Alright, Quinn, fine. You win. A lift back would be nice. Shadows know I've already sweat through this shirt three times already, and if I don't get a smoke soon, I might turn into a shifter myself."

"Good," Anya said, eyeing her. "But no smoking in the car. Seamus was very clear."

Chapter Nine

Her mother was sitting on the porch, cocktail in hand, when they pulled up. Virginia handed her gun and holster to Anya before she stepped out of the car, adjusting her suspenders. "It's just me, Mom," she called.

"Oh good, you're back," her mother said, rising up from the chair to set her glass on the railing. "I was starting to worry."

"Starting to?" Virginia asked.

"Were you arrested?"

"More or less."

Her mother shrugged, buttoning her cardigan, long-sleeved despite the heat. "I assumed as much. You never could keep yourself out of trouble." She glanced at the car. "Who's your friend?"

The way the word friend passed her lips sounded more like a curse than anything else, and Virginia blinked against the sun, waiting before she responded. "A colleague."

"You can tell your *friend* that it's rude to stay in the car," her mother chided, but tacked on a laugh at the end to soften the blow. "I made some fresh iced tea just a while ago, and there are leftovers from last night if you're desperate."

"She's a colleague, Mom," Virginia insisted, but nodded back to Jolie and Anya in the car that it was safe to exit.

Her mother descended the stairs like royalty, holding her hand out to shake Anya's. "I'm Ginnie's mother," she said. "You can call me Mrs. Cabot."

"Anya Quinn. Virginia and I have worked together on a couple of cases, now." Anya released her grip, toying with the hem of her skirt. "It's nice to meet you."

"Ginnie so rarely comes around, and even rarer does she bring anyone worth meeting," her mother said. "But I don't know why she hid you yesterday. It's not as though I had a problem with Juliette Ashling, Ginnie. Why would I have a problem with Ms. Quinn?" Her gaze slid sideways, the corners of her mouth in a smirk.

Rage bubbled up in Virginia's throat, but she swallowed it back down. Her mother was clearly reveling in punishing her with the past. Mercifully, neither Jolie nor Anya understood the relevance. "It's just such a long drive from Verdance, Mom," Virginia replied. "And there's so little that Birch Hollow has to offer." She knew that the words had been too barbed when Jolie shot her a look, but it was too late to take them back. "But iced tea sounds great. I'm parched."

Her mother glared. "In the fridge, bottom shelf. Help yourself. I'm sure you can manage to remember where everything is." She took Jolie by the shoulders, beaming at her like she was a prize from a cheap carnival. "Look at the state of you, my dear." She made a soft tutting noise, shaking her head. "It looks like you're wearing nothing more than Ginnie's hand-me-downs."

"I don't mind," Jolie said brightly, blissfully unaware that she'd said exactly the wrong thing.

"Well, I can't have that, not in my house," Virginia's mother declared, dragging Jolie up the steps by her elbow. "Ginnie was never petite, not like us, Jolie. I'm sure I have some things we can fix up for you."

The screen door slammed, and Virginia finally released the frustrated hiss that had been cloistered, pent-up in her lungs, begging for release. It came out first as a controlled exhale, and rapidly accelerated into a heavy, beleaguered sigh. "Fuck," she said softly.

"So, that's your mom, huh?" Anya asked, dropping the car keys into her satchel.

"Are you going to tell me that I should be nicer?" Virginia snapped. "That she's my mother, and I only get one? That she's getting on in years, and she won't be around forever, and—"

"No," Anya interrupted, her voice low. "I was going to say that she's horrible, and you should definitely get the hell out of this town as soon as you can."

Virginia stole a glance at her, but started marching towards the porch. "Most people don't really get that about her. Not at first, anyway."

"I run a shop, Virginia. I know people when I see them." Anya followed behind her, her steps light on the loose dirt. "I can see why you avoid this place."

"Shh," Virginia hissed, pulling open the screen door. No matter her age, her mother had always been frustratingly adept at overhearing just about anything. "Do you want iced tea?"

"I'd drink stagnant well water in this heat," Anya replied. "Iced tea sounds infinitely more preferable." She mopped her face with a fresh handkerchief from her satchel, sitting down in one of the antique wooden chairs, still polished to a lacquer shine. "I imagine Jo might be busy for a while."

"At least an hour, if I know my mother," Virginia replied quietly. "She tends to take an interest in waifs and strays." She held the rest of her tongue, which so desperately wanted to add, *how ironic.*

Anya watched as she poured tea into glasses, dropping tiny frozen cubes from the icebox into the drinks with demure splashes. "You know," Anya said, running a finger across the marble trivet in front of her, "I'm wondering if Heinrich Harrow was messing around with more than just a few lazy cons."

"Oh?" Virginia prompted, grateful that Anya had taken the reins of the conversation. "How so?"

"It doesn't make any sense, otherwise," Anya replied. "That was extremely potent magic. I've never seen it in real life, only read about it in books. Whoever was trying to hide him, hide that corpse..." she shook her head. "But something still doesn't add up."

"Whoever killed him was providing him with the magic to walk around as someone else," Virginia answered. "Is it similar at all to what you did for Ursa six months ago? The fake corpse in the river?"

"As similar as iced tea and stagnant well water, maybe," Anya said with a laugh, taking a sip of the tea. "Some of the basics are similar, but the execution is much different, far removed from anything I've done." She traced around a water ring on the coaster, dragging the condensation into a thin, perforated line. "Concealing living tissue is much more difficult than dead tissue."

Virginia nodded, leaning back against the counter to sip at

her own tea. It wasn't sweet enough, like always, and over-brewed, but that was new. "What are the odds that someone was only concealing the dead tissue, and there really were two different hucksters running around in town? That maybe James Folst took off already?"

"That depends on the kind of power we're talking about," Anya answered. "Judging by that trail, it's someone with access to extremely potent reagents."

"Like what?"

Anya sucked her teeth, staring at Virginia over the lip of her glass. "Given what happened last time, I hope you'll forgive my reticence in telling you."

"I'm not going to say anything to the VCPD," Virginia said with a scoff. "It's not like they even have jurisdiction all the way out here."

"You said that last time, and yet here I am in the middle of nowhere, having to dig through corn fields and scrape lichens off of pond rocks in order to replace what was lost." Anya finished the tea with a grimace, granules of wet sugar coating the bottom of the glass. "Given your... involvement with some members of the police, I can't risk it. Fool me once, you know."

"I'm not *involved* with the police," Virginia shot back, dumping the rest of her drink into the sink. The amalgamation of bitter taste and tepid temperature was too juxtaposed to enjoy the taste. She glanced towards the stairs, expecting her mother to appear and chastise her for lying, for not telling her what had happened when she was removed from the force, but she didn't. Doting on Jolie was a more rewarding activity, at least for the moment.

"That's not what it looked like the morning we planned

to raid Fiske's compound." Anya shrugged, but her brow furrowed.

"Let's go for a walk," Virginia said, pushing off the counter. "It's too stuffy in here, I can barely breathe."

Anya waited for a moment, and then nodded. "Who owns those fields out there?" she asked, nodding towards the window that faced the endless rows of stock-still corn.

"The farm over the road," Virginia replied, already heading for the door. "Why?"

"Webworms," Anya said simply, slinging her satchel over her shoulder as she followed Virginia out onto the porch.

"Worms?"

"Garden webworms," Anya clarified. "Harder to find in Verdance."

Virginia moved automatically, the steps leading to the small path heavily ingrained into her muscle memory, every crunch of patchy grass under her feet unlocking a new memory, every pebble that bit through the soles of her shoes an unpleasant reminder. "What are these worms for?"

"If I told you, I'd have to kill you," Anya replied easily.

"Right."

"Not many insects can metabolize the glow of a harvest moon, Virginia." She stepped over an exposed tree root, always graceful, always moving like a dancer through water, even as she ducked beneath vines that hung from a tree branch. "Once they're moths, it's too late. The metamorphosis destroys the compounds."

"Of course," Virginia replied, having no idea what she was talking about. "Moths."

"The process of histolysis," Anya explained. "Breaks them down to rebuild them, so the compounds get all messed around. You need the caterpillars, but it may already be too late in the season." She turned back, flicking her wrist casually. "No harm in looking, I guess."

"So this isn't an illegal reagent?"

"Not yet," Anya said, her tone bitter. "That's why I can't tell you what it does. You'd let it slip to Lindell, then before I know it, that's one more reagent on the list of things I'm not allowed to have."

Virginia stopped in her tracks, just shy of the one-track road separating her mother's property from the corn fields. "I already said, I'm not involved with anyone on the VCPD." She crossed, not even bothering to look both ways because no one ever went up that way, not unless they were on a tractor, and those could be heard from a distance. "Whatever you think you saw, you didn't."

Anya picked at a green blade sprouting from a stalk of corn, frowning. "No caterpillars."

"What are we looking for?" Virginia asked, irritated that Anya had ignored what she said, but not wanting to push any more than she already had. Allies were thin on the ground in Birch Hollow. "What do they look like?"

"It's easier to look for their impact. They chew early growth all the way down until there's hardly anything left, like a locust or a slug would." Anya checked several more stalks, moving quickly through the field, even as the corn was up past their hips. "Like I said, it might be too late, especially if the farmer is on top of treatments to keep them at bay."

"You really aren't going to tell me what these things do?" Virginia asked, curiosity getting the better of her.

Anya rustled her way through the corn, picking past one row, and then another. "What happened with Captain

Lindell?"

"I don't know," Virginia replied, and she was surprised at her own honesty. "It was fine, until it wasn't. We didn't talk much, unless it was about work." She sighed, examining a leaf with several large holes. "I was concerned about her sympathies towards the feds."

"Jo?" Anya asked, checking over Virginia's shoulder, shaking her head. "That's the work of something else. Looks like a billbug. See how the holes all line up?"

Virginia nodded, stepping over to the next row. The dust was already collecting in her shoes, and she tried to ignore the gentle grating of her heel against the leather. "The last thing Jolie needs is conscription. She's just a kid."

"Not by law."

"She's eighteen and hasn't even fully realized her abilities. She's got nothing and no one."

Anya glanced at her, shielding her eyes from the overbearing sunlight. "She's got you."

"She's just on my couch until she figures herself out. It's temporary," Virginia argued. "What am I supposed to do, throw her out on the street for another crew to chase her down?"

"Six months is an awfully long temporary situation, don't you think?" Anya bent, examining some damage, her full lips set into a frown. "Damn. More billbugs."

A subtle breeze fluttered down the perfectly geometric rows, whispering across skin, and Virginia shivered, rubbing the raised bumps from her arms. "Can't you get these things anywhere else?"

"No." Anya straightened, pressing at the small of her back. "Do you think I'd be roaming through dusty fields if I could?"

"Depends on your affinity for dusty fields," Virginia replied.

"Oh, they're my favorite," Anya said, chuckling. "These particular creatures are unique to this region. Too far east, and something about their physiology changes. They metabolize it differently, it's inert. Too far west, it's uncontrollable, unstable. Caustic."

The sun was just about overhead, leaning into the afternoon with weighty heat and a dusty, stagnant ripple through the crops. Virginia brushed sweat from her brow, blinking against the salt. "Right," she said.

"Plant and pest identification is very useful, you know," Anya chided. "Though I had the benefit of having the inside track with an entomologist." She laughed, thwacking her way across another row. "Shadows, that didn't last long."

"What a sordid past," Virginia said. "A torrid affair with a bug doctor."

"I wouldn't say it was torrid," Anya replied with an unsettling wink, "more tepid. Maybe that was the problem all along."

"Better luck next time, then. Maybe the next one will sweep you off your feet."

Anya tilted her head. "Sure, maybe."

Farms and fields and freighters. There was no end to it, not for acres, for miles, for hours and hours down the interstate highway. She was already sick of the sight of it, and she hadn't even been back for twenty-four hours. At least the cell at the station had been a vacation from the monotony.

Virginia bent, brushing her fingers over a skeletal leaf, nothing left but the delicate, fragile bones running along towards the stem. She swept along the stalk with her palm, and plucked a half-eaten shoot. "What do these things look like?" she called, now that Anya was four rows away.

"Green," she answered. "Fuzzy."

"I don't know if this is it, but whatever it is, that corn was its buffet." Virginia held the shoot in her cupped hands, not wanting to drop it. "Here," she said, handing it over.

"Well, that's our friend," Anya said, pinching the head from its body and dropping it into a soft linen pouch.

"No mercy for caterpillars," Virginia mused, raising an eyebrow. "That might have been the coldest thing I've ever seen."

Anya laughed again, inspecting the rest of the plant. "Ms. Vane, you have fired a gun at people. More than once, if I had to guess."

"People deserve it."

"Not all of them," Anya argued, decapitating four more caterpillars, one after another. "Left unchecked, these guys would raze the entire field. We can feed people or bugs, not both."

Virginia collected a dozen more of them, but left the processing to Anya. She checked her watch, squinting against the glare from the face. "Jolie might be out on parole by now."

"You should ask your mother if she knows anything else about James Folst, or Heinrich Harrow, whatever his name is," Anya said, picking her way back towards the broken wooden gate at the roadside. "I can't get out of my head how strong that magic was."

"Who knows, maybe Birch Hollow is hiding the next magical genius."

Anya stopped at the gate, turning around so fast that her skirts spun around her calves, fluttering in her orbit. "I just—

it can't be what I think it is."

"And what do you think it is?" Virginia asked.

"I don't even want to say it, because it doesn't make any sense." Anya leaned closer, her lips almost brushing Virginia's ear. "Fae," she whispered.

It was Virginia's turn to laugh, and she did, leaning back from Anya with a shake of her head. "Alright, you got me. Very funny, Ms. Quinn."

"I wasn't kidding."

"The Fae aren't real, Anya. They call them fairytales for a reason." Virginia swung open the unlocked gate, crossing the narrow road in two strides. "Those stories were all debunked."

"But the Rupture—"

"Didn't produce Fae," Virginia interrupted. "It's gossip for tabloids. It sells papers, that's all. There's never been any proof. People lie for headlines, that's all."

Anya followed behind, but slower. Quieter. "I just don't think you should write things off," she said softly.

"What would you even have to compare that to? When have you ever come into contact with known Fae magic?" Virginia asked, laughing again. "Come on, Quinn."

"I can't tell you that."

"Of course."

"You're not the only one who's allowed to have secrets, Virginia," Anya snapped. "It doesn't matter what is or isn't going on with you and Lindell right now, because if you do get back together, which you probably will, you'll spill your guts, and I'm the one dealing with the aftermath."

Virginia stopped in her tracks, waiting. For what, she wasn't sure. A nearby mourning dove cooed four echoed cycles before she said anything. "You have every right to withhold your trust," she said. "If you'd gotten my office tossed, I'd probably never speak to you again, so already you're far more magnanimous than I am."

"I'd say you were more tempestuous than magnanimous," Anya shot back, but this time her tone had softened, and she was looking past Virginia to the porch. "Hey, wow, Jo! Look at you!"

Jolie did a little twirl in the pink tweed skirt suit she was wearing. She giggled and then shrugged, letting her arms fall back to her sides. "What do you think?" she asked.

"Mom, I have to talk to you," Virginia said. "It's important." She turned to Jolie, the poor thing standing there in her mother's offcut wardrobe. "It's great, kid."

Her mother preened Jolie, fussing with her hair and frowning. "This would be so beautiful, maybe with a straightening oil—"

"Mom?" Virginia interrupted. "The sooner, the better."

"What's the big emergency? You're the one who spent all night in a jail cell because you tangled with Officer Carsh. He's always had it out for you, and you and I both know why that is." Her mother smiled at Anya, beckoning her up the steps. "Ms. Quinn, did you enjoy your tea?"

"It was wonderful," Anya replied. "Thank you, Mrs. Cabot."

"You should stay for dinner!" Virginia's mother replied, picking a bit of lint from the suit jacket. "I was planning on making something nice for the girls."

"She has work to get back to," Virginia interjected. "It would be rude of me to take up any more of Ms. Quinn's time, especially when she already went out of her way to give us a ride back up here."

"Where is your car, Ginnie?" her mother asked, pulling a pair of gold spectacles down over her eyes. "I hadn't even realized you weren't in it."

Virginia nudged Anya, trying to get her to leave. "Broke down," she said. "Off the county highway, over by the woods."

"What on Earth were you doing over there? That's a strange place to pull over."

"Like I said, Mom," Virginia said, poking Anya again, "I have to talk to you about that. There's something else going on. I followed that huckster of yours to the Speer place, and someone shot him."

"Shot him!" her mother echoed. "Eleanor Speer couldn't have had anything to do with that. She's older than I am and frailer than most." She already had the phone in her hand, tugging at the rotary. "Someone needs to call her."

"Mom, don't—"

"Eleanor!" her mother exclaimed. "How are you doing?" A pause, a performative gasp. "No! Are you alright?"

"I guess she found the corpse after you dispelled that illusion," Virginia whispered to Anya. "Sounds like no one managed to cover it again."

"Only a matter of time before someone found it," Anya replied.

"Take care, I'll check in with you soon," Virginia's mother said, putting the phone down. "Poor thing found the body herself," she said. "She's so shaken up. Her son had just dropped her home after a visit to his home last night." Wiping a ring of condensation from the table, she frowned. "I told you not to get mixed up in this, Ginnie."

"I should get back over there to question her," Virginia said, rubbing her hands against her knees as she stood.

"She's already been questioned by Officer Carsh at the station," her mother explained. "Eleanor said she doesn't know a single, solitary thing about that body. She wasn't even there, no one was. It must have been a break-in. Officer Carsh has cleared her and her family already."

Virginia scoffed. "I don't care what Eugene says. I'm going over there to question her, she might be the only one who has an idea of who did it."

Chapter Ten

There was an element of indecision as they pulled up near Mrs. Speer's son's residence, Anya at the wheel and Jolie sitting in the back.

"The two of you should stay in the car," Virginia directed, opening the passenger side door. "I'll be back in two shakes."

"Wait," Jolie protested. She climbed out after her, tucking in her shirt and straightening the button placket. "I want to go with you."

"This doesn't concern you, Firefly."

"But you said—"

Virginia shook her head, and it was enough to silence her. "I said you could come along on some field work, but not when it involves murder. This kind of thing can get pretty hairy, and I don't want you getting into any trouble."

"Ah, Virginia, let her," Anya chided, cracking open a worn book with a weathered leather spine. "What harm could it do? You and your mother agreed that Mrs. Speer couldn't have had anything to do with Harrow's death."

"Fine." Virginia wasn't interested in arguing, not when time was of the essence. The insistent pull of the highway tugged at her, freedom so close but just out of her grasp.

"Jolie, don't say anything. Just follow my lead."

The girl nodded eagerly, trailing along after her. "Why did we park so far away?"

"I find that people without time to prepare their answers are more candid. If they heard us coming, they might change their answers." Virginia stepped over an exposed tree root, motioning for Jolie to do the same. She wished she'd brought polish for her shoes. She wished she could ignore the temptation of the case, but she couldn't. She never had been able to let something lie.

The house was run-down, if sturdy enough. It had been built with a kit from a catalog, and there were dozens of them dotted around the county. Fifty years hence, they'd been a popular choice in cheap, reliable housing. Virginia climbed the steps quietly and then rapped on the screen door frame, the juxtaposition alarming Jolie as well as the inhabitants. "Investigator," she announced, preferring as always to keep her job title vague. "I have a few questions for Mrs. Speer."

Her son was already at the door, glaring out through the fine wire mesh. "She's already spoken to the police," he said. "She doesn't have anything else to say on the matter."

"I have reason to believe that the deceased stole money from your mother," Virginia said evenly, matching his stare blink for blink. "I just wanted to put one of the more uncomfortable theories to rest, if you don't mind, Mr. Speer."

He cringed. "Anthony," he corrected. "Mr. Speer was my father." His lip curled as he said it, pulling his frown into a strange sneer.

"Anthony," Virginia echoed. "I can promise you I won't be long in my questions. I respect that your mother has been through a lot and needs her rest."

"No," he said simply. "Whatever you have to ask, you can ask me."

Virginia glanced over his shoulder, seeing his mother sitting on an old sofa, knitting something long and vaguely misshapen. "It would be better if I could speak with her directly."

"That's not going to be possible."

"Were *you* there when the body was discovered?" Virginia asked.

He leaned closer to the screen. "No," he snarled. "And my alibi satisfied Officer Carsh, so I'm unclear what you're doing here."

"Oh, gosh, ma'am," Jolie called through the screen door. "Would you just look at that stitching? Truly, my tension is always just such a mess."

Virginia resisted the urge to shoot her a look, wishing she would just go back to the car where she would be safe and out of sight. Anthony leaned forward against the screen door, as if Jolie's words were an attempt to force her way inside.

"Oh, it's just practice," Mrs. Speer replied, holding up her work. "Nearly finished now." She stood, wobbling for a moment but regaining her balance. The floorboards creaked as she approached the door with her work, trailing blue wool across the floor. "It's going to be a shawl for poor Mrs. Brennan. She's been in my prayers of late, she lost so much to that con man. Rumor has it she'll have to go back to work. She hasn't a penny left."

Anthony grimaced, still maintaining the barrier between his mother and the door. "You should sit down, Mother," he chided. "You know what the doctor said."

"Why, Ginnie Cabot, is that you?" she asked, squinting through the mesh. "I haven't seen you in an eon, and I didn't quite recognize you, dear." Her gaze fell on Virginia's scars, and she had to resist the urge to look away.

"Hello ma'am, it's very nice to see you again," Virginia said politely. "I just had a few questions about that con man who turned up in your home."

"Oh, you'd have to ask Eugene about all that," Mrs. Speer demurred, waving her off. "I gave him my statement already on that mess. I have no earthly idea how he got in, I'm afraid I wasn't even home. Eugene said there were no signs of breaking and entering, but perhaps I left the door unlocked." She shrugged delicately and continued to knit, the metal needles clacking together in an uneven rhythm. "I'm afraid that's all I can tell you."

"Did he steal money from your son?" Virginia asked.

"Oh, Ginnie, who *didn't* he steal from?" Mrs. Speer replied sadly. "I think he had half the town bamboozled. Heavens only know how he did it." She paused her movements, brow furrowed. "Do you think he had us all under some kind of spell?"

"Unlikely," Virginia replied, realizing a moment too late that the woman had been looking for reassurances that she wasn't just an old fool. "But these con men have their ways, ma'am. They'll try anything for an easy buck. Gambling, lies, Nether..." she trailed off, hoping that one of the two Speers inside would fill the silence. When neither did, she cleared her throat and continued. "I'd like to come by again when you're feeling better," she said.

Before his mother could answer, Anthony interrupted. "I don't think that will be necessary. My mother has been more than compliant in this investigation, and I won't have her harangued."

"Just for a visit, then," Jolie suggested. "I'd love to learn how you get your stitches so perfect, ma'am."

"There are plenty of other places you can learn," he retorted. "As for you, Ms. Cabot, I suggest you find your way back to the city and leave criminal investigations to local police, they are the ones with jurisdiction here." He closed the interior door, throwing the deadbolt with a loud, decisive click.

Virginia backed down the stairs, but not before making note of the windows in front, the damaged roof at the eaves, and the stairs just visible through the airy lace curtains. "Well, that was almost a bust," she grumbled as her feet met gravel once again. "Nice save, kid."

"I guess we need to find Mrs. Brennan," Jolie whispered, peppering her walk with a bouncy skip every fourth step. "And something doesn't feel right about Mrs. Speer's son."

"He's hiding something," Virginia agreed, and then groaned. "I'll have to ask my mother about him."

***

There was the house, dark, unlit from within and the lack of light gave it a strange aura, like a memory resting just beneath the surface. Virginia climbed the steps but instead of unlocking the door, she waited for the figure in the rocking chair to speak. "You look like you still smoke," she said, an eyebrow raised. "Where are the other two?"

"Elsewhere." Virginia reached into her pocket for the cigarette case and groaned. There was nothing more than a mostly-spent matchbook and a tiny ball of lint. "I'm all out," she said.

"I wasn't asking for one, I was offering." Her mother reached into her small, hard-framed handbag, producing a gold case that matched the spectacles perched on top of her head. "Here, take one." She held it out, waiting for Virginia to take one. "I hope you still like Charmed."

Virginia nodded, grateful for the vice but the reminder of their similarities grated against her like rapids against rocks. "Thanks," she said, withholding the fact that they were the only brand she ever smoked. She lit her mother's, and then her own, blowing out the match once both ends burned orange in the inky darkness.

Fireflies twinkled across the parched grass, their delicate glow like whispered secrets in the night. Once, she would have trapped them in a jar, desperate to hold their beauty for a little longer, only to find them dead the next morning.

"What do you know about Anthony Speer?"

Her mother blinked, eyes glittering in the night. "Not much. Troubled when he was a young man, not unlike you. Quiet. Keeps to himself."

"Was he ever involved with anything illegal?"

"I don't know, Ginnie, what do I look like, the town crier?" her mother retorted, taking a long drag from her elegant cigarette holder. "Why don't you ask me something I can actually answer?"

The fireflies sparked along the tree line like embers, threatening a fire that would never come. The cicadas droned, and leaves swayed, and it was a beautiful night in Birch Hollow, reminding her too much of what almost was. But the past was the past, no matter how much it wanted to resurface.

"What did you mean when you said Dad was hiding something?" Virginia asked, once both of their cigarettes had burned down to the filter.

"We're going to need drinks for this," her mother said, pushing herself out of the groaning chair. She unlocked the door and vanished inside, only to reappear moments later with half a bottle of gin and two crystalline glasses. Easing herself back down, she poured herself a double, passing the bottle to Virginia. "In truth, Ginnie, I don't know. He wasn't around long enough to know him. Not really."

Virginia nodded, swigging directly from the bottle, despite her mother's impertinent glare. "He always seemed like he was hiding something."

"Ginnie, I need you to tell me why you're asking." Her mother pulled two more cigarettes from the case, lighting her own and offering the other to Virginia. "The real reason you came down here after years of silence."

"How long was that guy in town?" Virginia asked, not ready to broach the subject of mythic genetics. "The one you mentioned last night, what was his name?"

"James Folst," her mother answered after a long drag, talking through the smoke curling away from her mouth. "And I don't know, a month or so. He made the rounds at local churches, you know, making nice with old ladies like me."

"Unless that coroner's report surprises the hell out of me, his name isn't James Folst, it's Heinrich Harrow, and he's on the run after taking his family for all they were worth." Virginia inhaled, letting the acrid taste singe the back of her tongue. Most days, she craved it more than food. "He's dead now, anyway."

Her mother sipped at her gin with a quiet grimace. "He was raising money for charity, he said, something about a burned down church three counties over. A few folks found out he was lying, but no one had made a move yet. When you showed up yesterday, I thought it was the perfect opportunity."

"Yeah, too bad I wound up in a cell for it," Virginia grumbled.

"Eugene is throwing his weight around because you embarrassed him."

Virginia exhaled sharply, flicking ash over the rail into the waiting dirt. "Over thirty years ago. Shadows, and people say I hold grudges for too long."

"Who says that?"

"Arthur, mostly." Another inhale, the smoke embracing her lungs the way only poison could. "I disagree."

"Why did he leave?"

Virginia sighed, knowing she couldn't escape it forever. "He found himself a mistress."

Her mother nodded sagely, pouring herself more gin. "Plenty of them do."

"Yeah."

"Why did he go looking for a mistress?" she asked. "There had to be a reason."

"There were ten thousand reasons, Mom," Virginia replied, aware of the bite in her own voice. "Twenty thousand, maybe. We never should have gotten married."

"He was good for you."

"We didn't make sense together," Virginia shot back. "Never did."

The sound of cicadas swelled in the trees, drowning out her thoughts for one precious moment before they died back.

Cool air ghosted across her skin, and she reveled in the release from the day's oppressive heat.

Her mother sucked her teeth. "I don't believe that. You were inseparable as kids. Hell, you ran off to Verdance to follow him, lovesick and determined."

"That's not quite how I remember it," Virginia grumbled.

"It's the truth, Ginnie, and everyone around here knows it. I begged you to stay, but you wouldn't. You ran off, and that was that, other than showing up for half a day when they lowered your father's empty coffin into the ground. You couldn't even manage to speak to me that day. It was humiliating, but I've decided to forgive you for that." Her mother looked over, squinting through the darkness. "You're *welcome.*"

"And you wonder why I don't come back here," she said quietly, taking back the bottle of gin. "Everyone around here reads out of the same book of lies."

"Who's lying?" her mother demanded. "I hope you're not insinuating that—"

"You may not remember this, Mom, but when Officer Carsh dragged me in thirty-one years ago, it was because I exposed him for the up-jumped hack that he is. He botched Juliette's investigation from the start, and he couldn't bear that I was the one to show him up." Virginia stood, unable to dampen the need to be on her feet, to flee, to run into the corn and never reappear, because that was easier than the conversation she was having. "And you *left* me there."

"I told you to leave all that mess alone," her mother argued. "You were warned not to get into trouble, Ginnie, warned from the time you were small. Don't fall in with the wrong crowd, Ginnie, but you didn't listen to that. You didn't listen when I told you that Carsh would throw you to the wolves given half a chance, either."

Virginia brought the cigarette to her mouth once more, her hands shaking with quiet, impotent rage. "What was I supposed to do, other than leave?"

"Apologizing for embarrassing your mother would have been a good start."

Virginia barked out a laugh, flicking the stub over the railing onto the arranged rocks below. "Yeah, alright."

"This was my life, too!" her mother shouted, and the sound of it echoed out past the corn in an all-too-familiar way, reverberating amidst leaves and stalks and dozens of caterpillars, ripe for beheading. "You're so self-absorbed, Ginnie, you can barely see the forest for the trees."

"You didn't even care when Juliette went missing," Virginia accused, pointing across the porch. "You knew what she meant to me, and you barely batted an eyelid when she vanished into thin air."

"Girls like Juliette always wind up missing," her mother said calmly. The aloof air of it was suffocating.

Virginia flung open the screen door with such force, it smacked against the red brick exterior, denting the handle. "I have to make a call."

"Who are you calling?" her mother asked, unmoving from her position in the rocking chair.

"None of your business." Virginia combed through the drawer under the phone until she found the number for the local mechanic, and began to dial, dragging the rotary numbers across and focusing on each click the line made. It had been a mistake to go to Birch Hollow, no matter what Arthur wanted.

Her mother was now standing in the doorway, holding the screen door open with one hand, and the other clutching her still lit cigarette. "Your father was a seer, Ginnie."

Chapter Eleven

The phone lay in Virginia's hand as the other line rang fruitlessly. She stared at her mother, blinking with every drone that spilled from the receiver.

"I didn't want to tell you until you were older," her mother said, exhaling a final breath of smoke. She finished off the cigarette, stubbing out the remains in a stained glass dish on the counter.

"Forty-eight years old isn't old enough?" Virginia finally managed to ask, just as the line disconnected. She set the phone down, leaving it off the hook because she'd call again when the shock passed through her system. It wouldn't take long. Her mother had spent a lifetime betraying her in small, quiet ways.

"I wanted to tell you when you were twenty, but you left. Should I have written it in a letter?" She waved a hand casually. "Don't be ridiculous."

"That would have been a good start," Virginia replied. "Do you have any idea what you've done in hiding this from me?"

Her mother straightened, rigid posture engaged as she rose to her full height. "Protected you."

"*Protected* me?"

"You're not dead, and from the looks of you you're not hooked on that Nether nonsense, either. Nor were you conscripted by the federal forces, so from where I'm standing, I was right in not telling you."

Virginia blew out a derisive laugh, brushing her hair back out of her face. "That first thing nearly happened a few times, you know," she said. "Most recently six months ago when mythics were turning up dead all over Verdance." She pointed to a small scar on her cheekbone, dwarfed by the others but still pink and shiny. "I nearly got my head kicked in by a bunch of crew members saving Arthur's shadows-damned family."

Her mother raised an eyebrow, latching the screen door behind her. "I wouldn't have thought you'd be interested in saving the woman he left you for."

"Not all of us are so adept at turning our backs on people," Virginia snarled, and the rage was boiling up inside of her so fresh, so fervent, that she knew it wouldn't be long before she lost all control entirely.

"I don't know why you're so angry at me, it's not as though I did anything wrong. After the Rupture, I thought if you'd inherited his sins, you'd know. I waited for weeks, expecting you to turn up asking questions. You didn't, so I made the assumption that you hadn't." Her mother snapped her cigarette case shut, an achingly familiar dismissive gesture.

"I wouldn't have known if I was marked or not," Virginia said, pointing at the scars that dripped down from her hairline over her cheekbones. "I was indisposed."

"Still, you never showed signs of it as a child. I watched for years. Maybe being only half a seer means you're only half as powerful. I don't know, I don't aim to delve too far into whatever poured out of that rift that day." She tugged a gold cross pendant out of her shirt, laying it atop her cardigan. "I am a god-fearing woman, Ginnie."

"There is no god, that's the fucking point," Virginia snapped. "Don't you get it? If there ever was a god, he abandoned us a long time ago, letting us set fire to each other so long as the churches remain intact."

Her mother's brow furrowed, knitting ever closer together. "Don't say such things," she said flatly. "It benefits you, being what you are, to try a little harder to fit in with the beliefs of the people around you."

Virginia's fists clenched at her sides, tightening further until her short nails drew blood from her palms. "How long have you known?"

"I never knew for sure," her mother replied.

"How *long*," Virginia repeated, staring up at the ceiling because she couldn't bear to look her mother in the face. "I need to know how long."

"I suppose I suspected that there was something different about him from the moment we met. He seemed to know things no one else could. No one knew what a seer was then, myself included. He never told me what he was."

Virginia nodded, her eyes squeezed shut. She'd hoped her mother would deny the whole thing. Hoped that it was a fluke, a lie, some cosmic twist of fate and nothing more. Being a seer was like being a walking target, and everyone from crews to the feds wanted a piece. "Someone probably killed him for what he was, you know that, right?"

"Good riddance."

"Do you really believe that, or are you saying it to drive the knife in deeper?"

Her mother pulled out a kitchen chair, the legs scraping horribly against the floor. "I mean that since he was so happy to walk away from me, away from you, then he wasn't worth the trouble then, and he still isn't now." She sat down, drumming her fingers against the lace runner. "If he got himself into trouble, that's his own doing."

There was no such thing as quiet, not that time of year. Something rustled in the nearby trees, a coyote maybe, or a fox. Virginia glanced out into the darkness, seeing nothing, but bolting the inside door shut anyway. "You should have told me," she said finally. "I had a right to know."

"I know you won't understand—you can't, you're not a mother—but I truly was trying to protect you, Ginnie. I thought if something happened that made you question what you were, you'd ask. I thought for sure that the Rupture would have cleared anything up. I didn't hear from you, didn't see hide nor hair of you even after all that came to light." Her mother drained what was left of the bottle into her glass. "Grab me some ice, will you? It's hotter than hellfire in here now that you've closed the door."

"Sorry that I don't want to leave the door standing wide open," Virginia mumbled, digging in the cramped icebox.

"This isn't Verdance, you don't have to be quite so worried."

"It might not be the city, but I did just discover a dead body last night, so it's not exactly the world's safest backwater." She dropped the cubes into her mother's glass, regretting that she'd left her own flask in the car, resting safely in the glovebox. "Did Dad ever do anything specific? Did he, I don't know, meditate in a quiet room or something?"

"He wasn't one to meditate, unless slamming doors with

enough force to shatter the panes is considered meditation these days." Her mother delicately drained the glass of gin, putting the tumbler down on the table with more force than necessary, rattling the ice against the glass. "He wasn't the one who was here, you know. Not the one who raised you, who fed and clothed you, he wasn't here when you—"

"This isn't about chasing down some long-dead father-daughter memories, Mom, it's about figuring out what I am and how all this works." Virginia leaned against the back of the chair, rubbing her hands against the sticky varnish of the wood. "I can't keep on going through life not knowing this part."

"Visions, then?" her mother asked acerbically. "Prophecies?"

"Seers don't make prophecies," Virginia replied. "They can only see the past."

"I didn't ask about other seers, I am asking about you. What can *you* do, Ginnie?"

Virginia chewed on the inside of her cheek, most of her mouth already shredded from spending thirty-six hours in her hometown. "Not much," she answered, managing precisely how much truth she would allow to pass her lips. "A few spots here and there."

"What spots? Where?" Her mother leaned forward, forearms braced against the table as she waited for clarity. "I'm only asking so that I can help you sort it out for yourself. I only watched him for years, worried I'd see signs he'd leave again." She made a strange sound in her throat, something halfway between a laugh and a sob. "Which he did, eventually. Every time."

"I was working a case six months back, a crew back in

Verdance hunting down a—hunting someone down. Lots of mythics showed up dead, in the park, the shore, uptown, downtown, most of them baked on Nether. I infiltrated the compound. I could see things through the ring Fiske was wearing every time he punched me in the jaw."

"Well, you were always better under pressure," her mother mused. "You always did leave everything until the last minute."

"And now none of it works. It's as though it never happened."

"Then leave it, Ginnie. No one can kill you or conscript you for what you can't do."

Virginia turned away, wishing she could leap out the window and run all the way back to Verdance. "It's more complicated than that. Plenty of those crew enforcers will know, and will run their mouths to anyone who asks."

"Seers are required to report to federal agencies upon the age of majority or the realization of what they are," her mother said evenly. "You've missed both those boats by rather a wide margin. Pursuing this now will only cause you more problems."

"I'm going to shower," Virginia interrupted, moving to check the door's lock once more. "Two days of grime that I don't want to get on your sofa."

"Don't be ridiculous, you can sleep in your old room." Her mother gestured towards the stairs with a casual wave. "You know where everything is."

"Yeah. Thanks." She left her mother at the table and climbed the steps, skipping the third one partially out of decades-old habit, but also because she couldn't bear knowing if the screech of the boards really had been waiting for her all those years.

The house's second floor looked the same way it always had. Photos of grandparents and great-grandparents on the wall, displayed like deities as though they'd done anything more than beat their next generation down into the mud. The pink wallpaper blossomed with tiny, delicate flowers, all lined up in an orderly row.

She turned left into the bathroom, mindlessly pulling fresh towels from the linen closet and laying them on the shelf over the sink. The mirror was perfectly clean, and every surface had been recently scrubbed with bleach, the smell of the chlorine still lingering beneath the notes of dried potpourri from the crystal bowls littered across the counter. She was surprised to find fresh clothes already laid out for her, pulled from the bag she'd brought the day before. There was also an unfamiliar pair of pajamas, no doubt supplied for reasons of decency.

Virginia locked the bathroom door with the tiny, breakable latch, more of a polite suggestion than any kind of real security. The faucet's brass handle was polished to a shine, but the pipes still groaned with effort when she twisted it. Despite the summer heat of the day, all she wanted was a searingly hot shower to burn away all of her inequities.

Steam began to collect, and as soon as the mirror was clouded enough to only reflect blurry forms, she undressed, dropping each piece of clothing to the cool tiles with the soft echo of fabric on ceramic.

She wondered briefly what would happen if she never left the shower, if she stayed there long enough for the weak water pressure to wash her away, a little bit at a time.

Chapter Twelve

Virginia awoke to feverish pounding on the front door, rattling the screen in its thin wooden frame, slamming it against the brass lock. Stumbling off the couch, she rubbed her head and cursed when her shin met the sharp edge of the antique coffee table.

"Fucked shadows," she muttered, wrenching open the inside door. Sleep still swum in her vision, clouding it with drowsiness and the fierce desire for coffee.

Arthur stood on the porch, pacing in tight circles, rubbing his hands over his bald head. He hadn't stood on that porch in years. He'd probably been gone from Birch Hollow even longer than she had.

"What are you doing here?" she demanded, suddenly aware she'd answered the door in the ugly pajamas her mother had forced on her. She shifted, hovering behind the wood to cover the shame of baby pink pinstriped satin. It looked like something Astrid would wear, if Astrid wasn't always more interested in the art of seduction than the art of practicality.

"Ginnie, for fuck's sake," he replied, turning back to the door. He tried the screen again, but it was still locked. "I've been trying to call all shadows-damned day and night, but I couldn't get through so I drove all the way down here. Arrested, Ginnie? What the hell happened down here?"

Virginia left him on the porch, still busy wearing holes in the old planks of wood. "It's been dealt with."

"What happened?" he repeated, finally stopping his manic movements to stare through the screen.

"Eugene Carsh," she answered plainly.

He puffed out his cheeks before exhaling the air, scratching the side of his head. "Have you called your lawyer yet?"

"I try to avoid involving my lawyer unless it's absolutely necessary."

"Getting arrested isn't absolutely necessary in your estimation?" Arthur asked, now leaning against one of the porch's support beams. It was askew, but only slightly. A problem for the next owner of the house, more than likely.

The realization that it would be her was a wound she wasn't quite ready to face, so she ignored it. "It was barely an arrest. He didn't even let me pay bail," Virginia said finally. "Carsh is just trying to get me to leave town, rift only knows why." She stood back from the door, arms folded over her chest. "Happy?"

Arthur reached out for the handle again, but hesitated, hovering over it. "Are you going to let me in?"

"Fine," she replied. "But you don't have to stay, you know. I'm sure your wife is worried."

"No one knows where I am," he said. "I told Mona I was visiting my parents upstate. I told Lindell I was following up on a few leads regarding the homicides."

Virginia flipped the pin, unlatching the screen door. "My point stands that you shouldn't be here, Arthur. You have enough to deal with up in Verdance."

"Arthur Dixon, as I live and breathe," Virginia's mother said, descending the stairs already prim, proper, and dressed for the day in a tea-length sage green dress, three strings of pearls draped at her neck. "I never thought I'd see you at my door asking after our Ginnie again, that's for sure." She frowned at Virginia, tutting quietly. "It's not very seemly to answer the door in sleepwear, dear."

"Don't worry, Mom, Arthur has already seen plenty more of me," Virginia deadpanned, moving away from the door. If she had to be uncomfortable, she'd make it excruciating for everyone else, too. She stalked to the kitchen, angrily wrenching the handle on the coffee bean grinder. At least the roasted smell was a pleasant distraction from the scent of manure spread on the fields weeks prior. Still, it hung in the air, permeating every porous surface. "Arthur heard about Eugene Carsh and felt the need to intervene."

"It's so nice that you still care for Ginnie after everything that happened," her mother said, welcoming Arthur in with an embrace and a pinch of his cheeks. "I worry about her, all alone in that big city."

"Ginnie has never needed anyone," Arthur replied, laughing, damn him. "She does just fine on her own, most of the time."

Virginia's mother ushered him to a chair, straightening the lopsided lace runner. "It's such a delight to have you at my table again, Arthur," she said. "You always were the perfect guest."

"It's a pleasure to be back, ma'am," Arthur replied, smiling up at her from his seated position. "I've never once stopped thinking about those corn fritters you always used to make."

"Oh, you," Virginia's mother said, smacking him playfully on the shoulder. "Always such a charmer."

The ground beans sat in the pot, waiting for boiled water but the kettle had only just begun to heat. Virginia had grown so easily accustomed to the instant boiling that Jolie always provided at home, that having to wait grated at her almost as much as Arthur's presence and the irritation of the scratchy tag in the back of her horrible pajamas. "Don't encourage her," she muttered when her mother disappeared into the next room for a moment. "You know how she is."

"She's easier to manage if you play along, and you know that better than anyone."

Her mother flounced back into the kitchen, all smiles and enthusiasm, dropping a photo album on his placemat.

Virginia groaned, wondering how painful it would be to throw herself through the window. If Arthur wanted answers about what abilities she may or may not have, he could find them himself.

"Look," her mother said, flipping through the laminated pages of black and white pictures, each of them featuring happy childhood memories that had never really happened that way. "Here you two are when you were in your first year of school. Look how small you were, Sheriff Dixon!"

"Do you mind grabbing me a coffee, too?" Arthur asked, taking the book into his own hands, examining each page as though he actually cared about it at all. "I was driving half the night."

"I'm sure you remember where the beans are," Virginia replied.

"Ginnie, don't be rude," her mother chided. "He drove all the way down here to help you." She made a soft tsk in her throat. "Arthur, I'm so sorry, I don't know why she gets like this," she apologized, staring daggers across the kitchen. "At least, of all people, you know that I raised her better than this."

He shifted in his chair with a loud creak, trying to snag Virginia's eye contact. "I'm sure she's just tired. It's a long drive to come down here, Mrs. Cabot."

Virginia's mother tidied invisible mess, running a fresh rag over the unused counters, her heels too noisy against the wood floor for that time of the morning. "I was so upset to hear that you'd left for the coast," she said to Arthur, a sad frown painted across her face. "How are your folks doing?"

"They like it upstate," Arthur replied, closing the photo book and sliding it across the table. "The smell is better, at least."

"Well I hope you'll give them my regards. I always did admire their ability to find themselves on the up-and-up, even later in life."

Mercifully, the kettle began to whistle, the shriek ear-piercing and unpleasant. Virginia yanked it off the burner, extinguishing the flame. She poured herself a coffee, and slid Arthur's across the placemat. She sat at the other end of the table, fingers clenched around the dainty teacup and wishing it was larger, to fit more precious caffeine. "You should drive back to Verdance," she said again. "You're only going to draw attention being down here."

"Draw attention to what?" her mother interjected. "What are you trying to keep secret?"

"Nothing," Virginia replied. "Don't worry about it, Mom. It's nothing you should be concerned about."

"You're my daughter, I have every right to be concerned!"

her mother shot back, performative panic dripping from every word. "What kind of trouble have you gotten yourself mixed up in? What else does Eugene Carsh have on you?"

Virginia picked up her cup of coffee and pushed herself away from the table. "I'm going to call the mechanic. Is it still Stuart over there in Murph Township?"

"What's wrong with your car?" Arthur asked. "Brakes?"

She shot him another look, trying desperately to silence him. "No, the engine cut out over by the Speer place after I discovered the body." She hung up the phone's receiver, cursing herself for not having done it the night before.

Her mother hovered over Arthur, flitting back and forth in the kitchen with cream and sugar, fresh teaspoons, a plate. "Ginnie, I don't think all that is so important right now. You should be trying to clear this trespassing charge, not messing around with a murder investigation. Tell her, Arthur."

"I wasn't charged," Virginia snapped, already exhausted by the entire dynamic. She waited until her mother floated into the next room with a feather duster before she continued, her voice hushed. "And someone snatching up cash for fake investments is a damn good motive. My guess is that he pissed off the wrong person, that much is obvious. What isn't clear, however, is where in shadows he was getting high-powered illusion spells from." Her fingers still rested on the phone, desperate to call the shop to fix her car, but they wouldn't be open yet for hours. "That is another piece of the puzzle," she continued.

"Illusion spells?" Arthur echoed. "Maybe you should ask—"

"Anya has already seen it," Virginia interrupted. She yanked at the awful robe, willing it to cover more of her terrible pajamas. "She's down here restocking some reagents. Even if she wasn't already here, do you really think that she wouldn't have been my first call? She's the only illusion witch we know with that kind of knowledge."

"Is it a federal issue?" Arthur asked, leaning forward across the table. "What kind of time frame are we looking at, here?"

Virginia shook her head. "No feds," she replied. "The longer we can keep them at bay, the better. They'll freeze us out as soon as they get the opportunity."

Arthur nodded. "We should start with a list of victims," he said, stating the obvious. "Mrs. Cabot, who do you know in town who was impacted by these scams?"

Virginia yanked at the robe's tie once again, resenting the glare of the satin. "I have a lead on a Mrs. Brennan over by—"

"Oh, Arthur," her mother cried as she reentered the kitchen, topping up his coffee and pulling an accompanying cake from beneath a porcelain lid. "It's just been horrible. Once the younger generation all grows up and leaves small towns like this one, everything starts to crumble. Hucksters move in the moment we're all vulnerable, preying on the old folks." She tutted softly, shaking her head. "He made up some story about a business opportunity. He said that he was looking for investors. He made the rounds up at the old church, and over across the way in Murph Township, too. He swindled several in town here, Arthur. He took them for everything they were worth."

"Definitely sounds like motive to me," Arthur said, jotting something down in his florid, loopy handwriting.

"I'm going to go change," Virginia said, before her own

exasperation bubbled up in her throat as words she wouldn't be able to swallow back down. "Enjoy your cake."

"Yes, please do," her mother scolded, handing Arthur a large slice of coffee cake, the top loaded with a cinnamon sugar crumbled topping. It had been Virginia's favorite, once. Her mother stared across the foyer, her matching green eyes frosty. "Make sure you iron your shirt first."

Chapter Thirteen

Murph Township was an odd place, perhaps even more so than Birch Hollow. Similarly surrounded by endless freight train tracks, it was about a mile and a half up the road and a left turn at the junction where the old motel sat derelict on the corner, broken windows speckling its facade like a case of pox.

The two towns were linked by fields of crops, one cracked and poorly maintained two-lane highway, and the fact that the Birch Hollow police served both places. With populations so small, there wasn't usually much crime to go around.

Until there was.

Virginia had walked all the way there, stalking down that dusty highway for a mile and a half in the growing oppression of the heat. There was a breeze that morning, but its presence had been cruelly abbreviated. She wiped the back of her neck, the damp in the air equal to the moisture resting in her clothes.

She'd left the house without a word, afraid that if she even dared open her mouth, it would be the start of Armageddon. Hopefully, by the time she got back, Arthur would be long gone, driving back to the city, back to his wife and kids, back to his seat at the table.

A truck drove past, the chassis clattering angrily over every pothole, of which there were dozens. Infrastructure didn't matter that far out from the city. No one cared if a few folks out in the fields had a hard time of it. They weren't even worth their own votes.

She crossed the road, passing the sign welcoming people to Murph Township. It was new since she'd left, but still at least fifteen years old, the letters sun-bleached and faded, the rivets holding it together rusted, with delicate trails of iron oxide dripping down several inches. *Most improved town in the state*, the sign read. Virginia snorted. It wasn't much of anything to be proud of, given where it had started.

Stuart's shop baked under the sun, the asphalt in front already radiating heat back through the windows. The clocktower stood nearby, the town's crown jewel and the only thing they bothered to repair year on year. While the rest of the place crumbled into dust, there it proudly stood, ringing every hour, on the hour. Virginia yanked open the door, desperate for the relief of shade.

"Can I help you?" a woman asked from the next room, her disembodied voice floating over the counter.

"I'm looking for Stu," Virginia replied.

"He retired." The woman was wiping her hands on a rag as she entered, tucking the soiled fabric back into her belt loop. "The name is Sammy. Stu is my dad." She was young with a sturdy build, displaying a casual roughness that wasn't uncommon in those parts. "What can I do you for?"

"I, uh..." Virginia trailed off. "My car broke down over in Birch Hollow, out near the town line, just off the highway."

Sammy leaned over the counter onto her forearms, her

navy blue coveralls streaked with the same grease that graced her rounded cheek. "You could have called, we do have phones out here, you know."

"Yeah, I know. I'm from here. Well, from Birch Hollow, anyway." Virginia wiped more moisture from her brow, irritated that she seemed to be sweating more in the shade than she had in the unmitigated sunlight. "I knew your dad," she added. "A long time ago."

"It's a hell of a ways to walk when all I'm going to do is head out there to tow it back here," Sammy replied. "What's it doing?"

"Drove down the other day from Verdance. The engine was making a kind of clunking noise, now it won't start."

Sammy took a swig from a flask sitting on the desk, the leather casing engraved with something illegible. "More of a thunk, or more of a grind?" she asked.

"Thunk."

"Timing chain, maybe. Or a belt." Sammy set the flask down, twirling a set of keys around her finger. "It's a big job."

Virginia sighed, rubbing at her temples as though she could massage the growing headache away. "How long?"

"Not how much?"

"At this rate I'd pay just about anything to give me a faster escape," Virginia muttered. "Your dad was always fair and quick."

"My dad almost worked himself into an early grave," Sammy said. "You'll forgive me if I'm not aiming for the same fate." She lifted the hinged section of the counter, waving her through to the back as she rolled up her sleeves one at a time, revealing a patchwork of fresh tattoos across her olive skin. A snake, an apple, two gears, and the Murph Township crest. Strange skinfellows for someone so young. "Best case, maybe a week, but I won't know until I have a look."

"A week!" Virginia protested.

"It's likely to be a big job, ma'am, and I got three tractors in yesterday for servicing." Sammy shrugged lightly, showing off another tattoo peeking out from beneath the lapels of her coveralls. "You're welcome to take it elsewhere."

"There *is* no elsewhere."

"Then I guess you'll just have to wait until it's finished."

The building's walls were closing in around Virginia, and so was the entirety of Murph Township, the whole county, and the distant horizon, laying low and flat over the fields. "Can't I pay a rush fee, or something?" Virginia asked.

"You can't rush an engine block lift," Sammy replied. "It doesn't work like that. If you come with me to the office, I'll get you to sign off on the part order form. Will go faster than getting you to approve it later."

"Fine," Virginia relented, following her through the gap in the grimy counter. The back office was barely that, a tilted table piled high with handwritten receipts and invoices on manufacturer letterhead. There was a shelf to the side, stuffed full with part catalogs. The top shelf held three family photos in fingerprint smudged frames and an unlabeled binder.

"Sign and date the bottom, ma'am, if you please." Sammy handed over three pages, along with a pen sticky with grease. "Where are you staying?"

"Cabot residence," Virginia answered. "She's my mother."

"I wondered if that was the case." Sammy gave her a wry

smile. She tugged down the binder and leafed through it until she found what she was looking for. "My dad thought he was some sort of town historian," she said. "Followed any time Birch Hollow made the news, local or national."

Virginia stared down at the page, her own face, much younger, looking back at her. She was beaming as she accepted her detective badge from the police commissioner in Verdance. "Oh," was all she managed to say, as the half hour chime struck at the clocktower, the hollow metallic sound reverberating across the empty landscape.

"Be right back, I'll get you your copy."

Virginia flipped through the binder, skimming over news articles that spanned decades. Most of it was dull, half-baked interviews with local politicians waxing poetic about the clocktower bees as they cut ribbons and kissed babies. A few about the storm that decimated crops and would have killed dozens, had her mother not insisted that proper shelters be built six months prior. Everything was in perfect chronological order, one right after the next.

And then.

Juliette stared out from the page, her missing person poster preserved from the past. It was a sharp and immediate haunting, her eyes staring up at Virginia. She almost slammed it shut, but couldn't quite bring herself to say goodbye again. The page was cracked and yellowed, the edges torn even as they were taped down onto the cardboard. There was a small news clipping next to it, the only one that had been run about her, far back on page twenty-seven in the county paper. *Local Girl Goes Missing*, it read. Presumed runaway. No family. Inform local police if you see her.

The opposite page was Senator Jonathan Dean's swearing–

in, old J.D. himself, made from money and silver spoons but pretending at poverty. Virginia frowned, flipping through the rest of the binder. It was all about Senator Dean, following his meteoric rise to power. The following page was a society piece about his family's legacy at an ivy league school out east when he started there not long after Juliette went missing.

"Here's your copy," Sammy announced, sliding back into the office. The paper was black at the edges, a consequence of her profession. "As soon as I can, Ms. Vane," she said.

"Is your dad still in the area?" Virginia asked, turning back to the page with Juliette's poster. "I was wondering if he remembered much about this girl."

Sammy shrugged, downing a cold mug of coffee. "Beats me. I'd have to ask him. Bit before my time, you know."

"Do you mind asking him?"

"He's not been well, Ms. Vane."

"I understand, but I was hoping—"

"I said I'd ask," Sammy interjected. "But if you're looking for town history, you'll hear more of the unfiltered stuff out at the casinos, I'm sure you know." She set the mug on the desk, and it wobbled dangerously, the stack of files threatening to topple. "Was there anything else?"

Virginia stared her down, but Sammy didn't budge. "No," she said finally. "Thanks for your help."

***

Virginia walked the rest of the short distance into town, the sun rising like a threat in the sky.

She stopped into the local convenience store for a pack of smokes, purposefully avoiding the notice board where she'd once hung a missing person poster for Juliette. She could almost still see it in her mind's eye but the paper was long gone, replaced by notices about town tornado procedures, three requests for farm hands, and a leaflet promoting Jonathan Dean for Senator. *J.D. puts our nation first*, it read. She rolled her eyes at it.

"Fancy meeting you here," Jolie said, waiting outside the shop. "How did you know we'd be here?"

"I didn't," Virginia replied. "Had to come in to find someone to fix the car so we can escape this damned place." She lit a cigarette, stifling the contented sigh in her mouth when the smoke hit her lungs. "Where's Anya?"

"Here," Anya replied, emerging from an alley with an armful of half-rotted cornstalks. "I think we're just about set for the caterpillars, Jo. I got two dozen more from this batch. A great find, assuming I can dry these little buggers before they go bad."

"Dead caterpillars can go bad?" Virginia asked.

"They rot, just like people do," Anya replied, and her tone was somehow both blithe and deep at the same time. "I didn't expect to see you up this way, not with everything else going on." She tilted her head. "Any leads?"

Virginia inhaled again, grateful for the familiarity of the poison. "Juliette went missing thirty years ago, all the leads went cold a long time back."

"I meant about Heinrich Harrow," Anya said, her head tilted. "Are there any leads about him?"

"Oh." Virginia stubbed out the remaining embers against the weathered brick, stamping out the remains with the toe of her shoe. Of course Anya had meant Harrow. Why in shadows had Virginia thought she meant Juliette? She coughed, clearing her throat, a usual occurrence after a smoke. "Yeah, he swindled a bunch of folks between here and there. My guess is that's motive, and Arthur—"

"Dixon?" Anya interrupted. "What is Sheriff Dixon doing all the way down here?"

"He was overly concerned about my night at the station," Virginia replied. "Nothing to worry about. Are you heading back to the city, or do you have more reagents to dig up?"

The clocktower read noon, the loud chimes disturbing the bees at the top. The face of it was old and weathered, sun bleached and worn, the hands of the clock once black but now more of a brown, the unsightliness of it juxtaposed by the neat square of flowers that surrounded it, beautiful varieties of orchids and lilies that had been donated by the Dean family, according to the shining plaque that stood proudly in the middle of the blooms.

"I closed the shop for another week," Anya explained. "If I head back now, I'll just head straight into work. At least down here, I can pretend that I have more pressing matters to attend to."

Virginia resented that she knew it was Arthur's car speeding around the corner before he even came to a full stop and climbed out. "Ginnie," he said, slamming the door. "Thank shadows I found you."

"Where did you think I'd be?" She lit another cigarette, leaning against the convenience store. "Not many options in this county."

"You took off without saying anything!" he nearly shouted, straightening his suspenders with the loud snap of elastic against starched cotton. "With everything that's going on here and back in Verdance, I think it's best if you stick close to home."

"I'm a mile and a half away, Arthur."

"Your mother had no idea where you'd gone, she was in tears." He huffed quietly, his gaze sliding over towards Jolie. "It's nice to see you, Jo," he said.

Jolie nodded and didn't ask any more questions, for which Virginia was grateful.

"And Ms. Quinn, always a pleasure," Arthur said.

"Mmhmm," Anya replied, leaning against the door of Seamus' car. "Just drove down for some time away, you know how it is."

He walked past her, heading for the old clocktower . "I wonder if that old thing is still ridden with wasps," he mused.

"Bees," Virginia corrected. "They're bees. And yes, they are. You can see them flying in and out of the windows."

"Why don't they get rid of them?" Jolie asked, following behind Arthur. Her saddle shoes hissed against the hot pavement, the soles scraping against loose gravel.

"Superstition," Virginia answered. "Folks around here think the bees bring good luck. They've been there for a century at least." Something twinged in her chest, scar tissue tearing after too many years ignored. "Except the summer Juliette went missing."

"I don't remember that," Arthur mused, shielding his eyes to stare up at the tower. "Really?"

"You were already gone," Virginia replied. "You'd left for Verdance almost a year back by then. The bees vanished from the clocktower that summer, which only reinforced the superstition that it was good luck, good for the harvest, kept bad spirits away." She squinted against the harsh overhead light, her eyes already sore from it. "Of course, that was long before the Rupture."

Arthur turned back, looking at her for just a moment. He opened his mouth to say something, but nothing came. Nothing about the bees or Juliette, at least. He rubbed his head again, stepping back. "What about the Speer place? Do you think they were involved?"

"Mrs. Speer is about eighty-five years old," Virginia said with a heavy sigh. "So while it's not impossible, I feel it's unlikely that she managed to kill a conman in his prime. Carsh said she was pretty shaken up, and her son has an alibi, not that he shared it with me."

"Don't remove them from the running yet, Ginnie, there may yet be something there."

Virginia's shoulders tensed, the blades drawing closer together, stunting her breath. "There's certainly something, but it might not be what we think." She watched Jolie laughing at something that Anya had said, taking part in the strange ritual of dead-heading the spent flowers. "I'm looking forward to taking Jolie home. This place isn't good for her."

"You need to start making more permanent plans for her, Ginnie," Arthur said gently. "At some point, she's going to need to find her own way in the world."

Virginia stared at him, wondering how a man so elevated in his position could be so dense. "I'll see you when I'm back in Verdance."

Chapter Fourteen

Mrs. Candace Brennan lived in an old farmhouse not far from the clocktower, which loomed against the horizon, a permanent reminder of the passage of time even in a sleepy place like that. The house's white paint was peeling at the edges, long since yellowed by the elements. Virginia stepped out of the car and wavered at the base of the sidewalk, lined with what were once daffodils in spring, but were dead leaves in the height of a dry summer. "I won't be long," she offered.

Anya shrugged. "I'm happy to wait." She hesitated, her foot still on the brake before she put the car into park. "Are you sure you're alright down here, the two of you?"

"Sure thing, Quinn." Virginia glanced at the blue front door, beset on both sides by windows hosting empty flower boxes. "Thanks again for the ride."

"Given how fast Sheriff Dixon pealed out earlier, I assumed he hadn't offered." Anya tapped her long, elegant fingers against the steering wheel, the sterling silver of her rings sparkling in the sunbeams filtered down through foliage. "I hadn't realized you were married, once."

"It was a very long time ago."

"Explains a lot."

Virginia exhaled through her nose, shifting the weight of her bag to the other arm. "Water under the bridge and all that, I guess." The air was thick with the scent of summer, of stagnant mud and thirsty creeks, of too many memories and countless nightmares. "Hopefully Mrs. Brennan has something interesting for us."

"Mm," Anya demurred, still tapping her fingers against the leather cover of the wheel. "Whatever is going on here, it's not good." She let her hands fall into her lap with the quiet clink of the silver rings, one of them much darker than the others. "Maybe Mrs. Brennan will be the key that unlocks this whole thing, and then we can get out of here and back to the city."

Virginia laughed. "I wish, Quinn. I wish." The blue door creaked open, and Mrs. Brennan beamed out at her, welcoming and homey, even at a distance. "Keep an eye on the kid."

Midwestern hospitality was legendary, in that it was usually open, honest, and terribly naive. It wasn't hard to see why the likes of Heinrich Harrow targeted small towns like that one. Mrs. Brennan didn't hesitate to usher Virginia inside, pushing a glass of iced tea into her hands before she even knew the reason for the visit. "Ginnie Cabot," she said, gesturing for her to sit at the table. "I didn't know you were in town."

"Just back for a few days," Virginia replied. "Thank you for the tea." It was the opposite of her mother's, overly sweet and under-brewed, but wonderfully cold against her tongue. "Ma'am, I was wondering if I could ask you a few questions?"

"About what, dear?"

Virginia hedged her words, aware that the nature of the

con would likely embarrass the poor woman. "I heard that a man in town was up to no good," she offered.

"Ah," Mrs. Brennan replied, her face clouding over with shame. "Yes, well, the city's sprawl finds its way down here too, from time to time." She busied herself assembling a plate of stale cookies, half ginger snaps, and half oatmeal. "Did you hear that J.D. is going to visit the town next month? It will be nice to see our little place in the spotlight. Lovely that one of our own is out making something of himself, don't you think?"

"Certainly," Virginia lied, biting back sharp words on the topic. "It's wonderful that people are learning what a charming place this is. I'd forgotten just how pretty the drive down here is, Mrs. Brennan. I suppose it's no wonder that folks from the city find themselves down here from time to time."

"I was never one for the hustle and bustle," Mrs. Brennan said. She set the plate on the table directly in front of Virginia, urging her to take a cookie. "I prefer a quiet life. It's just harder now, without the farm."

"Who owns that land out back?" Virginia asked. For a stale ginger snap, it wasn't the worst thing she'd ever had. They were probably county fair winners when they were fresh.

Mrs. Brennan frowned, but only for a second before her face recovered, settling back into her default warm smile. "The bank does, now. Hard to keep up when the kids all moved away. All that land was too much for me, I was more than happy to sell it."

"Of course." Tea washed down the cookie, and Virginia found herself rescuing crumbs from the plate. "Some other folks in town seemed to have felt the same."

"I'm just so blessed to have as much as I do," Mrs. Brennan said, gesturing around at the small kitchen and the hand-made, unvarnished table they were sitting at. "So many have far less. I have the home I raised my children in, I have peace and quiet." She gestured at the plate again, wanting Virginia to take another. "More tea?"

"Yes please, ma'am," Virginia replied, vaguely guilty that she was indoors enjoying a cold beverage while Anya and Jolie waited outside. She'd pay penance for it later. "Sometimes I miss the calm of the fields down here." She'd intended it as a lie, but there was a strange granule of truth in it that made her uncomfortable. "Especially in the summer."

"Summers here are changing, Ginnie. It's getting harder for farmers to make a go of it. Strange, in a country where so many go hungry, you would think the ones growing the food would be revered, not reviled." The apron tied around Mrs. Brennan's waist was blue checked and embroidered with bright red tulips at the hem, one of the ties stained with what looked like tea or coffee. "People are desperate."

"Desperate people can resort to all kinds of things," Virginia offered. "Or be taken advantage of."

"Five years back you wouldn't have seen anyone with that awful Nether nonsense," Mrs. Brennan said. "Now it seems like everyone knows someone who uses the stuff." She shook her head, pitying the poor creatures she spoke of. "Whether people do or they don't, most are just scraping by." She added three more cookies to the plate, replacing the ones Virginia had eaten. "What did you hear about the man up to no good?"

"A clever thief," Virginia answered, taking another cookie. "Stole money from folks and disappeared." She left out the fact that he was already dead, the money likely long gone. "It's such a shame, because with a little more information, it would be easier to keep something like this from happening again."

Mrs. Brennan sat in the chair opposite, folding her hands atop the table. "I heard that he was selling people bad investments," she said. "Promised people that he could fix their financial problems, you know, get a good return, he said." She shook her head. "I'm afraid I don't much understand the ways of these things, Ginnie. My husband was the one who did all of that, God rest his soul."

"It happens plenty up in the city."

"Mmhmm, that's what they tell me. Anyhow, he took a bunch of folks for everything they were worth. Some tried to track him down, but no one has seen him in days, not since a few people figured it out. My guess is that he heard a few of the farmers near the interstate were talking about turning him into fertilizer." She allowed herself a devilish little smile, taking an oatmeal cookie for herself. "Seems to me he thought better of sticking around."

"I'm sure most folks wouldn't blame them at all." Virginia held out her glass, accepting a refill of iced tea. "Most folks would probably even say they were doing the world a favor, getting rid of a nasty piece of work like that." She gulped at the drink, surprised at her own thirst. "After all, what kind of person can steal what someone else earned fair and square? It's not as though money grows on trees, now is it?"

Mrs. Brennan nodded vehemently, crumbs falling into her lap, unnoticed. "I would say he deserved it," she said, and her tone had a new edge to it, a quiet, vengeful anger that sounded like brimstone. She smiled, and the anger was gone, swallowed back into herself along with an errant raisin from the plate. "Some of us wish we'd been given the opportunity to have a stern word with him before he went missing. Did you know that he took a whole lot from Mrs. Speer?"

"I had heard that, yes," Virginia replied, taking the last of the ginger snaps. Even stale, they were perfectly spiced. Either that, or she was hungrier than she had realized. "Terrible, terrible."

"It's such a shame about her son."

"What's that?"

Mrs. Brennan pursed her lips, as though she'd realized that she'd said too much. "He's had his troubles over the years, that's all." She patted Virginia's arm kindly before taking her empty plate and glass to the sink. "His poor mama has had a terrible time with him, and I suspect this fraudster hasn't helped matters at all. Not at all, Ginnie."

"Mm," Virginia murmured, letting her fill the silence.

"If that James Folst came to an untimely end, I can't say that many people here will be very bothered about it." She glanced back at Virginia over her shoulder as she filled the sink with soapy water, leaving the dishes to soak. "I don't think that would be a disappearance worth our time." She turned back to the counter, setting the white ceramic lid back onto the cookie jar. "Not like that poor Juliette Ashling," she said. "Did anyone ever find out what happened to her?"

The ginger snaps in Virginia's stomach seemed to solidify all at once, making a knot there. "No," she answered, dragging herself to her feet. "Thank you for the cookies, Mrs. Brennan. It was lovely to see you again."

"Stop in any time, Ginnie dear," Mrs. Brennan replied, following her to the front door. "I hope you won't be a stranger."

"I'll do my best." There was another strange truth to that, but Virginia would do her best to pretend it was a lie.

***

When they returned to Virginia's mother's house, Jolie was wearing the terrible pink skirt suit again, pulling at the hem as she climbed down out of the car.

"You don't have to wear that if you don't like it," Virginia whispered.

Jolie gave her a sideways glance, fussing with a button. "Maybe when we get home, we can burn it?"

Virginia stifled a loud laugh, swallowing it back with a theatrical cough. "Sure, Firefly."

"Are you two going to be okay here tonight?" Anya asked from the driver's seat. "You're not going to get arrested again, are you?" she directed towards Virginia. "Seems like that cop has it out for you."

"Oh, he does, but I'm about to call my lawyer. Should help clear some of this bullshit up." Virginia leaned through Anya's window, forearms braced against the door. "Thanks for the lift."

Virginia exhaled through her nose, shifting the weight of her bag to the other arm. The air was thick with the scent of summer, of stagnant mud and thirsty creeks, of too many memories and countless nightmares. "I'll get in touch if anything jumps."

"Did you tell the police about the illusion magic?" Anya asked.

"I did. He didn't seem to care."

"But did you tell him what I said I thought the origin might have been?" Her voice quavered, but almost imperceptibly. She tacked on a smile to the end, to cover her fear, or whatever it was. "The Fae?"

"I didn't mention your name, nor the origin," Virginia reassured her. "All I said was that it was high-level, complex magic. They don't know much about all that down here, they're more insular than somewhere like Verdance."

"Mm," Anya demurred, still tapping her fingers against the leather cover of the wheel. "Whatever is going on here, it's not good." She let her hands fall into her lap with the quiet clink of the silver rings, one of them much darker than the others. "Did that Mrs. Speer have an affinity for magic?"

Virginia shrugged, watching Jolie sit at the edge of the steps, pulling at the hem of the awful tweed skirt. "I don't know. I never heard anything when I lived out here, but people are secretive. I'm sure there's plenty about this place I don't know and never will." She brushed a droplet of sweat from her forehead and flicked it into the drying patch of yellowed grass. "It's probably better that way, if you ask me. I have enough problems up in Verdance already. A homicidal maniac, people looking for Jo, a backlog of boring cases."

"I don't mind sticking around," Anya protested, fingers toying with the keys in the ignition. "I don't think Jo will, either. Or Sheriff Dixon, for that matter, if he decides to come back down here."

"Sheriff Dixon has his own issues in the city," Virginia shot back, aware that her tone had overshot the mark. "And like I said, I'm calling my lawyer. She's expensive but she's good, got me out of hot water a few years back. Now she owes me a favor." She waited a moment, considering her options before she continued. "Some business with Astrid a few months back," she said simply, and to her relief, Anya nodded.

"Say no more."

"I'll catch you tomorrow," Virginia said. "I'll call if anything happens."

"Make sure you do," Anya replied, starting the engine. "Don't get thrown behind bars again, alright?"

"I'll do my best."

"And Vee—stay the hell away from that house. There's something off about the magic. I don't like it." Anya shifted the car into gear, but remained in place. "Tell me you won't," she reiterated.

"Alright, fine, I won't," Virginia replied, knowing she wasn't going to listen. Whatever was out there, she had to know what it was. "Have a good night, Ms. Quinn."

"And you, Ms. Vane."

Virginia rolled up her sleeves as the car trundled back up the long gravel driveway and disappeared around the corner, vanishing into the rows and rows of green crops. "You hungry?" she asked Jolie. "I'm sure we can rustle something up."

"I don't want to leave with Anya," Jolie replied. "I want to stay here with you."

"How much of that did you hear?"

Jolie shrugged. "Enough." She stood, brushing the dust from her skirt. "You shouldn't worry about those enforcers. I never told any of them my real name."

"No?"

"Nah. I don't think any of them even ever asked." Jolie fussed with the ends of her hair, untangling the tiny knots that had formed throughout the day. "So you can tell Sheriff Dixon that I'm not in any danger."

"I'll be sure to let him know," Virginia lied. Someone had handed over the kid's name, and if it wasn't an enforcer, then it was someone closer than they'd realized.

"What's the deal with these homicides?" Jolie asked. "Are they connected?"

Virginia nodded. "Likely." She sat down next to Jolie, looking out over the fields that stood unmoving in the stillness of the claustrophobic afternoon. "Would anyone else know what you are? Family or something?"

"No, I told you, I grew up in an orphanage," Jolie said. "Upstate, for a while. Then the one off Sixteenth street until I aged out. No one ever came for me." She dragged a fingertip through the dust on the porch, drawing disconnected lines and dots, little geometric shapes before brushing them away with an irritated sigh.

Virginia eased out a breath, half swallowing it back into her throat. "You let me worry about all this, alright? We'll get things down here done and dusted and go home."

"What happened here, really?" Jolie asked, leaning forward into the tiny hint of breeze emitting from the tree line. "It must have been bad."

"It was a long time ago," Virginia answered. "What's done is done."

"Why doesn't Officer Carsh like you?"

"I made him look foolish when I was a little younger than you are now. I don't think he ever got over it." Something like the smell of a campfire drifted lazily along the barely existent breeze, so faint that she almost questioned whether she'd really noticed it at all. "I had a friend who went missing.

They never found her."

Jolie nodded, solemn, her forehead so creased with worry that Virginia was regretting having said anything at all. "Do you ever wonder what happened to her?"

"Every day."

The screen door creaked, and it was obvious that their moment of honesty had come to an abrupt, necessary stop. "I was wondering when you two would show up," Virginia's mother chided, holding the door open. "I made us an early supper, assuming you're not about to disappear on me again."

"I had to get the car to the shop, Mom," Virginia said, pulling herself to her feet. "I told you that."

"You take it to Stu's?"

"Yeah. It's his daughter now, though. He retired."

Virginia's mother breathed out a laugh. "I doubt that. I just saw that man not two weeks back, up to his elbows in grease."

"I don't know, maybe it's recent then." Virginia offered a hand to Jolie, who took it, standing up and showing off a demure curtsy.

"Thank you for your hospitality, Mrs. Cabot," Jolie said. "I'm sorry that I missed dinner the past couple of evenings, I was helping a friend gather reagents."

"Reagents?" Virginia's mother pressed. "What kind of reagents?"

"Medicinal," Virginia said quickly, shooting a stare at Jolie. "She's a healer, that's all."

"I'll bet," her mother retorted, sarcasm dripping from both syllables. "Ginnie, Officer Carsh called looking for you after Arthur left this morning to find you."

Virginia ducked under her mother's arm to head inside, aiming for the phone on the side table. "Arthur did find me."

"It's not every day a man will drive hours for a damsel in distress, Ginnie. You should have held on tighter." Her mother latched the screen door once Jolie was inside and leaned against one of the kitchen chairs, the feet scraping lightly against the flooring. "Although you never know, I don't think he ever really got over you."

"Mom, enough," Virginia seethed through gritted teeth, holding the receiver in her hand. "Arthur has a wife and two kids."

"I always thought you two were so good together."

"We weren't." She dragged the rotary dial one number after another, trying to scrape the sequence from her memory. "Anyway, he's probably already back in Verdance by now, given how he drives like a bat out of the Rift." She paused before the final two numbers, unsure which order they belonged in. "Why did Eugene Carsh call?"

"He said there was a development."

"Perfect," Virginia grumbled, settling on a combination of numbers she hoped were correct. "Can you give me a minute? I'm calling my lawyer."

"More secrets?" her mother asked, painting a wounded frown across her lined face. "I'd hoped we were past all of that."

"Mom, please," Virginia hissed as the line began to ring.

"Sadie Sinclair, Esquire, we beat the odds for you!" a voice chirped. "How may I direct your call?"

"Tell Sadie it's Virginia Vane and it's urgent," Virginia said, and then added, "please."

"One moment!"

The line crunched with static, despite the clear weather. Nothing out in Birch Hollow had been upgraded for decades, not since the first lines were put in just before she left. Her mother was still staring, but her attention waning as she began to fidget with the sleeves of her lightweight cardigan.

"Ms. Vane," Sadie said evenly. "I was wondering when I would hear from you."

"I'm in a bit of a bind, and I need representation as soon as possible."

Sadie flipped through some papers, the rustling almost blowing out the line. "I have a four-thirty at the courthouse in an hour, I can swing by the precinct then. Otherwise, you may be in custody overnight."

"I'm not in Verdance," Virginia explained, relieved that her mother had wandered off, no doubt to dig up more awful clothes for poor Jolie. "I'm down south about three hours. Two and a half if you're a lead foot."

"I didn't realize you were out of town," Sadie replied. "I was under the impression that you rarely left the city."

"Unfortunately I got pulled into chasing a lead down here, and in amongst all that, I pissed off some of the locals. I was picked up for trespassing, and the department here is threatening charges if I don't get out of town, but I still have some work to complete." Virginia turned to face the door, putting her hand over her mouth to muffle the sound. "They have a bit of a grievance with me down here."

Sadie gave a soft *mmhmm* over the line as she took notes. "I didn't expect you would need my assistance quite so soon after your troubles with the State's Attorney six months ago."

"The State's Attorney also has a bit of a grievance."

"Where are you located now? I can arrange to move client

meetings in order to meet you there." Sadie cleared her throat quietly. "Although I should warn you, Ms. Vane, I'm not much of a lead foot, as you put it."

"Birch Hollow. They share a precinct with Murph Township just over the highway. The officer with a raging desperation to pin this on me is Officer Carsh. He's unhappy that I embarrassed him thirty-one years ago, and has decided to hold a grudge."

"Birch Hollow?" Sadie repeated.

"Yes."

She paused. "I'm sorry, I don't travel out that far for clients."

Virginia resisted the urge to smack the receiver against the coffee table. "You just said you would."

"I'm sorry, Ms. Vane, Birch Hollow is too far to drive in one day."

"Far? I told you at the start how far out I was, it wasn't an issue until—"

"I'll file some paperwork before end of day," Sadie interrupted smoothly. "I'll call the precinct there to make sure we can move this along quietly."

"What's the matter, Sinclair, afraid of a few cornfields?" Virginia teased, the edges of her tone barbed. "Can't handle a few hours' ride south in that nice new car you have?"

"Ms. Vane, I need you to understand me quite clearly in what I'm about to say, because I do not say it lightly." Sadie inhaled, and then hissed out a long, protracted sigh. "You should leave Birch Hollow, and do so as soon as possible."

Chapter Fifteen

Virginia probably shouldn't have waited until Jolie and her mother were asleep to sneak out of the house, quietly latching the screen door behind her. She shouldn't have been breaking into her mother's hidden bottle of gin, and she shouldn't have walked the mile and a quarter into town. She stopped at the one place that was still open, the twenty-four hour convenience store on the corner of Elm and Main to buy another small bottle of gin and a pack of smokes. The Speer place sat back in the woods, barely visible from the end of Elm. She stared at it, willing the answers to rise to the surface like cream.

Sadie Sinclair was one of the best lawyers in Verdance, especially if, like Virginia, the client was likely to have enough secrets to stop up the Rift itself. She'd thrown herself into the fray more than once—not for Virginia, but for others. Shifters, mainly, or other mythics who found themselves in hot water. Her insistence to leave Birch Hollow had lodged itself directly in Virginia's gut, roiling there in a mixture of bile and anxiety.

The gin helped to numb that particular impulse, and the smoke in her lungs was a prescient, necessary reminder that she hadn't died yet, no matter how much bullshit life had thrown at her. Juliette Ashling hadn't even been the start of all that. Virginia's father had been, with his understandable absenteeism and the unholy fights he and her mother would get into. They both gave as good as they got, until he stormed out and left them in peace for a few more weeks. Months, maybe, if she was lucky.

Alcohol slid down her throat, extinguishing the fiery rage a drop at a time. Arthur had been wrong, Birch Hollow wasn't the key to anything. It was just one more poverty-stricken backwoods town that the world forgot, and the only answers it offered up came in the form of more riddles than she cared to untangle. She hadn't been able to before she left, and she still wasn't.

Some things, at least, never changed.

The stability of the town's messiness wasn't a comfort, it was an alarm constantly sounding, blaring through con-sciousness and evaporating anything like sense that might have pierced through it.

Virginia stumbled over an exposed tree root and swore at it, regretting her loneliness at the same time that she was grateful for it. Jolie might be wise beyond her years but leaning on her was unfair. Anya was too afraid of the VCPD to be of much help, and she had enough work picking caterpillars off of leaves, anyway.

She hadn't meant to walk past the Speer place.

She hadn't meant to, and yet there it was, dark and dreary and empty, whispering secrets into the night's buggy din from the brick fireplace. Virginia squinted into the night, cursing the fact that she couldn't see as well as she once had. A tendril of smoke emitted from the home, but there were no lights, no pallid telltale glows to be seen. Strange. Odd. Whatever it was, she should ignore it and go home.

She inhaled another lungful of smoke and breathed it out into the crescent moon midnight, the tails of the smoke mirroring those of the house in front of her. Someone was in there, and they didn't want anyone to know. Given the hour, it was unlikely to be Mrs. Speer, though it wasn't impossible that a woman of her age took down a man in his prime. Virginia would believe it of her own mother, so why not Mrs. Speer?

Pausing next to a thick tree trunk, long since felled but still in the ground, the old remnants of lightning still blackening the bark, she leaned against it and breathed. She sipped at the gin, hidden inside a paper bag, letting the fiery liquid singe her esophagus. Calling Carsh was out of the question, he'd just haul her in again, and she'd be stuck until Sadie Sinclair sent paperwork through in the morning.

Really, she should turn around and march back up the path to her mother's house, creep past the threshold and find herself sleeping under the wool blanket that adorned the back of the couch, the fringe a permanent irritant. And yet, she remained, watching the house as though it would willingly give up all the answers she sought.

Moments crept by, one at a time. Owls called in the neighboring trees, and something small rustled in the underbrush. She stared, waiting for her eyes to adjust, but saw nothing more than she had before. Foxes and raccoons were rampant that far from the city, busy thriving outside the norms of human interference.

Virginia stamped out the remaining embers from the butt of the cigarette, driving her toe down into the earth until what was left of the orange glow flickered and then disappeared, plunging her back into the near total blackness beneath the thick canopy of foliage.

Against her better judgment, she approached the house, stepping from side to side to avoid snapping any twigs or rustling leaves in an alarming way. If it was Mrs. Speer, the last thing Virginia wanted was to give the old woman a heart attack. After all, in forty years, it could be her knocking around in an empty old house, terrified and alone.

From the trees, she stared into the house, willing someone to turn on a light, but no one did. Strangely, the hearth was cold and forlorn, despite the smoke trails from the chimney above. Virginia paused, watching, wondering, briefly, what the hell she was doing back out there again. It wasn't her mystery to solve, not anymore. Heinrich Harrow was dead, and good riddance, it seemed like. Not many would mourn him, least of all his family, and yet something itched under the surface of her skin, the unknowable dancing across every nerve and propelling her forward until she was at the base of the stairs to the porch.

She ran her hands over the wood, willing something to come to her, but nothing did. Her sight was as useless and void-like as it had been for six months. Nothing but darkness, and failure, and worst of all the loss of something she hadn't known that she wanted. There was an emptiness where sight should be, but it had taken her too many years to figure out the puzzle. Too many years, and now it was wasted, buried back somewhere inside herself that she couldn't reach.

"Ouch," she hissed, yanking her hand back from the railing, a nasty splinter already bleeding from the tip of her index finger.

All at once, the pain hitched in her chest, but it wasn't the splinter. It was explosive and had she been able to breathe, she might have cried out in pain, shouted for help because she was surely dying. Her mouth opened and closed wordlessly, and at the center of herself, a dam broke within, unleashing years and decades that she had never wanted to experience first hand.

Juliette, running down that same path, sunlight glistening against her skin and illuminating girlish freckles there, beckoning to someone behind her. Juliette, her pale hands pressed against Virginia's in the overwhelming moonlight so long ago. Juliette, her face wreathed in horror.

"No," Virginia said aloud, surprising even herself. She stared at the door, afraid it would open and expose her. It didn't, and the smoke continued to rise from the bricks above.

"No," she whispered again, shaking her head and clumsily biting at the splinter, desperate to get it out. It wasn't real, it was a fantasy. She'd been lamenting the loss of her sight and she'd had too much to drink. She shook the bag for the high-pitched swish of the few droplets left in the bottle. It was her own fault. She should have known better. Birch Hollow would always come knocking when you least expected or wanted it to.

She stumbled back up the path, shaken by the visions, trying to forget them as quickly as they'd come. The mile hike back to her mother's house wasn't enough to clear her head, and when her feet touched gravel the memories were still swirling in her mind's eye.

"Have a nice walk?" her mother asked, rocking back and forth in that shadows-damned chair.

"Yeah," Virginia shot back, ready to walk right past her

mother into the house. "Thanks."

"Ginnie."

"I'm tired," Virginia said.

Her mother nodded, the chair creaking softly as it wobbled over the loose porch boards. "Did you head back to the Speer place?"

"Maybe."

"Find anything?"

Virginia waited, her hand on the screen door's handle, the dented metal warm in her hands from the cloying, oppressive heat. "No."

"Shame. Seems this town could use someone with sight." Her mother shrugged and lit a fresh cigarette from a candle sitting on the table. "I'd offer you one, but from the smell of you I reckon you found your own stash."

"There was someone at the house, smoke from the chimney," Virginia relented. It was easier to tell her mother the facts than dive down into whatever had happened with Juliette all those years ago. "No lights, though. Did Mrs. Speer stay there, do you know?"

"I think her son came to get her. She was awfully shaken up after all that, I'm afraid."

"Someone needs to tell Carsh, then. But it can't be me. My lawyer has enough problems to deal with." Virginia sat on the steps, pulling out her own pack of cigarettes and lighting one up, despite the sick feeling in her stomach that always arrived when she'd had one too many. "I fucking hate Birch Hollow." She hadn't meant to say it aloud, but she had. To her surprise, her mother nodded.

"Not all of us had the option to leave, Ginnie."

"No one is holding you here, Mom. You can leave whenever

you want."

"You'll understand someday, when you stop running from everything that set you in motion. Until then, this place will only ever feel like a prison cell." Her mother shrugged, the same way she always had, that smug I-told-you-so air that she was so fond of. "You'll learn, even if it takes you longer than it takes most folks."

"Maybe it will be when you stop talking in riddles and tell me the truth," Virginia said acerbically, the sourness unpleasant on her tongue. She didn't want things to always be that way with her mother, but they were. Their curse was inescapable.

"I've never lied to you." Her mother drew in a breath, the ember at the end of her cigarette flaring in the darkness. "I've only done what was best for you."

"Fuck this, I'm going to bed." Virginia inhaled quickly, burning out the smoke much faster than she should have. "Enjoy your cigarette." She moved for the door, ready for the night to be over, to be one day closer to getting her car repaired, to escaping to the coast and never, ever listening to Arthur about Birch Hollow again.

"Your father once told me that pain helped him break through bad cycles. I never knew what that meant, but maybe you do," her mother said flatly. "You want to know more about him? There. Fine. Now you know more."

"What do you mean, bad cycles?" Virginia asked, hand poised on the handle but not yet wrenching it open. "What kind of pain?"

"I imagine you'll have to figure that part out for yourself." The cigarette flared in the darkness, illuminating only part of her mother's face. "I never wanted it for you, Ginnie. I'd hope you would escape whatever it was that made him that way, but maybe you didn't."

"You could have said something earlier," Virginia replied. "A hint might have been nice."

"How could I have known? You've spent years refusing to speak to me."

"Yeah, I wonder why."

Her mother leaned forward on her chair, the iron creaking against the damp humidity that flooded the air. "Did you ever wonder if everything that happened back then might have blocked you in some way?"

"Blocked?"

"You know, like a sink that drains too slowly," her mother offered casually. "Maybe it's just a case of dealing with things."

"Hard to deal with things when you're living on the streets."

Her mother coughed lightly, clearing her throat from the years of smoke that had damaged it. "You weren't on them for very long, you shacked up with Arthur the first chance you got."

"Not a hard decision when the alternative is freezing to death."

"You could have come back here, Ginnie. My doors, even with new locks, were always open to you. All you had to do was apologize and we could have moved forward from all the Juliette nonsense." Her mother began rocking to and fro once more, the motion strangely grating against Virginia's ears.

"Nonsense?"

"She ran around with half the town, Ginnie. Girls like that

tend to come to unpleasant ends. I tried to keep you from her, but you wouldn't listen. I tried as a mother to protect you from that inevitable heartbreak." Her mother sighed, coughing again. "You wouldn't listen."

"Juliette never would have left without telling me," Virginia shot back. "You didn't know her like I did."

"I think a few boys in town would have dared to disagree on that matter," her mother retorted. "You've spent too many years dwelling on this, Ginnie."

"She would have done the same for me."

"Would she have? Or perhaps Juliette Ashling would have moved on with her life and only remembered you once in a blue moon. Trash is as trash does."

"The only trash around here is us," Virginia said evenly. "Good night."

Chapter Sixteen

Her eyes flew open the moment she heard the glass shatter. Already reaching for her holster, Virginia tumbled off the couch, her legs tangled in the itchy wool blanket. Her knee slammed into the wood paneling and she swore loudly, throwing the fabric to the side. "Jolie?" she called out, willing her vision to adjust to the deep black of the night. It must have only been an hour or two after she'd gone inside. "Jolie!" she shouted.

"I'm here," Jolie replied, appearing in the hallway, the fire in her hands illuminating the long peach-colored nightdress she'd no doubt acquired from Virginia's mother. While it fit her better than Virginia's clothes, it still hung off her, making her look younger than her years. "What happened?"

Virginia picked a brick up off the floor, now visible. A note was hastily tied around it with a scrap of muddy twine, stiff and dry under her fingertips. She set it on the side table, pulling her revolver from the holster. "Stay here," she instructed, making a move for the door.

The night was quiet, except for the chorus of cicadas in the trees and the rustle of corn, the latter of which was suspicious in the stillness. Virginia tore off into the field, running nightblind through the stalks, gun in one hand, and her silver knuckles on the other. There was no path, no hints of the assailant's course, no matter how far she disappeared into the field.

Something scraped against her ankle and she bit back a surprised yelp. Whatever it was, it wasn't the assailant, and so Virginia continued to run.

"Stop!" she shouted into the night, pushing corn out of her way. "You're just delaying the inevitable, you know!"

Shots rang out, one of them whizzing past her ear. She ducked down closer to the ground, heart pounding in her throat. Bracing herself against the dirt, she fired back in the direction of where the muzzle flashes had come from, hoping to hear a body falling to the field, but there was nothing. Virginia waited for something: a sound, or a hint, or a vision to guide her way.

More cracks and flashes into the darkness, now from the edge of the field near the highway. Again she fired back, but again she missed, not even able to see who she was shooting at in the first place.

Virginia pursued, squinting, cursing under her breath as her pace quickened, willing herself to reach the field's boundary before the attacker escaped. The rubber soles of her shoes skidded against the loose dirt, the crops in need of a good rain. They wouldn't last long in the summer's heat without one. "Stop!" she shouted again, now not even expecting a reply.

"I've got you!" Jolie shouted from behind, sending a tall column of fire to hover above the corn, lighting the way but endangering the crop with the sparks and embers that rained down over mercifully wet leaves. The dew had come early.

"Jolie, no!" Virginia shouted, running back to where she'd come from, her mother's house still waiting for them both. She pinned Jolie's arms to her sides, and the column vanished into the night, throwing them back into bleak darkness. "Jolie, someone could have seen you!"

"What's the point of having this if I can't use it to help?" she demanded, wrenching out of Virginia's grasp. "I'm not a child!"

"We have to be careful out here, anyone would report you to the feds in a heartbeat so long as they got a bottle of cheap booze as reward." Virginia released Jolie with a frustrated sigh, pressing a hand against her own forehead. "Birch Hollow isn't safe for you."

"Neither is Verdance, according to Sheriff Dixon," Jolie shot back. "Or the coast, or anywhere."

"Things are complicated right now."

"I doubt that's going to change for someone like me." Jolie snapped her fingers at her sides, sending a spray of sparks down into the earth. "I don't want to spend forever hiding like you have."

Virginia stepped backwards, an unconscious move to protect herself from the impact of the words, but it did nothing to stem the tide of emotions rising up within her.

"Ginnie!" her mother shouted from the porch, her voice thickly coated in fear. "Ginnie, where are you?"

"We're here, Mom," Virginia called back, still staring at Jolie. "We didn't get whoever it was." She sighed, holstering her revolver in the waistband of the trousers she'd slept in. "We should get back to the house," she said evenly, walking past Jolie.

"I'm sorry," Jolie said, trotting after her. "I shouldn't have said that, it's just—"

"Don't worry about it, kid," Virginia interrupted, her feet already on the brick of the driveway, biting through her thin cotton socks. She should have slept in her shoes, too. "Mom, are you alright?"

Her mother was standing on the porch in her summer robe, the pink mauve of the satin glinting in the sparse light of the crescent moon. "Someone threw a brick through my window," she said, her voice uncharacteristically shaky. "They left a note."

"What does it say?" Virginia asked, nodding at the crumpled paper in her mother's hand.

"I don't know, I was too upset to look." She handed Virginia the page and turned away, sniffling. "I was so scared, Ginnie. I thought they'd taken you."

"No one is taking me, Mom." Virginia squinted at the paper, but couldn't read the words until Jolie sparked up a flame over her shoulder, shielding it with her hands. Virginia snorted a laugh. "Really? It just says that I should get out of town." She crumpled it back up, shoving the note into her pocket. "I've had worse."

"This is getting scary for an old lady like me," her mother said, sniffling again. "I wake up to the sound of broken glass and my daughter is missing." She reached out for Jolie, grasping at her nightgown. "And you too, Ms. Laar."

"It's probably Eugene Carsh," Virginia soothed. "He's throwing a little tantrum that I'm still here, and not running back to Verdance with my tail between my legs."

"Or it's whoever killed that man, sending a warning," her mother protested. "Ginnie, I don't think you should be involving yourself with any of this."

"A brick through the window is hardly anything to get excited about," Virginia said coolly, despite the bile that lingered in the back of her throat, and the adrenaline that still rushed through her veins.

"*My* window. It was *my* window," her mother pressed. "I never wanted you to get involved in all of this," her mother whispered, voice strangled with a fear Virginia had never heard from her before. "I think you should leave all of this alone."

"That's what you said last time." Virginia filled the kettle and was about to light the stove with a match when she threw out an exasperated sigh. "Well, there's no point in the pretense, is there? Jolie, do you mind?"

Jolie stared back at her, but flicked a tiny flame into the metal. "I'd like to help in ways that aren't just cheap party tricks," she said over the whistle of the kettle. "We could have caught whoever that was."

"And burned down half the damned field in the process," Virginia replied, steeping a herbal tea for her mother. "If you think the people around here are cagey and difficult to parse now, just wait until you endanger their crops. I guarantee you wouldn't leave this place unless it was in the back of a federal van."

"That's my choice to make," Jolie argued.

"I'm just trying to protect you!"

Virginia's mother laughed, taking the mug of tea into her hands. "And here I thought you'd have escaped all this by never having children," she muttered. "Looks like trouble found you all the same."

"Mom—" Virginia started, but cut herself off with an angry huff. "I'm going back to bed. I'll deal with Carsh and the damned window in the morning."

"Almost morning as it is," her mother said, gesturing towards the window, where the faintest glow of dawn was starting to glimmer against the distant horizon. "Maybe you should be making coffee, and not herbal tea." She slid her mug back across the table, an eyebrow raised in wordless challenge.

"Fine," Virginia relented, pouring the undrunk liquid down the sink and opening a cabinet door, hunting for the coffee beans. They weren't where she remembered them being.

"Third on the left," her mother supplied, her hands folded atop the lace runner on the table. "It's where we've always kept it."

Virginia didn't argue, she knew better than that. She ground the beans in silence, grateful that her hands had something to occupy them, so that the others wouldn't see that they still shook as she turned the crank of the hand grinder. She ground, she steeped, she poured, until there were three mugs on the table, each of them prepared just the right way.

"I thought you would have grown out of using that much cream and sugar," her mother mused, stirring her coffee with the irritating clink of silver against bone china.

"I guess not," Virginia retorted, blowing the steam away as it rose from her cup. "Jolie, are you hungry?"

"Too early to eat," Jolie replied, clearly still irritated about what had happened in the field. "I get sick if I eat too early."

"Are you sure she's not yours?" Virginia's mother asked with an indelicate snorted laugh. "Two peas in a pod. Coffee, gin, and cigarettes."

"I don't drink or smoke," Jolie said evenly.

"Probably best for a fire demon. I'd hate to see one of you when you're angry." Virginia's mother sipped at her coffee demurely, fussing with the tie of her robe. "I imagine that a fire demon could do a lot of damage."

"Jolie isn't dangerous," Virginia said flatly. "In case that was what you were hinting at."

"Ginnie, don't be rude," her mother chided. "Of course that's not what I am suggesting. Honestly, you read too much into things. Not everything is about you, daughter of mine."

Virginia suppressed a sigh, and it burned like fire in her chest. First murders, then bricks through windows.

"I have to call someone," she announced, standing up from the table with the scrape of the chair legs against the wood.

"Who are you calling?" Jolie asked.

"My lawyer. I want to know if she sent that paperwork through or not."

"It's barely five in the morning, Ginnie, I don't think lawyers are in the office quite so early. Why don't you and Jolie get cleaned up, and I'll fix us all some breakfast, and—"

"It will only take a minute," Virginia interrupted, already dialing Sadie Sinclair's home phone number. It rang seven times before anyone picked up.

"Sadie Sinclair, we beat the odds for you," she mumbled into the phone.

"It's Virginia Vane. Did you send over that paperwork to Birch Hollow yet?" Virginia asked.

"Ms. Vane, it's the middle of the night." Sadie breathed quietly. "The papers have been prepared, they will be couriered to Birch Hollow in the morning."

"Yeah, yeah, bill me a rush fee, do whatever you have to do," Virginia said. "Someone threw a brick through my mother's window about an hour ago. It's warning me to get out of town. I thought it might have been the cop with a grudge who's already arrested me twice in my life."

The crisp sound of a goose down comforter being tossed to the floor crackled over the line. "Ms. Vane, I will urge you again to leave Birch Hollow as soon as possible," Sadie warned.

"I'm hardly going to leave in the middle of the night with active charges against me, am I?" Virginia replied. "Skipping town before that paperwork is filed doesn't seem like a very good idea to me, Sinclair."

"I will handle the paperwork, as I promised."

"So handle it then," Virginia growled. "What the hell am I paying you for, otherwise?"

"This is favor for favor, Ms. Vane, if you remember." Sadie was more awake now, and sounding more like herself. She cleared her throat lightly, a more delicate sound than you might expect from a lawyer. "Ms. Vane, I will call the courier the moment we hang up. The precinct there will have the information before ten."

"That's hours away," Virginia protested, actually rather keen to follow the brick's advice, if for no other reason than for Jolie's sake. Of all the people in Birch Hollow she couldn't trust, her mother was unfortunately at the top of the list.

"Ten," Sadie repeated. "It's the earliest possible time, Ms. Vane."

Chapter Seventeen

Morning had passed slowly, inching by one sunbeam at a time, the harsh heat singeing leaves in the fields. Virginia paced the house, scoured the outside, the backyard, the tall iron fences, but found nothing in the way of hints or clues.

Once again inside, she picked up the note off the table, smoothing out the paper in the warm light of day, the air already too close and cloistered, suffocating in its humidity even as the sky remained cloudless. It was the worst part of summer. Everything cried out for rain, but instead water sat in their lungs, useless and drowning them slowly, week by week, until the relief of autumn arrived.

"Mom, do you know anyone with handwriting like this?" Virginia asked, as her mother sat at the table with Jolie, shelling a mound of endless peas.

"I didn't notice anything in particular, it was early," her mother replied, tossing another shell into the aluminum bucket on the floor. "Why?"

"It's distinctive." Virginia squinted at each character, the hastily scrawled loops, the unfinished letters, a t without the crossed bar, an open letter o that looked much like a letter u. "It could be a lead."

Her mother turned, squinting at the page from across the room. "I don't know anyone who makes note of handwriting." She shrugged, returning to the unshelled vegetables in front of her. "Doesn't look at all familiar to me."

Virginia turned the paper over, examining the wrinkles at the edges. There was nothing remarkable about it, just a scrap of plain paper that had been wrapped around a brick. "You know, Mrs. Brennan mentioned some farmers out by the interstate angry about James Folst—well, Heinrich Harrow really, but they don't know that."

"You know how they like to talk," her mother demurred. "It's all bluff and bluster."

"Maybe," Virginia agreed, thoughts lingering on Harrow's missing shoes. "But someone threw this brick, and I don't think it was Carsh."

"Ginnie, this is why I tried to keep you out of trouble, you know. Poking around in other folks' affairs is exactly how you wind up with these kinds of problems. If you would just keep yourself to yourself—"

Her mother's monologue was interrupted by the sound of Anya pulling the car up the drive, a pleasing rumble of tires. "Thank shadows," Virginia whispered to herself, already frustratingly aware of the growing tension in the house. It was far too familiar.

"Morning!" Anya called, climbing out of the driver's seat. "I thought I'd pop by. I brought pastries!" She held a brown cardboard box aloft, triumphant. "I went to the next county to get them. I heard they're the best you can get down here."

Virginia unlatched the screen door, holding it open. "Morning to you, too," she replied, relief flooding into her, quenching the quiet, burning discomfort that had only grown since the night before. "It's nice to see you."

"Oh?" Anya prompted, setting the box on the kitchen table. "Good morning, Mrs. Cabot, you are looking absolutely radiant today, a minor miracle in this heat!" She flipped open the box and revealed the pastry with a flourish. "May I interest you in something tasty?"

"I only like the apple jam tarts," Virginia's mother said casually, continuing with the peas. "And I doubt this fancy bakery had any of those."

"I got two, actually," Anya said, flipping one onto a spare saucer and nudging it across the table. "Please, help yourself! I already ate three on the way over here."

Virginia's mother stared at the tart in surprise. "Oh," was all she said.

"We had an eventful evening," Virginia announced, holding the brick in one hand and the paper in the other. "Someone smashed the window just to tell me to leave town."

"Ominous," Anya said, leaning on the back of a kitchen chair. Her cornflower blue dress hit mid-calf and fluttered there, the lightweight fabric dancing in the breezes of her every small move. "Who do you think it was?"

"Not sure," Virginia said. "Mrs. Brennan said that some farmers were none too happy about what Harrow was up to, stealing money from people. Could be that someone just wants to let sleeping dogs lie."

"More liked dead dogs. Harrow is very unlikely to wake up from that nap, I dare say." Anya took the paper, turning them over in her hand, her brow furrowed. "Might not hurt to ask around. Someone might know something, right?"

"I doubt we'll get much without an in." Virginia's hand closed around the mechanic paperwork in her pocket, folded and crumpled beyond recognition. "The old mechanic might know something about it."

"Alright, then we'll go," Anya offered. "Does Jo want to come?"

Virginia turned towards the corridor, hands cupped around her mouth. "Jolie! We're leaving in a few minutes!"

"I'll be right out!" Jolie called back, her voice muffled behind the bathroom door, the thick oak door absorbing most of the sound. She emerged, wearing the same thing she'd arrived in. Virginia braced for the inevitable.

"Jolie, what's the matter? Why aren't you wearing the clothes I gave you?" Virginia's mother asked, clearly playing up just how wounded she was. "Don't you like them? You look so much prettier when you're wearing things that fit you properly."

"I didn't want to get them messy, Mrs. Cabot," Jolie answered, somehow already an expert in top level communication. "I wouldn't be able to live with myself if I dirtied that lovely skirt."

"Perhaps Ginnie shouldn't be dragging you through the mud, then it wouldn't be of any concern at all," Virginia's mother mused.

"I think I'll grab a pastry for the road," Virginia interrupted, reaching over the table to select something so covered in powdered sugar, she couldn't even tell what it was. The stickiness coated her fingers before she thought to wrap it in a napkin. She sucked the sugar from her fingers, the taste more pleasant than she'd anticipated. "What?" she asked, noticing Anya staring at her.

"Uh, nothing, you have some sugar on your face," Anya replied, averting her gaze. "We should get going before it gets too much hotter, I can't imagine the heat makes anyone around here easier to deal with."

"You can say that again," Virginia replied, glancing over at her mother. "Some people are positively impossible in the summer."

Her mother picked at the tart with the tines of her fork, frowning down at the golden pastry and the glistening crystals at the edges. "What about my window?" she protested. "I want a quiet life, Ginnie. No more of this nonsense for me, I'm just an old lady waiting around for the end. I won't be around much longer, you know."

Virginia sucked her teeth, the decades-old guilt still rising to the surface like rancid cream. "We'll see you later, Mom," she finally said. "We won't be long."

The screen door was light in her hands, the soft wood lightly warped at the edges from the summer weather. She didn't turn back, she couldn't, not when she knew her mother would still be glaring out the kitchen window at them, silently outraged that her tactics hadn't been successful.

"Are you ready?" Virginia asked, climbing into the passenger side of the car. "If we're lucky, maybe we can dig up a lead."

"Sure thing," Anya said, thrusting the key into the ignition. "It's not hard to see why you left," she offered.

Virginia stared out the window as the car reversed back down the driveway, purposefully avoiding her mother's house. "I didn't leave," she said, but didn't offer any more.

***

The mechanic shop was full up that morning, cars crammed

into the tiny parking lot like puzzle pieces forced together. It was a labyrinth of metal and rubber, and impossible to navigate with their own car. Anya parked it on the street, looking back at it worriedly.

"Are you sure they won't tow it?" she asked. "I couldn't face Seamus if that happened."

"In a place where tractors drive to the local bar, it's not going to be a problem," Virginia answered, weaving between vehicles towards the front door.

"Hey, look at that car!" Jolie exclaimed, bending at the waist to peer into an early silver Jupiter model. "How old do you think it is?"

"Older than you by a year or two," Virginia supplied, trying to ignore her own elevated pulse at the sight of it. She shook her head, skirting around another truck on her way to the door. "Lots of crappy little scrap heaps around here still managing to run. It's not unusual in these parts."

She pulled the handle, the bells on the interior side jangling angrily, leaving Anya and Jolie outside. "Morning," she called out to the empty desk, peering past it into the shop through the door left just slightly ajar. "Sammy?"

"Just a second," she called from the shop, over the noise of a pneumatic drill and an air compressor. Sammy shimmied through the small gap in the door, it being unable to open further thanks to the stack of boxes up against it. "What can I do you for?" she asked, not looking up from the desk at first. "Oh. Ms. Vane, I did say I would call when I had news about your car."

"That's not why I'm here." Virginia's stare slid to the back room at the sound of a man's voice. "Is your dad here?"

Sammy tucked a rag into her belt loop, leaning against the

front counter. "Why?"

"I just had a few questions he might be able to answer. There was a murder, I'm sure you've heard."

"Something about it, yeah." Sammy scribbled into a worn notebook with the nub of a pencil that was so small, Virginia was surprised it was able to write at all. "Don't see what that has to do with us."

"Your dad knows everyone in these parts, and I thought maybe he'd heard something."

Sammy tucked the pencil nub into her ponytail and folded her arms over her chest. "My dad had a heart attack just a couple of weeks ago, Ms. Vane. Anything you have to ask him, you can ask me, are we clear?"

"Of course, and I hope his recovery is a quick one." The memory of the scrap book nagged at her, pulling at a thread she thought she'd long since snipped short. "I heard that some of the farmers were shooting their mouths off about the deceased," Virginia said. "I was wondering which farmers those might have been."

"Ms. Vane, I hope you'll understand why I'm not mighty keen on handing over those names," Sammy said. "Some of my customers might not be thrilled that I'm handing over their names to the police at the first mention of trouble. Some people prefer their privacy, you see." She wiped her hands on her coveralls, leaving long, greasy streaks against the twill. "Get me a warrant and I'll be more than happy to help you."

"I'm not with the police," Virginia said, always more than happy to sit both sides of the law enforcement fence, depending on what suited the situation best. "I understand that the deceased was hardly a paragon of the community. Some of the locals knew him as James Folst, some as Heinrich

Harrow. Regardless of what his name was, there's a chance this could be something bigger than it seems," she explained.

"I'm sorry, Ms. Vane, but I have my own livelihood to protect. Plenty of folks around here don't trust the authorities, and they trust private investigators even less. Few of them even got caught knocking boots where they shouldn't, if you know what I mean."

"Yeah," Virginia said with a sigh. "I know what you mean."

"I did get the chance to take a look at your car when it was towed in. Looks like a gasket and maybe a cracked oil pan. I've got the parts, so it should only be another day or so. Quick as I can, I'll get you fixed up." Sammy wiped her face with the rag, smearing grease across her forehead. Somehow, it seemed to suit her. "I'll let my dad know you dropped by. Again."

Virginia turned towards the window, watching as Anya and Jolie bent over some orchids that grew beneath the clocktower outside. Lilies lined the sidewalk there, their blooms vibrant hues of pink and orange. Tiger lilies. Those had been Juliette's favorite. "Please tell him I liked his scrapbook," she said, a little more loudly than she normally would have. Before Sammy could stop her, Virginia pushed past the counter towards the office, noticing movement within. "Not enough people care about the history of small towns," she said, smiling through the gap between the door and the frame.

"Ginnie Cabot, as I live and breathe." Stu beamed out from behind his desk, always with a wide smile and callused hand. "Your mama okay?"

"She's fine, sir, thank you for asking." Virginia pressed herself into the office, aware that Sammy was scowling at her back. "I was just in town on work. I was chasing down that fella who turned up dead at the Speer place, I'm sure you heard."

"I did, I did." Stu glanced at his daughter and back to Virginia. "Up to no good, so I hear."

"No, sir, not up to anything good, that's for sure," Virginia confirmed. "Stole a bunch of money from folks around these parts. I heard that some of the afflicted were saying an awful lot about what they thought his punishment should be. I was hoping you might have a name or two."

"Dad, you don't have to answer her questions," Sammy said, positioning herself between them. "You should be taking it easy, that's what the doctor said."

"I've told you a million times, Sammy girl, I'm just fine. Your old man's ticker isn't ready to stop ticking just yet." Stu paused, considering his words. "I think you'll find that most people are just talking, Ginnie."

"That's probably true, sir, but as I was just saying, this might could be something bigger than just a con artist who turns up dead." Virginia edged closer to the counter, in spite of Sammy's steely glare. "Sometimes, people see something that can turn the tide of a case. A partial license plate can mean no one else gets hurt. An eyewitness can be the difference between a guilty and an innocent verdict. I don't think those farmers had anything to do with it, but they might know who did."

"Sammy, go to lunch," Stu said, checking the watch at his wrist. "I'll hold down the fort."

"Dad—"

"I'm powerful hungry," he said, offering his daughter a smile. "Doctor said I have to keep my strength up, if I remember?" He clapped a hand on her shoulder, tucking a few bills into the pocket of her coveralls. "I'd really appreciate it."

Sammy hesitated, hands shoved into her pockets. "Alright, Dad," she said, before turning her glare on Virginia. "Ms. Cabot, I hope I don't have to remind you that he doesn't need excitement, not unless he wants to wind up back in the hospital."

"Crystal clear," Virginia confirmed. After Sammy left, and they'd settled into the back office, she waited, hands folded atop the desk as he searched for his words.

"Couldn't have been those farmers," he said finally. "The night that man was killed, the ones talking all that bluster were out at the barn at the edge of town. One of them lost a sum large enough to land him in hot water with his old lady. Other had to be taken home, could barely stand up for all the whiskey." He shook his head. "Even if I gave you their names, it wouldn't get you anything you're looking for."

"Did you see them there yourself?" Virginia asked.

Stu squinted, and then nodded. "I did. Don't want Sammy to know, it's a nasty little habit. Between you and me, it's caused a lot more strife than the work at this place did." He reached for the binder, opening it to the page with Virginia's photo. "She showed you this?"

"She did."

"I was glad when you got outta this place. Always wanted it for Sammy, but that girl is Hollow born and bred, this place is in her marrow, for better or for worse." He ran grease-stained fingers over the edges of the pages, a frown creased in his brow. "I'm always proud when one of us climbs up and out and makes something of themselves." He pushed it across the desk, almost asking her a question, but she didn't know what it was. "This town has had a lotta gems."

Virginia flipped through the pages, reminding herself of their contents. "The farmers—"

"Yes, the farmers." He tapped against the page with Juliette when Virginia stopped there, but wouldn't look at her. "She was meant to get outta here, too. Nice girl, even if she found trouble now and then."

"The best," Virginia agreed, swallowing back the painful lump forming in her throat. "No one ever found her."

Stu's stare slid to the opposing page, and then up to Virginia. "Not everyone forgot about her," he said simply, turning past the page before he lingered on it any longer. "It eats me up that girl never got justice."

The walls were starting to close in. "Me too," she managed to say, her voice barely more than a crack.

"Ginnie, I don't know who ended that man's life, but what I can say is that most people will think it's good riddance for someone who lied, cheated, and stole from folk." Stu closed the binder, but didn't put it away. "As a bit of an amateur historian, I do wonder how this will all play out, but I can say for sure that we probably won't ever know the true story. Headlines are headlines, not truth."

"Don't I know it," she replied.

He opened his mouth as though he was about to say something, but closed it, his brow furrowed as he shook his head. "You ever go up by that old clocktower?" he asked.

"Not been back in a long time, sir, but I know the one you're talking about. Bees like that place," she said, unsure what he was hinting at. "Why do you ask?"

"I just—" he chewed on his lip, fighting himself. He

checked the front window, nervous and starting to pace.

"Are you alright?" Virginia asked, aware that if he had another heart attack under her watch, his daughter would hold her personally responsible. "Why do you ask about the clocktower?"

"Saw something once, long time ago," he said. Stu shook his head again, plastering a smile across his leathered face. "It's nothing," he continued. "The barn is your best bet to ask some questions," he said. "But I'd be very surprised if you find any purchase there. People will always protect their own, even from imagined attacks."

Virginia stood, dragging her hand away from the binder, away from the reminder of Juliette. "Thank you, that's been very helpful."

"Some folk won't want you poking around," he warned. "Some things are better to leave them lie, if you catch my meaning."

"Thank you, sir," she said. "I do."

Chapter Eighteen

Virginia straightened the tie she'd thrown on that morning, emerald paisley on silk fabric. It was one of the nicest ones she owned, perfectly ironed to match her jade green starched shirt.

Moonlight kissed the edges of the old barn, a bright, artificial yellow glow seeping out from beneath the doors. It had been over thirty years since she'd set foot inside, and she wasn't supposed to be there back then, either.

"You ready?" Virginia asked, looking over at Anya.

"Ready as I'll ever be," Anya answered with a mischievous smile that curved the edges of her lips.

"That's all we can ask for, I guess." Virginia turned around in her seat. "I'd say to stay in the car, but I doubt you'll listen to that, so instead I will tell you to keep your head down, no fire, and try not to be too noticeable."

Jolie grasped the back of Virginia's seat, squealing quietly with excitement. "Okay! Yes, I promise, I promise," she said quickly. "I won't get into trouble."

Virginia climbed out of the car, stretching her arms over her head with the satisfying pop in her shoulder. Despite how much worse it could have been, it was never quite the same after taking that panther bite. "Let's do this," she said, aiming for the side door. "We should approach separately. I doubt they're watching who's coming in which cars."

"Thank the Rift for small mercies, I guess," Anya said, locking the door.

"I don't think we should be thanking the shadows-damned Rift for anything," Virginia retorted. "Caused more problems than it solved." She left Anya and Jolie at the car and shuffled through the grass, crispy beneath the soles of her shoes. She knocked on the side door, leaning against the door frame like she was drunk.

"Password?" a gruff voice asked.

"The password is I've got money to burn, so let me in," she slurred, holding up a crumpled one-hundred-dollar bill, knowing someone would be watching from inside. "And plenty more where that came from."

"Fine," the voice grumbled, and light spilled out as the door opened.

"Thanks," Virginia slurred, being sure to stumble over the threshold. If she acted inebriated enough, maybe no one would notice she was busy trying to glean information about Heinrich Harrow, the Speers, or who may have tossed a brick through her mother's window. Anya and Jolie would have to figure out their own way inside.

"What's your play?" the man asked, sitting on a stool inside the door. "Blackjack is on the left, poker on the right. Nothing else tonight, we don't have enough people to run other games."

"Blackjack," Virginia answered, a little too quickly. "Too drunk for poker," she added. "Maybe when I sober up."

"Yeah, if you don't lose it all first," the man muttered, but waved her off in the direction of the table.

She sat, tossing the crumpled money into the center. "I want to play," she said.

The dealer nodded silently, taking up the money and replacing it with a stack of red and yellow chips. "Red's five, yellow one," he said without even looking up, shuffling the deck artfully. He dealt the cards to the table, which included Virginia and four others.

Glancing at her cards, she made sure to grimace, despite the fact she was actually in rather a good position. It had been a long time since she'd played, but it returned to her just like riding a bicycle. "Stand," she said, unable to resist the temptation to win, even though that would draw more attention than she wanted.

She didn't recognize the others at the table. One looked to be someone passing through, she was far too pretty and put-together to be living somewhere like Murph Township. The other three were men of varying sizes, all of them grimy, probably farmers but none that she knew personally.

"Hit," one said, followed by another, and then the rest.

The dealer nodded, flipping over another card.

"Bust," one of the men grunted, tossing the cards back to the black felt table. "Damn."

"Twenty-one," Virginia said proudly, showing her cards.

"Twenty-one," the dealer echoed, shoving a small pile of chips in her direction.

"Beginner's luck?" the woman asked, sliding her own cards back to the dealer. "Bust here, too," she said.

"I don't know about luck, but I'm grateful," Virginia said. "Damned car took a dive a few days back." She checked the freshly dealt cards that landed in front of her. "Hit," she said, knowing another would send her over the limit.

"Shame about your car," the woman said, running her fingers across the felt. "Seems they always break down when you least expect it."

"You can say that again," Virginia agreed, just as the dealer flipped another card. "Damn," she said. "Bust." She pushed some of the chips back across the table, the felt soft under her fingertips. It was strange that an illegal gambling den so well-established would have brand new tables and twinkling lights that were strung overhead. If she didn't know any better, she might have guessed it was the basement of some club back in Verdance.

"The lady wins," the dealer said, nodding at the woman. "Er, the other lady."

Virginia tapped on the table, signaling she was in for another round. She'd have to balance her wins and losses carefully, in order to stay long enough to glean some information, and to avoid rousing suspicion or going broke.

"You from around here?" the man on the left asked, tugging on his blue cap.

"No," Virginia lied, hoping it wouldn't catch up with her. "Car broke down, like I said."

"Wasn't asking you," the man said. "You, in the pink there," he said. "You from around here?"

"Here and there," the woman replied. "I travel." She leaned towards Virginia. "What about you, do you travel?"

"Now and then. Hit," Virginia said to the dealer, more interested in the conversation than the cards. "Y'all are farmers?" she asked the two men at the table, letting an old, forgotten drawl creep up into her mouth. She hated the sound of it, the sound of her childhood, the sound of languishing summers, heartbreak, and loss. She hated the way the syllables tasted on her tongue, like milk gone sour.

The man in the blue cap nodded. "It's honest work." His brow furrowed as he checked his cards. "Hit," he said gruffly. "City folk don't understand."

"No, they don't," Virginia agreed, cloaking her disdain with a laugh that she forced through her teeth. "Salt of the earth round here." She ran her finger over the edge of the cards in her hand. "Shame that some people come down this way for no reason than to cause trouble."

The man glanced at her. "Mmhmm," was all he said.

From the corner of her eye, Virginia spotted Anya and Jolie, finally through the door. They sat at different poker tables, with Jolie already drawing the eyes of too many. She was young, pretty, and girlish. She looked like bait. Virginia couldn't help but watch Jolie from the corner of her eye, losing track of the conversation until the dealer cleared his throat.

"Ma'am?" he said. "Hit or stand?"

"Stand," Virginia answered. "Sorry. That beer went straight to my head."

Anya, for her piece, was gregarious and charming, leaning over the table to pick lint from a man's lapel. She laughed, and played with the hem of her dress. Virginia leaned against the table. Was Anya *flirting*?

"Bust," Virginia said again, sliding some more chips across the felt. She followed by tapping again, ready for another round. "How long are you in town?" she asked the woman.

"Not long. I flit through this way every now and then, for a day or two at a time. It could be worse," she said, tapping the table and waiting for another card. "It could be down south."

"We are south," the man in the blue cap said, trying to catch the woman's eye again. "South as this state goes, in fact."

The woman barely glanced in his direction. "Further south than this," she retorted. "Too hot for me, and everything is too far apart. I'm more of an east coast girl." She nudged Virginia's elbow, tilting her head. "The name is Melody Kingston," she said, adding, "where are you from?"

"All over." Virginia wasn't particularly keen to out herself as a native, nor was she about to share her name with a stranger. "Can't complain."

"What about now, where are you based?" Melody asked. She leaned in over the table, close enough to whisper against Virginia's ear. "I'm trying to figure out if I can orchestrate running into you again. It's rare that I come across someone interesting in places like this."

"The city," Virginia answered. Most would assume Verdance, but it could just as plausibly be another city down south. "And yes, maybe that can be arranged." She glanced over at Anya again, who was toying with a man's lapels and brushing a thumb over the back of his hand. Virginia coughed, leaning closer to the woman at her table. "It depends when you swing back this way."

"I swing wherever the wind moves me," Melody replied. "Work keeps me busy."

"Well then I hope work swings you into my path again," Virginia said. She tapped the table again, waiting for another card. "You know," she said, "I heard there was a murder here recently."

Melody didn't gasp or feign surprise, suggesting she was used to a more violent landscape. "Oh?" she prompted.

"Some con man," Virginia supplied. "Swindled a lot of folks out this way. People are saying it might have been one of them who did it."

"Horseshit," the man in the blue cap said, throwing his cards down on the table. "Bust." He pointed at Virginia, and then at the woman. "Neither of you should be shooting your mouths off about things you don't have a damned clue about. These snake oil salesmen that slither into town, the world is better off without 'em, but it's not the good folk round here who are responsible. That asshole was probably mixed up with the wrong sort, and wound up dead."

"What do you mean by the wrong sort?" Virginia asked.

"With all due respect, ma'am," he said sardonically, "use your head. God gave you brains, I think you should probably use 'em." He stalked off to the poker tables, sitting down next to Jolie with an angry thud.

The dealer cleared the table and shuffled, the sound of the cards lost in the din of the loud establishment. He raised an eyebrow at each of the women, silently asking if they wanted to be dealt in. Virginia nodded, and so did Melody.

"So you're in politics," Virginia said, still watching Jolie from the corner of her eye.

Melody laughed, her perfect teeth showing as she threw her head back. "What gave me away?"

"You meet enough of them, you start to notice," Virginia replied. "I imagine you've seen plenty of our nation's capital."

"You could say that. I do work for Senator Dean."

"What are you doing way out here?"

"Just passing through," Melody replied, rapping a knuckle against the table, her nails immaculately manicured. "Same as you, by the sounds of it."

"Something like that." Virginia scowled at the cards. "Bust."

The whole thing had been a bust, really. Nothing more than some angry farmers speaking in riddles. Any more prying and they'd see her for what she was, an up-jumped private eye with a very old vendetta and too many questions about things they worked hard to keep quiet. "There a ladies' room in here?" she asked, orchestrating an exit that wouldn't raise too many alarms or questions.

"Round back," the dealer replied. "Ain't no hotel, this is a barn, if you couldn't tell."

"Thanks." Virginia slipped out the back door, but not before being sure that Anya had moved to join Jolie at her table. She sidled back to the car, ignoring the latrine behind the barn because she'd rather drop her trousers in a thorn bush than risk whatever diseases lay in wait in that disgusting thing. Indoor plumbing was no longer negotiable, not since she moved to Verdance.

It was fifteen minutes before Anya and Jolie appeared, muttering in hushed tones as they approached the car.

"I didn't see where she went, did you?" Anya asked.

"No," Jolie replied. "Maybe she walked back?"

Virginia sat up, adjusting her hair from being pressed into the seats. "I'm in here," she said, reattaching her suspenders for good measure. If she showed up at home without them, her mother would make invasive assumptions. "Did either of you hear anything?"

"Some gossip about the Speer place at my table," Jolie said, gingerly hoisting herself into the passenger seat.

"You're jingling," Virginia said. "Did you cash out?"

"Beginner's luck," Jolie replied with a devilish grin. "I figured it could at least help pay the repair bill."

"Why don't you let me worry about that?" Virginia replied. "You keep that." She locked eyes with Jolie in the mirror. "I hope you didn't hustle anyone, people tend to remember that."

"Just a lucky hand," Jolie assured her. "Lost all the others." She adjusted her position in the seat as the engine roared into life, and the tires hitched along the dirt lot. "The man sitting across from me said he heard that the Speer son owns the house, not Mrs. Speer."

"Interesting," Virginia said, nodding. "It still doesn't answer the question of where that potent magic came from."

"Could she be an illusionist?" Anya asked quietly, turning onto the dark, deserted highway. "She'd have to be a damned powerful one, maybe even..." she shook her head. "No. Improbable."

"As far as I know, there aren't any witches or other mythics in Birch Hollow. Obviously that's untrue, but my point is that this far out, people tend to be better at hiding." Virginia drummed her fingers against the leather interior, trying to claw memories from the long-abandoned, dusty haze in her mind. "I don't recall her ever being anything other than old, even when I was young." She cringed at her past self. "I guess the passage of time stops for no woman."

Anya snorted. "The impropriety of youth," she offered. "You don't notice it until it's too late." She poked Jolie gently in the side. "It will happen to you, too."

"I don't know if fire demons age," Jolie answered, shrugging. "Maybe I'll have to look like this forever."

"You've aged until now," Virginia countered. "You're

as mortal as we are. Haven't you ever broken an arm or something?"

"My wrist, when I was nine."

Virginia smirked. "Case closed."

The car rumbled along over the poor roads, the tires finding every single hole. The crescent moon was oddly bright behind the clouds that concealed it, the glow emanating around the curvature of the water vapor and lighting the sky with the ring of haze surrounding it. Virginia leaned her head against the window's glass, the coolness a welcome relief from the stillness inside the car, but it brought forth goosebumps that scattered across her skin, raising the hairs at the nape of her neck. She hadn't felt so watched since she was a child.

Chapter Nineteen

The awful, incessant ring of the telephone screeched through the morning's fragile peace with all the fervor of an incensed zealot. Virginia resented that they had become so ubiquitous, so ready to demand attention, to satisfy the needs of whoever was on the other end of the line. She reached for it, still half-asleep on the couch.

"Hello?" she grumbled into the receiver, wiping sleep from her eyes. After a late night, she'd unintentionally slept in. She checked her watch, blinking the fog out of her vision. Eleven o'clock. Her mother would be in town already.

"What did you do?" Eugene Carsh asked softly, a reprehensible gentleness in his voice that Virginia wanted to forcibly burn from his vocal cords. "What have you gotten yourself into?"

Virginia sat up, throwing off the blanket, her heart already pounding in her throat. "It would help if I knew what in the hell you were talking about. Spit it out, Eugene."

He sighed quietly. "There's been another murder," he said. "A woman who you were seen speaking to at the barn last night."

If she hadn't known better, she would have sworn her heart

had stopped beating in her chest, leaving an empty, lifeless void in its wake. "No," she said.

"The land owner found her there about three hours ago and called me straight away. The man dealing the blackjack table said you seemed pretty darned cozy with this woman, Ginnie."

"I've been at home all night," Virginia replied coolly, despite the mounting panic in her spine. "And it doesn't mean anything that I spoke to her."

Carsh sighed again, this time with more pity than she could stand. "Another witness corroborated the statement." He cleared his throat. "Sammy saw you leave with her, Ginnie. You were the last person to see her alive."

Her heart pounding blood in her ears, she swallowed a mouthful of dry air that caught in her throat. "I didn't leave with her," she argued. "And Sammy wasn't even there last night. I left the barn alone, and drove back to my mother's with—" she stopped herself, not wanting to implicate Jolie or Anya in police questioning, especially when the feds were likely right around the corner to take over the Harrow case. "I left alone."

"Ginnie..." he trailed off, the sound of chair legs screeching against wood echoing out over the line. "Sammy saw you go off into the woods with her. She was there last night dragging her father home after he lost one too many rounds again."

"And was she *found* in the woods?" she shot back. "Or is this another piss-poor attempt by your department to close the books on a case long before it's solved?"

The line was quiet, and the mourning doves screeched their horribly repetitive song just outside the screen door. "You need an alibi, Ginnie."

"I was with my mother."

"And she'll testify to that?"

"She'd better, because I wasn't even out late. We had an argument when I got home about—" Virginia stopped herself short. "I was here, and she should confirm that."

"Where is your mother now?"

"In town, if I had to wager a guess."

"You haven't spoken to her this morning?"

Virginia checked her watch again, as if the time would have shifted. "No." She twisted the phone's cord around her fingers with such force that her knuckles shone white, and her fingertips were puffy and red. "I don't recall seeing Sammy or her father there last night, Eugene."

"They were there, and every poker dealer on shift can attest to it, along with the fact that you were also in attendance last night. Sammy is swearing on her mother's grave that she saw you go into the woods with that woman, Ginnie. How do you account for that?"

"Sammy is mistaken, or she's lying."

"Why would she lie?"

"I don't know, Eugene, you're the detective, aren't you?" Virginia snapped. "You've done nothing but try to entrap me since I landed in this shadows-forsaken place, and now you're trying to say that I'm a suspect for *murder*?"

"I'm just doing my job, Ginnie. You'd have done the same, if our situations were reversed."

"If our situations were reversed, Juliette never would have gone missing, and her killer never would have gone free." Virginia slammed the phone into the receiver, panic swirling in her lungs, her chest tight with it.

The kid. Someone would need to take care of the kid if her

alibi didn't stand up. "Jolie?" she called out, cautious, guilty that she'd even been accused of a crime she never committed. "Are you in there?"

Virginia knocked on the door, the sound terrible and hollow, signaling the emptiness within. "Jolie, I need to talk to you," she said, hating the waver she heard in her own voice.

The door opened, and Jolie, clearly half-asleep with a frizzy curl stuck to the side of her face, yawned. "What time is it?" she asked, her eyes resisting the bright sunbeam filtering into the hallway. Catching the expression on Virginia's face, she straightened. "What's wrong? What happened?"

Virginia chewed on her lip as long as she could muster, sensing that Jolie was growing impatient as she bounced on the balls of her feet. "Officer Carsh is trying to—" she began, and then stopped. "What I mean is, they found a body at that barn we were at last night. They're trying to pin it on me."

"Why do they think you did it?" Jolie asked in a small voice.

"A witness said they saw me leaving with the victim." Virginia pulled at the cuffs of her ugly pajamas, regretting their very existence. "It was corroborated by another."

"But Anya drove us back last night," Jolie protested. "Can't you just tell them that?"

"Firefly..." Virginia began, but trailed off. "It's not a good idea to be drawing you and Anya into this. The feds are probably already on their way down, given what Eugene said, and it's not a good idea for either of you to catch heat on my account."

"But—"

Virginia clenched and released her hands at her sides, a nervous habit born of sparring with Seamus. "My mother is my only real alibi."

"She'll say you were here, won't she?"

"I'm not sure," Virginia admitted. The situation was starting to spiral dangerously out of control. "I should call the sheriff," she said, already heading for the phone.

She dragged the rotary back and forth, the number long since seared into her muscle memory.

"Dixon."

"Arthur, it's me," she said, maybe for the millionth time in her life. "There was another murder."

"For shadows' sakes." He sighed angrily, and she knew he'd spent the night at his desk. "With feds comes the press, and everyone loves a serial killer."

"Yeah, except their victims." Virginia said, steadying herself on the sofa, sinking down into the thin, worn cushions until the furniture's frame bit into the backs of her legs. "It was in one of those old barns out past the highway." She stared at Jolie's door, willing it to stay shut. "I don't like this, Arthur. Something feels off."

Arthur muttered a stream of curses, more profanity than Virginia had heard from him in years. The city was starting to get to him. "You have to get out of there, Ginnie. The feds are going to—"

"I know," she hissed. "But I can't go anywhere until my mother corroborates my alibi."

"Your *alibi*? What in shadows are you talking about, alibi? What does this murder have to do with you, other than—"

"Someone saw me go into the woods with the vic," Virginia interrupted. "Sammy, the mechanic's kid."

"Shadows' sakes, Ginnie," Arthur said with a grunt. "What were you even doing out there?"

"I was at the barn digging up leads earlier last night," Virginia interrupted. "My car is still in the shop, and I certainly can't go get it now, not when my accuser is also the one with my engine block on a hoist. The State's Attorney would have me dead to rights for witness tampering."

Arthur huffed out a breath on the other end of the line, shifting in his chair so aggressively that the angry squeaks echoed through the phone. "Carsh isn't going to let you get out from under this, Ginnie."

"I told you it was a mistake to come back here, Arthur."

"Did you get any help from your mother about—well, about you-know-what?" he asked, whispering. No doubt federal agents were winding their coils around the whole of headquarters by then.

"Nothing," Virginia replied. "Nothing useful, anyway."

"Well, keep trying. Maybe if you can figure something out before Carsh drags you back in, they won't have anything credible enough to book you." Arthur sighed again, and it mixed with the buzz of the insects outside in an uncomfortably familiar way, something that almost brought a part of her to the surface.

"Call my lawyer, Arthur. Call Sadie," Virginia said, sliding her feet into her shoes. He'd know who to call, she was the bane of every detective in the VCPD.

"Ginnie, I'm buried under eight reams of paperwork here, I'll do what I can to stall them, but—"

"I have to figure out what this all is before my mother has the opportunity to make everything worse for me," Virginia said. "You know what she's capable of.

"I'll do what I can," Arthur replied. "Ginnie—" he cleared his throat of emotion, worry perhaps. "Take care of yourself.

Be careful."

Chapter Twenty

Brogues and slacks weren't optimal for evading arrest or questioning, but they would have to do. Burrs covered the deep green linen at her ankles, sprinkling themselves all the way up to her knees, stabbing their tiny spines through the fabric and reminding her with every prick just how dire the situation she'd found herself in was.

She exhaled softly, crouching behind a bush well behind the tree line, watching the rural county police department wrap a makeshift cordon around the crime scene. At that angle, she couldn't see anything other than a sea of outdated squad units, their tires beset with dust.

Of course there had been another murder, this time a woman she'd spoken to at the barn, and of course she'd been recognized, because it was rare that she wasn't. The scars on her face wrought too many stares and too many memories. Strange, though, that it had been Sammy to see her go into the woods with Melody Kingston, when Virginia hadn't seen Sammy or her father there at all. Maybe she was mistaken. Maybe she was lying, but why? To what end?

The town was rife with liars, that was why Juliette hadn't ever seen justice. Like covered for like. Birds of a feather, and all of that.

Virginia squinted into the trees, willing herself to make sense of rickety midday shadows that danced wildly against the knotted wood, the result of overhead foliage and a cloudless sky. It was almost impossible to make sense of any of it, not without getting closer. She wasn't under arrest, not yet, but showing up at the scene of the crime wouldn't help her story.

"Hey, hey!" one of the cops shouted at another. "Enough with the cordon tape!"

"I wanted to make sure!" the other yelled back. "Sheriff almost had my badge last time, he said it wasn't a thorough perimeter." He gestured at the woods, and Virginia shrank back further into the foliage. "Don't want any nosy Nellies creeping around in there, eh?"

"We're in the middle of nowhere," the first said, resting a hand on his holster. Almost every officer in Moassa County was a volunteer, and their inexperience showed when compared to the swift efficiency of any major city's department. He toyed with the grip of his revolver. "Roll up that tape and let's get the hell out of the way. The coroner will be here in a minute or two, and you know how he gets."

The second tossed the roll of tape into the back of the squad unit. "Yeah, fine," he grumbled. "But if the sheriff wants to have words about this scene, they're not gonna be with me."

"Bullshit, you'd never have the balls to say a damned thing to him," the first officer said. He jolted at the snap of a twig and wheeled on the heel of his scuffed patent leather shoe. "Sir," he said, making an awkward half salute before he realized it was unnecessary. One more strange holdover from the war. He was old enough to have been in it, and the way his arm fell limply to his side showed the truth of it. "Good to see you, sir," he tried again.

"Clear the scene," the county sheriff instructed, barely even acknowledging the other man's presence. "State police and federal units are already on their way, and the management of this had better not embarrass me." He strode towards the barn with all the unearned confidence of a rural man in charge of nothing. He was a king of the flat lands, empty and ignored.

Virginia watched him as he stepped over a muddy tree trunk in a uniform perfectly pressed, showing its disuse. He'd probably served as a volunteer for a few years, and then run for the elected position using his considerable inherited wealth. She'd seen it plenty downstate, where rich men moved to become paragons of their areas, unquestioned in their authority despite their complete and total lack of experience or insight.

The sheriff turned his head to gag, backing away from the scene. "My God," he uttered. "What kind of monster could do something like this?" He vomited into a bush, the sound echoing across the empty woods. "Do we have a name yet?"

"Melody Kingston."

"Find out more before state shows up. They always think we don't know what we're doing, and I'd love to prove them wrong for once." He scowled back at the scene, a strange expression, given the consequences. "Don't want another unsolved case pointing back at us, boys."

Virginia gritted her teeth against the frustration that he likely wasn't even talking about Juliette. She was no stranger to the fury of righteous anger. She'd joined the VCPD with a marked sense of injustice heavy in her soul, vowing that she'd do better than her predecessors.

She hadn't, not really.

No one had.

That was the point.

The sheriff hemmed and hawed as he approached the scene again, directing the photographer and gathering samples of soil, despite the fact that county forensics would take at least four weeks to get results back. Birch Hollow was no Verdance, and their testing backlog moved at a snail's pace. "I reckon," he began, striding around the outside of the tape with his thumbs hooked through his belt loops, "that this was a murder."

She rolled her eyes in the privacy of the trees. "No shit," she muttered under her breath, unable to swallow back the words.

"No natural thing could have caused this," he continued in his strange, wide drawl, indicative of a man who not only had rarely even ventured further than the county line, but one who prided himself on the matter. To downstate folks like him, the fields that stretched out to the horizon were more important than anything in the entire world, more important than any deity and certainly the center of the universe. He nodded. "Definitely a murder," he confirmed, as though Eugene Carsh hadn't reached that conclusion hours prior.

There was a thick, metallic scent to stagnant blood that made Virginia's stomach lurch, despite all the years of gore she had endured. It was a thick, arterial smell, one that bridged the gap between life and death, between hope and despair. It was earthy and wet, and lingered in her senses.

She crept around the side of the scene, craning her neck to see more than she could from the fringes of the woods.

One step closer at a time, she moved, inching nearer to the body, hidden by tree branches laden with leaves and bushes thick with berries. She knelt down around the back of the scene, only able to see the cuff of a starched shirt, dark with blood.

The sheriff inhaled noisily, looking around at the other officers. "Who else wants the opportunity to make their assumptions?" he asked.

Virginia leaned forward, biting her tongue when her palm found a thorned bush. The sheriff was out of his depth, cloaking his insecurity and lack of answers as an educational opportunity. She'd seen it before, especially within the confines of the VCPD. It was an expert maneuver in manipulation.

"Uh, we can't dust for prints," one of the officers said, brushing dirt from her cheek with a brandishing flourish. "There isn't anything with a smooth enough surface." She moved past the sheriff, scraping a finger against bark and frowning. "Without a murder weapon, it's going to be difficult."

"Right you are, Donahue," the sheriff agreed proudly, his chest puffed out with unearned glory. "That's the kind of thinking that will get you a promotion to detective, if you manage to keep it up." He clapped a patronizing hand on her shoulder, offering up what he probably thought was an encouraging smile, but it had more of an air of condescension and paternalism than anything else.

Donahue nodded. "Thank you, sir."

Bright sunlight beat down on the sheriff, and he mopped sweat from his brow with a crisp, unused handkerchief from his pocket, no doubt embroidered with his initials by his long-suffering wife.

"The safety of the town, of the county, lies with us," he announced, his admittedly pleasing baritone timbre booming out over the flat clearing, standing up to the wind that rustled through the corn in the distance. "We hold lives in our hands, folks. Without us, there is nothing more than chaos to behold, especially in this heat, and especially without the rain these crops are so desperate for." He strode back towards the cordon, head held high because he thought he had the right to do so. "I expect each and every one of you to maintain vigilance, to protect the people of this county."

Virginia bit back a half-snorted laugh, almost choking on it. Backwoods cops were hardly going to stand the line between citizens and murderers. Shadows, they could barely do it with hucksters, much less violent criminals.

"Donahue, please alert me to any news the moment those soil tests come through," he ordered. "Wake me up at home if need be. Don't worry, Carol will wake up. My wife has always been a light sleeper. I think I wake her up every night when I come to bed." He laughed to himself about this, that he'd spent the better part of twenty years disturbing his wife's dreams, as if it was just an inevitability of marriage, and not a conscious choice he made each and every day.

"Of course, sir," Donahue replied, extending the cordon to a tree six feet further away.

Virginia crouched, peering through the branches.

It was indeed the woman from the night before, Melody Kingston. The one who had flirted, if that was indeed what it was. Her corpse was propped up behind a half-felled tree, giving it the appearance of a podium. In one hand, political pamphlets for the various main parties, all three of them. In the other, a fist full of ten dollar bills. Her eyes were tinged with the purple-pink of Nether, of course. Virginia had anticipated that.

What she didn't expect was for the woman to be garroted, her throat all but torn out. The scene was drenched in blood, soaked into the parched, thirsty earth and leaving behind the scent that drifted heavy on the breeze. Her crisply starched white shirt was the scarlet brown of dried blood, leaving a trail that moved in a circle around her.

"Fucked shadows," Virginia whispered, and then cursed herself for saying it aloud.

The coroner who had finally arrived from the next county appeared. He recoiled from the scene, and in his examination, did his best to stay as far as he could from the body. More photos were taken, more flags were set down, and before long, she was taken down from her perch. Her body had been propped up to a standing height with a noose, but given the amount of blood, it was unlikely that it had killed her.

As they zipped her into the body bag, Virginia leaned forward, drawn to the strange yet familiar sensation of seeing the corpse of someone she'd seen alive and well just twelve hours prior.

"Where are the shoes?" the photographer asked, peering around at the flags.

"Weren't any," Donahue replied. "You're welcome to look, but as far as we can tell, we can't find 'em anywhere." She helped lift the cot into the ambulance, unzipping the bag once more. "No cuts on her feet or anything. I don't think she walked out here barefoot."

An unnecessarily theatrical scene.

Missing shoes that were nowhere to be found, just like the other murders in the city.

There was a serial killer in Verdance, and they'd followed Virginia to Birch Hollow.

Chapter Twenty-One

The Speer place haunted the woods around it, the strange resonance echoing through the branches like an old song that Virginia couldn't quite remember the words to. If she didn't know any better, she would have guessed that it was one of Astrid's, set about to evoke the feeling of sharp loss and bitter nostalgia. She'd always been particularly good at those, given where she came from. It hadn't always been plush velvet upholstery and the Sphinx. There had been a time that it was leaky bus shelters and threadbare cardigans, not that she ever let anyone else know that.

Abandoned by its occupants, the house was surrounded by an uneven square of yellow tape, adorned with a note scrawled in Carsh's uneven hand that it was an active crime scene, and to stay away. Virginia ignored that instruction of course, easily ducking under it to drag her feet through the dry dust, obscuring anything that may have been a footprint that could be traced back to her.

"I thought you might show up here," Anya said, emerging from the tree line.

"You shouldn't be here, you know," Virginia chided. "Didn't you read the sign?"

"Did you?"

"I have a vested interest in solving this, I'll have you know."

Anya threw off a light laugh, shrugging as her shoulders shook with it. "You're not the only one with secrets, Vane." She stepped around a thorny bush, yanking her skirts free when they tangled in the twisted vines. "Still wanted for questioning?"

"How'd you hear about that?" Virginia asked.

"Word gets around in a town like this, you know."

A cloud passed over the sun for just a moment, but it was enough to grant a passing of blissful shade as grey light filtered down through the trees. "Yeah, but not to outsiders," Virginia challenged. "They'd rather saw off their own limbs with butter knives than let something slip to a stranger."

"Let's just say I heard a few things in the diner this morning, then," Anya explained, straightening the pouch that was slung diagonally over her shoulder, the tan leather strap buckled where it met the bag. "You are quite the person of interest in Birch Hollow, you know."

"Why do you think I never come back here?"

"Not much to come back here for, looks like, unless you're after rare reagents." Anya turned, but shot her a look over a shoulder. "Which you needed to replace, after—"

"I got it," Virginia interrupted. "Shadows."

"Can I assume you're back to have a look at that murder scene, then?" Anya asked. "Because if so, I already got a window open around back."

Virginia tilted her head, always surprised at how much she didn't really know about Ms. Quinn. "Breaking and entering?"

"I didn't break anything," Anya replied, brandishing a long, thin piece of metal. "However, I may have entered."

"I'm not so sure that those semantics will hold up in court." Virginia trailed after her, carefully avoiding an upturned root that seemed grown specifically just to trip up anyone who wasn't supposed to be there.

Anya snorted an indelicate laugh. "We'd better not get caught then."

"No, I can't imagine that would go particularly well for either of us." Virginia eyed the open window with interest, wondering how much monitoring Carsh would be doing at the scene.

"Give me a boost," Anya ordered, hiking up her skirts until she flashed a slice of olive-skinned thigh.

"Weren't you inside already?"

"No, Virginia, I was waiting for you." She stepped into Virginia's cupped hands and grasped the edge of the windowsill, pulling herself through. "Here," she said, flipping an emergency rope ladder through the opening. "Makes things a bit easier, doesn't it? Nice that they prepared for an emergency."

Climbing the unsteady planks, Virginia held tight to the sides, the ladder swinging to and fro until she was through to the other side.

"Took you long enough," Anya teased, letting her skirts fall back to the floor. "I assume you can feel the magical resonance? Even non-mythics usually can when it's this strong."

Virginia nodded in affirmation. "There's something strange about it, like..." she trailed off, searching for the right words to explain it.

"An aftertaste," Anya supplied. She glided into the next room, kneeling down on the floor where the body of Heinrich Harrow had once been. With most of the illusion magic worn off, the blood splatter was not only visible, but substantial, even for Virginia, who'd spilled enough of her own to know the difference.

"Mm," she agreed, following Anya's lead. "Do you see any shoes anywhere?"

"Shoes?"

Virginia checked beneath the curtains and the sofa, finding none. Each time she found a new potential hiding place and found only emptiness, the knot in her stomach tightened. "Yeah." The closet near the door also didn't yield anything, holding only Mrs. Speer's shoes, an overcoat abandoned since winter, and three hats. "Shadows."

"Are you going to share with the class what you're doing, Virginia?" Anya asked, watching her from the corner.

"These homicides," Virginia said, shaking her head. "None of the victims had shoes."

"Wasn't one found in bed? And Harrow here, he was inside the house when he was killed."

"Yes, but then where *are* they?" Virginia asked. She gestured at the yellow flags on the floor, marking blood splatters. "They would have been left in place and photographed, but they're nowhere to be found."

Anya joined the hunt, searching back bedrooms and cabinets, even ones that wouldn't make any sense for shoe storage. "Nothing," she called from the hallway. "I can't find a single men's shoe. Any chance Harrow was wearing a nice pair of heels?"

"No, I saw him walking in," Virginia answered. "It was

dark, but looked like tan brogues." She hissed out a sigh, sitting back on her haunches. "I don't like this."

"Maybe we can find something else?" Anya suggested. "Maybe it's not all about the shoes."

Picture frames lined the mantle of the fireplace, each made from pewter and perfectly matched, holding memories of times gone past in chronological order. The latest one, all the way on the right-hand side, featured a family portrait of the Speers, all of them gathered around a table piled high with a festive feast, including a turkey large enough to feed a small army, despite there being only four of them.

Virginia took each frame in her hand, willing something to come, but nothing did. Every family photo showed neutral faces, intact without grief or regret, until she reached the one at the left edge. It was of the previous occupants, the Speer grandparents, standing outside the home the day it was finished being built. He held a large saw in one hand, holding his wife close with the other. She carried a basket of apples, laughing, her eyes squeezed shut in mirth. It was strange to see an old photo so candid and honest, the subjects lightly blurred with motion.

"Anything good?" Anya asked, leaning over her shoulder, her height making it an easy task.

Virginia shook her head. "Nothing," she lamented, putting the frame back in its place.

"Mm." Light crept through the closed curtains, a desperate attempt by Officer Carsh to repel any nosey onlookers that were brave enough to cross beneath the police tape. The sunbeams that managed to penetrate them laid against the wood floor, soaking into the bleached grain and illuminating delicate sparkles of dust that floated in the air, lazy and ostentatious. "There's a phonograph," Anya said, dropping the needle into a groove. "Maybe this will have some answers."

"What answers would those be?" Virginia retorted, crossing her arms over her chest as the beginning bars began to play. "I doubt the murderer recorded the killing."

Anya grabbed her hand, untwisting Virginia's arms. "Live a little, Vane," she said, swinging them both into the opening between the sofas on either side of the room. The music was jaunty and light, a jazzy little number that could have even been something played at the Sphinx. "When was the last time you danced?"

"With Arthur," Virginia replied, once again unsettled by her own honesty.

"Not since then?" Anya spun back, and then returned, the hem of her skirt twirling with the movement. "Not at all? What about at the club?"

"Despite appearances, Astrid doesn't much like dancing," Virginia explained. "And neither do I, so it wasn't a point of contention." She took the lead, just like she always had with Arthur, too. The man was as clumsy as he was irritating, and left to his own devices would step on every toe present on a dance floor. Briefly, she allowed herself to indulge in the wondering of whether that was something Mona had successfully trained out of him. If anyone on the planet could do so, it was her.

"Was it at your wedding?" Anya asked, always too blunt with her inquiries to the point of being improperly invasive.

"No, some benefit gala for the VCPD." Virginia spun her around, catching her by the waist. That wasn't a move she'd tried on Arthur, but then, he wasn't as tall as Anya. "Arthur and I were married at the courthouse. We were young and broke. No frills, no fuss, and it was what we both wanted."

The music bounced along, a driving rhythm carrying them across the Speer's living room floor. It was wildly reckless, but with every step, against her will, Virginia felt the tiniest bit lighter. "The gala was four months before everything went to hell."

"The Rupture," Anya agreed, and Virginia nodded, letting her believe that was what she'd meant.

The shellac record scratched and fuzzed as it led into the second song, a slow, methodical piece, pensive and beautiful. Anya didn't release her as she expected, instead pulling her into a tight frame, taking the lead. It was easy to follow her, given how tall she was, it felt strangely natural.

"What are we doing?" Virginia asked, her voice softer than she'd meant it to be. She cleared her throat, aiming to try again. "We should get back to looking for clues."

Anya responded by settling them both into a lilting waltz, carrying them across a small square on the floor, venturing out only to twist Virginia into an unwilling turn. "It will be over in a minute, Virginia. Just enjoy the moment before we both get arrested for trespassing."

She bit back the snide reply in her throat, acquiescing despite every instinct within her to break away from Anya's gentle grip and launch herself back through the window without a second glance.

She followed along begrudgingly, making sure to keep her mouth set into a deep frown throughout every beat despite some small part of her leaning into it, almost enjoying the nonsensical danger.

The record came to a close, the needle running against a

dead groove in the shellac. Despite the lack of music, Anya was determined to finish their dance, swaying gently under the amber glow that bled through the curtains. She finally stopped, releasing Virginia's hand, but not stepping back. "Thank you for the dance," she said. "I didn't think you would do that."

"You didn't give me much of a choice," Virginia shot back, comforted by the reappearance of her old defenses.

"I didn't hold a gun to your head, Virginia." Anya laughed, throwing her head back with the force of it. "If I did that, I think there would be a strong possibility that you'd shoot me first."

"There would be," Virginia replied, slinking away from the sunspot on the floor. "Though I would hazard a guess that you don't even own one."

"I do not," Anya confirmed, finally disenchanted enough with the moment to pick up the phonograph's needle and set it to the side, examining the record. "This doesn't tell us much, unfortunately."

"You never know." Virginia had returned to the family photographs, brushing her fingertips against each one. "Sometimes clues can surprise you, even in the least likely places."

"That's why you're the private investigator, and I am the witch," Anya explained with confidence. "However, we've yet to find anything particularly useful, and given where the sun is at in the sky, it won't be too long before that Officer Carsh decides to make his presence known to us." She squinted through a gap in the curtains, the sunlight flooding the tiny space on the floor.

Virginia trailed across the room, letting her fingers brush

against every surface, irritated when again, still, nothing came. She'd spent years, decades really, relying on her investigative skills, but the Speer place was untouched outside the blood stain in the knots of the wood. "There wasn't a prolonged struggle," she said finally, stopping in her tracks at the tiny, fragile, crystalline figure of a giraffe perched precariously at the edge of a shelf in the curio cabinet. "My guess is that he was disarmed, and it was done efficiently."

"How can you tell?" Anya asked, drawing the curtains once again, and shrouding them in warm, humid darkness.

"Heinrich Harrow was about six feet tall, average build," Virginia continued, bending to examine the remains of the blood splatter. "He wasn't sober, either. Any prolonged scuffle would have knocked something over." She gestured to the curio cabinet, dense with figurines all in their place. "Nothing did."

Anya raised an appreciative eyebrow, giving one shake of her head. "So it was quick, then."

"Two shots in quick succession," Virginia said, tracing the outline of the faded pool with an outstretched finger. "Almost immediately." She frowned, tilting her head. "Then the first one is missing." She sat back on her haunches, eyes squeezed shut as she considered all potential scenarios. "Harrow was only shot once, so where did the first shot land?"

She stood, examining the door frames and the walls, searching for a bullet hole that the local cops had missed. There was nothing on the far wall, or in the hallway, or the bedrooms. "It had to go somewhere," she said, running her fingers along a wood baseboard.

"Here," Anya said from the kitchen, pointing at a small,

ragged hole in the door frame.

The bullet was still embedded in the wood, the rough entry hole preserved. Virginia turned, looking back towards the front door. "Harrow was the first to shoot, would be my guess by the trajectory. Similar height, judging by the angle. Harrow shot first, and then the killer fired back and killed him." She tilted her head, trying to imagine the trajectory. "And then whoever that was took his shoes."

"Why the shoes?" Anya asked.

Before Virginia could answer, gravel crunched beneath tires as a car trundled up towards the house, ignoring the police tape entirely. They were out of time.

Chapter Twenty-Two

"Ginnie?"

Virginia groaned, straightening. "It's Arthur," she said. "Sheriff Dixon, that is." She opened the door to let him in, and he eagerly stepped over the threshold.

"Small mercies," Anya declared, dusting off her skirts, letting the fabric fall back to swish around her legs, the seams of her stockings slightly askew. "I think you've seen the inside of that cell enough for one trip, don't you?"

"Ginnie, thank God," Arthur said, rubbing his head in the harsh sunlight of mid-afternoon. "Your mother said—"

"I'm sure," Virginia interrupted. "What are you doing here?"

"Looking for you, obviously. I thought I'd find you here, but I hoped I wouldn't. Have you lost your mind? You need to stay far away from all of this until things get sorted out," he warned, stepping over the threshold to reveal Jolie sitting in the passenger seat of his squad unit.

"What is she doing here?" Virginia hissed, torn between slamming the door to keep her out, and beckoning her inside to hide her from passers-by. "I told you not to involve Jolie in this, Arthur. I told you that she—"

"Was worried sick and trapped with your mother?" Arthur shot back. "You of all people should know how sharp that particular punishment is. I could barely keep her away from the car, Ginnie. She's almost as stubborn as you are."

Virginia let out a noisy scoff, rolling her eyes up towards the ceiling. "You're telling me you couldn't fend off a teenage girl?"

"Not one that's a fire demon, no," he retorted. "Did you hear what I said? You need to steer clear of any active crime scene until your mother gives her statement."

She waved him off, backing into the house and leaving the door open. Someone else could decide whether the kid should be inside or out. "They're out at the barn at the edge of town," she said. "Local, county, state, and federal will all be occupied there for at least another hour."

"You should have waited for your mother's statement."

"And you shouldn't be lying to your wife about what you've been up to, and yet here we are," she sniped. Virginia gestured at the bullet hole with one hand, showing off the ripped wood. "He shot first, likely spontaneous. The shot was likely fired from the hip. Look at that trajectory."

Arthur's brow furrowed and he shoved his hands into his pockets. "They could have fought first, that would explain any strangeness in the angle."

"I don't think so, Arthur, that cabinet of curiosities is untouched. Two men of a similar height scuffling would have disturbed the shelf, but there they all sit." She resisted the urge to hurl the tiny giraffe against the wall in order to illustrate her point. "See?"

"The killer could have straightened everything before they left," he offered. "Unless... unless you *saw* something?"

"No," Virginia seethed, his words scraping against her like barbed wire. "I'm only using my skills as a fucking detective, Arthur, maybe you should try it sometime."

He walked the perimeter of the room, staring back and forth between the kitchen and the door. "Didn't you say those shots weren't fired immediately?"

"No, it was after a bit of time. I don't know how long, it was too dark to see my watch face. Twenty minutes?" she suggested. "Which suggests that something went wrong, or someone was hiding in the house."

"Did you hear anything?" he pressed, taking another step towards her. "Voices?"

"No, the house was closed up tight, even though it was hot that night."

Arthur pressed a hand to his chin. "No one entered the house other than Harrow?"

"No."

"You're sure?"

Virginia considered the question, closing her eyes to remember that night. "I'm sure," she answered. "There's no way someone could have broken in while I was watching without me noticing. So yes, I think either something went wrong, or someone was hiding, lying in wait." She frowned. "I feel like it was the former."

"Why is that?"

"Why would Harrow be here at all in the first place, if not to meet someone? Given what I've learned about Mrs. Speer's son, it seems likely that he was meant to be the contact, but according to Carsh, he has a rock-solid alibi."

Arthur examined the bullet hole again, kneeling in front of it to decide the trajectory. "I guess it would be too easy if he didn't," he said. "Open and shut case."

"Arthur, on those cases up in the city, did they ever find the vics' shoes?" Virginia asked.

"Shoes," he repeated.

"Harrow's shoes are missing, too. I saw him get tossed out of Club Cloud with shoes, and leave his vehicle with them on. The new scene up in the woods also doesn't have any shoes present," she said. "Near the barn at the town limits, you know the one."

"First victim was in bed," Arthur said. "I imagine his shoes were in his closet."

"And the second?" Virginia prompted. "He was in his restaurant, in the basement. Where were his?"

Arthur pulled a notebook from his pocket, flipping through the pages. "We noted that his shoes weren't present, but we didn't comb the place looking for them. It wouldn't be impossible that he felt very comfortable in an establishment he owned."

"And Harrow here?" Virginia asked, gesturing towards the blood splatter on the floor. "Not a single men's shoe in the place. Where are his shoes, Arthur?"

"What are you suggesting, Ginnie?" he asked quietly.

"I'm just pointing it out, I'm not suggesting anything," she replied, holding her hands up in deference. "But if the two up in Verdance were crew killings, then what in shadows is this down here? Two already, both Nethered up, neither with shoes."

"Does this shit ever stop?" Arthur asked, voice weary. He tugged at his suspenders, the sage green color incongruous with the rest of his VCPD regulation uniform.

"We're—you're a cop," Virginia answered. "No, it doesn't.

CHAPTER TWENTY-TWO

Did you head down here straight away?" she asked.

"Yes, why?"

She gestured at the suspenders. "Civilian," she said simply.

"Couldn't find my other ones, and Mona was still asleep," he explained. "I didn't want to wake her."

"How kind of you." He'd woken her out of a dead sleep at least half a dozen times for the same reason. Virginia sighed again, this time in resignation. "You should get back to Verdance. Don't you have a federal Nether trade investigation to be dealing with?"

"Feds are all over the shadows-damned place at headquarters," he muttered. "Lindell is ready to snap, one of them turfed her out of her office. Not much for us to do other than let them get on with it." He glanced at Virginia out of the corner of his eye, mouth pressed into a line. "I'm worried about you, Ginnie."

Virginia sucked her teeth. "Don't be."

"You're running from the police on a potential murder charge, and..." he trailed off. "And I assume things with your mother haven't been particularly smooth."

"No."

Arthur closed the gap between them, laying a hand on her shoulder, and for some reason, she let him, despite the overwhelming urge to either shrug him off or land her fist in the side of his jaw. "Ginnie," he said softly, whispering as if he didn't want Anya to hear even though she was standing four steps away in the corner of the room. "I think you should try to get a reading of this situation. You and I both know that it's the best way to figure out what in shadows happened here, and get all of this wrapped up so that once your mother corroborates your alibi, you can go home."

"The courts don't allow for seer testimony," Virginia replied evenly.

"No, but it could give us a solid lead, something more than we've gotten already."

"Fine," she deadpanned. "I'll do my best."

"I'm only trying to help. That's the only reason I drove all the way down here—again—it's to help, Ginnie. I know this place is hard for you." He wavered, as if he was trying to decide his next words carefully.

She nodded, even though he really had no idea just how hard it was for her. He'd been gone when the worst of it happened. He hadn't even known. He never had, not really. Juliette meant nothing to him, but she'd meant everything to Virginia. "Yeah," she agreed, and that was the best she could do. Anything more would betray not only Juliette's memory, but her own sanity.

"You're right, I should get back to Verdance," he said after a moment. "Mona will be wondering where I am if I'm not home for dinner."

"Better hurry," Anya said, and there was the slightest edge to her voice that hadn't been there before. "You don't want to hit traffic on your way back up there." She leaned out the front door, beckoning for Jolie. "She should stay down here if Verdance is still crawling with feds. They're down here now, too, but these aren't hearing whispers about fire demons or inferno witches."

"I agree," Arthur said, fidgeting with the tan leather holster under his left arm. "But I think she should stay with Virginia's mother. It will be safer there than running around in the woods with a wanted criminal." He tilted his head at Virginia, searching for something that wasn't there. "I'll drive her back to your mother's."

"Tell her I'll be around soon," Virginia said. "As soon as I get this figured, I'll come back and we'll drive out to the coast for a while. I think we'll both need it after all this, and it would be good to let things in Verdance die down before we head back to our usual routine."

"The coast," Arthur repeated slowly, in a way she knew meant he didn't approve and was about to make that known. "You're still thinking about that?"

"Yes." She stared him down, arms folded over her chest.

"What's on the coast?"

"Fewer people, hopefully." Virginia edged him towards the door, waving at Jolie in the squad unit, poised with one hand on the door. "At least, that's the likelihood. Once we get out there, the tourists will all have fled back home for the season."

"The more people that see her, the more risk," he said. "Do you really want that, with feds swarming across state lines?"

"She's not going to be hurling fireballs at boats, Arthur, I think we're safe." Virginia grabbed hold of the door, a silent signal that she was ready for him to leave. "And the east coast is at least four states away no matter how you slice it."

Arthur backed onto the porch, perhaps subconsciously. It wouldn't have been the first time she'd gotten him to leave without him realizing it. "East coast," he repeated. "I didn't think you liked it out there."

"You never asked."

"That place by the pier?"

Virginia nodded. "Best shadows-damned blue crab I've ever had."

He stood there, confounded, staring at her like he'd never laid eyes on her before. "I'd better go," he said again. "Think about what I said, you know, about the... about the thing."

"Uh huh," she said, closing the door. "Give Mona my best."

The latch clicked and she leaned against the heavy hardwood, a heavy sigh blowing out her cheeks before she remembered that Anya was still standing there. "Sorry," she mumbled.

"Don't mind me, I'm just in awe of your restraint." Anya threw off a delicate shrug as she straightened the seams of her stockings. "If I had to work with any of my ex-paramours, I'd find it hard to resist the urge to hex them nine ways from Sunday."

"Remind me to not piss you off."

Anya laughed, leaning against the wall, all ease and grace. "Too late," she said. "I didn't hex you, though. You seem like you have enough problems."

"Isn't that the truth," Virginia grumbled, making her way into the dining room.

A silver dining cart was pushed against the wall, stacked with plates, teacups, and cutlery. She examined it for any signs of use or clues, but the thick dust that had gathered on top suggested it hadn't been used in years. After all, the Speer's children had moved out long ago, and no one returned to Birch Hollow if they could help it.

The lack of clues or leads gnawed at her insides, and so did Arthur's words, his pleading for her to access her sight and deliver a perfect verdict that would tie up the case with a neat bow, gift-wrapped to perfection and delivered on a platter so silver and shining, it would put the dining cart to shame.

The carving knife's handle was smooth and inviting in her

hand, the blade sparkling with possibility. Her mother said pain sometimes helped to spur visions.

As Virgina drew the blade across her palm, she gasped, but before she could cry out, everything went dark.

Chapter Twenty-Three

When she came to, Anya was standing over her, lips pressed into a thin line as she dug into her pouch.

"I was trying to—"

"Hush," Anya interrupted. "I know exactly what you were doing." She knelt down, tying a strip of burlap around Virginia's palm to stem the flow of blood that had already dripped down into the rug under her. "Stay still."

The rough fabric ached against the fresh wound, but it was nothing compared to the herbed poultice that Anya rubbed beneath it, the leaves and nettles stinging mightily, so much so that Vrginia sucked in a breath through gritted teeth, resisting the urge to yank her hand away.

Anya glanced at her, an eyebrow raised before she continued. "You don't always have to do everything at your own expense, you know."

"The case needs to be solved."

"And this is worth it?"

"To get me off the roster of suspects, yes," Virginia challenged. "And my mother suggested that pain sometimes helped my father focus his sight."

"From what I've seen of your mother, I wouldn't trust her

as far as I can throw her," Anya said evenly, crushing another leaf between her thumb and forefinger until it released a greenish jelly that she spread onto the wound. "I don't know much about seers, your type being rather rare, but I do know that slicing into yourself isn't a sustainable methodology."

Virginia didn't reply, partially because she was being petulant about it, but also because the stinging pain in her hand was difficult to think beyond. The burlap felt like adding insult to literal injury, but she knew better than to question Anya's methods.

After a long silence, Anya buckled the latch of her pouch and crossed her legs beneath her, watching Virginia for whatever it was she was looking for. "Did you see anything?" she asked finally, her tone somewhere between curiosity and scolding. "Was it at least worth it?"

"I don't know, I blacked out," Virginia admitted, still angry at herself for it. Her intention had been to unlock her sight, solve the crime, and hide the wound from everyone until it had healed. "I didn't mean for you to see."

"You shouldn't have chosen your palm then," Anya replied acerbically. "It's rather obvious."

"I'm still trying to get the hang of this."

Anya nodded, her expression unchanging. "Clearly."

"You don't have to make a big point of it, I understand that you don't agree with my methodology." Virginia sat up, brushing Anya's hands away. "I'm fine. It's a cut, not a stab wound."

"You forget I've healed that for you, too."

The record player in the living room continued to rotate, the quiet sound obvious once again in the quiet of the still house. "I didn't forget."

"You're a frustrating woman to be around, you know," Anya said, untucking her legs and standing, checking her seams as she did so.

"Then go!" Virginia shot back. "Leave, then, if I'm so terrible to experience."

Anya stood there, jaw clenched as though she were swallowing back all manner of insults and reprisals in favor of a more demure response. "Someday you're going to have to stop setting yourself on fire."

"I'm not on fire."

"I disagree."

Virginia tugged at the cabinet of the serving cart, the track sticky with disuse. "If I'm lucky, there will be some gin in here." The cut on her hand hurt more than she'd anticipated it would, and already she was regretting the foolishness of what she'd done. The pain wasn't what made her black out, but whatever was sank deeper into the blackness of her mind, like a dream turned to sand upon waking. Her temples began to give a dull throb, pounding blood against bone. Reaching inside the cart, her fingers wrapped around the neck of a green glass bottle, dusty but intact. "Thank shadows," she mumbled, taking a swig.

"We should leave," Anya said. "Officer Carsh could swing back this way at any moment, and he'll come investigate when he sees that the tape barrier is down." She swung the pouch around to her hip, settling it in place. "I guess we can thank Sheriff Dixon for that."

"Arthur is used to being the biggest hog on the farm." Virginia climbed to her feet, one hand on the bottle, and another using the windowsill to hoist herself into a standing position. "Shadows," she hissed, sliding the small bottle into the pocket of her trousers. "I'd be surprised if he wasn't already at the Birch Hollow station causing problems. He's unusually good at that."

"And you aren't?" Anya asked sharply.

Virginia glanced at her, surprised at the stony expression she found there. "I try to solve a few, now and then."

Dust hung in the air, thick and particular as it drifted through the almost non-existent current in the house. It was tidy and well-kept, but even the most diligent eighty-year-old couldn't keep up with the demands of a large house, not on her own. "I'd like to see that," Anya said, climbing down the rope ladder at the window in the next room. "So far, I've only seen you get yourself into trouble."

"It's the job."

"It's you, Virginia." Anya landed softly on the grass outside, waiting for her to follow.

Virginia struggled with the rope ladder on the way down, her injured palm making the movements even more difficult and clunky than they should have been. She didn't say anything, because there was nothing she could say to that. "He'll know someone was here," she protested. "We should at least try a little harder to get the window closed."

"He'll definitely know someone was here if two someones are still here," Anya argued, pointing out at the road, where blue and red lights flashed in the distance. "We're out of time, Vane. Your little stunt cost us an extra fifteen minutes we didn't have."

"I was trying to help!"

"You can help by staying alive and intact, please," Anya said, dragging her back towards the tree line. "And I'm sorry I said that about you. It's only half of the truth."

"What's the other half?" Virginia asked.

Anya paused for a moment, examining her despite their lack of time to indulge in it. "I haven't figured that out yet." She tugged at Virginia's sleeve with brash insistence, pulling her deeper into the woods. "Come on, hurry up then. He'll be combing the woods in no time at all."

"Car?" Virginia asked, the dull throb of pain in her hand starting to edge towards a far more insistent stabbing sensation.

"Stashed."

"Close?"

Anya nodded. "The clearing ahead. I didn't want to take it further in, I wasn't sure Seamus' car could handle the terrain, not with that detailing."

"Probably not," Virginia agreed. "The man is obsessive about that car."

"He speaks very highly of you."

"That's only because he knows my right hook would put him straight otherwise." Virginia smirked to herself, face obscured behind the thick foliage Anya had just pushed aside. "He speaks highly of anyone who can kick his ass."

"He said you were training with throwing knives," Anya added, revealing the location of the car with a wide sweep of her arm, dragging away a large pine bough that had hidden its front end. "What's that all about?"

"Versatility."

"A gun isn't enough?"

"A gun is noisy," Virginia answered, climbing into the passenger seat of the borrowed car. "And sometimes, I'd rather not be. All that business at Fiske's compound made me realize that more than ever. Fucker might not have nabbed me if I'd had more options." She slammed the door and then winced at the sound, wary of attracting attention. "Sorry."

"We didn't talk much after that," Anya mused, looking over at her for a moment before she started the car, backing out of the clearing. "I don't know why I thought that would be different."

"I didn't think you wanted to."

"It was a near-death experience, it might have been nice to discuss it over coffee." The engine rumbled along quietly as she pulled out onto the unlit gravel road, the rocks crunching delicately beneath the rubber tires. "Jo blames herself, you know."

"She shouldn't."

"She does."

Virginia's jaw clenched, the tension born of ten thousand different guilts, all of them leading back to the same place she vowed she'd never return to. "Fiske would have found me sooner or later. Seers are high in demand. I'm surprised no one else has crawled out of the woodwork to try that trick again." Her fingers found the silver knuckles in her pocket, a defensive gesture that always brought her the tiniest modicum of peace. "Jolie needs to be protected."

"She's very capable, you know."

"Capable doesn't mean safe." She slipped the silver onto her hand, grateful that she'd chosen to wound her left hand instead. "I know she's capable. What I'd like is for her to drop off the crews' radars before someone else gets the big idea to imprison her."

Light from town sparkled in the distance, yellow light from the one bar on main street piercing the darkness around it. Virginia fumbled in her pocket for her cigarettes, setting one between her index and middle finger, ready to be smoked. The craving ached at the back of her throat, more insistent than the pain in her hand and harder to ignore.

"Seamus will kill you if he knows you smoked in his car, you know," Anya said, turning away from town and down a quiet side road, one that led out past the old barns and the fields towards the thick woods that surrounded the county.

"He's welcome to try." Virginia struck a match and lit the end of the cigarette, but rolled the window all the way down anyway. She'd apologize to Seamus later. She was always apologizing to someone, it seemed.

"You really shouldn't smoke so much," Anya said. "Why don't you just quit?"

Virginia considered ignoring the question, or changing the subject entirely, but something about the inescapable humidity of a high-summer downstate loosened her tongue. "It's the first breath of air after the smoke," she explained. "So crisp and clear you remember what it's like to live. In that one instant you have a tiny glimmer of hope that everything might not turn out as bad as you feared." She took a long drag, letting the taste of ash settle on her tongue. "It wears off, of course. Then you reach for the next cigarette."

Anya's eyebrows lifted one at a time as she shifted from skepticism to disbelief. "I think that's the most honest thing you've ever said to me."

"I've never lied to you, Ms. Quinn." Virginia shifted the cigarette between her fingers, keeping the embers from her skin. "In fact, I've been more honest with you than most."

Gravel turned to dirt, and with the change, the car's vibrations shifted from a heavy jostle to something smoother, but more perilous. "Be careful," Virginia said softly, unsure of how much guidance from the passenger seat Anya wanted. "Some of these roads have steep dropoffs where the quarries once were."

"I know," Anya replied, flicking on the headlights now that they were safely away from the vicinity of cops and feds alike. "This isn't my first time out here."

Anya pulled off, setting the car into park and hopping out. "Come on," she said. "We have about half a mile to hike."

"Where are we going?" Virginia asked, closing her door with more care than she had before, flicking embers onto the ground but immediately stamping them out with the toe of her shoe. "I don't think I've ever been back here."

"No, you wouldn't have," Anya said. "This is private property."

Virginia stopped in her tracks, ready to double back to the car. "Then what are we doing out here?"

"Trespassing."

"Hold on, I don't want to—"

Anya threw her head back and laughed, the silver of her hair sparkling like diamonds in the setting sun. "We already did that once today, and now you're shy about it?"

"Who owns this piece of land?" Virginia demanded, but gently. Anya didn't know all of the dark histories that Birch Hollow held. "There are some folks out in these parts who will shoot first, and ask questions after you're in the morgue."

"The owners won't be anywhere near here," Anya replied. "Besides, we go way back. They owe me a few favors."

"How many?"

"Enough."

Virginia trampled a string of vines underfoot, the stems

snapping from the pressure, and the thorns grabbing hold of the hem of her trousers. She chased the silhouette of Anya's skirts which somehow avoided every tangle that Virginia found. It was as if Anya had walked that way ten thousand times before and knew every step, every rabbit warren, every downed tree bathed in the golden glow of summer. "How much further?" Virginia asked after what felt like three miles of fighting her way through the unfamiliar woods.

"We're here." Anya stepped into a clearing with a large bell tent, cast iron sitting on top of cold ashes, and a makeshift table carved from a felled tree, the surface rough and unsanded. "What do you think?"

"Is this where you've been staying?"

"It beats your mom's house, doesn't it?" Anya untied the tent's flap, opening up the front end of it to show Virginia the interior. "She was right, though, there isn't much decent accommodation out here. I didn't want to drive twenty miles back and forth from the nearest roach-free hotel every day, and I've stayed here half a dozen times before. It's always served me well."

The inside of the tent was surprisingly comfortable, the wood plank flooring lifting it off the ground, and the faded rugs that covered them overlapping one over the other in a haphazard yet strangely cohesive way, as if they'd always belonged there in the first place. There were two blue bed rolls in the center, separated by a lantern with the wick turned down low, the glass smudged with black.

"I will admit, I didn't anticipate this when you dragged me out here," Virginia murmured, taken aback. If she'd known it was there when she was a teenager, she would have spent every night trespassing until the owners returned from whatever far-off place they'd been hiding.

"Hungry?" Anya took the lid from the cast iron, inhaling deeply. The coals which had looked cold, in fact were not, and the scent from inside was rich with garlic, thyme, and butter. "Looks like dinner is just about ready."

"You made this?"

"Some people cook, Virginia." Anya snorted a quiet laugh and doled out two portions of chicken and rice into metal bowls. "Be careful, it's hot."

Virginia took it, but quickly set it down on the table, the heat already singeing her skin. "Thank you." Her stomach rumbled, reminded of its purpose. "I don't think I realized how hungry I was."

Anya took a bite, closing her eyes to take in the aromatic flavors. "You can stay here tonight, of course. Jo had been using the second bed roll, but you sent her back to your mother's."

"It's safer there." Virginia fumbled with the fork and knife, her injured palm causing more frustration than she had anticipated. Despite her shortcomings, she managed to slice the chicken into six equal parts, and decided that was good enough for polite company. "If she's running around with me and I get dragged in..."

"And me?" Anya prompted, an eyebrow raised. "What if I'm here when you get dragged in?"

"You're a grown woman, for one, and you're also not a fire demon." Virginia thrust a forkful of chicken and rice into her mouth, resisting the urge to audibly groan at how wonderful it tasted.

"Fair enough."

They ate in silence, cleaned up in silence, and sat around

the embers in silence, each of them perched on a tree stump close enough to observe the heat as the air cooled around them. It wasn't enough to chill Virginia, and in fact, she welcomed the slight shiver as the breeze gusted across her sweat-stained skin.

Anya stood first, squinting into the darkness as she ventured into the tent, returning with the lantern. "Hand," she instructed, holding out her own. Virginia did as she was told, allowing her to inspect the wound.

"How much damage did I do?" she asked.

"Nothing permanent, but it needs re-dressing." Anya busied herself with this task, stripping off the old burlap and tossing it into the dying coals, where it sizzled and snapped when it met the heat. She cleaned the wound with fresh water from her flask, packed it with the same herbs she had earlier, and tied it with a clean bandage, this one mercifully cotton, albeit printed with a hideous floral design. "Beggars can't be choosers," Anya chastised, sensing Virginia's discomfort.

"I didn't say anything."

"Hmm." She sat back on her tree stump, stifling a yawn. "Morning comes early in these parts. We'd better turn in for the night."

Virginia stood, following her into the tent. "Alright," she agreed, even though a part of her nagged at the back of her spine. But then, something always did when she was back home, no matter the circumstances.

Chapter Twenty-Four

Birdsong came first, before dawn had even been given the opportunity to crest over the horizon and announce a new, terrible day. Sunlight was beaten by the birds, and it came through the canvas tent muted, filtered as if through a funeral shroud.

The day was already muggy, the wet hot summer settling on her skin and drawing superfluous sweat from her pores. It would sit there, untouched and unhelpful, until she brushed it away. Despite the rustic nature of the bell tent, it almost felt cooler than her room in her mother's house. Perhaps it was the lack of suffocation that helped.

Virginia stirred, unwilling to open her eyes just yet. It was early, so much so that fatigue still rested in her marrow, heavy and unwilling to allow her to wake from such a deep and undisturbed slumber. She hadn't slept that way in years, despite the birdsong, the sun, the heat, and the reminder that she was still, unfortunately, wanted for questioning in a murder case.

An idyllic tableau, except for the latter.

Her lungs inflated slowly, inhaling the damp air laced with honeysuckle, the sweetness dancing at the back of her throat, reminding her of hunger. It wasn't something she usually paid much attention to, her other vices taking far more precedence in her forethoughts.

Prying open one eyelid, she became aware of two things all at once. First, sometime in the night and without her consent, she had draped an arm around Anya's waist, her hand gently grazing a strip of bare, olive-toned skin. Second, if she moved, there was a strong possibility Virginia would inadvertently wake her, thus enshrining her shame in permanence, forever, with no escape from it.

She mouthed a stream of curses, not daring to let a single one actually find itself uttered into the present. Virginia tugged at her arm lightly, trying to dislodge it from its treacherous position without sounding the alarm that it had happened in the first place.

"Good morning," Anya said sleepily, stifling a yawn with the back of her hand.

Hoping she could get away with blaming it on the last vestiges of a nightmare, Virginia pulled her arm away, cradling it to her chest as though it was the injured one. "Morning," she mumbled, trying to sound as half-asleep as she could muster. Plausible deniability, isn't that what Sadie had said? Just enough doubt that she couldn't be convicted in the court of Anya's opinion that she'd done something she shouldn't have.

"Don't worry," Anya murmured, sitting up and stretching her arms over her head. "I won't tell Captain Lindell." She smirked at Virginia and pulled her shirt down, taking a small canvas bag from beneath her pillow. "I'm going to go clean up by the creek. I'll show you where it is when I'm done."

Virginia didn't even get the opportunity to stammer, or lie, or obfuscate about what had happened. As usual, Anya took it at face value, without judgment or comment, and granted her the swift relief of a mistrial. "I, uh, thanks," she mumbled, unsure of what else there was to say.

"Jo isn't here, or I'd ask her to heat those coals for us." Anya threw open the tent's flap, nearly blinding both of them in the process. "Shadows, that's bright," she grumbled. "If you don't mind building up the fire, Virginia, I think we could both use some coffee. There's bread in the basket with jam if you want something more substantial."

"Coffee is fine," Virginia retorted, surprised at the starkness in her own tone. She'd grown accustomed to her routine with Jolie, making the both of them a mug, reading the paper in silence, and heading to the office for a day's work. It was helpful that Jolie wasn't really one for mornings, either. "Thank you," she added, not wanting to give off the impression of being quite so unreasonable and frigid.

"You're the one building the fire," Anya said, tossing the comment over her shoulder along with a loose white towel. "Get to it, Virginia, you don't want to see me before I'm caffeinated." She disappeared through a thick hedge, and immediately her footsteps vanished into the noise of the forest, filled with more than just birdsong, but the lazy hum of cicadas as they woke from their slumber, warmed by the rising sun, and the crickets that sang from within the tall, untouched blades of grass, the greenery nearly a foot tall and falling over on itself.

Virginia stacked wood one way, and then another, striking flint against stone for several unproductive minutes before she remembered the book of matches in her breast pocket. She lit the pile of tinder, dry sheaves of wheat and yellowed pine needles from the floor of the woods. It went up quickly, and in the brief seconds before it died back down, she knew how Jolie felt to hold that kind of power in her hands.

The kindling went next, small twigs fallen from their trees just to be burned in effigy, a small sacrifice for caffeine. Flames licked along the larger logs, the bark blackening as it heated, snapped, and split. Proud of her minuscule achievement, Virginia sat back on her haunches, setting the percolator atop the grate over the fire.

"How did you do?" Anya asked, emerging from the invisible path. "I have to say, I've gotten spoiled with Jo around, but that's not a bad fire, you know." She sat down on the tree stump opposite, smoothing the fabric of her fresh dress, this one a duck egg blue, the collar embroidered with white flowers that seemed more specific than a daisy, but Virginia had never been much of a botanist.

"I know what you mean. Jolie heats stuff perfectly every time." Virginia watched the percolator for several uneventful minutes before the promise of bread called to her, breakfast being almost unheard of for her, but that morning it was dripping with temptation. She set two on the grate to toast, gesturing to Anya. "Want some?"

"Two please," Anya announced. "I'll watch this if you want to freshen up. It's just down the path between those two trees, you can't miss it if you just keep heading straight."

"Straight," Virginia repeated, and then shook her head. "Sure," she said. "Yeah, I'll do that."

"Be careful of the water," Anya added airily, waving a hand with a casual, nonchalant gesture. "Don't go all the way in."

"I'm a strong swimmer."

"There are naiads around here."

Virginia pursed her lips, irritated at Anya's assumption that she couldn't handle herself. "I've seen naiads before, they're nothing to be concerned about."

The foliage overhead hung heavy in the heat, the leaves stretched out from each twig to soak up the sun, to dry themselves out from the oppressive moisture, and to protect the path from harsh light. She was glad for the shade as she hunted for the trail, barely more than flattened grass and brush as the ground tipped ever so slightly downwards to the river. She was close enough to see it before the sound of waves against smooth rocks permeated the woods and fought back the noise of the bugs.

Ripples stretched out from each rock, every crash against them causing enough of a disturbance that despite the clarity of the water, the riverbed was incomprehensible, nothing more than a blur of rocks and detritus that had laid there, undisturbed, for months, maybe, or years. Overhead, a mourning dove cooed its thrice-driven song, one Virginia had always hated.

"Shut up," she hissed at the bird, tossing a small twig at the trunk of the tree. The bird stayed anyway, staring with its horrible beady black eyes, perched up high and safe from danger. It cooed again, just to prove that it could.

Virginia bent, letting the cool water rush over her uninjured hand, knowing well enough to keep her injury clear of potential pathogens. You never did quite know what was lurking upstream.

She laid her clothes out on a rock, washing herself quickly with the cool water. Even that far in the woods, it was an unsettling vulnerability that she was anxious to correct. Grateful for the refreshment of her skin, she lingered for just a moment, letting an eddy swirl around her bare legs, the current stronger than she might have imagined that deep into summer. It tugged at her, muscles fatiguing with the effort to remain still and upright.

Strangely, she felt the urge to descend deeper into the river, to let the water rush up to her waist, to her shoulders even. Gold glimmered beneath the surface, tempting with its sparkle. She reached out for it, but the reflection died in her hands, disturbed by the ripples. The glow vanished until she was still again, and then shone once more from beneath a large river boulder that bloomed up out of the water.

She reached out for the gold again, curious, stepping further down the bank until the river danced at her waist, pulling her further from shore. She was well-accustomed to it by then, the feeling that something wasn't quite right but being unable to pinpoint where the damage had already occurred.

Virginia was about to dunk her head under the water to get a better glimpse of the gold hidden beneath the foam when something grabbed at her ankle, sharp and insistent. She tried to back up onto the bank, but found the soil loose and unhelpful, sending her scrambling for firm land. She grasped at roots but found the plants coming free from the erosion, and she slipped beneath the waves.

Bright golden eyes stared up at her from the riverbed, three pairs of them, each with needy fingers that snaked around her legs and wrists, pulling her down to the depths where light glittered unkempt and wild, the tantalizing freedom of a quiet drowning. They were beautiful in a serene way, smooth skin striped with the thick scales of an alligator and plump lips that were hiding razor-sharp teeth ready to tear into her soft flesh.

She kicked at one, almost feeling guilty when it shrieked soundlessly, nothing more than bubbles emanating from its mouth as it slunk back into the darkness. Virginia pried their tentacled hands from her one by one, lungs screaming for the air she wouldn't find beneath the foam.

The last one held firm, staring into her eyes with a pleading sincerity that was difficult to ignore. They were starving, their bones protruding through thin, bluish skin. A hot, humid summer had chased away too many of the fish, leaving them to gulp nothing more than water, to fill their concave bellies with oxygen but never meat. Virginia almost let that one drag her down, to let it feast on her ruined flesh and have her death at least have meant subsistence for the naiads that dwelled that deep in the woods.

She pulled herself from the water, gasping and coughing up water, spitting it out onto the grass. Snatching at her clothes, she dressed quickly, as though thin linen would protect her from the creatures that still stared from their place in the tidal pool, their golden eyes a temptation for the easily led.

Though, she supposed, and with considerable shame, that had been her just a few moments prior.

Virginia stalked back to camp, squeezing the water from her hair and dreading what the river would do to it.

"You could have told me there were three of them," she spat, the taste of river still thick on her tongue.

"I told you to be careful." Anya slid a board of finely cut meat into a bowl. "They are just hungry."

"You're *feeding* them?" Virginia asked, incredulous. "Why?"

Anya handed her a plate with toast and two boiled eggs,

along with a mug of steaming coffee, the bitter scent beautifully welcome. "I'm feeding *you*, aren't I? Why should they be any different?"

"I don't try to tear apart anyone who gets too close," Virginia retorted.

Twigs crunched beneath Anya's feet as she headed back down to the river, bowl in hand. "Don't you?"

Chapter Twenty-Five

Day was moving on swiftly by the time Anya returned, every last vestige of meat gone, and the aluminum rinsed clean.

"Took you long enough," Virginia groused. "How long does it take to throw meat into a river?"

Anya packed the bowl into a small wicker basket, strapping it to the interior. "It's an exchange," she replied simply. "I feed them, they give me what I want."

"And what is it that you want?" Virginia asked, but at Anya's silence, held up her hands in defeat. "Right, I forgot, you won't tell me. Fine. I almost just drowned in the river, but fine."

"You didn't almost drown, don't be dramatic." Anya sat astride her tree stump, latching the basket closed. "They're starving, Virginia, they're no match for you." She eyed the bandage with a keen eye, tilting her head with interest. "You redressed your wound."

Fresh cotton looped around Virginia's palm, covering the poultice that laid beneath it. "I knew you'd give me hell for it otherwise."

"And the herbs?"

"I paid attention." Virginia nodded towards a discarded

pile of smashed leaves, the remains ready to become kindling on the fire, to smoke themselves out of existence until there was no sign they'd ever existed in the first place. Such was the beauty of cremation, the total erasure of self, even for a plant. "Hopefully."

Anya nodded, examining the stalks. "Good," she said simply, leaving them there. "You'll be a healer yet. Assuming you have an ounce of magic in you, that is. Crushing up botanicals is only half the work."

Resisting the urge to roll her eyes, Virginia stared up at the sun instead, letting the bright sun burn her retinas. "Did I miss saying the magic words?"

"I would imagine you missed the intention," Anya murmured, setting two more slices of bread on the grate. "But that's neither here nor there."

"Planning on feeding bread to the naiads, too?" Virginia snapped. If she'd have known how many were in there, she never would have ventured beyond the shore in the first place. "Shadows, why not just dump the rest of your reserves in there, too?"

Anya glanced at her over the moderate fire, the heat from the embers already almost unbearable in the summer's warmth. "They only eat meat," she said simply. "The toast is for me." Anya knelt down next to Virginia, taking her injured hand in her own and closing around it. She breathed deeply, quiet, and sat still for so long that Virginia was about to pull her hand free with a petulant yank just to avoid the awkward silence of it. "I think you'll be alright," she said finally, but didn't release Virginia's hand. "I'm sorry about the naiads," Anya said softly. "Perhaps I should have told you that there were three." She gave Virginia a tiny smirk with a raised eyebrow. "But I did warn you. Maybe you could listen to me once in a while?"

Virginia swallowed hard. "Maybe," she replied, unsure why she wasn't pulling her hand away. The gentle pressure at her wrist should have been enough to trigger that response, and yet, it hadn't. "Or maybe you could be more specific."

"I did use the plural," Anya corrected, teasing her lightly. "How specific should I be?" She trailed a fingertip across the top of Virginia's hand, following the edge of the bandage. "Virginia, there are between three and five naiads in the river that I have personally observed. Due to the heat of the summer, a new development a few miles north, and overfishing by the locals, they are starving, so I am offering them food in exchange for certain reagents. Okay?"

"Thank you."

Rainless clouds snaked their way across the sky, bathing them in grey light as they obscured the bright amber glow of the sun long enough for Virginia to blink back the spots in her eyes. It was a blissful if woefully temporary relief, and just as quickly as they had descended, the clouds dissipated into nothingness, leaving no more than wispy trails across the sky in their wake.

A twig snapped at the edge of camp, drawing alarm from both of them. They sprang apart, Virginia reaching for her silver knuckles, Anya hefting the cast-iron pan like a bat. "Who's there?" Virginia demanded, already off her tree stump and settled into a sparring position.

"Just me," Jolie replied, emerging from the trail with an uncharacteristic flourish. Her eyes darted from one of them to the other, biting back an amused laugh. "Did I startle you?"

"There's a serial killer on the loose. Yes, you startled me," Virginia grumbled, flipping the toast onto a metal plate. "Anya made breakfast. Jam is in the basket."

"Did you fall in the river?" Jolie asked, tilting her head at the dampness of Virginia's hair. "Did you see the naiads?"

"We're acquainted." Virginia left her stump for Jolie and leaned against a tree, enjoying the stretch in her legs. She missed her sparring sessions with Seamus. She was probably getting rusty.

Jolie crammed a piece of toast into her mouth, indelicately, but that's how she always ate, with unrepentant gusto and fervor. "What happened to your hand?"

"Barbed wire," Anya lied, slicing celery and carrots into the cast-iron. "Up at the Speer place."

Grateful for the cover, Virginia didn't object. She nodded with a shrug, adjusting the bandage to sit tighter around her palm. "Damned stuff," she agreed. "I didn't see it at first."

"Mm," Jolie mumbled, graciously focused on her meal and not the lie. "Sheriff Dixon said that the feds might come down this way."

"They're probably already here." Virginia lit a cigarette, ignoring Anya's quiet ire on the subject. "If we can figure out who killed Heinrich Harrow, and tie that to the woman who was murdered in the woods, we can get all of this wrapped up."

Jolie swallowed a bite of toast. "It was the same person?"

"Might be." Virginia polished her silver knuckles against the linen of her trousers, rubbing the smudges from the metal. "None of the victims had shoes."

"What if I was a witness?" Jolie asked. "I could tell them you were with me and Anya that night. Then you won't have to ask your mother to corroborate anything at all!"

Virginia shook her head. "Absolutely not. You need to keep away from this." She nodded towards Anya. "Both of you."

"Okay," Jolie replied, clearly not happy with the answer. "What about the magic?" She funneled the remaining toast crumbs into her mouth. "Any idea who could achieve that sort of thing all the way out here? Seems more like something you'd see back in Verdance, not in a tiny place like this."

Virginia shrugged, exhaling a plume of smoke. "Small towns have plenty of secrets." It was the truth, and one she knew better than most. "You'd be surprised at the kinds of things that get swept under the proverbial rug out here."

Virginia watched the bread crisp at the edges with a keen eye, knowing that despite being a fire demon, Jolie hated burnt toast. "Is my mother not feeding you?"

"There wasn't much in the house." Jolie poked at the bread's center, still too soft to flip. "I don't think she eats very much."

"She never has," Virginia replied, bringing the cigarette to her lips again. "Gin, menthols, and occasionally, takeout that she tosses half of." Saying it aloud brought forth a cringe at her own patterns, so perfectly mirrored, so woefully unexamined. "Are you hungry? Maybe Anya can hunt down a deer for you or something, seeing as she's some sort of wilderness survivalist."

"It's not the season for venison, Virginia," Anya corrected. "And these woods have been all but hunted clean of game anyway. Why else would the naiads be starving?"

"I thought they ate fish."

"They'll eat whatever gets too close." Anya's lips twitched as she bit back a smirk. "Deer, fishermen, or careless detectives are all on the menu from time to time."

Virginia didn't resist the temptation to roll her eyes that time, letting Anya see her derision. "I wasn't being careless."

"They wouldn't be able to take anything down in their current state, not when they're starving." The corners of Anya's mouth turned up prettily, and she wondered up at canopy, as if she were looking for answers in the leaves. "I should consult my books on the illusion magic at the scene of Harrow's murder. It's possible I'm wrong about the origin. I hope that I'm wrong, anyway."

"You have your books all the way out here?" Virginia asked, glancing inside the tent for some evidence of shelves or a trunk, and finding none. "Where are you keeping them?"

"There are a few in the car," Anya answered, only half of her attention on the conversation. "I didn't want them to get wet, in case it rained." Staring up at the sky, she winced. "Although, it doesn't seem like there will be much danger of that. I'd hoped that quick storm in Verdance before we left might have been the end of the drought, but I guess not."

"I don't think that rain even found its way all the way down here," Virginia said. She couldn't see the fields of crops from the forest clearing, and for that she was grateful, but she'd already seen enough of their stunted growth to know what the autumn would bring.

"Were there any disappearances around here?" Anya asked out of the blue, staring into the embers. "Any unexplained happenings?"

Virginia had no time to brace for the question, no caution with which to armor herself against Juliette's memory, nowhere to run from her ghost. "Yes," she said simply. "Not frequently, but it did happen."

"Were they ever found?" Anya asked, flipping Jolie's toast for her.

"No."

"None of them?" she pressed.

"No," Virginia repeated, the edge of her tone razor-sharp with unspoken warning. "She was never found."

Jolie grabbed the toast off the grate, slathering it with the last of the jam, but still looking between the two women as if there was something there to read other than irritation and obfuscation. "Juliette?" she asked.

Usually, Jolie was circumspect in her questions, careful to dance around Virginia's old wounds with grace, never mentioning too much, never prying past the point of decorum, never so desperate to uncover what had been long buried. "Is that who went missing?" she continued.

Unable to bring herself to say the words aloud, Virginia just nodded, pulling another cigarette from her tarnished silver case. Four left. She'd have to make them last—there would be no going into town until her name was cleared by the feds.

"How old was she?" Anya asked. "Grown?"

Crows flew overhead, screaming their ugly language that somehow communicated more than any delicate birdsong could. They were the harbingers of autumn, settling in the trees overhead. Their wings shone prismatic in the sun, their dark eyes always watchful, always knowing something that humans didn't, or couldn't. Sun filtered through the still-living and verdant leaves, even though another month would start to pull the green from the foliage, the frosted mornings and crisp dew one more reminder of human entropy.

"Sixteen," Virginia answered after the long, empty silence. "One year younger than me. Well, six months, really." She willed her hands to stop shaking, but they resisted her urges and quaked anyway, the motion betrayed by the movement of the cigarette as she lit it with the open fire. "Two years below Arthur—Sheriff Dixon. He didn't know her much."

"You were friends?" Anya asked, her head tilted.

Virginia didn't answer that time. She couldn't, not when the lump in her throat would so treacherously scream out the darkest of truths, where so much of it all had started. She inhaled, staring up at the crows in the branches, letting their screams fill the silence. Her cigarette burned down to the filter. Wordlessly, Virginia tossed the remainder into the flames and stalked off into the woods.

Chapter Twenty-Six

Despite her unfamiliarity with that area of the Birch Hollow woods, Virginia continued to climb a steep path, savoring the prescient burn in her thighs, made worse by improper footwear for the uneven mulch and detritus under her soles. She didn't know how long she'd been out there, walking, beating back memories in her head with quicker steps made to bring on the fatigue sooner.

A breeze rustled through the branches and she stopped for just a moment, letting it coast through her river-addled hair, the cool air a delicious relief against the sweat that had gathered at the nape of her neck.

She discovered that even one moment's rest was enough for memories to flood into her chest cavity, pushing out every breath she tried to inhale, so she set off again, climbing, always heading further north up the slope.

The path forked, the left leveling out towards a crystalline pond, stunning in the midday sparkles of sun that glanced between the leaves. The right continued to rise up out of the earth, a strange work of geographical fiction because Birch Hollow was never anything except flat, and yet she had been walking for what felt like hours.

She took the right fork, still craving the acute pain of fatigue. The pines turned to oaks, mighty and strong with their trunks, heavy acorns falling to the path weeks early. Just like Virginia, they were impatient for the season to change.

Birch trees dotted the horizon and soon dominated the sides of the vague path, their stark black and white bark a balm against an irritatingly blue sky, cloudless in its insistence to burn them all to a crisp.

The flora and foliage thinned as she approached the precipice, a stark cliff-face that looked over the town. A bench cast a shadow over the yellowed grass, wrought iron supports and rests with varnished planks of oak for the seat and back. Despite its exposure to the elements, it looked like it had been placed there that morning, so perfect and fresh in its exterior.

Virginia sat for minutes, or maybe it was an hour, wishing the path had gone on forever. If she'd have been lucky, she could have walked until she dropped dead. Perhaps the naiads could feast on her remains, if the crows didn't get to her first. The town was sleepy from that distance and elevation, but she knew better. Federal, unmarked squad units lined the streets, their identical black exteriors and shining fresh coats of paint a stark contrast to the kinds of vehicles that were common that far downstate.

"Hey," Anya said, emerging from another path from the right. "Are you alright?"

"Where's Jolie?" Virginia asked, already standing up from the bench.

Anya motioned for her to sit back down, and joined her, holding out a large flask of water. "I sent her back to your mother's."

"Thank you." Virginia drank from the bottle, draining half of it before propriety resurfaced in her mind. "Sorry," she said, handing it back.

"Don't be." Anya screwed the lid on and set it on the ground between their feet. "I thought you might be thirsty after that climb."

"How did you know I'd be up here?"

"I didn't," Anya admitted. "But I'm glad I was right."

Virginia stared out over the town. "You'll be a detective yet, Ms. Quinn."

"Oh, I don't know about that." Anya joined her in looking out over the horizon, the sun still overhead but beginning to dip down in the sky. "There are plenty of things I miss." She leaned back on the bench, crossing one leg over the other in a fluid movement. "Who was she to you? Juliette?"

Again, Virginia didn't answer, gripping the edge of the bench until her knuckles went white, the smooth wood splinterless but biting into her palm anyway.

"Best friend?" Anya tried, her voice lilting and soft, almost a whisper. The gentleness of the question threatened to draw tears to Virginia's eyes, so she shook her head instead of speaking. Anya nodded. "Oh."

"Oh," Virginia echoed, one part of her relieved that she'd figured it out, and the other horrified at the blatant, exposed honesty that had just laid her soul bare.

"Does Sheriff Dixon know?"

"No. Not that part, anyway." Virginia drew in a breath, reaching for her cigarette case. She dug in her pocket for the book of matches, but found only lint. Anya handed over her own lighter, bronze and engraved with some sort of rune.

"Here," she said. "Take mine."

Virginia lit the cigarette and inhaled, laying the lighter on the bench between them. "Thanks." The smoke was almost invisible in the harsh light, dissipating into the humid air too rapidly to perceive. "Juliette Ashling went missing on June fourteenth, thirty-one years ago."

She inhaled again, doing her best to steel her nerves, but failing. She hadn't spoken to anyone about Juliette in decades. Every memory of her was laden with such a deep and inescapable sorrow that even uttering her name aloud was enough to pull her under like a riptide. She clung to the cigarette like a life raft. "The police didn't even start looking for her for an entire week. They said she was a stray, you know, a runaway. She'd left home a few times before and headed south, but she always came back." She exhaled, her lungs fighting against the invisible thorns wrapped around them. "She always came back for me."

"No wonder you can't stand this place. It's full of ghosts for you."

"He was a rookie cop, you know, all filled up with piss and vinegar, thought he knew everything there was to know. Rumors circulated around the town, lies, you know how it is. Everyone wants to pretend their own morality would have protected them, so they invent stories about missing girls to protect their own backwards ideology."

The crows rustled in the branches behind them, wings flapping quietly, their usual cries muted and silent. She flicked ash to the ground, letting a few embers catch before she stamped them out. "They stopped looking after four days. Closed the case after two weeks." She inhaled again, holding the taste of embers in her throat, willing it to burn away the lump lodged there. "When she didn't show up after six months, they declared her dead and had a funeral."

"Did you go?" Anya asked, still keeping her gaze on the horizon, and for that, Virginia was grateful. "To the funeral, I mean."

Virginia nodded. "I did. I was one of the only people there." She picked up the lighter again, craving something to press into her hand, the sensation being the only thing keeping the undertow at bay. "I told Carsh he was a bad cop, that he probably killed her himself, a lot of things that weren't true. I was young. I was angry."

"And he threw you in jail for that?"

"No, he threw me in jail for breaking into the precinct to go through the files. I'd done it months earlier, but he didn't arrest me until after I embarrassed him at the funeral." Virginia shrugged at the injustice of it, the fire long since burned out of her marrow and replaced with a distinct heaviness she'd never been able to shift. "My mother threw me out after that, changed the locks. I wound up in Verdance. Was on the streets a while until I ran into Arthur at Seamus' gym."

"I'm sorry."

"I don't want your pity," Virginia snapped, and bit her tongue to prevent anything worse from escaping her lips. She took another drag, held it, and exhaled, the minty tang of the menthols a relief against the hot sun. "I don't need pity," she tried again, glancing at Anya from the corner of her eye. "What's done is done."

Anya shifted on the bench, uncrossing her knees and balancing her forearms against them. "It's not pity, Virginia."

"It feels like it."

"Okay." Anya took a long drink from the water flask,

wiping away the droplets that lingered on her chin. "I won't say anything."

"My mother knows," Virginia said. "There was no hiding anything from her. She was a one-woman panopticon. Things I was so sure I'd hidden, she figured out anyway."

The sun shifted again, another slice closer to sunset, which was still several painful hours away. Revealing secrets in the daylight always felt worse, somehow, than doing so under the cover of darkness. Virginia had spent a lifetime hoarding secrets, and to let that one fly free felt like her biggest mistake.

"She didn't want me to see Juliette, of course. She'll tell you now it's because she knew Juliette was trouble, that she didn't want me to get dragged down with her, but that wasn't really the reason." Virginia breathed in the final lungful of smoke, that truth being one of the more obvious ones. "You know."

Anya nodded. "I know."

Virginia sighed, the last vestiges of smoke leaving her body like so much penitent shame. "I don't know why I'm telling you all of this."

"You had to tell *someone* after all these years."

"All these years," Virginia repeated. "Fuck." A single cloud drifted across the landscape, lonely but superfluous.

"I couldn't have done it." Anya shifted her weight on the bench, the oak planks beneath them creaking against the black painted iron struts that held it all together. "I couldn't have come back here after all of that. Shadows, some days it's hard enough to wake up in the same apartment my aunt lived in, work the same job she worked, live the same life and hope that it's enough."

"Hmm." Virginia reached for another cigarette, swearing off all earlier vows to ration them until her name was off the roster. "You've saved a lot of asses in your time, Ms. Quinn."

"If I hadn't, someone else would have."

"Someone else wouldn't have dragged me back into that back-shop clinic when I had that shifter bite," Virginia pointed out. "I was half septic. You said I might not have survived the night."

"You were, and you wouldn't have," Anya agreed. "Maybe next time, you should listen to me, Ms. Vane."

Virginia lifted her bandaged hand along with a challenging eyebrow. "I am listening, Anya." She flipped the bronze lighter open, releasing a single flame that she used to light the next cigarette. "More than you know."

"From you, that's rather a high compliment, I would imagine." Anya took the offered lighter, sliding it back into her skirt pocket. "You should tell Arthur, you know."

"He wouldn't understand."

"I don't know, I think he would. He's loved people too."

"I've spilled an awful lot of secrets just now, Ms. Quinn," Virginia said after a protracted silence. "I think it's only fair you share one of your own."

Anya met her eyes, tilting her head with curiosity. "What do you want to know?"

"Promise me you'll answer it first," Virginia challenged. "Come on, after all of that, I think you owe me something to even the score."

"Fine," Anya replied, eyes narrowed in suspicion. "I promise."

"Why are you so afraid of the Fae?"

Anya drew in a deep breath, staring back into the birch

trees and all the crows their branches held, their dark eyes questioning and curious. "I've seen what they can do, Virginia. Terrible things, given the opportunity." She met Virginia's curious stare. "Their magic was never meant for our realm."

Chapter Twenty-Seven

The walk back to camp was quiet, nearly silent except for the summery din of the woods. Virginia was grateful to be left alone with her own thoughts, the shame of Juliette's unsolved disappearance as fresh as the day she'd gone missing.

Anya offered her water, and she took it, draining the flask.

"Thanks."

"Mmhmm."

A fire blazed at camp, and despite how she'd left, Virginia was almost glad to be back. It wasn't Jolie's fault for asking questions. None of it was her fault at all.

Jolie scrambled to meet them at the path's entrance, thrashing through the brush. "I'm sorry, Virginia, I didn't know—"

"It's alright, Firefly."

"No, you don't understand—"

Virginia clapped a hand on Jolie's shoulder as she passed, offering her a reassuring smile, only to come face-to-face with her own mother.

"So this is where you've been hiding." Virginia's mother gingerly stepped over a fallen tree, half covered with moss and lichens.

Virginia stood, skin already prickling with irritation. "How did you find us?" she demanded.

"Followed her."

Jolie shook her head vehemently. "No, I made sure I wasn't followed. I made *sure*, Virginia."

"And you?" Virginia asked her mother. "Did *you* make sure you weren't followed? Or are you leading federal agents and serial killers directly to us?"

Her mother waved her off, her lip curling at the sight of the camp. "Not exactly five star accommodation, is it?" She perched gingerly at the edge of the opposite tree stump, toying with a thin, weedy branch that had grown out of it. "And of course I wasn't followed. Some of us know how to lose a tail."

Virginia bit her tongue hard enough to taste iron, knowing that whatever punishment her mother would mete out would far surpass whatever the feds could do to her. Swallowing blood and bile, she found herself trying to press the wrinkles from the cuffs of her shirt, trying to fix the state of them, and when she realized, pushed them up to her elbows instead. "Go home, Mother."

"What, and leave my only daughter to the wolves?" Virginia's mother toyed with a pearl earring, turning it in place. It was a tell, and one she wanted Virginia to see. "I'm here to help."

"You can't."

"Of course I can, don't be ridiculous." Her mother tilted her head, frowning. "Why are you sitting like that? It's so unladylike. Cross your legs, Virginia, you're a woman, not a man." She sighed loudly, glaring at the percolator. "Aren't you going to offer me some?"

"It's not done yet," Jolie supplied, but was already reaching for a mug anyway.

"Mother, go home," Virginia said again, tension settling between her temples and beginning to pound, fierce and insistent. "I'll come see you when this is over."

"You've said that before, Ginnie, so forgive me if I decline that offer. I hadn't seen you for years before you showed up back here, asking all sorts of inappropriate questions." Her mother glanced back at the tent, her frown deepening. "I'm told you need me to corroborate an alibi."

"Don't worry about it," Virginia said airily. She didn't want anything from her mother, not when it always came gift-wrapped with strings attached. "I'll figure it out myself."

"What were you doing in the woods with that woman who was murdered?"

"I wasn't in the woods with the woman who was mur-dered," Virginia said. "Carsh is mistaken, and so is his witness. Probably drunk, if I had to guess. Shadows know drinking is the only thing to do in this place."

"Sammy hardly has the reputation to drink," her mother argued. "I imagine she'd be a star witness for the prosecu-tors."

"What do you want, Mom?" Virginia demanded. "Why are you out here, really? To gloat?"

"I'm not gloating, I am offering my help."

"If you wanted to help, you would have already. The fact that you're here and not in Carsh's office talking to feds is proof of that."

Her mother's brow furrowed, but only for a moment before her face returned to its usual neutrality. "I wanted to speak with you first, to make sure I was saying the right thing."

"Since when do you care about that?" Virginia snapped. "You've always been more than happy to let me rot in a cell, haven't you?"

"Is this about Juliette again?"

"*Again*," Virginia said with a scoff. "As if we ever discussed it in the first place."

"I wanted to keep you safe. That girl was always too volatile for her own good, but then, you always did like them a bit like that, didn't you, Ginnie?" her mother asked sweetly, as if it wasn't a summoning of Juliette's specter to hang over the camp. "Like mother, like daughter, I suppose. Your father was unpredictable, too."

Jolie poured coffee into a mug and nearly thrust it across the fire pit. "Here you go, Mrs. Cabot," she said. We don't have any milk, I'm afraid, but there's some honey in the—"

Virginia's stomach folded over on itself, the dynamic all too familiar. Regret and humiliation boiled in her throat hotter than the fresh coffee, and she took the mug from Jolie, wrapping her hand around the girl's for a moment. "I've got it," she said, and passed it to her mother. "She drinks it black." She took another mug for herself, reaching for a spoon.

"I've always said that you can accurately judge someone's intelligence by how much milk and sugar they take in their coffee," her mother said brightly, taking the mug. She scowled at the rim, wiping it with the side of her thumb.

"Pass the honey, Jolie," Virginia said flatly, holding her hand out. "And an extra spoon, please."

"No need to be so sensitive, Ginnie, you always take everything so personally." Her mother sipped at the coffee, staring at her over the top of the mug with one eyebrow raised in challenge. "Have you ever wondered if that's the reason people don't stick around?" The syllables dripped with snide irritability, every word a clear indication of her invisible, boiling resentment.

"And you wonder why I don't come back here," Virginia shot back, unable to contain the bitter defensiveness gathering on her tongue, singeing her taste buds more than the acrid, over-brewed coffee.

"I bet Arthur never speaks to his parents like this," her mother challenged. "He always knew the value of his elders."

"His elders didn't throw him out on his ass!" Virginia's chest burned with years, decades of unspoken sentiment, and it was dangerously close to bursting through her lungs and killing them all in one fell swoop.

Her mother ran one hand over the string of pearls at her neck, fingertip pausing at each one before she spoke. "I never threw you out. And besides, Arthur never got arrested."

"No, he just cheated on his wife and took up with a younger woman." Virginia poured the rest of the coffee over the still burning fire, only managing to douse half of it. She knew that if she tried to choke down the rest of the mug, it would only serve to bring everything back up at once, along with too many unrequited memories. "Talk to Carsh if you want, or don't. It doesn't matter to me one way or the other."

"Ginnie..." her mother tried, but stopped. "Fine. I'll do as I see fit." She stood to leave, disappearing into the hedges.

Virginia nudged Jolie's elbow. "Get your stuff. You're going with her."

"What? Why?" Jolie asked, her voice tight. "I want to stay here."

"Not with a serial killer on the loose, you're not. My mother is... challenging, but you'll be safer in that fortress than you would be out here."

"I don't want to."

"It's not a request."

Anya watched from the edge of the camp. "Virginia, maybe—"

"You know as well as I do that it's dangerous out here. It's unprotected. I don't want Jolie in harm's way."

"What about you?" Jolie demanded. "Isn't it just as dangerous out here for you? Come with me, I'm sure we can work it out, I'm sure she'll tell Carsh you were at home."

"Don't be so sure, kid." Virginia sighed as she handed over Jolie's bag. "And I'd rather be torn apart by a violent killer than spend another night under the same roof with that woman."

***

Virginia tensed as they approached the Dixon house, perched prettily on its concrete foundation, the cracks invisible at that distance but just as present.

Arthur's parents had always been lukewarm about her, despite her mother's status in the town. No doubt they'd been thrilled when he took up with Mona, all pretty and perfect and exactly the kind of socialite daughter they'd always envisioned for him. They'd moved upstate, leaving their house vacant, the perfect place to call her lawyer in peace. Anya had insisted on it after the argument at camp.

They pulled up the brick drive, a stark contrast to the dirt road that it met with. As Virginia had predicted, the house was empty, with no signs of occupancy.

"We should hurry," Virginia said. "I have more than one call to make." She jumped out of the car, leaping up the three steps onto the porch and prying up the third board from the left, the one that was slightly discolored from the rest. To her relief, the key was still hidden below, encrusted with a thick layer of dust. It slid easily into the lock and the door swung open, the hinges squealing from disuse.

"Wow," Anya said in approval, lingering in the doorway. "I guess being married to Sheriff Dixon was good for something, after all."

The Dixon house was exactly the same as she remembered. The money with which the house was built had immunized it against the inevitable entropy that had touched the rest of Birch Hollow, seeping into the cracks of every other foundation in town. It wasn't marred by the weeds and vines that snaked into the concrete and wood elsewhere, slowly tearing apart that which was lovingly created.

Virginia reached out for the phone, her fingers hovering in the air, waiting for the wail of sirens or specters or both, but neither came.

"What's the matter?" Anya asked, waiting in the open doorway.

"Nothing," Virginia replied, and then added, "I don't know." She picked up the receiver, almost anticipating the line would be dead, but it wasn't.

"Sadie Sinclair, Esquire, we beat the odds for you!" a voice chirped. "How may I direct your call?"

"It's Virginia Vane."

"One moment!"

"Have you been arrested?" Sadie asked, the telltale sound

of pencil scratching against paper.

"Not yet, but I might have a problem with an alibi."

"For trespassing?"

"For murder."

Sadie sighed, and even that was elegant about her. "I thought the charge was for trespassing."

"Yeah, don't worry about that one," Virginia said. "Someone says they saw me going into the woods with someone who was later found to be murdered in those same woods."

"That is... problematic, to say the least. What is your alibi that you're having trouble with?"

"I was at home with my mother, Anya Quinn, and Jolie. I don't want to bring the two of them into it because, well, you know."

"Indeed." Sadie put the phone down for a moment, speaking to her receptionist in a muffled voice. "And your mother won't corroborate?"

"I don't know. She's not particularly known for her maternal instincts." Virginia wound and unwound the cord around her fingers, letting the tips turn purple first. "I'm not sure how worried I should be here."

"Worried." Sadie shifted on the other end of the phone. "Ms. Vane, are you still in Birch Hollow?"

"I am."

"I did recommend that you leave post-haste, but I'm afraid that leaving now may only serve to implicate you further. Have you been questioned?"

Virginia cleared her throat. "Not yet. I'm sort of... avoiding the precinct."

"That may be wise until I can confirm what your mother may or may not have said. What is a good number to reach you on?" Sadie asked. "I assume that your mother's line is no longer an option."

"I'll have to get back to you on that. In fact, I'll call you this time tomorrow. I'll find someplace."

"Very good, Ms. Vane, I hope to have some answers for you then," Sadie said. "And once this issue is dealt with, I will strongly recommend once again that you exit Moassa county entirely and lay low for a few weeks until they arrest someone for this murder."

"Understood, but it's not like I want to be here," Virginia muttered. "I have a job to do."

"Do it elsewhere. I cannot overstate how dangerous Birch Hollow is," Sadie continued. "There are forces there that you cannot even begin to fathom." A bell jingled at the other end of the line, and Sadie paused. "Good afternoon, Ms. Frost," she said. "How good to see you again. Ms. Vane, I'm afraid I have some pressing business here. I will speak with you tomorrow."

The line clicked, and Virginia breathed out an irritated sigh. Of course Astrid was in trouble again. She was always in trouble.

"Well?" Anya prompted. "What did she say?"

"I have to call her back tomorrow," Virginia explained. "And she said something about there being forces in Birch Hollow that we can't even fathom."

Anya frowned. "That sounds ominous. I still can't get that illusion spell out of my head."

"Even if it was Fae, there's not much we could do about that, is there?" Virginia asked. "The Fae died out centuries ago."

"Not in my experience," Anya said. "I've seen things that

cannot be explained by usual means. That illusion spell at the Speer house was one of the strongest I've ever seen. Masking living tissue for that long undetected would take barrels full of reagents, Virginia. I've never met a living witch who could pull off something like that."

"What if Heinrich Harrow was an especially gifted illusion witch?" Virginia asked. "With access to barrels full of reagents?"

"Do you think you could get Sheriff Dixon or Captain Lindell to check the mythics roster?" Anya asked. "It's possible he avoided detection during the Rupture, but I doubt it. Most of us didn't." She tossed Virginia a sideways glance, her eyes lingering on her scars for a moment too long. "Except you."

"Not by choice," Virginia all but growled, an unintentional but unavoidable response to any recognition of the scars that dripped down her face from hairline to cheekbone. "It was news to me, too." She hung up the phone and picked it up again in preparation to call back to Verdance. "Arthur won't be back yet. It will have to be Shirin."

"Verdance police department headquarters," she announced to the operator. The line rang three times before the receptionist picked up. "VCPD HQ," she said in a bored tone of voice.

"Captain Shirin Lindell," Virginia said. "Please."

"Sorry, her desk is occupied. You can try again later." Papers shuffled in the background.

"It's, uh..." Virginia trailed off, hoping that the receptionist still remembered her. "It's Virginia Vane."

"Ms. Vane!" the receptionist cried, scattering paperwork across her desk. "Why didn't you say so?"

"I really need to have a check run against the mythics roster," Virginia explained. "I can't get it myself."

"Let me see if I can find the Captain." The mouthpiece clattered noisily against the desk, and Virginia had to hold the receiver away from her ear to reduce the volume of the sound. Yolanda's muffled voice faded away, replaced by the bustling sounds of the VCPD bullpen.

"This is Captain Lindell."

"Shirin, it's me," Virginia said. "I need you to run a check against the mythics roster for me."

"I thought you could manage your caseload on your own, if memory serves," Shirin sniped. "And what in shadows are you doing down there? Do you have any idea how much trouble this could cause for the department?" She was almost shouting, but cleared her throat, and continued on in her usual smoked honey tone. "This isn't good, you know."

"I'm aware." Virginia bit back another snide remark. "It doesn't matter how I got into this situation." She sighed, but swallowed the heaviest parts of it, leaving out the part where she was wanted for questioning in a murder. "The name is Heinrich Harrow."

"You think he might be a mythic?" Shirin asked.

"Could be," Virginia said. Shadows from the pruned cypress trees outside danced across the hand-woven rug, creating a strange, animated interplay with the fibers. "Have you got it? We think he might be an illusion witch."

Shirin paused from rifling through the cabinet, the abrupt halt obvious and irritating over the phone. "Can't you ask Ms. Quinn that?" The way she said Anya's name was acerbic, curiously dripping with disdain. "I would imagine she knows better than a roster what the denizens of Verdance City are up to."

"She doesn't know," Virginia replied, keeping her tone vague. "That's why I'm calling."

"Well, there's no Harrows listed in the city, not under Heinrich or any other first name," Shirin retorted.

"And what about in the state?" Virginia pressed. "I don't know if he was a Verdance native or not. His niece never said one way or the other."

"Fine." Shirin unlocked another drawer, rifling through files but sharper now, and the sound of paper sliced through the phone like an invisible but painful slice against skin.

"I appreciate this," Virginia tried, unsure of why the captain's demeanor had shifted quite so quickly. "Thank you."

"Nothing to thank me for," Shirin said. "Nothing statewide, either. No Harrows."

"What about James Folst?" Virginia asked. "He was using it as an alias down here, maybe he registered with it."

"I'll look," Shirin replied. Another cabinet door screeched as she yanked it out, the metal grinding against itself. "I'm not finding anything under that name either?"

"Okay, thank you," Virginia replied, shaking her head at Anya. "We should—I should go, try to follow up on a lead or two."

"We?" Shirin prompted, her voice tight at the seams. "Who is we? Is Jo there? You should keep her away from this, Virginia, it's not safe and besides—"

"It's Anya Quinn," Virginia interrupted. "We should go. Thank you for checking for me. It's not the outcome I wanted, but at least I know." A moment of silence oozed out over the empty line, hundreds of unspoken words letting their weight be known. "I'll see you when I'm back in the city," Virginia said finally, and hung up the phone.

"No luck?" Anya asked, one hand pressed against the door frame. "He's not an illusionist?"

"Not on the roster, anyway," Virginia replied with a grumble. "Whoever he was getting that spell from must have been someone important." She cast Anya a sideways glance, reluctant to even say it out loud. "You think it's someone Fae?"

Anya tugged at the short sleeve of her dress, folding and unfolding the hem. "I don't know," she admitted.

The brightness of the Dixon house was oppressive, like sunshine in the desert. It was too perfect, too curated, aside from the dust. Picture frames hung level and perfect on the walls, the tiny woodland figurines on their shelves were perfectly lined up one after the other, undisturbed by time. "We should go," she said finally, joining Anya at the door. "As you said, it won't be long before someone comes to check up on this place in light of my manhunt."

"Any other calls we need to make?" Anya wondered aloud, still standing in the doorway and blocking her exit. "Before we leave, I mean."

"Mm," Virginia agreed, looking back at the phone. No doubt Shirin was seething, stacking up resentments a mile high. "I don't know, that depends if you have any Fae on speed dial."

"I don't," Anya reiterated, derision and enough defensiveness in her tone to make Virginia wonder more about what she did or didn't know. "I don't know any Fae, and I don't care to, thank you very much, Ms. Vane."

"The idea of the Fae is hard to swallow."

"So was the Rupture," Anya argued. "But we all accept that as fact, now."

"There was no avoiding that, Ms. Quinn, aside from a tenth of the population being marked, there were rifts that opened all over the world. When you're staring at the earth tearing itself apart, it's difficult for people to ignore." Virginia edged past her, closing the door and thrusting the lock into the deadbolt. "It was impossible for anyone to have missed that memo."

"You said that, but—"

"I say that because it's true." Virginia pointed at her scars, long since healed but still slightly shiny in the late afternoon sun. "Even I knew everything that was going on, and I didn't leave the house for months."

Anya shifted, dragging her feet through the dusty earth. "Months?" She prompted. "You didn't leave the house for months?"

"People stare."

"Ah." Anya cracked a smile, flouncing back down the steps with her usual rhythm. "I'd think you would have been used to staring by then."

"No, why would I have been?"

"You're very striking." Anya hopped into the driver's seat, adjusting the mirrors even though no one else had driven the car since she'd parked there just a few minutes previous.

Virginia barked out a laugh, something edging towards discomfort settling in her throat. "Yes, Anya, that's the scars doing that."

"I don't know about that." Anya started the car, looking over her shoulder to pull back onto the dirt road from the beautifully laid brickwork of the Dixon's driveway, flashing

Virginia a smile. "I'll drive us back to camp, and you can carry my books in."

Chapter Twenty-Eight

Virginia grumbled as her shoe met another tree root, its twisting, sinewy trunk reaching up out of the ground. She squinted into the darkness, desperately trying to make out the path and differentiate it from the dozens of deer trails that forked off into the woods, leading towards ravines, ankle-sized holes, and that damned river with the naiads.

She hefted the strap of Anya's bag over her shoulder, knowing it would be bruised the next morning. A few books, Anya had said. What she didn't mention was that those few books were each the size of several, and so Virginia was carrying the better part of a small library through the wilderness.

At least three times she'd convinced herself she was on the wrong trail and doubled back, only to do the same again when she realized she'd been right the first time. The woods looked different in the encroaching darkness, every shadow a threat, and every leafy branch an attacker lying in wait. She'd slipped her fingers through the silver knuckles the moment she passed the tree line, and they'd stayed there, even as she caught herself twice, nearly falling down to the dirt.

Swearing under her breath once more, she emerged into

the clearing, relief flooding into her chest at the sight of the white bell tent, still starkly visible in silhouette. She lit the lantern first, flooding a perfect circle around it with yellow flickering light and tossing the spent match into the fire pit.

Anya hadn't left her with the lighter, but had given her a piece of flint, probably useless compared to a matchbook but Virginia was out of options. She smacked the flint against a rock, sending a shower of sparks down onto the tinder, where they died as instantly as they were created.

"Shadows be damned," Virginia growled, throwing the flint aside and sitting back on her haunches. "Literally," she said aloud, almost raising her voice at the trees at the edge of camp as their shadows twisted towards her, only cut short by the glow of the lantern. She checked her pockets once more for matches, finding none, and begrudgingly picked up the flint again.

She struck the flint again, harder this time. One hit, two, five, each one more forceful until she was throwing all of her weight behind the flint, squeezing her eyes shut against the inevitable shards that were sent flying from the repeated impacts. Finally, crucially, the tinder was set alight, catching the kindling first, and then the logs perched above.

Virginia sat back to admire her work, smirking at the fire as though she'd bested it in a sparring match.

The fire grew, but it would still be close to an hour before the coals were ready, and besides, Anya wasn't back with the supplies yet. Virginia swept the tent flap aside, taking the lantern with her. She sat on the floor, taking each book out of the bag one at a time. There was one on advanced illusion magic, one on the history of the Fae with a cracked green leather spine, and curiously, one on the physiology of seers.

The book was large and heavy, the cover black canvas with a gold embossed eye in the center. It had lost its dust cover, leaving only the fabric, the corners dented from use. The pages on the edges were painted black to match the cover, matte and almost tacky.

Virginia skimmed over the vague table of contents, the abbreviations and chapter headings written with florid prose not meaning much to her. She was new to things, after all, but being so out of her depth rankled.

She flipped through the first chapter, rife with diagrams and charts that didn't interest her much. Whatever it was in her head that made her what she was, she didn't care. It didn't matter what the biology of it was, only that it *was*, and that as a result she was saddled with something she'd never wanted in the first place. An upsettingly detailed and technical drawing of a bisected brain graced the tenth page, and she decided she didn't want to know whose it was or how it got there.

After the Rupture, plenty of mythics went missing, and in the chaos, most of those cases never got solved. No one cared if monsters were used as experiments.

As she skimmed the book, most of it seemed like horsehit to her. Meditations on focus had never done her good, not that she'd ever managed to meditate in the first place. There were a few recipes for poultices and teas that had been crossed out in pen, no doubt by someone who'd realized they didn't work.

There were notes in the margins about neurotransmitters, whatever those were, and how they impacted a seer's sight in accuracy and adaptability. Another chapter on the electrical signals that a seer's brain emitted during a vision, but nothing that would help her access what she needed. Virginia flipped forward several more pages, and then a chapter, and then found herself on the last page, where a note was scrawled in handwriting that didn't look like Anya's.

Under no circumstances should a seer undertake the use of Nether to access sight. The results are both unpredictable and unstable, and the brief power is never worth the risk.

The book didn't look old enough to be her aunt's, so perhaps it was a second-hand copy from somewhere else. She lifted the book closer to her face, trying to examine the tome. There was something rattling in the spine.

Virginia felt around the edges of the fabric binding until she found the loose stitches, pulling free a vial, the sparkling violet liquid drinking up the glow from the lantern and radiating it back out, albeit with more of a shimmer than the tent had before. *Nether.* What was Anya doing with Nether? She had insisted she didn't deal in that stuff.

She'd never tried it before, having seen what the addiction did to mythics on and off the streets. It was a potent drug, and an expensive one, the short shelf-life adding to the complexities of trading it for goods or for cash. Virginia swirled the tiny glass tube, the fire outside reflecting back at itself, unable to penetrate the drug. It was strangely dense, which was part of the danger of it. The body couldn't process it fast enough, and some people didn't care about their internal organs enough to stop for good.

It probably wouldn't take much to spur a vision, only a drop or two. She wasn't a regular user, and so had no tolerance.

No.

She went to nestle it back into the book, and lay the book back in the bag like she'd never seen it in the first place.

Sliding the book back into the heavy canvas sack, her fingers brushed against something else, something cool and smooth. Something ceramic. Pulling it out, she held the small giraffe in the palm of her hand, the same one that had informed her likely incorrect theory.

If that ugly ceramic giraffe held a memory, held something for her sight to see, it could solve the case in a few moments flat. She could figure out who Harrow's real murderer was and work backwards from there, finding the evidence she needed to solve the case, which could lead to the culprit for Melody Kingston's death, too.

The three of them could be on their way out of town in twenty-four hours, if only she knew where to look.

The coast would be peaceful. The coast would be nothing but sun and salty sea breezes, Jolie swimming in the waves with Anya while Virginia watched from the shore, and fresh blue crab dinners, and waiting out the feds back in Verdance. It would mean getting away from Virginia's mother, and Eugene Carsh, and the Dixon house, and the terrible, gut-wrenching memories of Juliette.

Virginia rolled the vial in one palm, holding the giraffe in the other, weighing up the cost of justice, the value of escape, and the price of peace.

She'd only use a little bit. One drop wouldn't be bad, not when bartenders at the Sphinx were serving up half-vials of the stuff with every other cocktail they passed across the polished marble.

The vial's cork was stuck tight in the glass, and Virginia had to pry it out, her fingertips slipping three times before it came loose. The liquid within glistened in the firelight, tempting with its promise of freedom suspended in the glitter. She pressed it to her lips, letting one drop drip across her tongue. She held the giraffe tight in her fist, waiting for a vision to overtake her.

She waited several long minutes, but nothing happened. There was no flash of light, no pain, no memories, and no sight. Virginia growled under her breath, irritated that her risk hadn't paid off. She tried for a second time, this time letting three or maybe even four spheres of Nether caress her tongue with a delicate sizzle that faded as fast as it had been felt.

Virginia closed her eyes, breathing deep the scent of burning firewood and the slight mildew of the tent's canvas. The ceramic giraffe bit into her palm, leaving a pleasant pressure.

Visions eluded her, leaving her with nothing more than darkness behind her eyelids and failure nesting at the base of her spine. Perhaps everything that had happened with Fiske had been a fluke, an accident of happenstance. Perhaps she was nothing special at all, nothing more than one more washed-up and disgraced private investigator.

Outside, the campfire blazed, crackling as wood was turned to ash, the shifting of the charcoal a strangely comfortable companion in the bleak, black loneliness of the woods. She shouldn't use more, not when she didn't know what it would do to her.

And yet.

Three more purple droplets laid against her bottom lip for just a second, lapped up by her tongue, still waiting for whatever it was she was waiting for. Visions. Power. Stability.

Love.

The final thought jarred her more than the rest of it, but she pushed it from her mind, cursing aloud at her own stupidity.

"Come on," she grumbled, squeezing the giraffe harder. The ceramic fractured in her fingers, the hairline crack barely visible but running across its neck down the spine of it. "Work, damn it."

She lifted the vial to her mouth once more, but she needn't have.

A rush of warmth spilled over her, and for an instant she felt safe, encapsulated in the unfamiliar peace of her own mind. The humidity faded away along with everything else, dulling the unpleasant sensations of sentience.

In a split second that felt like an eternity, she saw everything the ceramic had to offer in static snapshots that were slightly blurred at the edges. Heinrich Harrow in silhouette, standing at the window. He was smirking, waving his hand at someone, dismissing them. In the next fraction of a moment, he was gone. When he reappeared, he was lying on the ground in the Speer house, eyes wide in surprise, blood pooling against the waxed pine.

Virginia turned, expecting to find herself face to face with his killer, but there was no one there. It was nothing more than an empty house.

"He deserved what he got," a voice said, distorted by the vision. "Everyone who deserves their fate indeed finds it, sooner rather than later."

Gasping for breath, Virginia clawed at the floor of the Speer's home, trying to drag herself back to reality. She blinked, trying to clear the vision, but she was trapped in the home, staring out the front window, unable to move. Time shifted, speeding through years, only told through the rapid growth of trees outside.

Juliette, stealing strawberries as she laughed in the sunlight. Virginia at her side, holding her hand as they ran from their pursuer, Mr. Speer with a large broom. Juliette, alone this time, gathering raspberries in a basket. Virginia remembered that day. They'd eaten them in the shed they shared, a pauper's picnic in the twilight. Juliette, staring through the window as if she could see Virginia watching there.

Searing pain exploded across Virginia's forehead, shooting from one temple to the other. She groaned, pressing her palms flat against the wood and digging her nails into the soft pine.

Regret rose up in her, thick as winter sap, strangling in her throat. Juliette. Juliette. Juliette.

Chapter Twenty-Nine

Virginia was still heaving up bile in the bushes when Anya returned, crunching through the underbrush with careful practiced steps. "Hey," Virginia said, adjusting the lapels of her shirt with shaking hands. She was struggling to hold grip of the present, the drug in her system continually trying to drag her back into the past, long after she'd crammed the giraffe back into the bag. "Did you get anything good?"

"I brought some supplies, yes," Anya replied, not really answering the question she'd been asked. She cast a wary eye over Virginia, pausing from unloading the hemp satchel. "Are you alright?"

"I'm fine, why do you ask?" Virginia gripped the bark of a nearby tree trunk with white knuckles, praying to the rift Anya wouldn't notice in the darkness. "Just tired from dragging all your shit through the wilderness."

"I would have thought a woman who spars with a werewolf twice a week would handle a short hike just fine." Anya laid another log on the fire, positioning a large pan above the flames and pouring several glugs of oil into it, waiting for it to begin sizzling. "They didn't have any chicken, and they were about to close. I took what they had."

"And what did they have?"

"Catfish." Anya untied a brown paper parcel, winding up the twine to save it. She gutted the fish with alarming expertise, filleting the meat from the bones with precision. "What did you get up to while I was gone?"

"Not much," Virginia lied, hesitant with the truth even if it had solved her problems. "The fire took a while to get started."

"Mm," Anya murmured, chopping three potatoes into small chunks and dropping them into the pan alongside the fish, seasoning all of it with granules from a small pouch.

"What's that?" Virginia asked, gesturing, the small action almost sending her to the ground with dizziness.

"Salt and pepper." Anya glanced at her again, but didn't say anything. She moved the food around in the pan, shifting it from side to side with the edge of a wooden spoon. "Coffee?" she asked.

"It's late."

"You seem like you need it." Without waiting for a reply, Anya filled the percolator with fresh water and hung it over the fire, dumping ground coffee beans into it from a small fabric bag.

The truth loomed too closely, cresting at the edges of her perception. Virginia cleared her throat, lowering herself onto the stump across from Anya. "I guess I'm just tired. I had a vision while you were getting supplies."

Anya raised an eyebrow. "Oh?" she prompted.

The scent of seared fish filled the campsite, drawing a greedy growl from Virginia's stomach. "From the giraffe you stole from the Speer place," she explained.

"And?"

"There was a voice," Virginia continued, trying to catch her reflection in the bucket of water next to the fire, hunting for any hint of a purple tinge at her eyes. There wouldn't be one, of course not. She hadn't had enough for that to happen. "It said *he deserved what he got.*"

Anya's breath caught in her throat, and she coughed lightly before returning to the food she was preparing. "Did you recognize it?"

Virginia shook her head. "No. It was distorted, I couldn't have." She exhaled slowly, searching for clarity in the tree bark lodging itself painfully beneath her fingernails as she dug into the tree stump. "I don't know, I can't explain it. Harrow was already dead."

"Not all visions are reliable," Anya said carefully. "There's a book in the bag I gave you, it might—" she cut herself off, standing up. "I'll get it for you, just watch the food. Don't let it burn."

Virginia shrugged, not wanting to admit she'd already seen it. After the vision, she'd placed the vial back into the recess in the spine, the cork pushed in tight and the vial looking imperceptibly less full. She wasn't interested in another discussion about self-preservation with Anya Quinn. "I won't let it burn," she replied, poking at the fish with the wooden spoon.

Anya was only gone for a moment, dropping the book into Virginia's lap as she passed, taking back the wooden spoon. "There," she said, throwing off a casual gesture. "Some light reading."

"Thanks." Virginia thumbed through pages she'd already skimmed and dismissed, ignoring the one with the warning against using Nether entirely. As her vision began to clear, and reality sat heavy in her chest, the food was warm in her mouth but tasteless, any joy or pleasure stolen by her burnt taste buds. "So what now?"

"You tell me, Detective," Anya said, chewing a forkful of food. "I'm not the investigator here." She wrapped up the remaining fish, tucking in the ends of the brown paper to secure it. "I'll head back to the river in the morning." The stars peeked through thin clouds, glimmering faintly against the blackened backdrop. "Do you think your mother will corroborate your alibi?"

"No," Virginia said, swallowing the last of the food. Her stomach yearned for more, so she chased it with a swig from her flask, savoring the unpleasant taste of warm gin, the piney juniper almost stale at that temperature. "Part of me hopes that she doesn't. That's not a debt I'd want to repay. My mother is worse than the Fae in that regard." She tugged the pack of cigarettes from her breast pocket and lit one, taking three tries in the stagnant humidity. "But on the other hand, there's potentially prison, unless they find a better lead for the Melody Kingston murder." She inhaled, letting the smoke numb the persistent hunger in her belly.

Anya nodded, settling herself back on the tree stump and crossing her legs under her skirts. She glanced across the fire, head tilted. "When was the first time you had a vision?"

"I don't know, six months ago?" Virginia mused, averting her eyes to stare up at the celestial sparks instead. "During Benjamin's case, at his sibling's apartment."

"Are you sure?"

"What do you mean, *am I sure*? Of course I'm sure." Inhaling once more, Virginia stole a glance at Anya, who was still staring intently. "I think I would remember that."

"Perhaps, or perhaps not." Anya gestured at the book, looking rather wary at its proximity to ashes from the cigarette. "Some seers don't have visions until later in life. It's been documented."

"Or I'm not a seer at all," Virginia countered. "Maybe I'm just crazy."

Anya smirked, her skin glowing like embers in the light. "No one said you weren't."

Virginia rolled her eyes up to the sky, grateful for the familiar presence of the cigarette between her fingers. "Very funny," she grumbled, willing the constellations to unknot themselves in her blurred vision.

Virginia turned her face away from the light, staring off into the night just beyond the trees, a deep, inky blackness that was all but impenetrable that far out into nothingness.

Chapter Thirty

Virginia barely slept that night, haunted by the ghosts of seasonal visions rasping at the edges of her consciousness. Deer, crunching against autumn leaves. Snowdrops pushing through the final frost of winter. Footsteps against wet, dewy grass, and boots that she recognized as Anya's. Everything she touched dragged forth a weak sight, and it took her hours to figure out how to grasp reality in her fist once more. Dawn was peeking over the horizon, the first hints of pink clouds and the purple tinges beneath them beginning to light the sky when she finally dropped off.

If nothing else, her insomnia kept her from throwing an arm around Anya again. She'd take the deep exhaustion wrought by a lack of sleep over such piercing embarrassment any day, without question.

She'd slept maybe three or four hours when Anya stood up in the tent and stretched her arms over her head, the demure pale blue shift she wore pulling itself up above her knees. Virginia squeezed her eyes shut, trying not to see, and willing herself to forget.

"I know you're awake," Anya said through a yawn. "I heard your breathing change."

"Don't notice that," Virginia grumbled in response. "I didn't sleep well."

Anya tugged a fresh dress on over her head, this one a deep teal and belted at the waist with a line of buttons up the front. "I have some Valerian root in my pouch, that should help you for later."

"I don't know how keen I am on spending another night out here." Virginia sat up, pressing a hand against the small of her back. "These wood planks are murder."

"Murder is why you're out here, Ms. Vane," Anya chirped, throwing back the tent flap and stepping outside to secure it. "Well, that, and the very tense relationship with your mother. Breakfast?"

"Not hungry," Virginia replied, even as her stomach growled angrily. She was loathe to eat anything else after the catfish had roiled in her gut all night long, along with the half flask of gin she'd used to try drowning the discomfort and to send her to sleep. Unfortunately, it hadn't done either. She frowned at her shirt, stained from the previous day and torn at the elbow and cuff where she'd trekked through the woods at dusk. The thought of putting it back on itched at the back of her skull, so she didn't, tucking her white undershirt into her trousers. "But thanks."

"Toast?" Anya called.

"I said no," Virginia grumbled under her breath, irritated at Anya's pushing, always pushing her in one direction or another with her offers to help or quiet disdain.

"I wasn't asking you," Anya retorted with more cheer than should be allowed that early in the morning. "I think Jo just got here, she's just past the tree line. I heard the twigs snap." The flint striker echoed out over the clearing, once, twice, three times before the tinder caught, snapping sparks against the kindling. "Oh. Hello, Captain Lindell."

Virginia didn't even lace her shoes, stumbling out of the tent with one hand dragging her hair back into a low bun, the other catching her against the support post. "Shirin," she said, wondering if she was still asleep and dreaming. "What are you doing here?"

There she stood, impeccable in a freshly pressed uniform, cap tucked under her arm. She raised an eyebrow at Virginia, mouth set into a firm line. "I could ask you the same thing."

"I'm on a case," Virginia answered.

"Yes, I'm aware of that, my question is more pertaining to—" she shook her head and breathed out, nodding towards Jolie. "Ms. Laar brought you fresh clothes from your mother's house."

Virginia took the parcel of clothing from Jolie, the rest of her things stuffed into a paper grocery bag. "Thanks, kid," she muttered, but meant it. "I hope my mother isn't being too much of a nuisance."

"She keeps to herself mostly," Jolie replied, her face twisted into an unreadable expression.

"That sounds like her," Virginia said. "Do you know if she left to talk to Carsh?"

Jolie shook her head. "No."

"Virginia," Shirin interrupted, refusing the mug of coffee Anya had just offered her. "You need to get this sorted out. What's this I'm hearing about a witness seeing you wander into the woods with the victim the same night she turned up dead?"

"Wrong place, wrong time."

Shirin snorted a derisive laugh. "That seems to happen

to you an awful lot lately." Her eyes raked over Anya, brow furrowed to creasing.

"What are you doing down here anyway? Don't you have work up in Verdance? I can't imagine it's a very good idea to have the sheriff and the deputy fucking around downstate at the same time." Virginia ducked into the tent, tugging on a fresh undershirt and button-up, grateful for the crisp, starched cotton, smooth against her skin.

"The feds have taken over that investigation entirely. I don't even have a desk at present," Shirin muttered. "Besides, Sheriff Dixon is headed back north for the time being. I couldn't fend his wife off any longer, she was about to start a federal investigation of her own."

Virginia tucked both shirts into her trousers, wishing there was a mirror, and grateful there wasn't one. "Unsurprising," she said, emerging from the tent once more and taking coffee from Jolie. "Thanks," she said, taking a seat on the stump.

"Do you even have a plan? Or a lead? Anything?" Shirin demanded. She sucked her teeth, still refusing to sit, choosing instead to lean against a birch tree, the stripes of the bark a complement to her uniform. "You just need to find who did it."

"Thank you, Captain," Virginia said with a roll of her eyes. "I did manage to work out that much." She sipped at the coffee, the bitter liquid dragging her from the rest of her stupor. "I don't know if you know this, but that's easier said than done in most cases."

"You don't have the luxury of time," Shirin said, tone plain and flat but earnest. "So get it done so you can get the shadows-damned hell out of here. I almost blew a tire on my way down, and people out here look at me like I've got two heads." She begrudgingly took coffee from Jolie, but remained standing. "This place is hardly safer than Verdance."

"Arthur thought coming down here would be a good idea. I didn't agree, but here I am, regardless."

Shirin nodded, sipping at the coffee. "This is about as rural as it gets."

"Unfamiliar with the rustic trappings of the countryside?" Virginia asked, needling her.

"No."

Jolie coughed, breaking the awkward tension. She reached into the pan, grabbing the toast with no respect for the sizzling oil at all. "Thanks, Anya," she said, crunching into the first piece.

"Sure thing." Anya tossed two more slices of bread into the pan with a drizzle of oil and two eggs. "Jo?" she asked, nodding at the pan.

"Please," Jolie replied. "Over-easy."

Shirin rubbed her hands against her knees, having deposited the empty mug on a stone surrounding the fire pit. "You've got quite the operation out here, Ms. Quinn. How did you find out about this place?"

"I've known about it for years," Anya replied simply. She shuffled an egg onto Jolie's plate, where the yolk broke over the bread, the orangey yellow liquid like gold in the morning sunlight. "Virginia, have you changed your mind about breakfast?"

"Toast," Virginia agreed, sensing there would be an argument if she didn't. "Thank you." She took the lightly crisped bread and bit into a slice, irritated at how her mouth watered the second it passed her lips.

"Since when do you eat breakfast?" Shirin asked with a laugh, shining the badge on her arm.

"Since now," Virginia shot back. "Don't you have something you need to be doing? I don't need a nanny, I'm perfectly capable on my own, thank you."

"Yes, so capable that you've yet to solve the case you came down here for, and you're on the verge of being implicated in another." Shirin raised an eyebrow in challenge, standing up to assert her height and broad frame once more. "Seems like maybe you do need supervision."

Virginia brushed the toast crumbs into the fire, watching as each one flared and disappeared into the ashes. "Go back to the city, Captain Lindell."

Shirin shifted in the loose dirt, kicking up a delicate cloud of dust that settled on her patent leather brogues. "I think I should stay here until the sheriff recalls me," she protested. She flicked an irritated glance at Anya, who was busying herself with her herbalist pouch, sorting through some of the worms they'd collected. "I know you didn't kill that woman."

"Thanks for the vote of confidence, Captain," Virginia replied.

"Where did you call the precinct from?"

"Arthur's parents'. They don't live there anymore, but the line still works."

Shirin scowled, tugging her cap on over her head as the sun rose high enough in the sky to cascade down through the branches, shooting sunbeams directly into her eyes even as they bounced off the dark wavy locks tucked behind her ears. "That was a risk," she chided. "Something like that would make you look guilty, and you know you'd think the same from the outside of this situation. And what about me?

You think that the feds would look kindly on a police captain assisting someone who may or may not be a suspect in an ongoing murder investigation?"

"It's not as if we had many options, you know," Anya interjected, keeping her stare fixed on the pouch. "It's all well and good to swan down here with your badge and your squad unit, which I hope you stashed somewhere, by the way, seeing as we're discussing risk, but it's a far sight different dealing with things on a daily basis."

"Your presence isn't needed here, Quinn, is it?" Shirin sniped. "From what I can tell, all you've done is make things more complicated."

"Lindell," Virginia warned, grabbing her by the elbow and dragging her off towards the tree line, "enough." It was the most proximity they'd had in months, and the charge of it was still there, but polarized in another direction, like two magnets that had begun to repel instead of attract. "Anya has already saved my ass down here," she said, setting her hands on her hips once they were far enough from camp that their voices wouldn't carry. "Don't antagonize her."

"Is that what this is, then?" Shirin asked. "I show up and you're climbing out of a tent half-naked?"

"I wasn't, but even if I was, it's hardly any of your business."

Shirin reached out, brushing a thumb over the line of Virginia's chin. "Isn't it?"

"We've barely spoken in months," Virginia challenged, but didn't stop her. The polarities were shifting again, and she hated herself for it.

"Only because you won't return my calls, and run from a crime scene if you so much as suspect I might be there,"

Shirin said softly. "I thought we had a nice time together, Virginia."

"I didn't want Arthur to find out that I was fucking his deputy sheriff," Virginia retorted, and meant for her tone to be sharp, but that's not how it came out. "Things are complicated enough without adding that, too."

"What's complicated?" Shirin asked. "We aren't coworkers, although that clearly never stopped you before. According to payroll, you're a contractor. There's nothing unethical, nothing to worry—"

Virginia pulled back, shaking her head because maybe it would rattle something loose in her brain that would allow her to return to her senses. "It's not about ethics, Shirin. I don't want every detail of my life to be public or common knowledge."

"Why would it be?"

"You haven't been around long enough to hear how people talk." Virginia rolled her sleeves halfway up her forearms, sweat from the humid air already collecting on her skin. "Besides, we basically hate each other. All we do is argue."

"That's what makes it fun, no?" Shirin asked, her strange accent a little thicker than usual. She sounded as if she'd lived two dozen different places, and perhaps she had, picking up little linguistic tics in every new locale. Her honey-gold eyes sparkled in the light that filtered down through the canopy, her cheekbones prominent and cutting with shadows. "Sheriff Dixon didn't tell me to come down here, you know. I came because I wanted to help you."

"Help me get arrested maybe," Virginia grumbled. She swatted at an errant mosquito as it buzzed near her face, dreading the number of bites she'd probably earned during her sleepless night. Itchy little bastards loved the horrible Birch Hollow summers, breeding in every stagnant puddle that collected in the verges along the highway. "Go home, Shirin."

"Do you even have a lead?"

"It's in progress." Virginia leaned against a thick tree, already knowing what she was setting herself up for, but there was something within her that she couldn't really deny. It was an odd instinct, whichever one it was that always led her to the same shadows-damned conclusions.

"Who is it? Mayor of the town, or something?" Shirin asked, advancing on her with a calculated lean forward through the brush, somehow keeping her uniform free from snags.

"No, not the mayor," Virginia said. "I don't think anyone has seen him for a couple of years, anyway. Not much to be mayor of. He lives up the highway, past exit forty-two, right at the town limits. Big house up on a hill. Strange guy, collects old atlases."

Shirin pressed a palm against the tree bark, moving in closer. "What's the lead, Ms. Vane?"

"I need you to do something for me."

"Oh?"

Virginia looked up at her, trying to keep her stare steely. "I need you to find out if the feds are starting to investigate those murders as if they were connected," she said.

"Why?"

"I have a theory."

"Which is?"

"Classified," Virginia replied.

Shirin pressed herself against Virginia, hands running over

her hips and catching at the empty belt loops. "You don't always have to make it so difficult, you know."

"I thought you said that was part of the fun."

"Hmm," Shirin growled, and then kissed her full on the mouth, drawing a light gasp from Virginia's lips that she hadn't meant to let escape. She tasted like fresh coffee, with an unidentifiable sweetness that lingered on her tongue. "The theory, Virginia," she repeated, pulling back, but only just. "Tell me what it is."

"The homicides up there and down here might be connected," Virginia answered. "Arthur knows."

"The sooner you can clear your name, the sooner we..." Shirin trailed off, but caught Virginia's jaw between her thumb and forefinger, drawing her back. "Or are you happy here with Anya Quinn?"

"It's not like that," Virginia replied, resisting another kiss. She ducked beneath Lindell's arm, freeing herself. "Go back to Verdance. There are enough complications here without this, too."

Chapter Thirty-One

Anya returned to the camp from her journey to town with a wide smile and her arms thrown wide. "Your lawyer says you're in the clear," she announced.

"My mother supported my alibi?"

"She must have, because your lawyer called the precinct, and you are no longer a person of interest."

"Wonders may never cease." Virginia groaned, knowing that her mother's loyalty always came with a price. She stood to hang her river-washed clothes on a makeshift line. In that humidity, everything always felt a little bit damp. "Anything else from town?"

"No," Anya replied. "But now that you're a free woman, we should get out of here. I don't like Jo staying with your mother. She's not saying it, but I know she's not happy there."

"I don't want her there any more than you do, trust me," Virginia replied, grumbling under her breath. "And we'll leave when the job is done."

"But the feds—"

"Were more than happy to look in my direction once. I don't want to give them the chance to decide my mother's affidavit isn't worth the paper it's printed on. Family corroborations always get looked at twice in unsolved cases."

Anya frowned, adjusting the laundry on the line so that the seams lined up at the edges. "I don't think it's a good idea to stay out here, even if there's a chance someone is looking for Jolie up in Verdance. Surely she's safer there, rather than—"

"She was kidnapped in the city before, or don't you remember?" Virginia snapped. "Those crew murders are going to dredge up more scum who would be more than happy to accept a reduced sentence for leading the feds to an unregistered fire demon."

"I would have thought you were desperate to get out of Birch Hollow," Anya retorted. "Between your mother and the murders, I'm starting to think you like the frustration of all of this."

Virginia bristled at the accusation. She couldn't really blame Anya for not understanding the strength not just of the vision of Juliette, but the gravitational pull of her disappearance. Maybe if she could truly close that chapter of her life, things would be different. Maybe it would quiet the voice loud in her mind of her incompetence and inadequacy, maybe it would mend the wound of her lost first love and the aftermath of a botched case.

"I don't have much of an affinity for camping, you know. I'd rather be sleeping in my own bed, not on a pile of mossy boards in the middle of the woods, rinsing my shirts in naiad-infested water," Virginia said. What she didn't say was that she wasn't sure she could bear leaving Birch Hollow without answers about Juliette's disappearance again. It had nearly killed her the first time.

"You have to admit, they're much more docile when

they're fed." Anya shook a small blue vial at her, the cork firmly in place. "And I'll have enough of this to last me at least a year and a half once we're out of here. A good thing, too. They're becoming rarer and rarer, even in rural areas."

Virginia rolled her eyes. "Docile, sure. They only half looked like they wanted to feast on my flesh when I was down there this morning. I'm sure given the opportunity, they'd drag me under and have me for dinner."

"Waste not, want not," Anya retorted with a smirk. "Can you even blame them?"

"Yes, actually, I can." Virginia flung the final shirt over the line, tying the sleeves to keep it from falling into the mud that had collected at the edges of camp, the result of damp boot treads and thick dew. "Maybe it would be okay to have Jolie out here with us."

Anya nodded and scribbled something into the pages of her leather–bound notebook, frowning at the shavings gathered in the crack of the spine. "Good idea." She glanced up at Virginia, pencil still poised in her hand. "Captain Lindell was in town again this morning."

"And?"

"And I thought you told her to go back to Verdance."

Virginia heaved out a sigh, again wondering why it was her responsibility to keep everyone else on the straight and narrow. "I did," she replied. "But Captain Lindell doesn't seem to be one for following orders."

"Not when it comes to you, anyway." Anya returned to her notebook, drawing out what looked like a complex formula.

"What is that supposed to mean?" Virginia demanded, but then added, "What are you working on?"

"A spell, maybe, if I can figure out the amounts." Anya

growled in frustration, the sound small and demure in her throat. "It's not always easy to accurately measure reagents, and I don't want to waste the rare ones."

"You've been scribbling in that book for days, maybe you should take a break and go for a walk or something." Virginia gestured towards the odd trail that led up to the cliffs that didn't exist. "It wasn't so bad up there."

"You go, I'd rather work on this," Anya said. She leaned forward, jostling the coffee pot hanging over the grate. "Besides, I haven't had any coffee yet. I need at least two to function."

"You had coffee this morning," Virginia challenged. "So much for your stellar memory."

"I haven't had *any* this afternoon," Anya deflected. "And I'd have thought you'd jump at the chance to imbibe some more caffeine."

Virginia paced the length of the camp, aware that her steps were already wearing a weak trail into the dirt as she retraced her steps over and over again. "Fine," she relented, reaching into the tent for the grinder and dumping more beans into the hopper, twisting the crank that squeaked just enough to draw an irritated glance from Anya. "Don't give me that look, you're the one who wanted coffee."

"Sorry." Anya hissed out a sigh, slapping the cover shut. "I've never been very good at spell development."

"I don't know, that banshee was pretty impressive. Saved our asses, anyway." The handle crunched against the gear, depositing more ground coffee into the receptacle. "I think you're selling yourself short, Quinn."

"That was my aunt's spell. She was incredibly adept at spell creation, she was renowned in this part of the country.

She wrote a few books, actually." Anya traced an embossed symbol on the cover, the tip of her finger following along the groove in the black leather. "I never quite got the hang of it."

"What kind of spell are you working on?" Virginia asked. Despite the Rupture happening years before, she hadn't worked closely with many witches. Most of them preferred their solitude, and given conscription laws, she didn't blame them. "Healing?"

Anya tucked the notebook back into her satchel and cinched it shut, taking the hopper of ground beans from Virginia and dumping them into the pot. "No," she said simply. "I'll tell you if I manage to figure it out."

"It's not like you to be so cagey."

"I learned from the best."

Virginia huffed out a reluctant laugh, the answer being both unexpected but irritatingly true. "I'm not cagey," she replied. "I'm private."

"Same difference," Anya replied, filling the pot with fresh water. She let the space between them hang, filled only with the lazy chirp of a cricket somewhere near the edge of camp and the noisy chatter of sparrows littered in the trees. They started their dawn chorus long before pink grazed the horizon, and carried on past twilight. It was their season and they knew it, gloating to anyone unfortunate enough to hear their mocking chirps. The water boiled in the pot, and she filtered it through a fine sieve into their two metal mugs.

"Thanks," Virginia said, internally lamenting the lack of milk. She added an extra cube of sugar for good measure, trying her best to cut the bitterness. As much as she'd become reliant on caffeine, she preferred it milky and sweet. "You know, my car is probably ready to be collected," she mused.

What Stu said about Juliette's disappearance still roiled in her mind, digging up resentments she thought she'd long since buried. The pull to solve her case for good, to find peace for Juliette, was so much stronger in Birch Hollow that it felt like she was suffocating. The only way to breathe was to keep looking for the truth.

"If she said a week, you have a few days to go," Anya replied with a laugh. "But my bet is that you want to ask why she said you were walking into the woods with that woman."

Virginia nodded. "That wouldn't hurt." She sipped at the coffee, wincing at the taste. "And it would be good to see her dad again. I think he knows more than he's letting on."

"About Harrow, or Melody Kingston?"

Virginia didn't answer, not wanting to admit her renewed drive to find justice for Juliette. "It would be good to get back up there, regardless. He's a town historian, maybe he knows something about this illusion magic. Maybe they've seen it before."

"Mm," Anya murmured, still lifting her face to the sunlight as it filtered down through the abundant foliage. "If Harrow was getting that magic from the Fae, they would have had a contract. They love their contracts, you know. Rules and loopholes form most of their society, at least as far as the writings suggest." She ran a finger around the rim of the mug, slowly dragging it through beads of condensation that gathered on the lip. "My aunt had some dealings with the Fae when she was young."

"You left out that particular detail," Virginia accused, sitting forward on the tree stump. "What kind of dealings?"

"She wanted some rare reagents for a spell, the kind that only the Fae could provide." Anya shrugged casually, opening her eyes one at a time as she bent her head back down to earth. "Spent the rest of her life paying off that debt. It's why she was never able to really turn Moonshadow Apothecary into something sustainable." She drained the remainder of the pot into her empty mug, refilling it until it sloshed over the sides, dripping down into the parched earth where the moisture soaked into the cracks wrought by the heat of the nightly campfires. "The reagents worked, though."

"What were they for?"

Anya inhaled, holding the air in her lungs a long moment before she spoke. "Severing spells. She didn't charge for them, either. Plenty of women coming through her door with bruises, you know, desperate to be rid of whatever cursed idea of love they were in the grips of."

"I assume she used it for herself first," Virginia said quietly.

"She did, yes."

"What were the reagents?"

"Oh, you know," Anya said, waving a hand in the air and sending another wave of coffee into the dirt from the motion, "a little of this, a little of that. Things only the Fae can get a hold of. I can make severing spells now, but they aren't nearly as potent, nor as permanent. It will last a few days, maybe a week at best, and in many cases that isn't long enough."

Virginia nodded, having seen enough of that over the years, and not just in her time with the VCPD. "I've turned away more than a few rats looking for their missing wives," she said. "I could always tell the ones who were up to no good."

"Visions?" Anya asked.

"No," Virginia responded. She sipped at the coffee, the

taste more palatable with the gathered, undissolved sugar at the bottom of the mug. "They always gave those cases to me when I was still on the force."

"Because you're a woman?"

"Because the women asked for me," Virginia said. "Word got around." She shifted her shoes in the dust, kicking up a cloud that quickly settled back to the earth. "Arthur was really the only one of the men who took it seriously enough. The rest waved it away, sent the men home after a night in a cell." She sighed and set the mug on the stones around the fire. "Arthur got the women out, found them halfway houses out of town, and got them what they needed to start over. It wasn't much, but it was better than the alternative."

The lone cricket chirped again before it ceased its strange song, allowing the sparrows to take the melody of the forest. "I grew up witnessing it," Anya said softly. "It's one of the reasons I decided to follow in her footsteps, seeing how those severing spells changed so many lives. Dozens, probably. Most of them would show up six months later, bright and rosy, a spring in their steps, giving my aunt whatever they could spare as a thank you. It was never much, but their joy was reward enough for her." She grimaced, forehead creased. "I just hate that I can't get more of the stuff without selling my soul to the Fae. Truth be told, Virginia, I wouldn't even know where to start even if it was a sacrifice I was willing to make. My aunt died indebted to four banks and who knows who else without so much as two pennies to rub together. I just don't know if that's something I can sign up for."

"What were the reagents?" Virginia asked, and sensing Anya's hesitation, held her hands up in surrender. "You don't have to tell me."

"My aunt never kept them out in the open," Anya said. "She knew that a raid was a possibility, especially after the Rupture. Once those rifts opened, all bets were off. You remember."

Virginia nodded and poked at the fire with a long stick, letting the end of it catch on fire and burn up the length a little before stubbing it out in the ashes. "People wanted normal back, they wanted to scrape any trace of magic and mythics off the face of the earth."

"She kept them in her apartment, the one above the shop. Warrants don't usually extend up there because the police don't think about the difference in dwelling." Anya cleared her throat and bit her lip, stealing a cautious glance at Virginia. "I hope you won't share that with your paramour."

"She's not my paramour."

"I mean it, Virginia."

"Alright," Virginia relented. "I hear you. My lips are sealed. I didn't mean for that to happen last time, you know. The VCPD had me backed into a corner." She snapped the stick into three parts and tossed all of them into the flames, savoring the sharp cracks as the moisture within burst forth from the bark. "I won't let that happen again."

"A severing spell requires a balance of reagents," Anya explained. "More powerful spells call for more powerful reagents, and unfortunately in this case, the most impactful ones are very difficult to source. There is a particular sap from a tree that can't be found on our plane of reality. That sap, mixed with a specific root tuber that also can't be found here, along with four other ingredients that can, creates a powerful severing spell."

"Sap," Virginia repeated.

"Yes, from a tree that looks much like our birch, but shot through with platinum. Our birch trees have a sweetwater sap that can be tapped in the spring. Fae birch is thicker, and far more magically resonant." Anya gestured towards a tree near the edge of the camp, the sharply contrasted bands of white and black stark against the deep chestnut brown of the other trees around it. "The root tubers grow near the base of them in the Fae realm. They look like sweet potatoes, but are much more fibrous. You have to steep them to create a sort of tea."

An ember escaped the fire pit, landing near Virginia's shoe and smoldering dangerously next to a fallen leaf. She stubbed it out with her toe, crushing it into the earth. "Thank you for telling me," she said. "If I ever have occasion to steal a Fae tree for you, I'll let you know."

Anya snorted a laugh. "Virginia, if you find yourself in the Fae realm, you're going to have far more problems than digging up a tree." She doused the fire, sending up a plume of steam and smoke that rose up through the trees, dissipating into the sky. "Come on," Anya said, dropping both of their mugs into the wash bucket. "I'm tired of waiting for something to happen. I have an idea."

Chapter Thirty-Two

Anya twisted in the driver's seat. "You should probably stay in the car for this part."

"Why, am I too recognizable?" Virginia asked wryly, lifting an eyebrow.

"Yes. The family knows who you are already, and I was hoping to take a different approach that relies on me not showing up with you."

"They're not going to let you in, you know. You aren't even a friend of the family. Mrs. Speer is of sound mind as far as I'm aware, and her son isn't particularly fond of her being questioned." Virginia rolled down the window to light a cigarette. "I don't think her son will take kindly to a stranger showing up at the door, and he already doesn't like me."

Anya unbuttoned her dress, paying no mind to Virginia's averted gaze behind her. She tugged on a white blouse and matching pair of trousers, a red stripe embroidered onto the collar and sleeve. "I'm a nurse sent to check up on the poor dear."

"Where in the hell did you get that?" Virginia asked.

"Found it in the trunk," Anya replied with a shrug. "Seamus must have left it in there."

"For shadows' sakes," Virginia grumbled. "I think that his ex-boyfriend's uniform."

"Why would it still be in here?"

"Because maybe the ex part isn't as set in stone as Seamus suggested," Virginia said. "So, Nurse Quinn, what's your plan here?"

"See if she remembers anything." Anya buttoned the trousers, the strange fit at the hips obvious but not so unusual. Most nurses wore skirts. The ones that didn't, took the men's uniforms. "I don't know, Virginia, we don't have many other leads, and you don't seem like you want to leave here without solving the case." She opened the car door and stepped out, tucking in her blouse. "You're much too intelligent to spend the rest of your life chasing ghosts down here."

Her words were more accurate than she realized, but before Virginia could protest, Anya was marching up the path to the younger son's home. The eldest had died overseas before the Rupture, from cholera, so she'd heard. He was the only surviving child, and as such, the one who'd whisked his mother away from all the upset and overwhelming drama of the crime scene to his house two counties away. It was smaller, more run-down, and much further from town than his mother's house.

The driveway was gritted with gravel, but Anya was even-footed as she approached the front steps, knocking on the screen door with an air of confidence that Virginia found surprising. It seemed that Anya Quinn took to lying rather well. Much to her surprise, she was let inside, disappearing behind the simple pine door that closed with a sharp snap of the lock that echoed out over the delicate parcel of land, fenced on all sides in a way that seemed more like it was keeping the house's residents in, rather than keeping strangers out.

She shifted against the leather of the seat, already feeling suffocated despite the open window. Between the situation and the humidity, she started to feel like she was drowning. Throwing it off, she opened the back door and crept out onto the path, closing it behind her with a latch too noisy for her own comfort. Shifting into the trees, moss deadened her footsteps, for which she was grateful.

Having visited the house already, Virginia already knew the best place to eavesdrop. There were two windows around the sides, and three across the back. The steps leading up to the cramped porch were peeling with faded light blue paint, sun-bleached and weather damaged from too many years out there in the corn-fed wilderness.

Anya's voice echoed from within, but muffled, her bright, chirpy tone a perfect dupe for a home nurse. Virginia ducked beneath a window around the left-hand side, keeping one eye on the car as if it was about to drive itself away. The glass was pushed up to its maximum height in a fruitless attempt to encourage a breeze to cool the interior. The leaves and branches remained painfully still, allowing the wet air to hang like a threat.

"Yes, as I said, the local hospital sent me out just to check everything is alright," Anya said, the sound of her feet shuffling against dusty floorboards. "The Birch Hollow police department was concerned that the, uh, horrors of the situation might be a little tough to bear for your mother, Mr. Speer."

"Anthony."

"Thank you, Anthony. I'm Nurse Quinn." Anya hesitated.

"These kinds of events can cause a person a great deal of upset, you know, especially for a woman of your mother's age."

"She's fine."

"It would be good if I could speak with her, even just for a moment," Anya pressed. "If I go back to my supervisor without a report, it will be my head on the chopping block, I'm afraid."

Virginia moved to the second window, having pinpointed where the sound was loudest and clearest

"Fine," Anthony relented. Virginia could hear him shuffle up the stairs, one creak at a time. "Ma!" he shouted, his voice a deep, pleasing baritone even when he was dealing with something he'd never signed on for. "The hospital sent a nurse around for you. She needs to speak with you about your health. It's just a precaution, she says."

"I already told Officer Carsh everything," she said, weariness dragging at her voice. "I don't know why I have to go through all that again."

"She said she just needs to tick a few boxes, make sure you're up and around."

Mrs. Speer sighed loud enough to hear it all the way down on the ground, and Virginia winced from the guilt of interrupting an old woman's nap. Footsteps tapped across the upper level and down the staircase, pausing in the living room. "Yes, dear, I'm alright," she said. "It was a terrible shock, to be sure, but I didn't see it happen."

"Hello, ma'am, I'm Nurse Quinn," Anya said, introducing herself. "I'm glad to hear that you're alright. Do you mind if I ask you a few questions?"

"I suppose not."

"Good, good. First off, are you having any nightmares?"

"No," Mrs. Speer replied confidently. "I've never had a problem sleeping. I can sleep anywhere, at any time. It's the only talent I retained from my youth." She laughed, but it was short and thin, the telltale sign that she was lying. "In fact, I was just upstairs having a little lie down."

Anya dug in her pouch for something, discernible only by the clink of vials. "I'm terribly sorry to disturb you, ma'am." It was strange how even Anya's fake apologies sounded genuine. Most people didn't have that skill. "It's just for work, you see. People are worried, and want to see you safe."

"I can assure you that I'm doing just fine," Mrs. Speer said politely. "I'm not sure how much more I have to say on the matter."

"Sometimes, a shock like this can take some time to sink in," Anya said. "It can cause not just nightmares, but ulcers, upset, or melancholy." Though her tone was neutral, Virginia could hear the genuine concern for the woman. "It's for the best that we follow up on these things, if you think about it."

Mrs. Speer shifted in her seat, clinking metal against porcelain. "As I told Officer Carsh, I was here with my son for a couple of nights to visit. He needed some mending done, you see. He returned me home that morning before he went on to go to work. There was nothing out of the ordinary, no broken glass, no forced entry. It wasn't until I unlocked the front door that I saw the body on the floor near the window, covered in blood. I called the police right away, of course, but there wasn't much for them to do other than to call the coroner and take a few photographs."

"Were any windows open?" Anya asked. "Left open, or

opened the previous night?"

"I don't recall," Mrs. Speer said. "I would imagine not, but I suppose it's possible that I forgot to close one the night before. Regardless, none were open when I returned home."

Virginia shifted, silently cursing the thin twig that snapped beneath her shoe. No open windows, no sign of a break-in. Someone's alibi didn't line up.

"Mrs. Speer, just a couple more questions for you," Anya continued, her voice drifting closer to the window. She glanced out and down, raising an eyebrow at Virginia before turning back towards the old woman and her son. "Have you been having any headaches, any nausea? I imagine that would make mending and knitting rather difficult to focus on."

Awkward stillness permeated the air, the heaviness sinking all the way down into last autumn's decaying leaves under Virginia's shoes.

"Mrs. Speer?" Anya prompted. "Headaches or nausea? It would be a shame for that shawl to go unfinished, I see it draped over the back of the chair. It's beautiful."

"I, uh..." the old woman trailed off, indecision hanging in the balance. "I'm not feeling well, Anthony. I think I should return to my nap. Thank you, dear, for the check-in, but I'm quite alright other than the perils of old age. Please fill your forms out saying as such, my son will be more than happy to sign off on whatever it is you need."

"Of course, ma'am," Anya replied gently. "Would you like me to help you upstairs?"

"No, no, my son will do that," Mrs. Speer deflected. "Leave your forms on the table in the kitchen and he'll see to it they're returned to the hospital tomorrow. We'll be out that way anyway to see to some errands."

Anya shifted, the heels of her sensible leather shoes scraping lightly against the unfinished wood floors inside. "I'll do that, thank you so much for your time. I hope you have an enjoyable rest here with your son, it's good that you two are still so close. A blessing, many would say."

"I'll drop those forms off tomorrow morning," Anthony reiterated, making it clear that Anya was about to overstay her welcome. "Please tell the hospital we appreciate their concern, but that we don't require any more surprise visitations. She's had enough upset already, dealing with a known con man turning up dead in our home and being questioned by the police. It's quite enough now, Nurse Quinn."

"Go," Virginia hissed under her breath, willing Anya to get out of there before her cover was blown. She was too curious, trying to wrest more information out of the son after they'd made it very clear she wouldn't get more. Virginia gripped the edge of the windowsill, resisting the urge to pull herself up to see inside. If Anya didn't blow their cover, that certainly would.

"Thank you again," Anya said over the sound of the screen door hinge squealing in protest. "Much appreciated. We understand how busy this time can be, and—"

Virginia stood off to the side, just on the other side of the trees, motioning for Anya to leave. She jerked her thumb back towards the car and backed up into the shadows, hoping Anya would follow.

The door snapped shut, the metal screen rattling in the swollen wooden frame, the paint peeling at the handle. Anya traipsed down off the steps, sauntering back towards the car with a confident gait that pulled something from within

Virginia she couldn't quite pinpoint. Familiarity, maybe, or strangeness. It was frustrating how often those two things overlapped.

"You talk too much."

Anya flashed her a grin as she threw the car into gear, turning around in the wide drive. "They didn't notice anything."

"Barely," Virginia challenged. "You're an incredible witch, but you're not much of a private investigator. You can't keep pushing just because you didn't get what you wanted yet, you'll blow your cover."

A branch scraped against the car window, the glass screeching. "I'm not an incredible witch," Anya said after a moment.

"What are you talking about?"

"I'm competent at best. My aunt was incredible." Anya turned onto the main road, glancing both ways before she did. She proceeded down the gravel-ridden street, tapping each of her fingers against the steering wheel in succession, the silver rings there glinting in the summer sunlight. "She's being poisoned."

"What? Who?" Virginia asked, taken aback by the abrupt shift in conversation.

Anya tapped faster as the car picked up speed, leaning into the uneven rhythm of her movements. "Mrs. Speer."

"How do you know?"

"I've seen it more than once. She's stiff and is having muscle spasms. Her reluctance to answer me about nausea and headache suggests she's also having those." Anya checked the rear view mirror, staring at the car behind them until it turned off onto a narrow dirt track. "My guess is strychnine."

CHAPTER THIRTY-TWO

"Rat poison?" Virginia asked, sitting up. "How do you know just from that?"

"Wild guess, judging by the bottle of it in the kitchen. It was sitting out on the counter."

Virginia gritted her teeth. "The son. Anthony."

"It would be easy enough for him to hide it in her food, and with her all the way out here, no one would be the wiser. No doubt they wouldn't even do an autopsy, she's elderly for one thing, and for another, she's had a terrible fright."

"She sounded alright to me," Virginia said. "She didn't sound traumatized."

"You didn't see her." Anya chewed her lip, tightening her fingers around the wheel. "We can't just leave her there, Virginia. Neither the police department nor the hospital are actually going to send someone out to check on her, and even if they did, he wouldn't let them run the necessary tests. He made that much clear."

"It would also alert Anthony that someone is onto him, which..." Virginia trailed off, hoping that Anya would put the pieces together.

"He'd just kill her faster," Anya finished, the blunt edge of her words uncharacteristic and surprising. "In order to cover his tracks."

"Little shit probably wants his mother's money," Virginia said, the invisible compression of being trapped in the back seat creeping up her spine and settling in her shoulder blades, making it harder to breathe than she'd like. "Wouldn't surprise me if he killed the con man trying to beat him to the punch." She squeezed her eyes shut, remembering the disembodied voice. "She gave a statement to the police about his alibi."

"His mother is covering for him," Anya agreed, smacking the steering wheel. "She has no idea he's trying to kill her. Mrs. Speer trusts her son and thinks he's doing what's best for her, and he's trying to poison her in order to get his hands on a bigger house." She locked eyes with Virginia in the mirror, crystalline eyes clouded with rage. "You saw that place, it's a far cry from the Speer house."

"There's nothing we can do, Anya. Not without making everything worse."

Anya shook her head, jerking the car off the road into their usual clearing. "No. I don't accept that." She threw it into park and jumped out, pacing between two leafy birch trees, the low heels of her shoes sinking lightly into the earth with every step. "I don't accept it." She reached for her herb pouch, resting on the dashboard. "I'm not going to accept it."

"What are you doing?" Virginia asked, scrambling out of the car to block her path. "Don't do anything foolish, Quinn, we have an investigation to—"

"Get out of my way," Anya said, brushing past her. "I'm going to make sure he can't hurt that poor woman any more than he already has."

Chapter Thirty-Three

"How long has she been in there?" Jolie asked, waving a hand towards the tent. Her ginger ringlets were tied back with a large purple bow, and she was dressed in a matching skirt suit, though she'd already given up on the shoes, which she abandoned next to the fire circle with an aggressive toss. "What's she doing?"

"Beats me." Virginia knew better than to interrupt Anya any more than she already had, having been knocked back the last time she poked her head into the tent. "All I know is that I was told to stay the hell out of there until she was done." She poked Jolie in the arm. "I imagine that goes for you, too."

"I don't know, she's been teaching me some stuff."

"Oh yeah? You're a witch now, are you?" Virginia asked lightly, motioning for her to light the log beneath the aluminum percolator. "Being a fire demon wasn't enough heat, you wanted to add something else to the pile?"

"Not spells, I wouldn't be able to do those anyway," Jolie said, opening her palm to send a wide spray of fire into the pit, her eyes sparkling as she did so. "Poultices mostly."

Virginia opened her mouth to explain the situation with

Mrs. Speer, but coughed through them. The kid was still a teenager, she didn't need to get all bogged down in the absent morals of adults. She'd seen enough.

"Anya, are you done in there?" she shouted through the closed tent flap, fists balled at her side. "I don't want to sit around all day waiting for you to finish whatever the hell it is you're doing in there, I'd much rather figure this all out and get back to the city as soon as possible."

The flap wrenched open, the canvas fabric gripped in Anya's fingers. "No, I'm not done yet," she replied flatly. "If you're so desperate to solve this unsolvable case, then go." Anya thrust the keys out of the tent, and they landed in the dirt, emitting a small cloud of dust. "Take the car, get arrested for all I care, but make sure you leave Jo out of it. Not everyone needs to get mowed over by your impatience."

"Fine!" Virginia sniped, waiting until the tent flap was closed again to bend over and pick up the keys. "Jolie, let's go. We'll leave Anya to work in peace."

Jolie hesitated for a moment. "Maybe I should stay."

"To learn magic?"

"To help." She leaned in close, whispering in Virginia's ear. "This isn't like her."

"No, it isn't," Virginia agreed. "I should go get something for us to eat."

"Chicken?"

"I don't know, Firefly, we'll see." Virginia laid a hand on Jolie's shoulder. "Be safe. Don't let her blow up the camp."

Jolie giggled. "I won't."

"I'll be back in a while, okay? I might be an hour or so, I wanted to go and check something."

"What are you checking?"

"I'll let you know if it turns into anything." Virginia cast a glance at the tent, Anya muttering angrily within. "Make some more coffee. That always helps."

***

She could have gone anywhere in the woods, and yet she was drawn back to where she'd always gone with Juliette. Some part of her still believed in its power, that childish, naive fancy that a secret place hidden amongst the trees would answer questions over three decades old.

Virginia had tried to resist it, happy to let Anya drive while they were in Birch Hollow because at least that meant Virginia wouldn't take the sharp left off the road onto a dirt track, following it right where it forked. The trees grew thick and impassable, concealing safety in their branches. She'd have to walk the rest of the way.

The car came to a stop perched on top of yellowed grass, wilted, each blade bent double, almost as if they wanted to escape back into the coolness of the earth. She walked along a deer path, wondering if they still went the same way down to the large lake near there. But deer out there were as reliable as the sunrises and sunsets, and she began to recognize gnarled branches and oddly shaped boulders as she picked her way through the trees.

The canopy of birch trees shielded the worst of the sun, but the humidity was still cloying, and after a short while, sweat soaked through the collar of her shirt again. She yearned for a shower, even if it was the one at her mother's house. After all, beggars couldn't be choosers.

It was strange how accurately her legs remembered the

325

way, even as her mind second-guessed every step she took. One landmark, one sharp memory after another lined the way. A twisted tree trunk, marred from a storm thirty-two years hence. A copse of mushrooms, growing in intersecting rings. Initials carved into the side of an old shed, the exposed wood long since grown over with moss. The letters were illegible, but she knew what they were, and the sight of them yanked air from her lungs with such force, she wondered for a moment if she'd ever recover. She wasn't even sure she wanted to.

JA+VV

Virginia reached out, brushing her fingertips against the gashes she'd carved so many years earlier. She blinked, and in an instant the carving was gone and the wood whole and unblemished. The edges of her sight were tinged with blur, but not enough to protect her from the shock of seeing Juliette in front of her, throwing her head back and laughing.

"Ginnie, you always make me laugh," she said, reaching out for Virginia but not quite making contact with her. That name in her mouth throbbed like a stab wound. "What do you want to do next?"

"I don't care, as long as I don't have to go home," Virginia said automatically, once again unsettled at the sound of youth. "You know how she gets."

"We could go back to the lake," Juliette offered. Her hazel eyes shone in the green-tinged light of the woods, every fleck of gold and grey a work of art. "It's hot enough to go swimming."

"I didn't bring my stuff," Virginia protested.

Juliette raised a conspiratorial eyebrow. "So?" she teased, moving closer. The silver locket she wore caught the light. "That's never stopped us before."

"That was at night."

"Then we'll wait until night." She sat down in the corner, stretching her legs out in front of her, her tan trousers cuffed at the hems and the neckline of her blue sweater stretched out to bare her left shoulder. "As long as you think you can stay out that long without her calling the police again."

Virginia groaned, and that time she was surprised at how familiar the sensation was. "I don't care anymore," she lied. "My mother can do whatever she wants. She does anyway, it doesn't even matter what I do or don't do."

The shed was still shabby, but slightly newer, with fewer lichens, and less moss danced across the roof boards. It was an old hunting blind, long since abandoned after the farmers had preemptively hunted the deer right out of Birch Hollow. It had been years since anyone had tasted fresh venison.

"Only a few more months until we can get out of here," Juliette mused. "Just as soon as I can earn enough money, we'll hitchhike out west and put this place behind us forever." She rolled onto her stomach, looking up at Virginia. "We'll never come back here, Ginnie. She'll never find us."

"She'll try."

"We'll change our names," Juliette assured her. "We'll get jobs, find a little apartment, make it ours. No one will be able to tell us no, least of all her." She laughed again, the sound like sequins sparkling in twilight, just a little bit dark with a hint of mystery. "I love you, you know."

"Yeah, I know," Virginia replied, and even as the words left her mouth, cursed herself for not saying it back in kind.

The past couldn't be changed, no matter how many times she relived it in vivid, excruciating detail.

"Where out west should we go?" Juliette asked, unfazed by Virginia's answer because she'd heard it dozens of times before. "The coast?"

Virginia nodded. "The coast. Somewhere warm, where the winters don't suck the soul right out of your body. We can go swimming every day."

"Ice cream," Juliette added. "Whatever flavor we want." She toyed with the end of her long, shiny braid, the end of it secured with a fat green ribbon wrapped around it three times. "And sunshine, and freedom, and a new start." She looked up at Virginia again, a look of intensity there that threatened to unravel the very core of her being. "And you."

"And you," Virginia echoed, and in that moment she wanted nothing more than to scream that they should leave right then, no waiting for enough money to go, that they should hop a freighter and figure it out on the way. That it was the only way they could be together, that something terrible was coming.

She reached out for Juliette but she dissolved in front of her, leaving a red-handled pocketknife in Virginia's hand as she sobbed, carving the tenth scrape in the wall. A new vision, a new memory sprang forth.

Ten days since Juliette had gone missing.

That was the day Carsh announced he wouldn't keep looking for her.

Virginia sank to her knees, dropping the knife to the damp floorboards with a dull clatter, the metallic sound deadened by the moss growing up between the cracks. She buried her face in her hands, more physical pain than she'd ever felt on the sparring mat. It was sharp, and it was unavoidable, and despite her constant renewed vows that she'd never relive that moment again, there she was, neck-deep in the same shame and guilt that never stopped trying to creep through the cracks in the windows back in Verdance.

Juliette was as inevitable as breathing, until she wasn't.

She'd disappeared without a trace, without a goodbye, no letters or notes, no hint as to where she'd gone. Virginia had always known something happened, but no one would listen. No one but her even cared about Juliette. She was an orphan, a poor kid in an even poorer county where folks had very little to spare for their own children, much less someone else's.

Case closed.

No justice.

The world shifted around her once more, one vision bleeding into the next. The notches on the wall grew in number by five and then stopped, the grooves scabbing over with moss and the thick slime of summer algae. Virginia looked down at the pocketknife and watched as it was slowly reclaimed by the shed, first growing over with vines of clover, and then the steel blade turned to rust.

Another hand reached forth to collect it, and Virginia would have recognized that bracelet anywhere. It was one she'd given her mother when she was small, before her father left. They'd chosen it together.

"Where have you gone?" Virginia's mother asked, pulling the knife free. "Why did you leave?"

The leaves outside the shed yellowed and dropped to the forest floor, awaiting their destruction into decaying fertilizer for spring flowers. It was winter, and her mother had discovered her hideout. She knelt on the ground, hunting for some sort of sign that Virginia couldn't even imagine. Her mother buried her hands in the snow, digging down into the frozen earth. "Where?" she shouted, rage beginning to color the edges of her tone. "Why?"

Virginia wanted to scream, but couldn't. She raised her hands to her mouth, and though nothing felt amiss, her jaw would not release and her voice would not sound. She wanted to scream *What do you mean, why did I leave?*

Her mother wouldn't hear her.

She never had.

Virginia curled up on the floor of that dirty, dilapidated old shed, staring at the place where Juliette had just been. "Come back," she said, running her hands over the wood. She reached for the vision again, willing it to replay, to see Juliette again and to hear her laugh.

"Just once," Virginia pleaded, pressing her fingers into the notches, but no vision came. She reached for the pocket knife that had long since been freed from the wood, losing the margins between vision and reality. She'd have happily risked tetanus for one more moment with Juliette, but it wasn't there.

Virginia punched into the wood, denting the moist earth below it and splintering the mold that held the shack together. She bled, but still the vision remained elusive.

"Juliette," she whispered, pulling the stolen bottle of Nether from her pocket. She'd taken it while Anya was working on her spell. She hadn't meant to, but maybe she had.

The contents of the vial were bitter on her tongue, but she swallowed them eagerly, ready to descend into Juliette's warm embrace, no matter the cost.

Chapter Thirty-Four

Snow sparkled along the path to her mother's house, the pristine white frost crystallized on the surface. There had been a blizzard, although that wasn't so unusual in those parts.

Virginia trudged through it, pausing to knock on the front door but it was already open, a tree lit with glittering tinsel and ornaments in the corner. December, then. She couldn't quite remember how she'd gotten there, or why. Everything felt a little hazy at the edges, like waking up too early after a long night, or the hour before a particularly bad headache set in. She was supposed to be looking for something or someone, but the need drifted off somewhere she couldn't reach.

Her mother was sitting at the table, wrapping a box in brown paper. The radio was playing jazz orchestrated for a large ensemble, but every crescendo sparked static at the edges, blurring the melody.

Virginia took another step inside and it was autumn, the leaves outside orange and gold, falling to the ground with every gentle gust of wind that blew across the empty fields outside the window. Her father was sitting in the chair in the corner, reading the newspaper, frowning at headlines about the Rupture. Strange. He'd gone missing before that.

She sat on the sofa and it was spring, daisies poking their heads out from beneath recently frozen earth, and daffodils in full bloom in the beds outside, surrounded by the previous year's decaying leaves. She watched as every bloom rotted and fell to the ground, the yellow petals fading into nothingness.

Summer, autumn, winter, spring.

Every movement shifted her into another season, each of them as mundane and useless as the last. It was an awkward, oppressive calm, like having the air slowly sucked out of a room, and not knowing until it was too late. A far cry from her childhood of chaos, with doors ripped from their hinges and wallpaper showing off brand new holes. It was death by another name, and she knew she had to get out before it was too late.

"Virginia," her mother said from the table, somehow still there with the half-wrapped box. "I told you, I don't want you seeing her. She's poison."

"She's not poison," Virginia argued, the script of the moment so deeply embedded within her that it was as automatic as blinking. "She cares about me."

"She doesn't care about you." Her mother creased the paper for a neat fold, securing it with a sliver of tape. "She's using you."

Virginia stood, all the old emotions rushing to the surface. "For what?" she demanded, striding into the kitchen. "What could she possibly be using me for? She just wants me to be happy!"

"I thought the same thing about your father, and look what happened," her mother said, bitterness aching at the edges of her voice. "He's been in and out for years, only coming back when he needs something. Food, a bed to sleep in." She stared up at Virginia, eyes cold and emotionless. "Other things."

"She cares about me more than you do," Virginia snapped. "Just because you couldn't keep a man, doesn't mean I won't be able to keep her."

"And where will you live, Virginia?" her mother asked. She turned, and it was summer again, and she was pouring herself a glass of gin in the heat of a humid morning. "Who is going to put a roof over your heads? Lord above knows two teenagers can't make it on their own, and her parents knew enough to leave her here when they hitched the first freight train out of this place."

"I love her!" Virginia shouted.

"Love doesn't pay the bills, Ginnie." Her mother lifted the glass to her lips, and the tree outside the kitchen window sped through another year's seasons. When it came to a rest in early autumn, the yellow-green leaves bright within the wooden frame, she was crying, her head buried in her hands. Virginia flinched from it, trying to back out of the kitchen, but her feet were rooted in place, and she was forced to behold the inevitable, irrevocably scorched into the past.

She knew from the slight brisk in the humid air and the thick rows of unharvested corn in the fields that it was September. Her mother's dress was burned into her memory, that awful yellow floral print with huge marigolds pressed into ivory satin, snags visible at the hips from where Virginia's fingers had clawed at her from inside that jail cell, begging her to bail her out. Half an inch of the hem was torn where her mother had wrenched the fabric from Virginia's grasp as she turned her back and left the station, leaving her there to rot behind iron bars.

No, no. Virginia shook her head, willing herself to awaken, but she couldn't, trapped in the dream, the nightmare of it, locked inside by her own hubris. Her mother's shoulders shook with wracking sobs, mascara smeared across her porcelain cheeks, still young, devoid of the deep lines that had come to rest there in the ensuing thirty-one years. She squeezed her eyes shut, willing the seasons to shift again, but they wouldn't, secured in place and determined to punish her for her mortal sins.

"I told her to stay away," her mother wailed, pounding her fist into the kitchen table until the legs rattled in their loose sockets. "I told her!" She picked up the half-full glass of gin and hurled it against the opposite wall, where it smashed into ten million glittering shards, the lethal dust left hanging in the air, illuminated by bright moonlight. The bottle of gin sloshed in her hand as she brought it to her lips, draining it dry before sending that to the same fate.

Glass collected on the floor in a pile of chaos, her mother's one and only masterpiece. She never had liked oil paints much, too unpredictable, she'd said. Perhaps she preferred to be the only instability in the room, which is why she'd always had a quiet hatred for Virginia. She reflected back that which her mother hated most about herself.

The draft creeping under the door grew frosty, and the icicles off the gutters appeared and lengthened until they were a dangerous threat to anyone who was foolish enough to pass beneath them. Her mother stood at the counter, staring out at the window in her bathrobe, the tie cinched at the waist as she clutched a fresh cup of coffee. Soft snakes of steam rose up from the chipped ceramic towards the ceiling, curling past wallpaper that had begun to peel at the seams.

"I know you're there," her mother said evenly, not even bothering to turn and face her. "After all this time, there you are again, trying to weasel your way back into this house without an apology, without so much as a mea culpa as you wipe your muddy boots on my front mat."

Virginia looked around, but saw no one. "Are you talking to me?" she asked. Whatever memory this was, it wasn't hers. It was a fabrication, a confused hallucination created from an amalgamation of years spent in that house, none of them happy.

"I always told you not to come back," her mother continued. "I told you time and again that you weren't welcome." She turned now, looking past Virginia or through her, it was hard to discern with the black, cloudy rage in her eyes. "Get out."

"I can't leave," Virginia tried to say, but her voice had gone silent. No sound passed her vocal cords, and no amount of frantic clawing at her throat would fix the problem. She reached for her silver knuckles, a reflexive gesture in the face of threat, but her pockets were curiously and unusually empty.

"Get out!" her mother screamed, pulling a large knife from the block on the counter. "I told you that if you ever came back here, I'd kill you myself."

The room grew thick with static, the white snow gathering at the edges of Virginia's vision the same way they did when she took a particularly nasty hit to the head. She knew she was about to go down, but couldn't quite put her arms out to stop herself before her mother's kitchen snapped to black.

***

"Ginnie," her mother said.

Virginia opened her eyes, unsure if she was witnessing a memory or reality. "Mom?" She sat up, rubbing at her temples. She'd fallen asleep, or passed out on the floor of the shack. "How did you know I was here?"

"Jolie came to the house looking for you. I didn't think there were many other places you might be." Her mother was standing in the doorway, looking down at her. "You look like you've been dragged backwards through a hedge."

"Thanks," Virginia grumbled. She coughed and tried to check her reflection in the broken glass of the shack's window, but the moss and years of water stains concealed her visage. It was probably for the best. "I'm fine, you can go."

Her mother just stared.

Virginia rolled her eyes. "What?"

"No thank you for your alibi? Or for finding you in the woods? I'm getting on in years, you know, one tree root could see me breaking a hip."

"Thank you for telling the police the truth, I suppose," Virginia snapped. "And you didn't have to come and find me, I would have woken up and gone back to camp."

"You could come home, you know."

"No thanks."

Her mother breathed out a sigh. "What were you doing out here?"

"Nothing."

"Ginnie—"

"You know, Mom, we don't have to do this."

"Do what?"

"Pretend we care."

Her mother wavered on the spot, but just barely. She tilted her head. "Did you find what you were looking for?"

"I wasn't looking for anything, I just wanted to see if it was still here." The day had turned to dusk, and fireflies blinked in the gathering darkness around them. "I fell asleep, that's all. I don't sleep well at the campsite."

"Did you have a vision?"

Virginia finally returned her stare, but didn't know what to say. She wasn't sure how accurate her visions had been, or if her mother really had gone to the shack after she left for the city. She wasn't even entirely sure if her mother was actually standing there or not. Her mind was muddled like she'd had far too much gin, or spun in circles for hours like she had as a child.

"Ginnie," her mother prompted. "I'm just asking if you had a vision."

"No," Virginia lied. "Still busted." She climbed to her feet, dusting off the knees of her trousers in a fruitless effort to improve her appearance. "How did you get here? It's too far to walk."

"I got a taxi to where the highway splits onto that dirt path. He wouldn't go further, said it was hell to clean out the wheels."

"He's not wrong." Virginia cast one last glance at the notches on the wall, committing them to memory once more. "Come on, I'll drive you home."

Her mother held the keys out, just out of reach. "You left them in the car. I'll drive."

"No, Mom, I'll drive."

"It's been far too long since I've had the pleasure of a steering wheel," her mother said, already making her way back to the path. "What are you going to do, steal the keys back from an old lady?" She flicked a glance over her shoulder. "I sent Jolie back to camp, it sounded like she was needed there, but there's a police captain waiting for you at the house."

"Why?"

"I haven't the foggiest idea, Ginnie. You're the one who can't stay out of trouble."

Chapter Thirty-Five

"Are you going to come quietly, Virginia?" Shirin asked, holding the passenger side door of her squad unit open. She lifted an eyebrow, and Virginia returned the look with a scowl.

"Am I under arrest? I have a right to an attorney."

"No, your mother corroborated your alibi," Shirin said. "Nice to see you again, ma'am." She tipped her cap, and it was wholly unnecessary and clearly for show. "You were one of the only people to speak with Melody Kingston the night she was murdered, so they have a few questions."

"I know how these things go, Shirin," Virginia said. "They're going to try to sweat me, but if I'm not under arrest, I am under no obligation to cooperate."

"They'll just subpoena you when it goes to court," Shirin said. "I'm sure you'd love the opportunity to visit your mother again."

"Fine." Virginia turned to say goodbye to her mother, but she was already halfway up the path to the front door. "Let's go, then." The haze of the Nether was turning into the feeling of knives in her throat and mallets in her brain, hammering at her skull. "Did you find out if they're investigating the murders up north as connected?"

"I did."

"And?"

Shirin glanced over as she tucked her cap into the corner of the dash. "There are some theories, let's put it that way."

"Since when are you so cozy with the feds?"

"I don't think it's a good idea to share that with you before you're questioned. If you let anything slip, it could make you look guilty."

Virginia scoffed, folding her arms over her chest. "Want to give me a preview of those questions, Captain Lindell?"

"I am not privy to their questions, I am just bringing you in."

"So it's the feds, then," Virginia said, sitting forward in her seat. "You wouldn't hide any questions Carsh might have, so it must be federal." She swore under her breath, wondering how much it would hurt if she threw herself from a moving vehicle. They weren't going fast, but the roads were all gravel. "Shirin, the feds are going to dig anything they can out of me."

"Better to get it over with, and then you can go home."

"I'm not done here yet."

"These cases are turning federal, Virginia. There's no reason for you to stay down here. If your main concern is Jolie, then just lay low for a while until we clear out some of the crew that would recognize her. We can have them transferred to state or county, less of a chance they'll be able to drop intel on her that means anything." Shirin had one hand on the steering wheel, and the other resting on the window of her door, skin soaking in the cool night air. "This is the last step to get you out of here."

"I assume they took over the precinct."

"They did."

"I'll bet Carsh is spitting tacks."

Shirin smirked. "He is somewhat less than pleased, but then, local PDs are never thrilled when feds come in." She glanced over at Virginia. "I'm sure you'd agree."

"Feds like to steamroll and take credit," Virginia said. "They'll steal whatever cases they can, if it means more government funding when the new budget takes effect."

"Mm."

They rode the rest of the way in silence, and when they reached the precinct, Shirin acted as though they'd never met, pushing her through the door by her shoulders and calling for an interrogation room.

So much for preferential treatment.

***

Taking the rest of the vial of Nether had been a mistake. Her head throbbed with every pulse of her heartbeat, and her throat ached as though she'd spent the night screaming or trying to swallow fire.

"I could use some water in here," she called out hoarsely. They were trying to sweat her out, make her nervous. Despite her alibi, someone wasn't buying it.

The door creaked open on its ancient hinges, the rust probably fifty years thick. "Ms. Virginia Vane," an agent said, taking one look at the uncomfortable chair and choosing to stand instead. He frowned at it and tugged at the badge that was hanging on a chain around his neck. "You're not under arrest, so there's no need for an attorney. We're just asking some questions today."

"Whether I am under arrest or not, I can have my lawyer in here if I choose," Virginia said coolly. "Can I have some water? You're not allowed to deny me that, it's against my rights."

"Apologies, we forgot you were in here." The agent propped open the door with a sturdy book from Carsh's bookshelf, the loud whomp of it hitting the unwaxed tile like a bomb in Virginia's sensitive ears. "Water in here, please," he called, and almost immediately a rookie fed who looked like he was scared of his own shadow appeared with a large glass of water, which sloshed onto the table in front of her and settled easily into the grooves carved by years of Moassa county citizens sitting in lockup overnight for a drunk and disorderly.

"You forgot I was in here?" Virginia asked, raising the glass to her lips. The water was tepid, almost warm, and the sedimentary taste of the well it had come from almost brought it straight back up immediately after she swallowed it. She'd mostly had coffee since arriving in town, and had forgotten how accustomed she'd become to city water back in Verdance. "I find that hard to believe."

"We're federal agents brought in to look at the issue of Nether distribution," he said, leaning against the back of the chair, his oversized black suit baggy at the shoulders, as though he'd inherited from someone. "My name is Agent Campbell, I work for the Federal Authority for Freedom. I'm sure you're aware of the new federal law that makes distribution a terrorism charge worthy of treason." He took a beige folder from his briefcase, scanning over a file with a furrowed brow. "Did you know this Heinrich Harrow person? The deceased?"

"I was running him down for a client," Virginia answered, still desperately thirsty but unable to bring herself to drink any more of the well water. "Real prince of a guy, took his family's money, assets, and took off. Found him down here, where he'd been conning elderly folks into handing him all kinds of stuff. Fake investment scams, low-grade blackmail, you name it. Also went by the name of John Folst."

"And the other deceased, Melody Kingston?"

"I spoke to her briefly the night before, but I'd never seen her before. Haven't seen her since I went home that night." She gestured towards her front pocket. "I'm a private investigator up in Verdance. You can check my license, it's current."

"That won't be necessary," he said, snapping the file shut. "We're well aware of you who are." He turned, making note of the clock on the wall that hadn't changed since she had arrived.

"It's nice to be noticed," she said sweetly, but let the snide sarcasm color the edges of her tone. "Especially by the feds." Her stomach clenched as she said it, imagining conscription or worse at the other end of the negotiation. If they'd discovered she was a seer, through some rumor tumbling out of the mouth of one of the Ruby Thorns who had witnessed her pummeling six months prior, then there would be no escaping the incessant and dangerous drudgery of a federal desk.

"It was hard not to, Ms. Vane. The witness who reported seeing you wander off into the woods with Ms. Kingston was only too keen to speak to us." Campbell glanced at her, and it was dismissive yet interested. "Care to explain that?"

"I left the premises alone and didn't return. As to how this witness saw me going off into the woods with a woman whose name I barely knew, I can't explain that, no."

"We haven't been able to dig up any connections between you and Ms. Kingston," he said.

"Almost like I didn't do it," Virginia said.

He stared, examining her face, eyes falling to a rest on her scars for a moment too long. "I did discover that you had an arrest in conjunction with Nether up in Verdance, as well as a tenuous connection to another potential homicide four years back."

"The charges were dropped."

"So they were," he said. "But your connection to a known distribution location does raise questions, Ms. Vane."

Shadows fucked, Astrid again. Always, always Astrid and the gravitational pull of her own misguided self-reliance. "You'll find I've had no connections there for quite some time," she replied, gritting her teeth. "It was only six months ago that the State's Attorney tried dredging all that up again, to no avail."

He shrugged and ran his hands over the top of a filing cabinet, frowning. His nonchalance was a thinly veiled threat. "You've worked in law enforcement, Ms. Vane. What precisely would you have me do at this juncture? You are our only lead, and we have an eyewitness willing to swear to that fact."

She rested her wrists on the table, the scarred wood biting into her skin. "I have a knack for being in the wrong place at the wrong time." She didn't challenge the report, wanting to ferret out more information about it before she did. More knowledge of a situation was always preferable to shooting blind.

"Most private eyes do." He examined the dust on his fingers, rubbing them together until a fine powder dislodged and floated slowly to the ground. "Civilians rarely have the same sort of skill set or resources that we have."

The dig burned in Virginia's chest, but she breathed in the shame of it anyway, knowing there was no other option. He knew it, too, which is why he was needling her. "No, I suppose not," she finally managed to say.

Campbell dropped the file on the table and leaned against it, his palms flat against the surface. "What do you know about these cases?" he asked, staring her down.

"Not enough," Virginia admitted. "If I knew more, I doubt I'd be sitting here, being questioned despite my alibi."

Campbell paced the length of the small station, his standard issue uniform shoes clicking against the floor with every determinate step. "Officer Carsh mentioned that you grew up around these parts. I don't suppose you know of anyone or anything that might be of use? Anyone who might be a cause for concern?"

"This is the first I've been back in a very long time," Virginia said, doing her best to keep her tone level even as her stomach climbed further into her throat, only exacerbated by her physical condition. "What kind of things would you be looking for?"

"Mythics, of course," he spat with derision. "Powerful ones, capable of what we've seen down here." He stopped his pacing, tugging at the badge around his neck. "They're more trouble than they're worth, if you ask me, but the military finds that some of them can be useful for conscription." He turned on his heel to face Virginia again, his face surprisingly light. "So, Ms. Vane, who do you know in town who may or may not be mythic? Someone involved with the Nether trade?"

"Not that I recall," Virginia answered.

"I'm trying to help you, Ms. Vane, I implore you to not make this more difficult than it needs to be." He stopped his pacing, flipping through the file once more. "I will ask you again if you know of any mythics or any activity in the Nether trade in this county."

"That sort of thing would kick up a lot of dust in a place like this."

"Indeed," he agreed. "And have you noticed any newcomers in town? Anyone unusual?"

She wouldn't have believed that her organs could contort themselves any further, and yet the sharp pangs as they did so proved her horribly wrong. "I wouldn't know," she said. "As I said, I've not been back in a good long while. I wouldn't know who is or isn't new, and besides, I've spent most of my time with my mother." Worry for Jolie wound its way through her chest, the barbs palpable. Half a dozen people would be able to describe her as a newcomer to the area without much trouble.

Campbell tilted his head, but only slightly. "Not the past few days, though," he said. "Officer Carsh assured us he'd checked for you there several times a day, and you were nowhere to be seen."

"I was camping."

"Where?"

"The woods," Virginia replied, trying and failing to contain the razor edge in her tone. "That's still legal, last I heard."

Campbell stared her down, willing her to flinch, but she wouldn't. He sighed, running a hand over his close-cropped grey hair. "Ms. Vane, I'm going to level with you. We don't want to be down here any more than these fine folks want us rifling around in their business. We'd rather solve this nonsense and head back to headquarters in the city. The faster people around here help us do that, the faster we'll go." He slid the folder across the table until it was within her reach. "I have the power to make this go away, ma'am, all of it. I also have the power to suggest to the State's Attorney that your alibi be thrown out. A credible witness saw you leave the barn with Melody Kingston and go off into the woods, now what am I supposed to do with that?"

"I don't know what you want me to say, Agent Campbell. I was at the barn, yes, fine, you got me there, but I was there looking for leads on the Harrow case. I left because there was nothing to be had, and I went home to my mother's house. That is the whole story."

"No powerful unregistered mythics out here?" he asked innocently, draping his hands into his pockets and resting there as if they were having a casual conversation. "No pockets of Nether trade?"

Virginia shifted in the uncomfortable chair, feeling the edges dig into the backs of her knees. "How would I know if someone is a mythic or not?" she asked, matching his unassuming vocal timbre at the same time she worried that he would read that as mocking, because it was. "After all, the Rupture was a long time ago. Marks have long since faded."

"What would you do in my position, Ms. Vane?" he asked. "One suspect, two murders that seem like they may be connected, and you were at both crime scenes, or near enough. The way I'm looking at it, your mother's affidavit isn't going to hold up with the State's Attorney, so how about you help me out, here?"

"I'm not aware of any unregistered mythics in Moassa County," she stated firmly. Maybe Anya was already bundling Jolie into the car and getting her far from town. Maybe she'd still be safe, despite the feds looking to pin the deaths on anyone else. "And if I were you, I'd be taking a closer look at the disgruntled mortals in town. After all, they're more than capable of committing atrocities."

He nodded, brow furrowed in concentration. "Ms. Vane, I'm not trying to be mythiphobic, I'm just trying to keep people safe. Mythics are known to be tied with the Nether trade across the country. This Ms. Kingston was known in political circles to be whipping votes for certain laws in Congress for Senator Dean." He folded his hands in front of him. "So unless you can explain this eyewitness that saw you with her, or offer up other information in the way of mythics or Nether, I won't have any choice but to detain you."

The room was dark, lit only by the charcoal light of the outside that filtered through the thick glass of the windows, made darker by passing clouds. "I wouldn't know anything about any of that," she said. "I don't keep track of politics. It's one of the reasons I didn't continue to speak to Ms. Kingston that night, I found her boring and a bit insuffer-able."

"What else did you talk about?"

"She said she hates the south, and wanted to get out of here as soon as possible," Virginia said. She left out the part where the victim had asked to see her again. "I'm sure the dealer has already told you that."

Agent Campbell nodded. "He did."

"Then we don't have anything else to talk about."

CHAPTER THIRTY-FIVE

"When did you leave the barn?"

"Shortly after that," Virginia said. "Maybe ten-thirty at the latest." She leaned across the table. "Your eyewitness didn't see what she thinks she saw," Virginia said. "Her father is a compulsive gambler, I'm sure she was a bit too preoccupied to have paid much attention."

"Then how would you explain the victim's death?"

"I don't know, Agent Campbell, the federal agencies have so much more information than civilians."

Agent Campbell smiled, and it was snakelike, flat and mirthless as it melded into his face. "Ms. Vane, you don't strike me as a serial killer, but then, I am not seeing anything else more likely."

"So you've connected the dots, then," she said.

"It's a theory, we're waiting on whatever forensics we can get."

"Then Agent Campbell, you're asking the wrong questions. If you're investigating all four murders together, then you'll want to know my alibi for the first two, won't you?" Virginia smiled at him and took another sip of the water, immediately regretting it.

"And what would those be?" he asked. "Your mother, I presume? Or a lover, perhaps?"

"No, sir," she replied. "I was with two members of the VCPD, Captain Lindell and Sheriff Dixon." She sat back in her chair, the sides digging into her hips, but she maintained her position. "I can understand why you'd want to throw out my alibi down here, I would too in your shoes. But you can't suggest they're all connected and try to tie me to all of them. It won't work."

The room began to spin, and no amount of grasping at the

table was helping her to set it right again.

"Hmm," he said, facing the wall. "And the Nether trade here?"

"I don't know anything about the trade here," she admitted. "I don't spend enough time down south to know. What I know of Verdance, you likely do, too."

"And you don't know anything else about Astrid Frost?"

"No more than I shared in court six months ago," Virginia said. "We are no longer affiliated, and haven't been for some time."

He nodded, still facing the broken clock. She couldn't figure out what he was looking for, either in the motionless hands or in her story. "Don't leave town, Ms. Vane," he said. "And we'll need your notes on the Harrow case."

"Of course," Virginia agreed, but her stomach was threatening to empty its contents all over the desk. She swallowed back bile, sure that she was coming down with something terrible, despite the warm weather. "I am happy to turn over my notes. I imagine Captain Lindell already took them from my mother's house."

He turned, narrowing his eyes, but then they widened. "Ms. Vane, are you alright?"

"I am not feeling my best," Virginia admitted.

"Water!" he shouted, but before it could appear, Virginia slumped down in the chair, her face meeting the cold, slimy wood of the table.

Chapter Thirty-Six

"Virginia."

Light flickered overhead through closed eyelids, the fierce pounding in her brain only having intensified. She groaned, hoping whoever it was would just let her sleep.

"Virginia, you need to open your eyes, or I'm going to get the smelling salts." It was Anya, and there was none of the usual lightness in her voice. "You're not going to like it."

"I'm fine," Virginia croaked, keeping her eyes firmly shut against the intrusion of the incandescent bulb. "Leave me alone."

"Those agents said you had some sort of fit," Anya said quietly, as though someone could be just outside the door listening. "You're lucky I was in town when they were asking where the nearest hospital was, or you'd be in intensive care right about now, surrounded by a team of at least six different doctors, all of whom would be happy to note your mythic status in your chart and turn you over for conscription."

"Agents," Virginia said, and pried open one eyelid. For a split second, disorientation made the room spin, because she wasn't in the clinic room of Moonshadow Apothecary back in Verdance, she was in her mother's house.

Great.

Out of federal custody, into the fire.

She moved to sit up, but Anya pressed her back onto the chaise lounge. "No," she insisted. "Give yourself a few minutes."

Virginia pushed her hand away. "I said, I'm fine," she growled, drawing herself into a seated position. "Shadows," she swore, pressing two fingers to her temple. "Can't say I anticipated that."

"I assume it wasn't a stroke, then."

"No."

"Did you have a vision?" Anya asked, watching her with a wary stare from three steps away. "And where the hell did you go last night?"

"The woods," Virginia answered, and then added, "I was looking for something."

"What on earth could have been that important?" Anya demanded. "I assume you didn't find whatever it was, or—"

"No," Virginia interrupted. "I didn't." It was morning, but early. Just past dawn, if she had to guess. "It was stupid, I know."

"What were you looking for?"

"I don't want to talk about it," Virginia replied, the words more a resigned sigh than a coherent sentence. "Listen, I'm fine now, just let me up."

Anya ignored her as she dug through her medicinal pouch. "I'll let you leave when I am satisfied you're not going to keel over."

"Feds seem satisfied it wasn't me, at least. They've connected the murders in Verdance and here, and my alibis up north are with Lindell and Arthur. I wouldn't say I'm entirely off the hook, because they're still looking for other mythics down here and won't let up on asking." Virginia gripped the edge of the chaise, digging her fingernails into the plush upholstery and willing it to give her the balance she so desperately craved. She'd had enough uncertainty for one day. Hell, she'd had enough for an entire lifetime.

"And you're concerned about Jolie?"

"Obviously," Virginia grumbled, pain radiating down her neck and into her spine. "I was hoping you'd gotten her out of here already." She hissed out a breath, willing the light pressure of the upholstery staple on the underside to clear her mind enough for a real thought to surface. The metal was warm, heated by the oppressive summer's day, and it dented her fingertip admirably. "Where is she?"

"In back," Anya said. "She's alright, if worried." The clasp of the medicinal pouch rattled as it opened and closed three more times, with dried ingredients being tossed into a small wooden pestle. "She feels responsible, you know."

Virginia tossed off an incredulous laugh that she meant to dull the guilt taking root in her chest. "Why would she be responsible?"

"She told your mother you were missing, you wound up back here, and Lindell took you in."

"None of that is her fault."

Anya's eyes flicked over to her. "Maybe not, but she feels it anyway."

"I'll talk to her."

"She looks up to you, you know." Anya ground up the ingredients with a mortar, releasing a sweet, fruity scent into the air that was a pleasant relief from the fertilized corn across the road. "Here," she said, dissolving several heaping teaspoons into a glass and stirring vigorously. "Drink this."

"I don't like lemonade," Virginia protested, refusing to take the glass. The pale yellow hue had been adulterated by the greyish-blue powder that hadn't yet dissolved, still swirling in its own private typhoon.

Anya set the glass down on the small end table, an aggravated growl not quite dormant in her throat. "Fine."

"Alright, shadows," Virginia seethed, taking the glass. "What's in it?"

"Still don't trust me?"

"I want to know what to expect."

"Vegetable charcoal, cuttlefish ink, and bilberries," Anya explained. "Should help with the fainting."

Virginia tried to keep the look of disdain from her face, but from the blurred reflection in the glass table, she knew she hadn't succeeded. "Bottoms up," she said, and drained the glass quickly, doing her best to let it pass over her tongue without tasting it. Much to her surprise, the aftertaste was vaguely sweet, although the grittiness left something to be desired. "Not terrible, I guess."

"You're not drinking it for pleasure," Anya shot back, slightly defensive in her tone and her stance. "If you can't remain upright until we get out of here, I'm not so sure that we *will* get out of here. Not any time soon, anyway." She sat back on her haunches, her teal skirt draped over her knees as she organized the reagents back into her pouch, frowning. "What was Captain Lindell still doing here, anyway?"

"Beats me." Virginia swirled the few droplets left in the glass, collecting what was left of the sediment before tossing it back. "I have a feeling that the two of them volunteered to be the VCPD liaison. Did you happen to see Sheriff Dixon, or is he back in the city?"

"I heard he just got back into town here this morning," Anya said, buckling the clasp on her pouch. "He probably heard that you were in for questioning."

Morning sunlight streamed in through the stained glass windows, casting shadowy rainbows to dance along the tiles. "I guess I must have been out for an hour or so."

"Something like that. You weren't here long before you came to." Anya leaned forward to take the glass, her fingers brushing against Virginia's for just a moment before she drew back again, brow knit into a deep furrow. "Tell me you didn't," she said, staring her down.

"Didn't what?"

"I can see it, Virginia. Don't *lie* to me."

The familiar toxic cocktail of fear, shame, and guilt flooded into every pore, poisoning every crevice of her being until she was sure she would succumb to the noxious gas of it. "See what?" she asked, hating the trepidatious croak in her voice. "What are you talking about?"

Anya stared, her glare affixed. "Where did you get it from?"

"If you don't tell me what you're talking about, there's no way I can answer that," Virginia shot off. "Even if I am a seer, I'm sure as shadows not a mind reader."

"You know shadows-damned well what I'm talking about." Anya stood, arranging the pouch to hang at her waist. "Where did you get it from? It could have been adulterated, you know as well as I do that plenty of that stuff that winds up on the street is cut with who knows what, and I can't treat these fainting spells if I have no idea where you've—" she stopped herself, letting her hands fall to her sides. "Oh."

Virginia didn't say anything, because there was nothing

to say. She'd been caught in a net of her own making. The sensation was overly familiar.

"You didn't have the right," Anya said softly. "I trusted you."

"What in shadows were you doing with it anyway?" Virginia demanded. "It's all well and good to be high up on your self-righteous horse, but I wasn't the one traveling downstate with it." She resented that the lemonade mixture was clearing her head just in time for another argument with Anya, right when she needed the trouble the least. "What if you'd been arrested, too? Where would Jolie go then?"

"Virginia, you are aware that I work as a healer, correct?" Anya asked coldly. "I would have thought that someone with your experiences would know what happens when a shifter addicted to Nether drops off cold turkey." She exhaled a dangerously controlled breath, her icy eyes flashing with disdain. "But then, I also would have assumed that you would know better than to even think about touching the stuff."

"I was trying to trigger a vision," Virginia explained, alarmed at how she was already standing up and pacing along the floor, despite the vague shifting that still happened in her periphery if she moved too fast. "Some of us want to figure out what all this is about before Jolie winds up on the conscription rolls, or, I don't know, before my mother drives us all completely fucking insane!"

"You and I both know this has nothing to do with Jo or your mother," Anya hissed, her volume a desperate bid to get Virginia to match it. "You're so twisted up over the unsolved case of Juliette Ashling that you can't even see straight."

"Oh, sure, I'm the one not seeing straight," Virginia retorted, barking out a laugh. "I seem to recall that it was you in that tent yesterday, whispering and chanting over crystal bowls of bullshit. What even was that, anyway?"

"It doesn't matter, because it didn't work." Anya grasped the leather strap of her bag, clinging to it like a lifeboat in a flood. "At least I was trying to do something productive, something to help protect someone, and not drowning my own sorrows in my mother's house."

"Well maybe if you hadn't been hiding out in isolation, I wouldn't have left," Virginia said. Even as the words left her mouth, she knew that they were unfair, but she folded her arms over her chest anyway, defiant in her opposition. "What else was I supposed to do, just sit around and wait to get hauled in, despite my alibi?"

"You did anyway!"

"But not Jolie! They didn't find her because I made sure they didn't." Virginia raised an eyebrow, wondering if she'd won the argument.

Anya made a soft clicking sound with her tongue and sighed. "And they aren't looking for a fire demon down here?" she asked, crossing her arms to mirror Virginia's.

"No." Virginia shrugged, unfolding her arms and sitting back down because the remedy hadn't finished its magic just yet. Her head continued to swim with remnants of the vision, or Nether, or both.

"So where were you last night, really? Where were you trying to trigger this vision?"

"It was an old shed out on the east edge of town that I used to spend time in when I was younger."

"So nothing about Harrow, or Melody Kingston, or...?" Anya let the unmentioned name hang unspoken in the air, the tension of Juliette's disappearance thicker than the encroaching humidity.

"I told you, it was nothing." Virginia ran a hand through her hair, disgusted with her own condition and in dire need of a shower. "Where did my mother wind up? Is she here?"

"She's here," Anya said carefully.

"What did she do when I went in for questioning?"

Anya sat down next to her, picking at the buckle of her pouch. "She didn't stick around for too long. I don't know, she was gone by the time I got here."

"Why didn't it work?" Virginia asked. "The spell you were working on, I mean."

"Not good enough."

A crow gargled its call in the nearby cornfield, no doubt alerting its siblings to the existence of free, unprotected food. They'd long grown too clever to be disabused from an open buffet by ratty clothing stuffed with hay. Virginia glanced out the window, watching five more of them descend on the field. "The spell wasn't?"

"I wasn't." Anya sighed again, dropping her hands to her sides. "I saw my aunt conjure that spell dozens of times. I don't know what I did wrong."

"Don't be so hard on yourself," Virginia said, nudging Anya gently in the shoulder. "What were you trying to do?"

"Nothing." Anya splayed her fingers out over her knees, the silver rings catching the colored light from the front window. "It doesn't matter."

"Well, whatever it was, I'm sure you'll figure it out." Satisfied that her own inquisition had ended, at least temporarily, Virginia tried to offer Anya an encouraging smile. "You can always try again, right?"

"Sure."

"And you could stay here tonight, instead of the camp, if you want. Might be nice to sleep in a real bed after almost a week in that tent." Virginia was surprising even herself in extending the invitation, even if it was born more out of guilt more than anything else.

"No, I'll head back tonight. Maybe I will give that spell another try." Anya stood, clearly still irritated, or worried, or both. "At least you're no longer a wanted woman."

"Small mercies," Virginia said, standing to match her but coming up six inches too short. "I should get cleaned up. You sure you don't want to stay?"

Anya hesitated by the door, one hand on the carved frame, her fingers tracing the swirled ridges in the pattern. "I'm sure."

Chapter Thirty-Seven

Virginia undressed with her back to the bathroom mirror, an unconscious habit she'd formed in childhood. Even before she was scarred, something about her own reflection was a striking discomfort that she couldn't escape. She'd stare into the rifts themselves without flinching, but making eye contact with herself was strictly out of the question.

It was a mercy when the tiled bathroom filled with steam, clouding the mirror with wanted fog. The heat that was almost unbearable clothed was a relief when accompanied by strong water pressure. She stepped into the deep, claw-foot bathtub, letting mud run down off her legs and down the drain. She'd always hated camping. It reminded her too much of those early days in Verdance.

Long minutes ticked by as she stood beneath the stream, letting it soak through her hair and drag the matted curls straight until they brushed past her shoulders. The tangles would be murder to comb through.

She hummed to herself, trying to distract her thoughts from the inevitable carnage of the vision she'd had. The sound in her throat grew louder as the memory grew more insistent, clawing its way to the surface until she was bracing against the edge of the tub, taken to her knees. It had always burned her that they'd never found Juliette. No body, no crime. No evidence, no justice.

Eugene Carsh had only been part of the problem.

The real rub was the entire culture down in Birch Hollow, that selfish and myopic worldview which allowed people to dismiss anyone who wasn't exactly like them. The old boys' club thrived there, from those illegal gambling barns to covering up each other's embarrassing indiscretions. She'd seen it time and again, and so had her mother, who helped them do it more often than not.

Almost every local politician had been in their home at one time or another when she was growing up. They all went to her mother for help, begging her to fix their campaign, or to assist in hiding some old flame with a child out of wedlock. Sometimes it was both.

Virginia's mother had helped everyone except her.

She'd never understood it, and the memory of that parade of desperate fools marching through their foyer sitting on that same chaise lounge burned her so much that she had to lean over to the sink to splash cold water on her face.

Maybe it was too warm for a hot shower.

"Ginnie?" her mother called through the door, punctuated by three sharp knocks.

Virginia didn't answer, still holding fast to the porcelain despite the slick surface.

Her mother rapped against the wood again, this time more insistent. "Ginnie!" She tried the door, finding it locked. "Why did you lock the door?"

"Probably because you just tried to come in," Virginia grumbled, pushing herself onto unsteady feet, a danger through the water pooling around her feet. "What do you want?"

"What did the police ask you?"

"It doesn't matter."

Her mother made a strange sound in her throat that echoed through the heavy door, and the muffled noise still managed to echo off the hand painted tiles that stood from floor to ceiling. "Police or federal agents?" she pressed.

"Yes, the feds," Virginia answered, already tired of the inquisition. She was tired of all of it: the questions, the harassment, and the pressing suffocation of her hometown. "I took care of it."

"What did they want?"

"It's about the murder of Melody Kingston, which I can assure you has nothing to do with me." Virginia twisted the knob, shutting off the water. The enchantment of a hot shower only lasted as long as the peace did, which was never very long in that house. "And Agent Campbell seems to think the murders are all connected by the Nether trade."

"Are you going to open the door?"

"When I'm dressed." She looked for her clean clothes and cursed herself for leaving them on the table in the hall, so desperate to be clean that she'd mislaid them. "Can you—"

"Why do you think I'm standing here? Unlock the door, Ginnie, it's not as if you have anything I haven't seen." Her mother's heels tapped against the waxed floors in the corridor as she waited, her impatient gait picking up rhythm the longer that she waited. "What's the matter, did you get stuck?"

"No," Virginia snapped, wrapping a towel around herself. "Just wait for a second." She secured it under her arm, keeping the overlapped seam at her side. The lock slid easily, releasing the door and with it, a plume of steam into the rest of the house.

Her mother stepped through, holding out the pile of clothes but turning her face away from the bathroom. "You are the only person I've ever known to take a hot shower when the weather is this humid," she mused, but her musings always sounded more like criticism than jokes. "You've always been a glutton for punishment."

"I spent several days in the wilderness, pardon me for wanting to get clean before I dirty up your upholstery," Virginia shot back. "Irritating you is far more a punishment than a little bit of warm water."

"There's mud on the chaise."

"Great." Virginia took the clothes, rolling her eyes and foolishly making sure that her mother saw it. "Thank you," she tacked on as an addendum, but the words came out tangled with indecision and irritation. "You can go now."

"Oh, can I?" her mother sniped, still standing in the way of the door. "You didn't have to spend days and days out there camping, you know. All three of you were more than welcome here."

Virginia disappeared behind the shower curtain to dress, becoming very aware that her mother had no intention of offering her even the slightest modicum of privacy. *Your welcomes are hardly the gold standard* is what she wanted to say, but she pressed the words back down into her chest, letting them burn holes into her ribs instead. "It's complicated," was what she said instead.

She buttoned her trousers, biting back a contented sigh at the feel of fresh linen against her skin, and tucked in her shirt before drawing back the shower curtain. "Thank you for keeping an eye on Jolie."

"She's a sweet girl."

"Yes," Virginia agreed. "She is."

Her mother's eyes roved over her, looking for even the smallest imperfection to linger on, to critique, to point out in the name of self-improvement. "What is her story, really?" she asked, having found nothing with which to verbalize her permanent distaste. "She should be in school."

"She's eighteen, she can do what she likes."

"Where are her parents?"

Virginia dried herself with the towel, regretting the steam. "You'd have to ask her that," she replied, wanting to avoid any conversations that even remotely danced too near the truth. "We haven't discussed it often."

That much was true. Jolie was tight-lipped about her family, and given her own, Virginia allowed it without much pushing.

"Is she an orphan?" her mother asked, always intrusive, always asking too many questions, always knowing more than she should.

"I don't know."

"Aren't you concerned about what she might be running from?"

Virginia caught her mother's eye in the reflection of the mirror as she tied her wet hair back into a low bun. "No."

"Why not?"

"People run for all kinds of reasons." Virginia wiped the rest of the condensation from the mirror before she left the bathroom, flicking the droplets into the sink. "Some run from loan sharks, some run from bad partners, some from bad family." She edged past her mother in the doorway, taking her muddy clothes with her. "And some run from themselves."

"She's very bright."

"She is."

"Aren't you worried about conscription?" her mother asked, following her into the bedroom as Virginia stuffed her clothes into a small net bag that fit neatly into her weathered tan suitcase.

"Of course."

"If she's really a fire demon, then—"

Virginia yanked open the door of the oak wardrobe, shoving the suitcase inside. "You aren't telling me anything that I don't already know, alright?" she snapped, barely resisting the urge to kick it shut again. "I never wanted to come back down here, not with the way things were, or are, and certainly not to get barged in on in the shower."

"I didn't barge in on you, I knocked. You opened the door, Ginnie, not me."

"Only because it was locked!"

Her mother folded her hands in front of herself, falling primly atop her matching pale green skirt suit. "You could stay here for a time, if you wanted. Both of you, until things cool down."

"Judging by Melody Kingston's murder, nothing is going to cool down any time soon." Virginia's irritation seeped through her every pore, fingers reaching deep into her pockets for the familiar. "I need a cigarette."

Her mother pulled a bronze case from her skirt pocket and held it out, her face neutral despite the gesture. "Here," she said casually. "I assume you're out."

"I'm good, thanks," Virginia said, even as she realized that her mother was right. "I don't want anything from you."

"You're very hard work, you know," her mother replied, sliding the case back into her pocket. "Maybe if you didn't spend half of your time getting tangled up in cases that don't concern you, you wouldn't be spending the other half in cuffs."

Virginia snorted a derisive laugh, already feeling like a caged animal. "Heinrich Harrow *was* my case, actually, I told you that."

"Once he turned up deceased, that should have been the end of it," her mother said, tone far too calm for the conversation they were having. "But you couldn't leave it alone, as always."

"Always?" Virginia asked, incredulous. Frustration was a rising tide within her again, and the riptide would drown her if she wasn't careful. Along with it came the shame and guilt of the dream she'd had of her mother crying at the table. But that hadn't been a vision, the timing was off, and she was asleep, besides. It hadn't been real.

She breathed out a dangerous sigh, flexing her hands at her sides. Her fingers felt bereft without the silver knuckles, but she'd left them on the sink in the bathroom. "You know what? Never mind."

"Did you have a vision?" her mother asked, so plainly that it was startling.

"No," Virginia lied.

Her mother stared for a moment, but said nothing, backing out of the room until she was half-hidden by the doorway. She hovered and opened her mouth like she was going to say something, and didn't.

"What?" Virginia prompted, a little too sharply.

"You'd tell me, wouldn't you?" her mother asked. "If you had?"

"Sure."

"Why did you go out to that old shack last night?"

Virginia grimaced, turning back towards the mirrored wardrobe because having to face her own reflection was preferable to facing her mother, no matter how uncomfortable it was. "I don't know."

"This would be easier if you would just tell me," her mother said. And then, gentler, "Ginnie, did you have a vision, or not?"

"I don't know why you care so much." Virginia wanted to punch the mirror, to feel the shards of glass shred through her skin, because at the very least the distraction would be rather palatable. "It doesn't have any impact on you."

"I would rather that my only daughter wasn't conscripted." Her mother remained in the doorway, standing half inside, and half out, rocking her weight between the two satin heels that matched her outfit. "Don't you know what they do to conscripted mythics?."

"Of course I know," Virginia said with a scoff. "I am more than aware, thank you."

"It's no kind of life," her mother chastised. "Not for you or that girl. Senator Dean is busy penning legislation that would make life for registered mythics more difficult than it already is." She took the cigarette case from her pocket again, sliding one out for herself. "He'll do whatever he can to shore up mythiphobic votes." She scowled and held the cigarette between her middle and ring fingers on her left hand, always such a strange way to do so. "Your life would be much easier if you'd just listened to me."

"Just because everyone else around here worships the ground you walk on doesn't mean I have to." Virginia spat the words out one at a time, regret growing heavy in her lungs with every passing syllable. She headed for the front door, but before she went, she grabbed her silver knuckles from the bathroom sink.

Chapter Thirty-Eight

Virginia's car was waiting in the driveway, freshly fixed and detailed. The black paint sparkled in the afternoon sun, the windows clear and without a single streak. No doubt Sammy had wanted to avoid a confrontation with her after swearing to the cops and feds alike that Virginia had been the one to go off into the woods with Melody Kingston, but she wasn't going to get her wish. Virginia would have words with her soon enough.

As she wrenched open the door, Jolie came tearing up from behind the house, calf-length chiffon skirt hitched in one hand. "Wait for me!" she shouted, practically throwing herself into the passenger seat. "Don't leave me here again," she pleaded, pressing her hands to the dashboard.

"I thought you left with Anya," Virginia said, guilt rumbling within her. "I would have come to find you otherwise."

"I thought you were angry with me."

"Angry?" Virginia asked, thrusting the key into the ignition. Mercifully, the engine roared into life, with no trace of the disgusting clunking noise that had landed her dead in the water back by the Speer house in the first place. "Shadows, this car hasn't looked or sounded so good since it was new off the lot, I'd expect." She circled the horseshoe driveway before pulling out onto the gravel road, tires inflated and the chassis balanced. "Why would I be angry?"

"I told your mom you were missing, and then you wound up in questioning with the feds," Jolie explained, her voice quiet and sheepish. "Because of me."

"That would have happened anyway," Virginia grumbled. "And don't worry about my mother. She finds out everything in this town anyway."

Jolie sank down in her seat, covering her face. "And I accidentally led her to the campsite, too. I was so sure I hadn't been followed. I kept checking, I doubled back on myself at least four times, I didn't leave a trail, either."

"I wouldn't worry about it," Virginia said, trying to soothe the kid's guilt. "Even good private eyes get tailed sometimes. Happens to the best of us, and my mother has more of a knack for it than anyone in the VCPD." It felt good to be behind the wheel again, the leather warm and smooth under her fingertips. "I'm not angry," she reiterated, sneaking a glance at Jolie and nearly slamming on the brakes when she spotted the holster under the girl's arm. "What in shadows are you doing with that?" she demanded.

"I just thought—"

Virginia eased out a breath, trying not to lose her temper. "Why do you have my gun? I was sure it had wound up in police or federal custody," she said. "While I am glad it didn't, I do worry about you carrying it around like that."

"I had it hidden in the kitchen," Jolie explained. "Underneath the cake plate."

"The cake plate." Virginia shook her head, laughing, because all she could imagine was her mother's abject horror if she'd only known. "You should be careful. I wouldn't want anyone yanking that out of its holster just to use it against you."

"I can shoot fire from my hands," Jolie protested. "I'm fine."

"You shouldn't be doing that, not where anyone can see you, and not now," Virginia chastised. "Things are only getting worse for powerful mythics in this country, and federal agents are just looking for an easy scapegoat to pin crimes on so that they can all go back to their wives or mistresses or both back in Verdance."

"Both?"

"You'd be surprised."

Jolie nodded sagely, unbuckling the holster. "Where are we going?" she asked, placing the gun and the holster down on the floorboards. "Back to the campsite?"

"I don't know," Virginia admitted, and then added, "Probably." Briefly, she considered trying to track Shirin down, if for no other reason than getting the intel from back in the city. She was quietly hoping that another murder in Verdance would drag the feds away to some midway roadside motel, grouchy and out of the way. Then, she could quietly pack all of them up and head back without the eyes of six federal officers staring down anyone who crossed out of the city limits.

But Shirin was becoming more of a liability than an asset, more of a threat than a comfort. Perhaps that had always been the case with Captain Lindell. For the first time in a long time, Virginia wished that Arthur was around.

Her jaw set firm, and she turned left towards the woods, instead of right towards town. They couldn't take the risk of anyone asking Jolie any questions, not when they were so focused on the idea of outsiders. "Let's head to the campsite, maybe we can help Anya pack up and we can all head home. I'm tired of this place, I don't know about you."

She wanted to get Jolie out of Birch Hollow before someone mentioned her to the feds. She wanted answers for Juliette, but the vision continued to haunt her, tugging at memories and guilt she had long since buried.

"It's a good thing they got the car fixed up quick," she mused, but Jolie only nodded. Virginia tapped her fingers against the wheel, grateful for the freedom that a working vehicle had returned to her. "You okay, Firefly?" she asked gently.

"Yeah." Jolie shifted in the seat, pulling her knees up to her chest and leaning her head on her forearm, facing out towards the fields. "I'm just tired."

"You sure?" It wasn't in Virginia's nature to push, not when she wasn't interrogating someone with information to hide, but it was plain as bright daylight that something was eating away at the kid little by little. "You can tell me, you know."

"I told you, nothing."

The obvious lie rankled Virginia, but she wasn't quite sure why. "If you say so," Virginia replied, doing her best to keep her tone light and airy but it fell flat against the leather interior, drowned out by the sound of the wind rushing past the windows. She grasped for something that might pull Jolie back to her. None of it was Jolie's fault, even if she'd chosen to take on that guilty burden for herself. "We can stop in town for some grub, if you're hungry."

"Sure, whatever." Jolie sighed, but if Virginia hadn't been

listening for it, she would have missed it entirely. It was so quiet and swallowed that only the rise and fall of the kid's shoulders told the story of it. "We should get Anya something, too."

"We will."

"What spell is she working on?" Jolie asked, probably as grateful for the subject shift as Virginia was.

"She didn't tell you?"

Jolie shook her head. "No."

"She didn't tell me, either," Virginia admitted. "I think it might have something to do with Mrs. Speer, but I can't be sure. We were out there yesterday, her son's house that is, and Anya thinks he might be poisoning her." It was the most Virginia had shared with Jolie about a case since they'd arrived in Birch Hollow, but even as she said the words, wondered if she might come to regret them.

"Poison!" Jolie exclaimed, sitting up in her seat. Her eyes sparkled with intensity as she leaned forward against the dash, resting her forearms on the hot leather. "Why would he poison his own mother?"

"Money, I expect," Virginia answered. "It's always money, kid."

"Imagine poisoning your own mother," Jolie said, shaking her head.

Virginia didn't offer up her own truth, which was that the thought had crossed her mind once or twice over the years, especially around Juliette's death. The betrayal that had come after made it far too easy to sever that cord.

Her hands tightened against the steering wheel, uncon-scious in their pressure. If only she could sever herself truly, for once and for all, from her mother, from Birch Hollow, from all of it.

Perhaps she would have been someone else, if she'd managed to escape it all sooner.

"Virginia?" Jolie prompted, her head tilted.

They were stopped at an intersection, the car idling. Virginia wasn't even entirely sure how long they'd been sitting there, staring at fields and empty roads. "Yeah," she said, easing the car across to the other side. "Was just making sure no one was coming."

"Can I ask a question?"

"Shoot," she replied, hoping the question was something innocuous.

"What was it like growing up there, in that house?" Jolie asked, shrinking back into her seat like she was anticipating an inevitable, volatile reaction, but one that wasn't quite bad enough to discourage the asking in the first place. "I can't even imagine. The orphanage was all dirty, unwaxed wood floors and beds with broken springs."

While Virginia was no stranger to a harsh life, it had started much later than it did for most. Her upbringing had never left her hungry, at least. "I struggled," she answered honestly. "I'm sure you can tell that my mother and I don't really get along very well."

Jolie nodded lightly, tapping her fingers against her knees. She didn't ask any more questions, but for some reason, Virginia felt compelled to fill in more of the blanks. Maybe it was the kid's sad and frustrated demeanor that day, such a departure from her usual sunny self, or maybe it was the creeping emotional rot of her hometown, she'd never know.

"She had me locked in my room the night Juliette went missing." Virginia hadn't spoken those words aloud in three decades, not since she sat at Eugene Carsh's desk, begging him to investigate. "I was never able to forgive her for that."

"And then what?"

"And then the police here did a very poor job of finding out what happened to Juliette. I tried to investigate myself—I was a little younger than you are now—and they didn't appreciate my efforts, especially when I started asking questions about who might know where she went that night." Virginia was stopped at another intersection, foot pressed into the brake pedal. "Carsh warned me to let it go, but I couldn't. Not when it was—not for Juliette, I couldn't. He threw me into a cell to teach me a lesson." She inhaled, and her lungs resisted the life-giving inflation that the oxygen was offering. "I need a cigarette," she muttered.

Digging through the glove box, she found her case, mercifully intact with two left inside, hiding beneath the tarnished silver. She held it out to Jolie with a raised eyebrow, asking the question she wouldn't voice.

Jolie chewed her lip but shot a tiny spark at the end of the filter, setting it ablaze.

"Thanks." Virginia inhaled, the smoke filling her mouth and coating her tongue and *shadows*, she was grateful for its poisonous familiarity. "My mother left me in that cell. I begged her to get me out, pleaded, but she left anyway."

She was smoking the cigarette too fast, and it was churning in her stomach, but she didn't care. Virginia flicked ash out the window onto the waiting pavement below before she released the brake and carried on down the road. "As soon as Carsh let me out, I made my way to Verdance. She'd made it clear I wasn't welcome at home, so that's what happened."

"No wonder," was all Jolie said. It was validation, at least, even if it came from an eighteen-year-old girl.

When they reached the usual spot to park near the campsite, there was a strange, unfamiliar energy in the air that crackled almost like a static shock. The hairs on Virginia's arms stood up, and it was the same sensation that she sometimes got just before a big break in a case.

"Does it feel—" Jolie started, climbing out of the car.

"Yeah," Virginia interrupted, reaching back inside to grab the holster off of the floorboards. "Be careful." She buckled the leather strap around her shoulders, keeping the revolver loose in its sheath. Birch Hollow had caused enough problems for her, she wasn't about to let it cause more.

Chapter Thirty-Nine

"Anya?" she called through the birch trees, their starkly contrasted bark juxtaposed against the verdant canopy above.

When there was no answer, she made her approach quietly, motioning for Jolie to follow close behind. She couldn't leave the kid in the car, not when something about the impending clearing ahead felt so wrong. Virginia picked her way through the brush, resisting the urge to do so with her gun at the ready.

"Are you out here?" she said loudly as she reached the clearing, fingers already secured within the silver knuckles in her pocket. "We came to see if you wanted to get the hell out of here, we thought maybe—"

Virginia stopped short at the sight of the camp, overturned and strewn to the edges with refuse and discarded reagents. Half-burned candles littered the boards around the tent. "Shadows," she swore, nudging at a cast iron pot with the toe of her muddy brogue. "Anya?" she called again, reaching for her gun this time. "Are you alright?" She may not be able to shoot magic, as Anya had so eloquently put it, but the safety the weight in her hand gave her was undeniable.

"Good morning," Anya muttered from inside the tent.

She pulled back the flap and rubbed her eyes, red raw from reagent or upset, Virginia couldn't tell.

"Are you alright?"

"I need coffee," Anya replied, securing the flaps to their posts.

"Coffee," Jolie repeated with a nod, holding her hand out towards the fire pit.

"Yeah, of course," Virginia replied. She holstered her gun, tightening the buckle back into its usual position. "Are you sure you're alright?"

"I'm fine," Anya grumbled. "Just a rough night."

"What were you doing?" Jolie asked, her brow knit into a concerned frown. And then, quieter, "Why didn't you ask for my help?"

"Can't help with this one, Jo," Anya said. "Tinctures and poultices are one thing, spells are another." Her mouth set into a firm line. "And it didn't work, so it doesn't matter anyway." She reached out for the cup of water that Jolie was handing her, setting it down on the floor where it left a water ring on the untreated wood. "I saw my aunt do this a hundred times, but..." she trailed off, shaking her head. "I must have missed something. I thought maybe... but no." She looked up at Virginia, a bemused look coming to a rest on her face. "Were you going to shoot me, Virginia?"

"No, I was going to shoot whoever did that to the camp." Virginia stepped back towards the tent's entrance, her back to the canvas. "I wouldn't shoot you unless you really deserved it."

Anya chuckled a quiet laugh and tugged the hem of her skirt back down over her knees. "Good to know. I was worried our working relationship had shifted into untenable territory."

She sighed angrily, smoothing back the silvery locks framing her face that had come loose from their long, intricate braid. "I was working. I thought maybe if I just added a bit more of the active ingredient, it would work." She grimaced at the state of the tent. "It didn't."

"What exactly were you trying to do, again?" Virginia probed, wondering if her usual interrogation techniques would work on her. She was probably too smart for that, but maybe the all-nighter had shaken something loose. "What spell was this?"

"Don't question me, Virginia, I'm not a suspect," Anya chastised. "And I told you, I couldn't just sit around and let Mrs. Speer be poisoned. That poor old woman won't last much longer with that much strychnine in her system, she's already unsteady enough as it is. That lousy, good-for-nothing son Anthony deserves prison."

Anya swept a leafy green reagent into a small pile, using a bent piece of paper to funnel it back into a tiny glass jar. "It was supposed to be a severing spell, but something kept going wrong. The reagents were unstable, it wouldn't work." Anya tightened the jar's lid with a smooth, deft gesture, setting it gently into her pouch. "It doesn't make sense. I've done them before with birch sweetwater for a mild result, but maybe it would have been enough to get her somewhere safe, I don't know."

"What do you mean, unstable?"

"The coated candles, the soaked twine, all of it kept flaring before the ritual could be completed." Anya said, bitterness coating the sides of her tone. "I don't know what I did wrong." She moved to the next overturned jar, sweeping what she could back into the glass. "What a waste of reagents.

Foolish."

"No one can blame you for trying," Virginia offered. "Maybe we can try to figure out something else." She wasn't sure what, not without alerting the authorities to the fact that they'd been snooping around in the first place and drawing attention back in their direction before they were able to get Jolie out of the area. "How long do you think she has? Maybe if we can solve this case quick, then—"

"Days," Anya interrupted. "If I had to guess. She's not doing well, Virginia, and I can't stand the thought of leaving her out there with her awful son. You and I both know he's just waiting around for her to die so he can have the house to himself."

"You'd think he'd be happy to wait a few more years, instead of risk prison," Virginia mused. "It's not as if she's a spring chicken."

"Greed and avarice are rarely logical." Anya stood, steadying herself on the central pillar of the tent. She buckled her pouch around her hips, letting it rest on the left side before she moved to the front of the tent, securing the flaps open once more. "Jolie, that coffee smells amazing. You are an absolute angel."

"Demon, actually," Jolie replied, grinning from the other side of the fire pit.

Virginia snorted a laugh, the sound echoing around the campsite.

"Enough for two cups each," Jolie said, pouring freshly brewed coffee into a mug.

Anya sat down on the bench, taking the mug and sipping deeply, groaning with the pleasure of the taste. "Perfection."

Jolie glowed under the praise, and it struck Virginia that

she probably spent more time criticising and warning than anything else. That specific realization stung more than any hive of angry wasps. "Coffee?" Jolie asked Virginia, holding the kettle aloft.

"Er—yeah," Virginia replied, passing her a mug. "Thanks." She added honey to the coffee once she found it under an overturned pot, but there was no milk to be had. She took a sip, pleasantly surprised that it wasn't too bitter. "I could talk to Arthur about Mrs. Speer. He'd probably listen."

"Are you entirely certain he wouldn't tell the feds how he came to know that she's being poisoned?" Anya asked. "You have to be sure, or they'll pick you up for questioning again before we can make it out of here. Not to mention, they'd likely nab me for impersonating a nurse. I may know more than one, but that doesn't stop me from being prosecuted for it."

"He won't say anything, Anya." Virginia sighed into her mug. "As much as it pains me to admit it, I would trust Arthur with my life."

Chapter Forty

Virginia slid into the booth at the burger joint, the familiar scent of burnt grease already permeating its way through her clothes. She'd have to toss just about everything when she got back to the city, there would be no washing the miasma of Birch Hollow out of the fabric. "What's good?" she asked. "Or what's bad, given the situation?"

"Ginnie," he said, blotting sweat from his shining head with a cheap paper napkin. "How did you know where to find me?"

"I always know where to find you, Dixon."

He waved at the waitress and held up four fingers, pointing at the menu to indicate what he was ordering. "I took the liberty of ordering you a vanilla milkshake and a large portion of fries." He gave her a cautious glance, waiting for her inevitable reaction.

She wanted to protest the order, but he'd remembered her favorites, even after all those years had gone by. "Thanks," she said casually. "Where's Lindell?"

"I sent her back to the city." He drummed his fingers against the scratched wood table, his gold wedding ring sparkling in the light through the large window beside them.

"Told her not to come down here in the first place."

Virginia raised an eyebrow, but didn't say anything else. The waitress dropped the order down in front of them with a casual pleasantry, along with a paired salt and pepper shaker set. The fries were perfectly crispy, irritatingly still the best she'd ever had, even up in the city. The cold milkshake slid over her tongue like water after a drought, the frozen concoction a delightful respite from the heat.

"This is all getting out of control, Ginnie," he said.

"Agent Campbell assures me that they have everything completely under control."

"And you always trust a fed, right? No doubt they..." he trailed off long enough to take a large bite of his cheeseburger, the tomato sliding off the patty and onto the plate. "I just worry about you being down here. I didn't think it would be this hard."

"Okay." Virginia knocked back another swig of the milkshake, having realized just how much she had missed them since she'd left. "And?"

"Did you talk to your mother?" he asked quietly. "About, you know..."

Virginia swallowed back a grumble, chasing it with another fry to dampen the bitter taste of it. "She doesn't know anything."

"And have you—" he prodded the tomato, but decided to leave it on the plate after his inspection. "Have you been able to access anything?"

"Nothing useful."

"So you have?" he prompted. "What was it?"

"*Nothing useful*," she repeated, this time with more insistence. "I'm not hiding anything, Arthur. It's just old memories, dredged up bullshit."

"What about this Heinrich Harrow character? Or John Folst, whatever his name was." Arthur took another bite, this time unseating the large leaf of lettuce that dangled out of his mouth for a few seconds until he crammed the rest of it in with his fork. For a man raised on manners, he'd forgotten most of them in his time working on the force. "Leads? Anything? How about Melody Kingston?"

Virginia shrugged, because she couldn't very well tell him that she'd had a vision featuring nothing more than a quiet, disembodied voice. He'd never let it go, picking at the clue, if that's even what it was, until her memory was red-raw. "Nothing concrete," she said. "And it's not like they're our cases anymore, Arthur. It's now in the hands of the feds." She dipped a fry into her milkshake, enjoying the disgusted face it pulled from Arthur. "Although it seems like Mrs. Speer's son may be poisoning her."

"And how did you work that one out?" he asked, mouth full.

"He wants the house, he's down on his luck," she said. "And now he's got her isolated out in unincorporated land just the other side of the county line."

"And you went out there?"

She swallowed another mouthful of milkshake to buy herself just enough time to come up with a plausible answer. "Maybe," she said, which was plausible but not particularly convincing. "I can't say."

"Ginnie—"

"Just try to get someone out there, alright?" she interrupted. "Work your magic on Eugene Carsh. Tell him he's a good cop and a brilliant investigator, lie through your sparkly white teeth about his abilities and he'll fall over himself."

"I'll go out there myself." He reached across to her plate, stealing a fry, and she let him. Some allowances were too ingrained to fight against, even though the last time he'd done it they were still just kids. "One less thing to worry about."

"Yeah, I think I've had enough of this place for a while, to be quite honest with you." She took the abandoned tomato with her fork and plopped it onto her own plate, cutting it into thirds. She ate the two pieces that didn't have his bite mark on them. "It would be nice to tie all of this into a neat little bow, but I'm getting the feeling that we won't be able to, especially not with the feds sniffing around."

"Ginnie…" he tried again, staring across the table with that shadows-damned furrowed brow she'd always hated so much. The concern apparent on his face was enough to turn her stomach, the acid of the stolen tomato mixing with the frosty dairy of the milkshake in an insidious way. "Maybe I shouldn't have pressured you to come back down here."

"You think?" she asked with a derisive snort. "I told you so, Arthur. I specifically said that coming back down here was a bad idea. I was pushed into it by Nina Harrow, by you, by Lindell."

"That's not true," he protested. "You could have said no."

"And then heard about it from now until kingdom fucking come." She sipped at the milkshake again, willing it to soothe her nerves and her stomach. "My mother doesn't know anything useful about seers, bodies are piling up, Juliette—" she stopped herself short, cramming another fry into her mouth. "I got dragged into this mess, is it so bad to want to see it through?"

He squinted, leaning across the table on his forearms. "No, you know something," he said in a low voice. "You have a theory, at least." He pressed in further, bent almost entirely in half over the wood in an almost comical pose. "You forget that I know you, Ginnie, I know when you're hiding something."

"I'm not hiding anything," she lied, returning his glare with enough force to hopefully deter him from any further prying. "You're just paranoid. Too many years on the force, maybe, or maybe it's just Verdance specifically that brings it out in you."

"It's not the force, and it's not Verdance," he said, eyes flicking from one side of Virginia's face to the other, desperately seeking the answers she wasn't willing to divulge. "Tell me what it is."

"I only know what I've already told you about the active cases," she deflected. "Shoes, Nether. Nothing else." She stole a pickle that was hanging off his burger to the side, popping it into her mouth, and immediately regretting the flavor profile of vanilla and dill. "But that's not your jurisdiction. It's state, or, the rift forbid, the feds. I doubt you or I will even get a glance at those case files from here on out."

"It's tied to a missing person report in Verdance, I have every right to investigate."

"That's horseshit, Arthur," she said casually. "And you're starting to sound like me, or, shadows forbid, Lindell."

"Lindell is by the book," Arthur challenged. "More than you ever were."

"Until she wants something, maybe." Virginia sat back in the booth, folding her arms over her chest in a defensive position.

"And what about her?" he asked, and without saying, Virginia knew who he meant, even though they'd rarely even discussed her.

"Of course not," she snapped. "That was thirty-one years ago. The case is colder than a Verdance puddle in winter, no evidence, no suspects, no leads. I accepted that a long time ago."

"I've seen her photo on the board in your living room," he said gently. "I remember how you used to—"

"The only thing you remember is how desperate you were to throw me under the bus when we worked together, and just how gleeful you were when you met Mona. No doubt having a beautiful woman fawn over you was a sensation so potent that even a Dixon couldn't resist it." It was a cheap shot, and they both knew it.

He leaned back, considering her, and she knew he was about to either defend himself or leave the diner. "Please, Ginnie," he said casually. "As if you don't also know the wonder of a beautiful woman."

A laugh strangled itself in her throat, too confused to exit her mouth through usual means. "That's not what I expected you to say."

"People change."

"You don't." She ate another fry, the grease starting to cool and the crisp beginning to turn to mush. "I don't."

Arthur sighed and pushed his plate towards her, having left a third of it. "What vision did you have?"

Virginia matched his shrug motion for motion, adding a dismissive roll of her eyes. "The real lead wasn't from a vision," she said casually. "And not every lead is actionable.

Some people have high-powered lawyers, or diplomatic immunity, or—"

"So whoever this lead is about has immunity," he said, scribbling a note in his pad.

"I didn't say that."

"You didn't have to, I read between the lines." He jotted something down, the graphite of his pencil smearing across the pristine page. "Alright," he relented, but clearly wasn't happy about it. "You'd tell me if you were in trouble, right?"

"Called you from a jail cell, so yes, I would."

The light in the diner shifted, a cloud passing over the sun. "Weather is turning," he said casually, following the sky as it changed. "Might finally be a relief to all this heat and humidity, what do you think?"

"Sure," Virginia said.

"I wonder if the storm will reach up to Verdance. It's just about as hot there as it is down here," he mused. "Mona is fed up with it."

Storm clouds swirled in the distance, gathering out past the edges of Birch Hollow. "Looking a little green," Virginia said, leaning forward across the table. "Reminds me of that big one back when we were kids, remember?"

"Took out half the fields that summer," Arthur agreed. "Talk of the the town for months." He gave her a sideways look, unsure if he should include his addendum. "Your mother saved this place back then."

Jaw clamped firm, Virginia nodded. "So they say."

"None of the farms would have survived without investment into the town, enough to tide folks over until the next harvest."

"You don't have to remind me, Arthur," Virginia grumbled

under her breath. "Shadows know half the people in this town think she's a gift to humanity." Just as she was about to lay into her absent mother's character, the waitress stopped by the table again, refilling their water glasses. A metal frame on the wall held a signed photograph of Senator J.D., as if he were a film star and not a politician. She scowled at it, and Arthur turned in his seat, following her glare.

"Good Ol' Jonathan Dean," he muttered. "My parents had stories about that family."

"Stories?" Virginia asked. "What kind of stories?"

"Oh, you know, the same sort that always crop up in places like these. Corruption, hush money, connections." He sipped at his water, rubbing the condensation from the glass where the diner's logo was stamped. "Wouldn't be surprised if he made a play for president, sooner or later. President Ariano's term is up in a couple of years, and that would be a perfect time for Dean to make a play."

"Mm. Few folks around here don't have much good to say about him."

He met her eyes and raised an eyebrow. "Not him, Ginnie?" he asked. "How would he have anything to do with Harrow and Kingston?"

Virginia shook her head. "Not them. Juliette."

He nodded slowly, eyes wide. "Taking down Jonathan Dean would be—"

"Impossible, I know." She shook her head. "You don't have to tell me that."

"Not impossible," he argued. "Not if we start with the little fish."

Chapter Forty-One

The Speer family residence came into view, the canopy of trees waving gently in the precious breeze as shadows danced along the path. Virginia blinked against the memory of the vision, Juliette's visage in her mind like a knife between her ribs.

"How do you want to play this?" Arthur asked. "Her son is going to start hollering the second he sees us."

"Hollering," Virginia repeated with a smirk. "You're downstate for five minutes, and already you sound like you never even set foot in Verdance." The car lurched to a stop, and as it did, she squinted at a strange pock in the home's exterior. A missing brick, but not the kind that had smashed through her mother's window. "I was kind of hoping that would have been the brick that got thrown through the window," she said, pointing.

"I guess Anthony wasn't the only one who didn't want you sticking around." Arthur took the keys from the ignition and ran his hands along the steering wheel. "Let's get in there. Maybe we can get him to let something slip. He knows more than he's letting on."

"I wouldn't count on it. We're the last people he wants

to see. He's going to—" she stopped herself short, leaning against the dashboard. "What in the hell is Anya doing here?"

"Not part of your plan with Ms. Quinn?" Arthur drummed his fingers against the steering wheel, brown skin against black leather.

"We didn't have much of a plan," Virginia admitted. "But if she's here, that may just offer us some cover." At Arthur's questioning, skeptical raise of an eyebrow, she sighed. "Anya posed as a nurse from the county hospital to get in last time. Don't say anything to anyone, and don't make a big deal out of it. She was trying to help."

Arthur sighed. "That was one hell of a risk, given how things played out."

"Not complaining now though, are you?" she asked, climbing out of the car. "Leave it here. We might need a quick exit if he decides to answer the door with his daddy's shotgun." At the sound of her own words, her hands brushed against her holstered revolver. "We can only hope things don't quite go in that direction. I'm not really in the mood for a tourniquet today."

"Doubt a tourniquet would save us," Arthur muttered.

"You never know, we might get lucky," she replied with an artificial chirp. "It could be loaded with bird shot."

"Lots of little holes, instead of one big one. Fantastic."

Virginia kept her hand at the holster's buckle as she approached the steps, wary of the silence within. Maybe Anya was speaking with an unusually hushed tone. Maybe it was something worse. "You're the one who wanted to start with the small fish," she sniped. "Can't nail J.D. to the wall for a damned thing, we don't know which fish is busy murdering folks up and down the interstate, but we can damn well save an old lady from her only surviving son." She blew a breath out from where it had been held in her cheeks. "Fuck," she grumbled. "What a life."

Virginia climbed the steps, squinting through the mesh of the screen door. "Hello?" she called, unable to see anyone in the shady interior.

The door opened with a whisper across the wood floor. "Virginia!" Jolie said, throwing her arms around Virginia's neck. She looked past her, waving at Arthur. "And Sheriff Dixon, too!"

"What are you two doing here?" Virginia asked, aware that it sounded more like an accusation than a casual question. "Where's Anya?"

"In the kitchen," Jolie answered. "She wanted to check something, but she didn't say what."

"More of you?" Mrs. Speer asked from the sofa, hands busy with her knitting even as they shook. "Who are you and what do you want?" she asked.

"It's me, ma'am, Ginnie Cabot," Virginia answered, cringing internally at the use of the name her mother gave her but hoping it would be the key she needed to assuage the woman's concerns. "My mother wanted me to stop by with her warm regards. She heard that you've been ill."

Mrs. Speer's brow furrowed, increasingly focused on her work as she struggled with each stitch. "Vivian Cabot, of course," she said, fumbling her needles.

"Virginia," Anya said from the kitchen, leaning her head out of the doorway. Her brow was furrowed in confusion, or concern, or both—it was hard to discern such an unusual look on her face. "What are you doing here?"

"Could ask you the same thing." Virginia sidled around the

wingback chair, the upholstery in fashion twenty years back and the threads worn at the points of contact. Mrs. Speer had left her husband's chair exactly the way he'd left it.

She closed the kitchen door, hoping to earn them a little bit of privacy. "Where is her son?"

"I don't know. She said he was out back, but Jolie didn't see anyone or anything out there." Anya wiped at the splatters of cold tea dripped on the counter. "I wanted to check on her. Turns out the place was cleared by the feds so he moved her back here." She sighed, squeezing her eyes shut as she craned her neck to face the ceiling. "Small mercies, I suppose."

"How is she?"

"Worse. I was trying to—"

The screen door slammed shut, the wood audibly splintering as the crack echoed across the living room. "What the hell is going on here?" Anthony roared.

"Show time," Virginia grumbled, keeping the catch of her holster open. The son was angry, volatile, and she'd already taken note of the shotgun over the fireplace on their last visit. "Anthony," she said, easing out into the living room with her palms facing upwards. She caught Arthur's eye, and he nodded, a steely glint in his own. "We just had a few more questions for you."

"Already told you people everything," he retorted, setting a brown paper sack on the floor, the top folded over to conceal the contents. "Locals, county, and feds have been in here day in and day out, harassing my mother. It's time you greaseball grifters left us the hell alone already." He gestured towards the door. "Go on, get. Don't make me show you the way to the door, I'm sure you found it just fine on the way in." He waited a beat, and when no one moved, he reached for the shotgun. "And she ain't no hospital nurse, neither," he uttered, taking a step towards the kitchen. "If I didn't know any better, I'd say she was a damned dirty witch, and unless she wants me reporting her to the feds, she'd better make tracks along with the rest of ya."

"Tony, don't be rude," Mrs. Speer said softly, hands trembling as her stiff, trembling fingers tried to grip the smooth, aged ivory of the needles. "Ms. Quinn just wanted to check on me again, and these others here are just trying to do their jobs to find out why that man was killed in our front room."

"If they haven't gotten an answer figured yet, they're not gonna," he said, snapping the shotgun shut. "Y'all have one last chance to leave here before I feel the need to defend myself and my property from people trespassing on my land."

"Your mother's land, I think you mean?" Virginia asked with a slight smirk, goading him. It wouldn't be hard, not with a man like Anthony. "It's not yours. Not yet, anyway." She glanced at the bag on the floor. "What have you got there?"

"None of your beeswax, Cabot." He glared, hand already placed on the trigger. He swayed on the spot and then steadied himself. His eyes were glazed over, purple-tinged at the edges.

Virginia checked her watch. "The feds won't be long," she lied, trying to rile him into a confession. She sucked her teeth, taking several steps towards him. "What's in the bag?"

"Fuck off," he said, pointing the barrel in her direction. "Get out of my house."

"Your mother's house," Arthur corrected, picking up

where she'd left off. They always had played off each other nicely, and she hadn't realized how much she'd missed their games of cat and mouse with suspects. "But then, it's practically yours, isn't it?"

Anthony nodded. "Yeah."

"Rightfully so, with your father and your brother gone." Arthur tucked his thumbs into his belt loops, taking Anthony's focus long enough for Virginia to shoo Jolie out the front door, easing the hinges shut. Whatever was about to happen, the kid didn't need to be seeing it. "After all, you never did get your due in life, did you?"

"No," Anthony said, shaking his head. "School of hard knocks because my brother, the devil rest his soul—"

"Tony!" his mother interrupted, hand held over her mouth in shock. "How dare you talk about your brother like that?"

Anthony rolled his eyes, turning his back to her. "The devil rest his soul, my brother got all the tuition money. I got squat." He laughed, keeping his hand on the trigger. "Fat lotta good that did them. He died overseas anyhow."

Anya hovered at Mrs. Speer's side now, holding out another cup of tea, which the elderly woman gratefully took, sipping deeply. "Thank you, dear," she said, before turning her attention back on her son. "Tony, put your daddy's shotgun back up on the wall." She set the tea cup down on the coffee table and brushed his arm affectionately, staring up at him with pleading eyes. "Please, son. Just this once, do as I say." She patted his elbow with reassurance, nodding. "I'll make us a nice dinner tonight. Our neighbor from up the road a piece brought over some fresh catfish earlier, I'll fry that up with some cornbread. Go have a lie down, son. Lord knows you need it, with all that running around you've been doing for me."

He grunted, keeping the shotgun as he rounded the corner into the hallway. "Do as I please," he growled.

"Does your son do most of the cooking?" Anya asked, exchanging a look with Virginia.

Mrs. Speer picked up the tea again, sipping at it. "Oh, heavens no," she said. "That boy can barely heat beans in a tin can. I always did hope he'd find himself a good woman who could take care of him." She stared off out the window, frowning. "Maybe he will, once I'm gone and this place is his. Girls don't like boys that still live with their mommas."

Keeping watch on the hallway, Virginia rested her palm against her holster. Anthony was mean, unstable, and armed, always a terrible combination. His aim wouldn't need precision with those double-barrels. If he wasn't slipping poison into her food, how the hell was she winding up with enough strychnine in her system to subdue a fleet of Verdance rats? "I'm sure you have plenty of good years left in you, ma'am," she reassured the woman. "My mother says you're healthy as a horse."

"That may have been true once, but I've been on the decline for months," the woman said, finishing the tea. "I'm not sure how long I have left."

A shot rang out from the back bedroom, and Virginia moved in tandem with Arthur, both moving swiftly towards the source of the noise with weapons drawn. "Anthony?" she called, stepping carefully into the back bedroom. He was sprawled on the floor, blood pooling beneath what remained of his left hand. She whirled around, somehow expecting to see someone other than Arthur behind her. "Call an ambulance," she shouted past him.

"Looks like he passed out," Arthur added, no doubt trying to calm Mrs. Speer's nerves, and for that, Virginia was grateful. He turned Anthony over, making a tutting sound in his throat. "So much for the bird shot theory."

"The hell was he doing in his mother's room?" Virgina wondered aloud, stepping over his unconscious frame to inspect an overturned bottle of perfume, the smell of berg-amot, iris, and vanilla pungent and overwhelming in the small room. She coughed, covering her nose. "Shadows, it burns," she uttered, her eyes watering. Perfume sediment spread itself across the vanity, gritty and white as it collected along the shards of yellow glass. "We need to get him out of here," Virginia said.

Before they could drag him out, his mother was there in the doorway, hand over her mouth as tears collected in her eyes. "Tony, Tony," she cried, "what have you done to yourself?"

"Ma'am, you should stay in the living room and wait for the ambulance," Virginia cautioned.

"I'm a medic," Anya announced, pushing her way into the room. "Move." She bent, tearing a strip from her skirt to apply a tourniquet above Anthony's wrist, checking his vitals one at a time. "He has a pulse, but his breathing is ragged." She gagged lightly, covering her mouth. "What is that?" she asked, staring over at the spilled bottle on the vanity.

"My perfume," Mrs. Speer said defensively, clearly used to the effect it had. "My husband would buy me a bottle every year on my birthday. In a way, he still does. I have to buy it for myself now, though." She glanced sadly at the vanity, emotion clouding her face. "I always decanted it into that bottle, though. He bought me that the year before he died."

"Poison," Virginia said as Anya worked to stem the flow of

blood. "It was in the perfume. The strychnine will be on his person."

Arthur nodded, disappearing into the hallway to comfort Mrs. Speer.

Kneeling down next to Anthony's unconscious body, Virginia checked his pockets, finding a small, empty bag with powdery residue. "The poison," she said quietly. "He was about to dose that perfume again. You were right, Anya."

"Of course I was right about the poison." Anya cinched the tourniquet and elevated his arm above his head. "Can you get that gun out of here?"

"Sure," Virginia replied, setting it outside in the corridor. "Everything okay?"

"I think it was me."

"What was you?"

"This," Anya said, gesturing at Anthony. "The gun accidentally firing."

"Don't be ridiculous, it was just an accident from a drugged-up, angry man. Doesn't take much for these types to fly off the handle."

Anya shook her head. "You don't know, Virginia. You didn't see what I saw." She took his pulse again, frowning. "My severing spells result in fender benders, late nights at work, a fistfight at a club. Never much, but enough of a delay, sometimes, for someone to get away. But my aunt..." she trailed off, shaking her head. "Sometimes it was worse."

"I thought you said that the reagents on this plane weren't strong enough? And you said that they were unstable at the campsite, and—"

"I know," Anya interrupted. "It doesn't make sense, but maybe it does." She looked up at Virginia, her face grave.

CHAPTER FORTY-ONE

"What if there's a Fae portal somewhere in Birch Hollow?"

Virginia snorted a laugh, but swallowed it when she saw how serious Anya was being. "No," she said. "That couldn't be. Something would have happened long before now, there would be—" she shook her head. "There would be suspiciously strong Nether in these parts from an open rift."

"And strong illusion magic," Anya added in a whisper. "Don't say anything to anyone, not yet." The flashing lights of the ambulance cascaded against the faded wallpaper, and in the next minute, Anthony was being loaded onto a stretcher.

"Where are they taking him?" Mrs. Speer asked.

"The county hospital," Virginia answered. "I'm sure they'll let you visit once he's stable." She snapped the holster shut, finally, and breathed a sigh of something that wasn't quite relief. "I can take you when the time comes."

Anya settled the woman back on the sofa, clearing away the empty mug of tea, staring intently at the leaves left at the bottom. "Hmm," she muttered, but didn't offer anything more than that.

"Arthur?" Virginia called, knowing he hadn't left the house. Jolie had come back inside after the ambulance arrived, and was sitting on the wingback chair, legs tucked under her as she chewed on her nails. "How are you doing, Firefly?"

"Fine." Jolie gestured at the bag. "So what's in there?"

"Good question." Virginia opened the paper bag with a crinkle, apprehensive of what she might find, knowing it could be just about anything. "Oh," she said softly.

"What is it?"

"Several dozen vials of potent Nether," she answered.

Anthony had triple-bagged them to contain the purple-pink glow that radiated throughout the inside of the paper. "Well I'll be damned."

Arthur emerged from Anthony's bedroom, holding a large bottle of rat poison in one hand, and empty vials in the other. "Ginnie, we need to get Eugene Carsh down here," he said gravely.

"You don't have jurisdiction here, Arthur Dixon," Mrs. Speer spat, reaching for the vials. "You're Verdance police, not Birch Hollow. I won't have you railroading my only living son."

Arthur pulled the vials out of her reach. "There's a federal warrant in place for this property, ma'am. It's up to them, now." His mouth pressed into a thin line.

"I thought the feds were focusing on the Kingston murder," Virginia said. "Which federal agent executed it?"

Shirin Lindell swaggered through the front door, a new bronze badge on her arm and matching bands on her boots. "I did," she said.

Chapter Forty-Two

Virginia took a step backwards, as if the presence of a newly minted federal agent would detect what she was just through proximity. "What the fuck, Shirin?" she asked, the notes of quiet betrayal singing from the gritted edges of her voice.

"Agent Lindell, actually," Shirin said, offering a smile so genuine and proud that Virginia had the unmistakable and almost irresistible urge to slap it off her face. "The federal agents in town needed a Verdance liaison for their inquiries here, given the provenance of the first victim, and also the Nether that was found in the system of both." Shirin stood, broad-chested with her hands in her pockets. "Mrs. Speer, ma'am, I'm going to have to ask you a few questions."

"I told him to stop," Mrs. Speer said. She sank down onto the sofa, and Virginia guided her down onto the cushions until she was settled, wearing a black cotton dress as though she was still in mourning for her husband and her eldest son. "I told him it was all a terrible idea to get involved with all of that."

"Stop what?" Shirin asked, slipping a notepad out of her pocket and nodding to Arthur. "What was your son up to?"

Mrs. Speer shook her head, folding her hands in her lap.

"He's my only son," she said. "No matter what he's done, he's still my only son."

"He was poisoning you, ma'am," Virginia said. "Your son wasn't who you thought he was."

"Poison!" Mrs. Speer shouted, burying her face in her hands. She stayed there, shoulders still, tension lining her petite frame. "No, that isn't true. Anthony is... troubled, perhaps, but he'd never do that."

"It's true," Anya offered, still covered in the blood of the woman's son. "We'll take you for treatment soon, get you all patched up." She bent, taking Mrs. Speer's hand in her own. "You're safe now," she said. "No one is going to hurt you."

"My perfume," Mrs. Speer said, sniffling softly. "How could he do such a thing?"

Shirin moved closer, towering over the sofa. "Mrs. Speer, are you aware that the sale and distribution of Nether is illegal?"

"Of course," Mrs. Speer answered. "I'm old, not senile." She sighed, dabbing the tears from her cheeks with an embroidered kerchief from her pocket. "Anthony was always in money troubles. Gambling, poor investments, con men, he was always finding himself entangled in a new bout of nonsense. It wasn't his fault, you see. His father was just the same. It was a curse of his birth, inescapable. There was no stopping it." She stifled a sob, her hands clenched together tightly. "All I could do was try to keep the poor boy on his feet."

"So how did he wind up distributing Nether?" Shirin asked, always a one-track mind, especially in the middle of an interrogation. "Where was he getting it from?"

"I don't know," Mrs. Speer answered. "I never saw him. I

only know it was a man because I heard his voice once."

"How many people did he distribute or sell to?" Shirin asked, leaning forward, the bronze of her new federal badge catching what little light there was to be had in the Speer living room with the curtains drawn. "Was he selling to anyone in Verdance?"

"I don't know!" Mrs. Speer shouted, more anger than upset boiling in every syllable. "I don't know, I don't know."

Virginia sat down next to her, placing herself between Mrs. Speer and Shirin, shooting the latter a look as she did so. Shirin might be a good detective, good enough to worm her way onto a federal task force, but her bedside manner was lacking in more than one area. "Mrs. Speer, did your son have dealings with Heinrich Harrow—well, I suppose you may have known him as James Folst?" She patted Mrs. Speer's hand and nodded in encouragement.

"I don't know," Mrs. Speer answered. "It could have been him. I'm not sure." She released her grip on her skirt to toy with a mother-of-pearl button at the edge of her cuff. "I tried to raise him right, but nothing like morals ever took with him. I think he was a bad seed, you know. Nothing I ever tried to teach him set into stone. I never quite could understand what went wrong with him."

The old woman squinted, as if she were trying to remember something. "The man whose voice I heard," she started. "He had a flashy car, red, I think. I saw it out the window of my bedroom the time he came here."

"Harrow's car," Shirin said, making a note in her pad. "When was that?"

"A month or so ago," Mrs. Speer said. Anthony was frustrated, he'd wanted me to visit his home that night, but I felt ill, so I stayed here. He wanted me to stay in my room, so I did.

"Shir—Agent Lindell, please get Officer Carsh on the line," Virginia said. "Tell him we have a new witness statement for the Harrow-Folst murder, and tell him that a potential collaborator was taken to County General hospital."

"It's done," Arthur said calmly, thrusting his hands into his pockets with just a little too much force. "I used the phone out there. He'll be here in thirty minutes." He waited until Shirin collected the Nether and took it out to her new federal squad unit before he continued. He tossed Shirin a steely glare. "You can go, then," he said. "I imagine your new superiors will want an update on the Nether trade here, and how it may have intersected with these murders."

Shirin almost looked wounded for a second, but she straightened, placing her cap back on her head. "Thank you, sheriff," she said curtly. "I believe I will. There's more to be done here, more to learn about who's to blame for these deaths."

"I'm sure you'll learn plenty," Arthur said in a flat tone.

"More than the rest of you did, certainly," she replied with a smirk. She turned on her heel and left the Speer's home, descending the front steps with sharp clicks of her polished patent leather brogues.

"Drink up, ma'am," Anya said, returning with a steaming mug. "That mint will help the nausea."

Mrs. Speer nodded, taking the mug from Jolie. "Thank you, dear," she said graciously, her ingrained manners rising straight to the surface. "There were more meetings, more drop points, more strangers showing up at the house here." She sipped at the tea, some of the tension in her shoulders ebbing back into the sofa. "It wasn't much of a surprise, I'm afraid, when that man turned up dead just there." She shook her head. "Only a matter of time, I suppose. I don't know what we'll do now."

"We can make sure he doesn't return here," Anya said. "Whether he winds up in more trouble or not, this is still your home."

"You're not from the hospital, are you?"

Anya shook her head. "No."

"I can't just leave him out in the cold. He's my son, no matter what he's done." She inhaled, her breath shaky as it inflated her lungs and finding itself trapped there for a few moments too long. "I wanted him to be a good man, a strong man, like his big brother. I never wanted this."

"I know, ma'am," Virginia said kindly, patting her gently on the arm. "I'm going to leave you in the care of Ms. Quinn now, she'll treat you for the poison."

Anya nodded, fiddling with the buckles on her satchel. "Of course," she replied.

Virginia escaped into the kitchen, following Arthur. She sighed, bracing a hand against the marble countertop. The cold was a sweet relief. "So much for a peaceful questioning," she said quietly.

"Some things never change."

"I'm thinking there's more Nether in this house some-where. Why else use his mother's house as a drop point unless she has a loft or a crawlspace?" She drummed her fingers, craving something more than a cigarette. "I hate this, Arthur. I hate that even though we managed to figure out who was running Nether out here, we can't figure out who killed Harrow or Kingston."

"There's a shed out back," Arthur offered. "That's my best guess at a stash point for more of this stuff, but that bag in the living room suggests he was on his last vials, ready to sell them to his customers."

Virginia took a deep breath. "Arthur, I'm going to say something crazy, but I need you to listen to me."

He raised his eyebrows. "Okay."

"I think it's the Fae."

To her surprise, he didn't laugh or scoff, but nodded. "Could be."

"That's not what I thought you'd say." Virginia rifled through the cabinets, hoping that Anthony had stashed a bottle of gin or some cigarettes, but no luck. "It would explain the Nether, at least." She didn't say anything about Anya's spell. Some things, she had to keep secret, even from Arthur. "With Harrow out of the picture, maybe that aspect will calm down here. Who knows how much he was shifting."

"Enough to load into cars headed to the city," Arthur grumbled. "I doubt the vacuum following his death will remain unfilled for long. Someone is going to miss their money, one way or another."

Virginia nodded. "So Harrow was getting Nether from the Fae, and that made someone very angry indeed. I don't know what the connection to Kingston is yet, but we'll find it." She cast a sideways glance at Arthur. "Did you know about Lindell?"

Arthur scowled, his fists flexing in his pockets. "News to me."

"Guess you'll have to find a new deputy sheriff."

"Guess so." He exhaled a barely controlled sigh that whistled in the back of his throat and he rubbed a hand over his head, perhaps trying to polish the skin there to a sharp shine. "Nearly hit the roof about it, Ginnie."

"Because she didn't tell you?"

He leaned in close, his voice a heavy, dangerous whisper. "Because now she's a fucking fed, and she knows about Mona and Penny."

"They weren't on the register?" Virginia asked, surprised that Arthur would evade the law of the land. "Not even Mona?"

"No," he replied. "No, no. She's worked very hard to hide herself after the Rupture. Her family comes from money, and—"

"I'm aware," Virginia interrupted, knowing she shouldn't have. "Go on."

"They wanted to remain hidden. When the Rupture happened, they were well-connected enough to figure it all out before the press did. Stayed inside for weeks until the marks faded, and in the chaos, no one really noticed. Hired mortals to run their errands in the meantime." Arthur drummed his fingers against the marble, a percussive, damning rhythm. "And now a fed knows, and it's all my fault."

"It's not your fault," Virginia said, echoing back what he'd said to her all those years ago. "Shirin won't say anything."

"Are you sure about that?"

Virginia wasn't sure, so she just stared at him instead, part of her wishing she could give him a hug. "I don't know. Shirin is a hard woman to figure out."

"Really?" he asked, the terrible realization dawning on him and his face contorting between surprise and discomfort. "*Shirin?*"

"No," she replied defensively, knowing even that had given

herself away by using her first name in Arthur's presence.

"You two fought like cats and dogs."

"Arthur, leave it." Virginia moved to push past him, but he caught her by the elbow.

"Why didn't you tell me?"

She rested her hand on the doorknob, waiting for divine inspiration that might absolve her. "I don't know," she admitted. "I guess because some element of me always knew it wasn't right. Too close to the feds."

He nodded. "Clearly." Anya's soothing tone and the grind of her marble mortar and pestle were muffled through the heavy oak door as she tended to Mrs. Speer, and Arthur sighed again. "I hope you didn't tell her about your—"

"I didn't."

"Good."

"More worried about Jolie, to be honest with you." She caught his stare and released her grip on the door. "Turns out I understand that kind of worry, Art. The kind you have for Penny."

He nodded. "I know." He reached out for an embrace, hesitating, but she returned the gesture. They stayed there for a long moment, their mirrored anxieties hovering above them, and for the first time in a long time, Virginia was grateful that he was there.

Chapter Forty-Three

The drive to Murph Township was a quiet one, other than the grating sound of gravel and dirt crunching beneath the rubber tires as they drove. Anya and Jolie followed in Seamus' car behind, Mrs. Speer having been taken to the hospital for further treatment and observation. Carsh had arrived as they were leaving to take note of the empty shed and the freshly sourced Nether in Anthony's bag, doing his part to do the feds' work for them.

"So what now?" Arthur asked. Pine trees lined one side of the road, and birch the other, both competing for the right to uproot the unkempt highway that was already riddled with fissures.

"Back to Verdance."

"And that's it?"

Virginia's hands tightened around the steering wheel. "And that's it. Not much else to do down here now, is there? Feds will either decide to link these murders, or they won't. Best case scenario, a serial killer isn't running up and down the state, and we don't go home to more bodies." Sunlight flickered across the dashboard, and something like regret pricked at the hind side of her consciousness. "Maybe we get lucky, and we get a few quiet months."

Arthur barked out a sarcastic laugh, more himself than she'd heard him be since he'd found her at that crime scene six months back. "Fat chance of that," he muttered.

"Mm."

He looked over at her, considering her face with the familiar deep furrow between his brows. "And Juliette?"

"Dead ends, Art. One old man's suppositions aren't enough to build a case on. I can't take down Senator Dean with a loose theory and a scrapbook."

"I wish I'd known what she meant to you," he said softly, turning to stare out the windshield as they drove. "I think maybe I would have understood you more."

"Yeah." Words caught in her throat thicker than molasses, and sharper than the questions she hadn't found answers for. A killer, still on the loose. Her abilities, still unpredictable. Juliette's disappearance, still unsolved. "Maybe I should have told you." The clocktower came into view along with the short, quaint main street, quiet that time of day. Quiet all the time, if she was being honest. "Stu said something about the clocktower," she said evenly, pulling the car over before she had too much time to consider what she was doing. "Said he saw something the night she died, but..." Virginia trailed off. "I don't know. It was so long ago, most of it feels like a dream. Like it was someone else's life entirely."

Arthur nodded. "I know exactly what you mean." He exited the car and crossed the empty road to the clocktower, beckoning her over. "Remember when we used to dare each other to sneak in and climb up to the top?"

"Yeah, you were always too chicken," Virginia replied. She pocketed her keys and left her hands there, her right caressing the safety of the silver knuckles there. Something was pulling at her, and while half of her wanted to give in, the other half was knotting her gut into an impressively detrimental twist.

"I don't remember you going up either," Arthur chided.

"I had my mother to consider. Don't you remember how she always knew what we were up to?" Anya and Jolie parked up behind them, the latter jumping down from her seat. "You okay, Firefly?" she asked. Virginia always worried about the toll that following her around might take on Jolie, up to the point she was starting to wonder if Arthur was right. Maybe she did need to consider other options for the kid.

"I want to go home," Jolie said, pulling her arms tight around her chest. "I'm tired."

"Yeah," Virginia replied, all notions of finding her a new home evaporated into the air faster than acetone. "Me too." She glanced up at the clocktower, the face intact and the hands pointing to half past the hour. "Those bees never do stop, do they?"

"We don't say busy as a bird, now do we?" Anya asked. "It's a damned good thing they don't stop, either. Do you have any idea how often I use honey as a binding agent in poultices?" She poked Virginia in the shoulder, her finger meeting scar tissue. "You might have died from that panther bite without bees."

"Yeah, okay," Virginia relented, irritated by the memory of her failure. Benjamin had died because she was too laid up after that bite, because she'd been too weak to stay awake. "All hail the bees, fine." Virginia laid a hand on the iron railing, moving to pull herself up and over one of the cracked steps.

She couldn't breathe.

Her fingers tightened around the bar at the same time as she was desperate to release it. Something was smothering her, ripping the air from her lungs even as she stood there.

"Virginia?" Anya asked, but then she was gone, faded into the black mists of memory.

Two figures in the night, dragging something into the clocktower . Strange. No one ever went in there, not so long as she could remember. They didn't want to disturb the bees.

Whatever it was thudded against each of the concrete steps, whole then, the railing polished to a shine. The sound was hauntingly hollow, a sick, bone-cracking sound. She knew what—who—it was even though she was being dragged up the spiral steps in a laundry bag.

It smelled like lilies and orchids, the scent thick like a mortuary.

Virginia followed, unsure how she was managing to climb the steps without breathing. It was dark, probably past midnight if she had to guess, the sun that had been shining through the foliage just a moment ago vanished into the blackness of evening. One of the hooded figures swore under his breath, hissing out curses like they were just misplaced, irreverent prayers.

The other looked down the stairs and right through her, the glint of the badge on his arm reflecting the waning crescent moon.

Forty-seven steps to the top of the clocktower. She stood at the landing, watching as the figures dumped out the laundry bag, propping a cold, lifeless body in the corner. Her head lolled to one side, rigor-mortis not yet set in. The blood oozing out onto the floorboards was fresh but quickly thickening, dripping down between the slats into the unseen, untended emptiness below.

Juliette.

Her eyes, lit by stars, revealed a shocked pleading, an unseen threat, an unanswered question. The hooded figures dissipated, and so did the flesh from Juliette's bones, and so did the cold glow of midnight.

Virginia stared, breath stalled in her lungs.

No, no, no.

She'd known for years, but a spark of hope had remained in the crevices of her heart. The remaining embers of justice had been snuffed out by a violent truth.

Light filtered down through the remaining florid wrought iron, and it danced horribly across dust and bones. Bees hummed around their lively hive, collecting in one corner and then another, the sound of their wings a terrible, familiar hum.

The pollen they'd spent years carrying to and fro was the only hint of any flowers that had ever touched Juliette's hidden grave.

Virginia's stomach clenched hard enough to drag a retch into her throat, but the air tangled there and the bile burned. There were no words, none that she could say aloud. There was nothing. She was standing on sun-bleached boards but she was lost, trapped between knowing and unknowing, wishing against every shadow that she'd never returned to Birch Hollow.

She'd always thought that knowing would bring her peace and a sense of finality, but instead she was left with a thunderous void. It was draining whatever was even left of her, pulling it from her bone marrow only to deposit it somewhere deep in the earth, unreachable and unrecoverable.

She reached out for the bones, trembling with an impulse she couldn't refuse. Knowing was terrible enough, but now that she'd fractured the seal of it, she had to see more. She had to hear Juliette's voice one more time, even if it was a horror she'd never recover from.

"Virginia," Jolie whispered, grabbing her wrist. "Don't."

Opening her mouth to protest, Virginia was disgusted to discover that the only sound that made it past her lips was that of a strangled sob.

"We should go," Anya said from the top of the stairs, her voice uncharacteristically low and careful. "Virginia, we should go."

Virginia shook her head, inhaling sharply now that her lungs had remembered how to inflate. "Chain of custody," she managed to eke out. "We should stay until the police arrive. I don't trust—" she exhaled slowly, swallowing back the hard lump in her throat. "I don't trust Eugene Carsh with this." Haunted by the vision, by Juliette's remains, and by the sparkle of that badge, she began to understand the seduction of vigilante justice.

"Ginnie!" Arthur shouted from the stairs. She hated herself for finding the sound of his voice comforting. "Ginnie, what—" he stopped short, just behind Anya, staring past all of them. His eyes fell on what remained of Juliette Ashling. "Fucked shadows," he murmured.

"She was here the whole time," Virginia said, strangely aware of how flat her tone was. "We never thought to check."

"Are you alright?" Arthur asked, hesitating on the stairs.

"Of course she's not alright," Anya hissed, moving out of the way so that he could pass her. "Would you be alright?"

"Jo?" he prompted, tugging at his belt loops. "What about you?"

"Fine," Jolie replied, lodging herself between Virginia and the pile of bleached bones. "Sheriff Dixon, we need to contact the state police. You don't have jurisdiction here."

Virginia nodded, grateful for Jolie's attention to the case and her understanding of protocol. When all else failed, protocol stood as a pillar, a testament to normality.

He watched the bees froth and buzz, what was left of their hive glistening softly with honey. "I never thought…" he trailed off. "I'm sorry, Ginnie."

"Why?" Virginia asked. "It's not like you're the one who killed her." She peered over Jolie's shoulder, her breath catching once again. What was left of a blue sweater sagged against the ground, half-rotted from winter moisture and almost white from every summer sunset Juliette had never seen. A necklace, tarnished silver with engraved initials, tangled in her bones.

"Someone did," Arthur said, bending down to examine the remains but not touching them. "Trauma to the skull, likely a gun shot." He squinted, sitting back on his haunches. "Fractured tibia. Compressed vertebrae, though both of those may have been post-mortem."

"Shh," Anya hissed, looking like she was torn between remaining where she was and physically stopping him from his examination. "She doesn't need to hear that."

"I want to know," Virginia interjected. "I need to know how she died so I can tear apart whoever did it."

Arthur stood, blocking her view of the bones. "I don't know if that's such a good idea," he relented. "You said yourself that there's no viable evidence, that Carsh botched it all."

"Carsh botched it on purpose," she snapped. "What would you do if it was Mona? Would you let the state police handle it, or would you burn down every fucking evidence locker until you found something that would bring her some justice?" She moved around him, kneeling on the floor next to Juliette. "How would you feel to learn that the bones of your first love had been rotting away in a fucking clocktower for thirty-one years?"

"I didn't know," he whispered. "Probably something that would get me thrown off the force."

"Go call the state police," Anya urged him. "They'll come faster if you call, you know they will." When Arthur didn't move, just continued to stare at Virginia over the pile of bones, some of them sticky with errant honey from the bits of hive the bees had built in the ribcage, Anya tried again. "Sheriff Dixon."

"They'll be busy with calls about the Melody Kingston murder and the federal jurisdiction on that," he said. "Hopefully it won't take too long to get through." He stood, laying a hand on Virginia's shoulder. "Why don't you come with me, Ginnie?" he suggested. "No one knows more about this case or about Juliette, not even Eugene."

"Especially not fucking Eugene," Virginia growled. She didn't want to go. She didn't want to leave Juliette's side, not again, not when she still needed her to fix everything, to solve the crime, to do something that wouldn't bring her back but might bring her peace in whatever fucked sort of afterlife there was or wasn't.

"If we go now, we can circumvent dealing with the local department entirely," Arthur urged.

"Fine," Virginia said. "I'll go with you."

Chapter Forty-Four

Arthur sighed. "Ginnie, you said you'd go with me to the station where we'd wait for state officers."

"Your first mistake was letting me drive." Virginia pressed harder into the accelerator, willing the car to go faster, even as it struggled over the uneven road surface. Shoulders hunched over the wheel, she seethed, the memory of her vision burning a hole in her consciousness.

"Are you at least going to fill me in?" he asked, bracing himself against the dash. "Shadows, woman, are you trying to kill us both?"

"Don't worry, if anyone dies today, it's not going to be either one of us," she reassured him as the tire hit one of the county's largest and most aggressive pot holes, throwing them both forward.

"For fuck's sake, Ginnie!" Arthur shouted, holding the back of his head where it had connected with the top of the car's interior. "Do you want to explain to Mona why I wound up with stitches today if you don't calm the hell down?"

She jerked the car onto a side road, the left side nearly leaving the pavement as she did so. "It was Carsh," she growled.

"What was Carsh?"

She glared at him from the corner of her eye, willing him to understand what she had meant. "Carsh," she repeated, unable to say more than that. "Vision," she added.

"You had another vision!" he almost shouted, leaning over towards her seat. "About Carsh? About what?"

She'd always thought that the knowing would allow her to move past Juliette, to confirm she hadn't been left, but that happiness had been violently stolen from her, just like everything else, but the only thing left was the rage. It boiled beneath her skin, urging her forward towards Officer Eugene Carsh so that she could exact the revenge Juliette had so deserved for years. "It was him," she whispered. She dare not speak louder, knowing her voice would crack if she tried. "Juliette. It was him."

Arthur sat back in his seat, palm pressed to his forehead. "What in shadows?" he asked, but it was rhetorical. He wasn't looking for an answer. He stole a glance at her, no doubt worried she would turn her ire on him. "Carsh?"

"Him and someone else," Virginia replied. She cleared her throat, but no amount of delicate, controlled coughs would clear the emotion that lay there. "Dragged her up the steps in a laundry bag." She shook her head, trying to clear the tears that were already flooding her vision, dangerous when driving that fast down country roads. "Smelled like a funeral."

"Lilies," Arthur agreed. "The Deans were famous for them and for those damned orchids. Greenhouses out back were packed with them."

"I'll kill them all," Virginia said, throwing the car into park so fast that the engine protested with a loud clunk. No doubt it shouldn't be abused so thoroughly so soon after being serviced, but she couldn't bring herself to give a shit. "Carsh!" she shouted, stomping up the steps to the Speer residence.

"He may not even be here anymore Ginnie, he might have—"

"Eugene Carsh!" Virginia yelled again, glaring through the dark mesh metal of the screen door. "Come out or I swear to every rift, I will drag you out by your thinning hair."

He sidled out the door, trying to look angry, but landing somewhere between fear and a bruised ego. "What do you want now, Ginnie?" he asked, doing his best to draw himself up to his full height. His shoulders were still rounded, his eyes wide as he leaned backwards into the house. "Haven't you had enough of this place yet?"

"Get out here," Virginia hissed, grabbing him by his collar.

"Ginnie!" Arthur shouted, attempting to intervene. He tried to insert himself between them, wedging himself in front of Eugene's pathetic, hunched posture.

"What are you doing?" she snarled, ready to punch him, too. "Get out of my way!"

"Trying to keep you from getting arrested again," Arthur bit back, prying her fingers from Carsh's collar. "Have you forgotten that feds are still in town? That state police are already on their way? That both of those agencies are more than happy to throw the book at anyone assaulting an officer, regardless of the context?"

"I'm sure they'd love to know the context, wouldn't they, Eugene?" she hissed, taking a step backwards. "Maybe I should fill them in on what you did thirty-one years ago, I'm sure they'd find that very illuminating."

Carsh faltered as she released him, stumbling until he dropped to a knee. He stayed on the ground, looking up at her. "Tell them whatever you want, Ginnie." He sighed, squeezing his eyes shut. "I'm tired."

"Tell them what, Ginnie?" Arthur prompted. "That you had a—" he stopped himself short, eyeing up Carsh. "That you had an idea who killed Juliette Ashling all those years ago?"

"That Eugene is at least partly responsible, that's what I'll tell him." Instinctively, one had rested on her revolver, almost hungry for Eugene to give her a reason to use it, or to break his jaw, or gouge his eyes out, or—

"You don't know what you're talking about!" Carsh shouted. "You were just a kid, you have no idea what actually happened, just flights of fancy and revenge!"

Virgina leaned into his face again, her nose only an inch from his. "I'll drag your name into the gutter, Eugene," she snarled. "I'll make sure everyone knows what you did. I know everything. It's taken me years, but I finally know why you never investigated. You were in on it, Eugene."

He searched her face for mercy, but found none. "I tried, Ginnie," Carsh said, emotion pulling at his voice. "I tried, I tried, but I was a rookie cop, what was I—"

"Rookie cop, please," Virginia retorted. "You forget that Arthur and I were once rookie cops too, we sure as fuck weren't murdering young women and hiding the bodies, now were we?"

"Ginnie—"

"Shut up, Arthur," she snapped. "Let me have this."

He held his hands up in surrender, but stayed between her and Carsh.

Virginia grabbed Carsh by the ear, dragging him towards the tree line. Mrs. Speer had enough blood in her house in the recent past to last her a lifetime, she didn't need more of it on her porch. "Talk," she barked. "Tell me what you did to her."

He shook his head, breaths shallow and fast in his chest. "Ginnie, no," he pleaded. "It wasn't me, he—"

"Please," she oozed, ready to drag out her questioning for fifteen consecutive days, if she had to. "Don't lie to my face, Eugene. I think we can both agree that you've done quite enough of that."

Eugene was holding his hands up to guard his face, cowering in front of her and the shine of the silver knuckles she had poised right next to his face. "Ginnie, please, just listen!" When she nodded, he drew in a shaky breath, propping himself against the trunk of a tree. "I was a rookie cop, Ginnie. I was a rookie cop and he was..." he swallowed hard. "This can't go past us," he said. "It would put every one of us in danger."

"He was what?" Virginia pressed.

"He was my friend." Eugene buried his face in his hands, a quiet, shameful moan escaping his mouth. "You don't know what it's like to grow up with nothing."

"I know damned well what it's like to have nothing."

"Not then, you didn't."

She sat back on her haunches, staring a hole through his forehead, knowing he was right about that, at least. "Go on."

"His family was very highly positioned in this county. Hell, in the whole damned state. We went to school together."

"J.D.," Virginia said. It wasn't a question, it was the confirmation she needed.

"He called me late, Ginnie. Said he was in trouble. I thought he'd gotten pulled over for drunk driving or something, maybe he'd hit a deer, one of those protected ones." Eugene shrugged, but it was mournful. "When he opened the trunk, I thought that's exactly what had happened. Blood..." he shook his head. "Thought she was a deer, Ginnie, until he told me."

"A deer."

"I told him to meet me at the clocktower. I was just getting off shift. You know how folks feel about deer around here, damned things eat all the crops. No farmer in a twenty-mile radius hasn't shot at least one and fed their families on secret venison." He lowered his hands finally, digging his fingertips into the dirt. "Not anymore, of course. You don't see them round these parts now. Haven't for years."

Virginia just continued to stare at him, willing him to keep talking, and terrified that he would. Deer. Juliette. Visions. *Pain.*

"I didn't know what to do when I realized. I told him he had to turn himself in. He said it was self defense—"

"Horseshit," Virginia spat.

"Said she broke into his house," Eugene continued. "He was drunk, he shot her before he realized it was just a girl. He said she had a fistful of his mother's jewelry, ready to climb out the window when he found her."

"He shot her in the back of the head, Eugene," Arthur said. "I saw the remains with my own eyes. She was on her way out, she was no threat."

Eugene swallowed hard again, and then nodded. "I know, Arthur. I saw it too, just... fresh."

"And you botched the investigation?" Virginia demanded.

"You had the opportunity to make it right the next morning and you decided you wanted access more than you wanted justice?"

"No, Ginnie." Eugene closed his eyes as if to remember, shame etched across every fine line that lay there. "I took it to my superior. I took it to the sheriff. I told him what I'd done, offered to resign, to be a witness for the prosecutor, to do whatever it took." Eugene looked at her, guilt weighing heavy in his gaunt cheeks. "He told me that I must be mistaken, and that if I wasn't, to leave sleeping dogs lie. He said that the Deans had enough power to make or break not just my career, but his, and the entire department's budget. He retired eighteen months later with two brand new model V cars in his driveway."

"The Deans are untouchable," Arthur agreed, rubbing a hand against the dark skin of his bald head.

"What about the next sheriff?" Virginia asked. "Why not take it to him?"

Eugene sighed. "Bought and paid for. Elected thanks to the Deans."

"And you? What about when you took up the mantle?"

"Ginnie, I..." he trailed off. "It had been so long, and he's a shadows-damned senator now. I'm just a small-town cop. What the hell can I do?"

Virginia blew out a breath, pulling the cuffs from Arthur's back pocket. "I'm placing you under a citizen's arrest," she said slowly, clasping the metal around Eugene's wrists. "You're an accessory, Eugene, and that's not even talking about obstruction charges, or the fact that I'm not so sure I even believe this story of yours. For all I know, it was the both of you boozing it up, and maybe you shot her with your service pistol, all hot-headed and egotistical with your new powers as a cop."

"Ginnie, don't," he whispered.

"I'm sure state police will be very interested to hear what you have to say when they arrive tomorrow morning." She glanced at Arthur, who nodded, confirming her assumed time frame. "If you want to save yourself, you can turn state's evidence against Senator Dean, I'm sure they'll work out some sort of deal for you. They usually do, for the rats who squeal."

"They'll kill me," Eugene said softly.

Virginia leaned in, her nose less than an inch from his. "That's not my problem."

***

Night came, dampening the sky into a sickly black, the stars distant pinpricks of light but still brighter than they would be in Verdance. The chicken shop glowed bright in the darkness, the windows bleeding light.

"Here," Arthur said, sliding a box in front of her. "Got one of the last portions."

"I'm not hungry," Virginia said. "This is taking too long, I'd hoped that tomorrow morning was an overly generous estimate. Didn't you tell them that you're the sheriff in Verdance?"

Arthur pushed a fork at her, ignoring what she'd said. "Yes, Ginnie, but there's enough red tape with the feds crawling all over the woods that jurisdiction is taking some time to iron out. Sounds like someone on the phone decided all murders must be connected to the same federal investigation." He sighed. "I suppose she missed where I said this one happened over three decades ago."

"I suppose you'll be looking for a promotion to state now that Lindell has defected to the feds," Virginia said, bracing herself for what seemed inevitable.

"I don't want to move back downstate," Arthur said. "Mona wouldn't want to, either."

Virginia picked up the fork, poking at the chicken. "Not even if it gave you some leverage to keep their names off the conscription rolls?"

"I don't know." He put his honey butter biscuit into her box, gesturing with his spoon. "You know I never liked those as much as you do."

"I told you, I'm not hungry."

"You have to eat, Ginnie."

"I need a smoke." Virginia slid out of the booth, pushing out of the shop past the twenty other people waiting for their orders. The police department headquarters was dimly lit from the inside, Eugene tossed into the same cell she'd been a guest of twice. He hadn't fought. He seemed resigned to his fate.

She struck a match against the brick and lit a cigarette, grateful that Arthur had handed his over without complaint or argument. They weren't menthols, but they would do, and she'd already breezed her way through most of the pack that afternoon.

Reaching under the passenger seat of her car, she freed the flask of gin she'd hidden there and drained it in one string of gulps, the fiery juniper cooling the rage that boiled between her every synapse. She chased it with another inhale of the cigarette, sliding the flask back into its place.

It wasn't dissimilar to her mother's behavior.

The thought flashed against her like razor wire but she pressed herself to the car door, inhaling again, willing herself to forget the memories seared into her broken consciousness. Juliette's broken body, dragged unceremoniously up forty-seven stairs to rot in a clocktower for thirty-one years.

Flaring orange in the darkness, she took another drag. Of course. That was the summer the bees had disappeared. She'd been so obsessed with finding Juliette that she hadn't even stopped to wonder why.

"Ginnie," Arthur said, carrying the two boxes in his hands. "We shouldn't just wait here all night. He's not going any-where, and the state officials won't be here until morning."

"Fantastic." She tossed the filter to the ground, crushing it beneath the heel of her ruined shoe. "We should find Jolie and Anya. No doubt they're at my mother's house, it's at least more comfortable than that campsite."

Chapter Forty-Five

Virginia sat in the car, refusing to go in. There had been enough pain that day without adding insult to injury.

"Ginnie, come inside," Arthur said, descending the porch steps for the third time. "She's already asleep."

"I doubt it."

"Anya wants to talk to you." He leaned against the driver's side window. "Jolie went to bed an hour ago."

Regretting that she'd already drained the flask, part of her wondered if it was worth the risk to raid her mother's cabinet. "Tell Anya I'll be at the campsite, and we can leave first thing in the morning."

"Just come inside and we'll figure out a plan," Arthur offered. He flipped a fresh pack of cigarettes through the open window, shrugging at her. "It's all I've got, Ginnie, take it or leave it."

"Fine." Virginia stepped out of the car and accepted the flame from his lighter, the ember lighting the darkness with a quick, unsteady flare. "I didn't want to come down here, Arthur."

"I know."

"This place is poison."

He sighed, taking a cigarette from the pack when she offered it. "I know." He inhaled deeply, blowing a plume of smoke into the night air, illuminated only by the yellow glow of the porch lamp. "Once state police take over, we can go."

"I'm almost surprised that Shirin hasn't reappeared, trying to play some jurisdictional game to get her hands on this, too."

"Lindell is talking a big game, she'll have her hands full with these homicides." Arthur gripped the cigarette between two fingers, crushing it between his knuckles. "She just wants you back in the city."

"Yeah, to monitor me."

"Or to make sure you're safe."

Virginia made the sound of a disgruntled scoff in her throat. "Shirin likes control, that's all. She's probably embarrassed we were the ones to nab a lead for the Harrow murder, especially if it's connected to Melody Kingston and all the rest of them." She inhaled, exhaled, and swore. "Shit."

"Mmhmm," Arthur vocalized. "You can say that again."

"Shit," Virginia repeated. "What a fucking mess, all of it." She flicked ash towards the ground, and the embers melted into the ground. "Looks like it might rain." Clouds circled around the moon, diffusing the light. The heat was beginning to break, leaving a cool white shine in its wake.

She climbed the steps one at a time, finishing the cigarette. It was a poor substitute for what she really wanted, but it would have to do for the time being. The heavy door swung inward, the stained glass inset perfectly soldered with hundreds of tiny pieces.

"How are things here?" Virginia asked. Anya was sitting at

the table, reorganizing her satchel of reagents into tiny glass vials that were separated by thin fabric dividers. "Where is Jolie?"

"Asleep," Anya replied. "Finally." she shook her head. "She was asking a lot of questions. I'm afraid I didn't have the answers for her."

"That makes two of us," Virginia replied with a heavy sigh. "And the ones I do have don't do anyone very much good, least of all Juliette." She sat across from Anya and toyed with the handle of the teapot waiting there, the porcelain long since gone cold. "She's still dead, regardless."

Anya nodded slowly, her attentions focused on the task in front of her. "Sometimes closure isn't what we want it to be." She twisted a ring around her finger, searching for words that wouldn't come. "Sometimes, trying to right a wrong just complicates matters further."

"I intend on uncomplicating them."

"Ginnie," Arthur said gently. "It's probably best if we just try to take it easy tonight, alright?"

"You can wait in the car if you can't resist the urge to manage me," Virginia retorted. "You talked me into coming in here, now you'll just have to sit down and shut up or leave."

"Anthony Speer was my fault," Anya started to say, but her voice faltered halfway through whatever it was she was trying to get out.

Virginia played with the worn cork lid of one of the tiny vials, rolling it around in her palm. "He deserved to shoot his hand off. He's lucky you were there to make sure he doesn't lose the rest of his arm, too. Or bleed out. If I was his mother, I'd have let it happen."

"That poor woman."

"I hope someone keeps an eye on her," Virginia offered. "She's going to need someone to take care of her while she recovers from that poison, if she's even able to purge it all from her system in the first place without lasting consequences."

"Don't worry, she'll be well looked after," Virginia's mother said, hovering silently in the hallway, a specter, a ghost who had the ability to waft from room to room undetected, listening in on everything that had been said. She'd always been that way, as long as Virginia could remember. "Folks around here won't leave her to fend for herself." She pulled out a kitchen chair, perching at the edge in a crisp white dress with blue flowers, pearls hanging at her neck.

"I thought you were asleep," Virginia accused.

"I was, but when you stomp around, it tends to rouse a person from her slumber." Her mother gestured for Virginia to sit down, waving her hand in a way that implied it was a command, not an invitation. "Ms. Quinn told me what you found today. I'm sorry to hear it."

Anger wasn't an unfamiliar emotion when it came to her mother, and yet it always seemed to take her by surprise. "Somehow I doubt that."

"I am sorry to hear it," her mother echoed.

Virginia hoped that Arthur and Anya would leave, but they didn't, remaining in the room as witnesses to her faulty past. "She was murdered."

Her mother raised an eyebrow as she poured lemonade from a pitcher into a glass, pushing it across the table. "Oh? It could have been a number of people, I imagine."

The words seared into her chest, burning their way into her bone marrow. "We have a solid lead," Virginia said. "We found her in the clocktower. She was there for some time, probably from when she first went missing."

"Nothing you could have done, then," her mother said casually. "All that effort, all those arrests, and for what? You couldn't have saved her, Ginnie." She fussed with the rope of pearls at her neck, tugging them back into place. "I told you as much years ago, from the moment she didn't show up for your little midnight tryst."

Virginia stared, fingers wrapping around the edge of the chair, her fingernails digging crescent moons into the wood. "I never told you that."

"Told me what?"

"I never told you we were supposed to meet that night."

Her mother scoffed, pouring a second glass of lemonade. "Don't be ridiculous. Of course you told me, why else would I have kept you in the house that night?"

"I never told you *anything*," Virginia said. "I made damned sure I never told you anything, especially not about her, and especially not about *that*." She resisted the urge to reach across the table and snap that silly string of pearls, to claw and thrash and scream until it made everything right again.

But nothing would make it right again.

It wouldn't bring her first love back to life.

"How did you know?" Virginia asked evenly, her shoulder blades so tight she knew she'd feel the aftermath in the morning. "Mother, how did you know I was supposed to meet her that night?"

"You were always sneaking out to see that girl," her mother said, dismissing the concerns that hung in the air like a thick, viscous tar. "It wasn't a far leap."

"*Always*," Virginia said with a scoff, leaning over the table.

"Please."

"Ginnie," Arthur tried, waiting by the door for her to bolt, but she wouldn't. Not that time. "Let's go sit in the car."

Virginia didn't even bother turning to look at him. "Stop it, Arthur," she said, a steely calm about her voice. "You can leave, if you're so desperate to." She pushed herself up off the chair, bracing her forearms against the table. "Tell me how you knew I was supposed to meet her that night you shut me in my room with a fucking padlock."

Her mother shifted, the first sign she'd shown that she was even remotely uncomfortable. "You forced my hand," she said. "What else was I supposed to do? No amount of ordering you to stay in the house, no amount of begging nor pleading ever made a whit of difference to you, so deluded you were by that girl."

"You put bars on my window, Mother," Virginia said. "You hid my things, you locked me in and she *died* because of it."

"Did you not think it might have been you, too, if you'd been there?" her mother snapped, standing up to match her height. "That maybe I knew that girl would wind up in the gutter one day? And look at that, she did! You didn't, though, did you?"

"You don't know half the fucking gutters I wound up in, thanks to you!" Virginia shouted, the rage bubbling up and threatening to leak out of her eyes as tears. "Juliette died because I didn't show up that night, she went off on her own trying to—" she couldn't finish the thought, not when the weight of it would crush her. Juliette had been stealing from the Deans to get them enough money to skip town together. If Virginia had been there, she wouldn't have let her do it. Money didn't matter then. It never had. They would have hopped on a freighter and gone to sleep with empty stomachs but Virginia would have stayed *whole*, not picked apart by the uncomfortable truths of reality.

"I let you out the next day at lunch," her mother said casually.

Virginia smacked her palm onto the kitchen table, rattling the screws beneath the leaves that held the wood together. "When she was already dead!" she shot back, the realizations coming thick and fast like a tide coming in much too soon. "I'm going to give you one last chance to tell me how you knew I was seeing Juliette that night."

"Or what?" her mother asked innocently. "What will you do to me, Ginnie? Rough me up like one of your bail jumpers?"

"Arthur, leave," Virginia ordered. "Take Anya."

"Ginnie—" he started.

"*Leave.*"

She waited until the door slammed closed before she bent over, positioning her face right next to her mother's. "You're a seer, aren't you, Vivian?"

"I don't know what you're talking about."

"It's obvious to me now, you know. There's no sense in lying about it." Virginia huffed out a derisive laugh, the hatred crawling its way across her skin and settling there like a blanket of invisible parasites. "You always knew everything about everyone, and I thought it was because you were an insufferable, unrepentant gossip, but no, no. That wasn't why." She cracked her knuckles, an empty threat. There was no sense in hitting her mother, and besides, it had never been Virginia's purview to hit someone who wasn't already swinging. "Interesting choice to blame it on Dad, though."

"That man couldn't see a shadows-damned thing with his eyes wide open," her mother replied with a sneer. "A useless rat of a man and I'm glad he's dead and buried."

"Why lie to me?" Virginia asked. "Why not tell me when I was younger?"

"You showed no signs as a child," her mother explained. "I half expected you to come running back here after the Rupture, filled with questions about what you were, but no." Her eyes fell on Virginia's scars once more, and something blinked across her face, too quick to discern. "But it would appear that you were indisposed. I had no way of knowing because you were too far gone from me and you always refused to return to Birch Hollow, so that was that." Her mother folded her hands in front of her, shoulder squared. "You have no one to blame but yourself."

"You're a real piece of work, you know that?" Virginia turned on her heel, knowing that if she didn't get out of that house in the following four seconds, she'd tear the place apart with her bare hands, brick by brick, dismantling the entire house with nothing more than rage and sheer force of will.

Bricks.

"It was you," Virginia said coolly. "With the brick through the window, it was you."

"I don't know what on earth you're talking about," her mother retorted. "Don't be ridiculous. Why would I destroy my own property?"

"I don't know, why would you do anything that you've already done?" Virginia strode to the phone rifling through the drawer of the side table it sat on.

"Ginnie, stop it."

Virginia produced a note with the familiar looped scrawl, just a bit tighter than it had been on the note wrapped around that muddy brick. "What did you do, use your left hand to write it?" She slammed the drawer shut after stuffing the note back inside. "Why? To what end?"

"Ginnie, don't get mixed up in this," her mother warned, her voice a harsh snap. "It will be your undoing."

"Oh yeah?" Virginia asked, wheeling around once more. "What more could life possibly take from me that I haven't lost already?"

"The Deans are persistent and persuasive and they will drag Eugene Carsh down into the mud. They will pin the whole thing on him, they're already making moves." Her mother moved towards her, but it was a jerky gesture, riddled with frustration and rage. "They own half the state police force and they'll already know."

"You can't see the future, you're no oracle," Virginia snapped. "Someone has to pay for Juliette's death, I won't let them escape justice. How the hell are you so connected with the Deans, anyway?"

"You're not the only one with regrets, Ginnie."

Virginia stared, considering, and marched through the door to the porch, gulping the cool night air she so craved.

"Ginnie—" Arthur tried again once she was outside.

"Fuck off!" she shouted, pushing him aside.

He grabbed her by the wrist, yanking her backward. "You can't just keep doing this, you know. Running, pushing me away. I'm trying to help you!"

Virginia wrenched from his grip, barely resisting the impulse to sink her silver knuckles into the soft flesh of his cheek. "Get away from me," she snarled, stalking off into the empty field, praying that was what left of the stalks would hide her silhouette in the darkness, even as the heavy clouds blocked out what was left of the moonlight. She stumbled, running as far as she could until her muscled ached from the effort.

Shame washed over her like flood water, murky and tainted. She buried her face in her hands and for the first time in years, she wept. Sobs wracked through her, dragging up through her lungs and echoing out over the fields, a pathetic, beleaguered sound that she would never forget, no matter how many glasses of gin she tried to drown it with.

Thunder rumbled in the distance, quiet at first, and then growing louder as the storm approached. She remained kneeling in the field, the first drops of rain taking another piece of her with them as they sank into the earth. Electricity hissed beneath her skin and she knew, a deep inexorable knowing of the suffering that was yet to come.

There was no escaping what she hated most, because it lived in her veins, too, just as toxic, just as potent as the source. Bitterness and resentment, filed away in place of what she'd spent forty-eight years searching for, but had never found.

Lightning sliced across the sky like the glint of a knife, followed by an angry roar. Virginia stayed there in the field, her head in her hands, praying the torrential rain would drown out her crying. Linen stuck to her legs as it soaked through with water, loosening the clumps of dry, crusted mud that rested there, alongside burrs and dust.

She couldn't run from it, not when it coursed through her as obvious as oxygen.

They were the same, Virginia and her mother. They

couldn't bear to see the truth reflected in the other.

Mothers and mirrors, always destructive, and just as always unavoidable.

Chapter Forty-Six

Dawn hovered at the horizon, pink and gentle, despite everything that had happened. Her mother's warning about the Deans hung heavy on her shoulders, tying her to ground that she couldn't get away from fast enough. "You know, Arthur, if I never see this shadows-damned place again, it will be too soon."

He nodded, reaching out for her cigarette and taking a puff. "Don't I know it," he agreed. "I was gone long enough that I forgot how things happen out here. Quiet. Covered. Everything brushed under the rug, secrets in every corner, and the days continue as if nothing happened." He inhaled, exhaled, and then spoke. "I'm sorry I wasn't here for you when all that happened with Juliette."

"Not your fault you're two years older, it was time to move on." She took it back, just for one breath, and gave it back to him. "You picked me up off the streets when you caught up with me in Verdance."

"Seamus did that."

"You both did that." She squeezed her eyes shut, willing the last week to vanish into a fever dream or an ill-conceived vision. "I still don't have it figured out, you know," she said.

"The seeing."

He patted her knee. "You will. Probably for the best you're not some oracle, not with the feds so close." He gritted his teeth and ground them, folding his arms over his chest. "I still can't believe I didn't see that coming."

"Lindell probably has more secrets than we know," Virginia offered. "She has never been very forthcoming with her history, even as she digs into everyone else's."

"I had her over to my house!" he barked. "I invited her into my home, my wife cooked her dinner, and more than once, and for what? To limp back to the city with a knife in my back made of federal protocol?"

"Yeah, you're telling me," Virginia said, seething right alongside him. She finished the cigarette and stamped the butt out, sighing at the rays of sunlight at the horizon, giving the fields of corn a strange, ethereal glow. "I'm thinking about making a big mistake," she said, nodding at the door of the police department. "You coming?"

"I get the feeling it's probably better that I don't see what you're about to do, or hear what you're about to say," Arthur said, an eyebrow raised in question.

"Probably right."

"Yell if you need me."

Virginia stood, bracing her hands against her thighs. "If you hear yelling, it won't be me." She crossed the empty street, the silence of the morning a balm to her noisy, crowded thoughts. Grief was a strange predator. She thought she'd cried the last of her tears for Juliette years ago, but they gathered in her eyes regardless. The riptide of pain was as strong as it had been thirty-one years prior. It was as if she was left alive only to suffer another day.

She pushed inside, the glass door squeaking on its hinges. "Eugene," she said calmly, seating herself across from the cell. "We have things to discuss."

"I have nothing to discuss with you," he said sharply from the inside of the singular cell. "This is a matter for state police, thanks to you."

"If you could just talk to me like I didn't arrest you, I'd like to have a few questions answered before the state police get here in about an hour." She folded her hands atop the desk and stared him down.

"I bet you've waited this day all your adult life," he grunted. "The justice of seeing me behind the same bars I locked you in."

"I'm not interested in revenge," she said softly. "Not anymore. Not about this." She glanced at the clock on the wall, noting the time. Six in the morning. Too early for breakfast, but she passed a day old donut through the bars anyway. "I brought you this."

"Poison?" he asked, taking it. He took a bite before waiting for her to answer and swallowed, sitting against the concrete blocks behind the narrow bench. "Not quite your style. What did you do, pinch some of the strychnine from the Speer place?"

"If I wanted to kill you, Eugene, you'd be dead already." She smirked, unwrapping another for herself. Her chest heaved with sadness again, and she set it aside, her appetite ruined. "Why?" she asked.

"Why what?"

"Why did the chief back then cover it all up? Money, sure, and fear of the Deans, but shadows, Eugene, he could have involved state police. The Deans had power in this county, maybe in a few, but he wouldn't have escaped justice forever. Now he's..."

"Untouchable."

Virginia nodded. "Untouchable," she repeated.

"I don't know," he answered. "And Virginia, I spent the past three decades and then some with the same sick feeling in the pit of my stomach." He took another bite of the donut. "Strange that I feel freer in this cell than I ever did outside of it."

"Not so strange, maybe."

He set down the wrapper and grasped the iron bars with both hands, leaning forward until his face was an inch away. "I'm sorry," he said, his voice cracking with emotion. "There's no excuse for what I did, and I'm so sorry that girl never got justice. Virginia, I—" he swallowed back a strangled sob, leaning his forehead against metal. "The damage that all did, not just to you, but to the town. It's mired in muck, and I helped. Now J.D. is making a name for himself on the backs of mythics, and my chance to make it right is done." Eugene brushed tears from his eyes and rubbed the moisture onto the knees of his uniform. "And what happened with you and your mother, that was my fault, too."

"Nah," Virginia countered. "We were always going to wind up where we are." She sucked her teeth. "Too similar, maybe."

"We should have hashed all this out when you came back for your dad's funeral."

"I probably would have punched you square in the jaw," Virginia replied. "This is a new me, Eugene. I won't punch you unless you deserve it."

"And you don't think I deserve it?"

She sighed heavily, sliding her fingers in and out of the silver knuckles in her pocket. "You forget, Eugene. I was part of the VCPD for years. I've seen how things work. Or rather, how they don't, sometimes."

He nodded. "It's a profession that attracts the do-gooders and the criminals alike," he commiserated. "Everyone else gets caught in the crossfire."

"Over and over," she agreed. She dropped the knuckles back into her pocket, the weight of them pulling at the linen of her trousers. "The Deans will put all of this on you, Eugene."

"I'll talk to the prosecutor," he said. "I'll tell them everything."

"If they don't have you killed in custody." She sighed again, rubbing her hand over the smooth scars on her forehead. "I'm going to do something for you, Eugene."

"I'll tell state police as soon as they arrive," he said, regaining some of his long-lost integrity, and the lightness pulling him to sit straighter. "It's time to have the truth be said."

Virginia picked up the ring of keys from Eugene's desk and put the key into the lock, turning it until the deadbolt released. "I may have performed a citizen's arrest and called the state police, but as it turns out, you managed to escape the cell before any of the officers arrived." The door swung wide, and Eugene still sat there, stunned. "You can do more for Juliette out there than you can in here," she said.

"Just like that?"

"You'll be dead before you get to county otherwise," Virginia said. "What good does that do? You didn't kill her,

Eugene. I know you didn't, because you don't have the spine for blood."

He stood nervously, like he was afraid it was all some trick. "I can't tell if that's a compliment or an insult."

"That's how you know I'm being earnest," she replied. "Go, get out of here before they show up. You don't have long to get across county lines, and you'll have to steal a car to get shot of this place."

"Why?" he asked. "Why not just let me die for what I did? It's at least some justice for Juliette."

"Because I know that if I let you go, you're going to do your shadows-damndest to make sure J.D. pays the price." She tore a piece of paper from the inventory of his personal items and scribbled some information down. "You can find me at this address in Verdance," she said. "Use that judiciously."

"Thank you, Virginia," he said, laying a hand on her shoulder. He squeezed, but only briefly. When he slipped out the back door, she made sure that she didn't watch where he went. The less she knew, the better.

***

Shirin was standing out front, arms folded over her chest as she leaned against her VCPD squad unit. The new bronze badge had come quickly, clearly the vehicle would take a little longer. "What was that all about?" she asked.

"Nothing," Virginia lied. "Just getting my cigarette case back." She flipped it out of her breast pocket as proof and slid it back inside. "Bastard never returned it."

"I heard you found some remains yesterday."

"Word always did travel fast in this place." Virginia leaned against a concrete pillar, shielding her eyes against the growing light of the day, uninterrupted by clouds or foliage. "I assume you're already neck-deep on that lead we dug up on the Harrow murder."

"Yes." Shirin nodded, slowly, and she took off her cap, ruffling her salt and pepper hair. "Virginia, I shouldn't even tell you this."

"But?"

"The feds know about Jolie. They—we—have a renewed effort to track down unregistered mythics. There are more in this state than most, so it's a priority."

Dread snaked up through the cracks in the street and wound itself around her veins. "How?" Virginia managed to ask. "How did they find out about her?"

"A lead. Tit for tat, information given to save someone's ass." Shirin kept her cap in her hands, as if she was apologizing for someone else's sins.

"Those enforcers," Virginia supplied, her hands curling into fists involuntarily. She'd use those assholes for sparring practice, given half an opportunity.

Shirin shook her head. "It wasn't them," she said. "They didn't have the right information, anyway. Something about an inferno witch, some tall tales about a banshee that disappeared." She tried for a smile, but faltered. "Virginia, it was Astrid."

Her hands tightened, and then relaxed, leaving her nothing to grab onto. She was falling into nothingness, and while she shouldn't have been surprised, some part of her still was. "Astrid."

"She wanted to shore up the club's viability and her own immunity going forward. She agreed to be an informant.

Jolie's was the first name she supplied."

"So you're going to take her in, I imagine?" Virginia's voice was low and tight, a barely restrained growl. She wasn't sure in that moment who she hated more: J.D., her mother, or Astrid. Shirin was a close runner-up. "Going to throw her to the shadows-damned wolves, Shirin, going to let her break herself on the front lines of whatever the fuck the government is up to these days?"

"I'm telling you in order to warn you, Virginia," Shirin said carefully, her own defenses just below the surface. "I'm risking my job to tell you this."

"Your brand new shiny job with the feds, what a fucking shame," Virginia snapped. "Maybe it wasn't Astrid at all, Shirin, maybe it was you who gave her up."

"I wouldn't do that."

"Wouldn't you? Arthur didn't even know you were leaving until yesterday. You couldn't wait to join the feds, you were practically giddy about it." Virginia took out the cigarette case, grateful that Eugene hadn't smoked them all. She lit one, hands shaking. She had to get Jolie away from the feds in town. She had to hide her somehow. "You've been looking for a way to get back at me, and you decided this was how to do it."

"Virginia—" Shirin released a frustrated sigh, her shoulders tight with the tension of it. "I'm giving you a head start. Get the girl out of the state, but you can't go with her, they'll know. Astrid told them she was staying with you. You can't keep her, Virginia. She'll get picked up, and so will you for concealing an unregistered mythic."

"Is that a threat?"

"It won't be me picking you up, or her. Please, just this

once, stop fighting me and listen!" Shirin replaced her cap, folding her arms again. "Yes, I wanted to join the federal bureau. I want scum off the streets, and they're going after the big fish. Yes, I jumped at the opportunity when it was offered to me. No, I didn't tell Sheriff Dixon beforehand, because I didn't know until I knew." Sunlight glanced off the metal of her service revolver until she shifted her weight away from the glare. "I'm telling you because I know what that girl means to you. If you get her out of the state, you might be able to buy her another six months."

"Six months," Virginia said. "And then you'll have her anyway? She's just a kid, Shirin."

"I don't make the laws, I just enforce them."

"That's a weak excuse."

Shirin blinked at her, and then shook her head. "What was I supposed to do, Virginia? Once Astrid gave up the girl's name, there was no way I could keep her name off the list. This is the best I can do, and even this is a risk."

"I'll see you back in the city," Virginia said as she walked away. "Or, if we're both lucky, maybe not."

***

Virginia could barely stand to face the clocktower, squeezing her eyes shut as she entered the mechanic's waiting room. Despite her refusal to see, she could still hear the chatter of nearby squad units as they processed the scene of the thirty-one year old homicide.

"Just a second," Sammy called from the back.

"Mmhmm," Virginia intoned, not wanting to give herself away before she could face her accuser.

Metal clanked against concrete in the shop for several moments before the quiet hiss of swearing. "What can I do ya for today?" Sammy asked as she rounded the corner. "Oh, it's you." She wiped her hands on the blue towel hanging from a belt loop and stared across the counter. "I returned your car earlier."

"Yes, thank you."

"Something wrong with it?"

"No, nothing wrong. Runs like a dream, actually." Virginia approached the counter, leaning over it to look down towards Stu's office. "Is your dad in?"

"No, he's not."

Silence hung tense and heavy, punctuated by the muffled toll of the clocktower's bell. It was strange that no one had silenced it. Maybe they couldn't.

Virginia breathed in a long, slow breath, and let it out as a quiet sigh. "Please give him my thanks for what he said the other day. Helped solve a case."

"The girl who went missing?"

"Juliette Ashling, yes." Virginia still stood, still staring. It was difficult to know what to say to someone who had tried to put her away for murder, but had also returned her car in pristine condition. "So if you could let him know, I'd appreciate it."

"Yep."

"Sammy, you know, I—"

"It's probably for the best if you leave now, Ms. Vane," Sammy interrupted. "Your bill has been settled, we have no more business to attend to. I'm sure you have plenty of work to be getting on with back in the city."

"Bold of you to suggest we don't have any business speaking when you told the feds that you saw me going off into the woods with Melody Kingston the night she was murdered," Virginia snapped. "Do you have any idea how much trouble I might have been in? Prison, Sammy, and for what? Because you don't like that I was asking your dad some questions?"

Sammy pressed her fists against the counter, eyes glowering. "I told the cops that I saw you, because I *did* see you. Now, I can't pretend to know what happened beyond that tree line, and you seem to have convinced the authorities that you had nothing to do with that mess, but I saw what I saw. Nothin' you say is going to convince me different."

"It couldn't have been me," Virginia said simply.

"Ain't no one else out here look like that," Sammy retorted, gesturing at her own face. "I saw you, Ms. Vane. I'm not saying you're a murderer because I think if you had the stomach for it your mother would have been six feet under years ago, but I am saying I think you know more than you let on." She gestured at the door. "I trust you can find the exit without assistance."

Chapter Forty-Seven

Virginia didn't stop at the door to the Sphinx, pushing straight past the bouncer that tried to call after her. "The name is Vee," she said, grabbing a bottle of gin from behind the bar as she passed. "Tell Astrid she can put this on my tab."

"But—"

She slammed the door that led to the private residence behind her, pulling the cork out with her teeth. The taste of juniper warmed her throat, the liquid long craved on the seven hour drive back upstate. She hadn't even gone home to her apartment yet, instead she'd driven straight to the club without stopping.

When she threw open Astrid's door, there she sat, the queen betrayer herself, perched in front of her vanity and examining her eyelashes one by one.

"Vee!" Astrid shouted, standing up from the chair so fast that she nearly knocked it over. It wobbled on three legs as she threw her arms around Virginia's neck. "Shadows, I thought I'd never see you again, I thought—"

"Shut up," Virginia growled, pressing her back against the wall and holding her chin between thumb and forefinger. "I don't want to hear it."

Astrid nodded. "Okay," she replied, exposing her throat to Virginia's teeth. The tie on her pink silk robe dropped and the front fell open, previewing the matching lace underthings. Her dark skin glistened beneath the fabric, showing through between the gaps.

She smelled like tangerines, the sweet tendrils of summer curled around her. The citrus memory of the coast in June pulled at something in Virginia and she pressed Astrid further, kissing her hard on the mouth.

A quiet, desperate gasp escaped Astrid's lips, and Virginia knew that she had her. Astrid had always liked when she was harsher, sharper, cut with too many rough edges.

Before she could second guess the mistake she was almost certainly making, her hands were at Astrid's hips, roaming over silk and lace, pursuing skin. She found it beneath the seam of her underthings and popped the buttons free one at a time until fabric fell to the floor, whispering secrets against expensive, hand-woven carpets from overseas.

Astrid didn't reach back for her, she never had. It was always the way of their dynamic, Virginia was always the hunter, Astrid always the prey, except that she was really more of a snake, a siren who had never learned to master fighting her own nature.

Although, Virginia supposed, few ever did.

She dragged a hand up between Astrid's thighs, drawing a sharp intake of breath from her full rosy lips, and the power of that was too intoxicating to eschew. It was the only time, the only place she had the upper hand with Astrid, the only occasion where she had the opportunity to sneak past the gates around her and strike at the heart of her. Virginia never imagined she would use their connection like that, whatever it was, but the betrayal had been six months in the making, starting with Astrid allowing for Jolie's kidnap, and culminating with giving the girl's name to federal agents. It was the third and worst of her misdeeds, and the one Virginia couldn't let her get away with. It was unforgivable, a sin worthy of worse penance than even she would mete out.

"Don't *tease* me, Dollface," Astrid pleaded, her breathy voice lingering against Virginia's neck. "You've already made me wait so long."

Virginia kissed the words out of Astrid's mouth, tongue against tongue and it was languid, slow, a torturous experiment in waiting and denial. She took as long as she thought Astrid would stand before she started to complain before she dipped to her collarbone, pushing the silk robe off her shoulders. Her lips trailed down over breast and ribs, lingering at the sides as she knelt on the floor, holding Astrid against the wall by her hip.

She crept closer to where Astrid's thighs met, waiting there, tormenting her spoils of love and war like a cat with a mouse dangling from its mouth, unwilling to end the game just yet. Virginia buried her face there, finally, pulling an uncharacteristically guttural whine from Astrid that was both satisfying and the worst kind of temptation, calling her to abandon what she'd showed up for. She kissed and nipped, teasing, taunting, and tormenting until Astrid's breath quickened, resting right on the cusp of the cliff-edge.

Virginia leaned back on her haunches, taking another swig of the stolen gin.

"What are you doing?" Astrid demanded, slumping down against the wall now that no one was holding her there.

Virginia stood and leaned in close. "Don't," she said, kissing her. "Ever." She thrust her tongue into Astrid's mouth before she pulled away again. "Call me again." She released her again, taking another shot from the bottle before setting it on Astrid's vanity. "And you'd better watch your back, because I'm not watching it anymore."

"Wait," Astrid said, trailing after Virginia as she cinched her robe back together. "Vee, wait!"

"As far as I'm concerned, you're dead, you've ceased to exist, do you hear me?" Virginia paused on the stairs to look back at her one last time, the vestiges of whatever they once had sparking into inert dust. "I've seen the inside of a court room enough times on your behalf, Ms. Frost, and I'm done."

"Vee, hold on, just—" Astrid pulled at her sleeve, an uncharacteristic desperation lodged deep into fresh lines on her face. "What was I supposed to do?" she whined. "They had me backed into a corner, Vee, you saw how close they got to nabbing me on some trumped-up charges last time, I never would have slipped the net again."

"How is that my problem?"

"I didn't have a choice!"

"Go fuck yourself, Astrid," Virginia said, returning her attention to the stairs as she went. "You always had a choice. You just chose yourself, like you always do."

Astrid stopped trying to follow her, which was for the best. The last thing either of them needed was to make a scene in the club, even before it was open. Being at the club at all was a risk that had dragged Virginia in front of a judge more than once, so if her plan was going to work, she had to keep her nose clean.

She shoved past the bouncer on the way back out too,

ignoring his angry shouting. He didn't matter. None of it did.

"So you're sleeping with her again?" Agent Lindell demanded, incredulous, standing there in front of her sleek new federal agent's car with that ugly bronze badge pinned to her bicep.

Virginia wiped her mouth with the back of her hand, staring back at her. "You tell me, since you seem to know everything. What did you do, track me down with your new special federal agent resources?"

"It's not like it was hard to find you," Lindell replied acerbically. "You're unbelievable, you know that?" She ripped the cap from her head, raking a hand through her hair. Heat radiated up from the pavement, even that early in the day. "It's a wonder you've managed to escape prison, considering your desperation to run back here at every opportunity."

Something pricked at Virginia, but she ignored it, drowning it in cold indifference instead. "And yet, here I stand, free as a bird."

"I warned you that they were onto her," Shirin spat, throwing a folder to the ground. White pages scattered across the dew-speckled asphalt, darkening where paper met moisture. Virginia knew that Shirin meant for her to gather them, so she stayed, folding her arms over her chest.

"How magnanimous."

"I risked my position with the bureau so that you could get her out of the city. I tried to help that girl out of some misjudged affection for you." Lindell rested her hand against her service revolver, but moved to mirror Virginia instead.

"Do you want a medal?" Virginia asked coolly. "The feds shouldn't even have Jolie's name, but now they do. You could have steered them away from Astrid, away from Jolie, but you didn't." She pulled a cigarette from its tarnished case, lighting it with a match. "So if you don't mind, I will refrain from prostrating myself at your feet."

"This was the best I could do," Lindell insisted. "What would you have me do, Virginia? Burn down the records office? Falsify accounts, forge signatures?" She huffed out a derisive laugh that was more an exasperated sigh than anything else. "Did you think I'd break protocol before I even got my federal badge?"

Virginia exhaled a soft plume of smoke, letting it eke out from the side of her mouth. "Do you really think I care about federal protocol more than that girl?" She shook her head slowly, maintaining eye contact with Shirin. "You are sorely and dangerously mistaken."

"Are you threatening me?"

"I'm not threatening you, Shirin, I'm telling you that you're mistaken if you think I would care about your ladder of professional successes more than Jolie." Virginia inhaled, swallowing back the taste of ash and the burn of impotent rage. "They aren't going to stop looking for her just because Anya has her out of state. The first hint of a threat to national security and they'll have agents combing every interstate from here to the coast looking for her. She's too valuable to lose."

"It's the law for mythics to register," Shirin said. "I don't make the laws, I just enforce them. I went to bat for her, kept her out of immediate danger, but you—"

"They're going to tear her apart, Shirin," Virginia interrupted with a snap. "You know it, and I know it. She isn't even nineteen and you want to send her to the front lines."

"She wouldn't be the first teenager on the front lines, Virginia, and you know it."

"Other teenagers aren't my responsibility, she is."

Shirin sighed. "I did what I could. I guess I thought you'd appreciate that."

Virginia nodded, letting the embers of her cigarette burn the edges of her fingers. "It's not good enough, Shirin."

"It's better than nothing. I thought you'd be grateful, but no, you're running around town fucking the first woman you trip over." Lindell flexed her fists, skin pulled tight over her knuckles. "Plenty could happen in the next election. They could stop conscription, Senator J.D. said that—"

"They won't."

Lindell threw up her arms in exasperation. "Aren't you going to apologize?"

"For what?"

"Honestly, Virginia, you are one of the most infuriating women I've ever had the misfortune of meeting."

Virginia exhaled a laugh through her nose, the last lungful of smoke huffing into the air. "And I suppose you think you're somehow *not* infuriating?"

"I at least tried," Shirin said. "That's more than the rest of them can say."

"You have no idea what you're talking about. You think you know, but you don't."

"Then tell me."

"No," Virginia said, shaking her head. "I was afraid I couldn't trust you. Now that you've handed Jolie off to the feds, I see that I was right."

"I didn't—"

"Go home, Agent Lindell," Virginia interjected, saving her

admission for the right time, and early morning in the Sphinx parking lot wasn't it. "You don't belong on this side of town."

"So that's it then?"

Virginia nodded, crushing the burning filter under her heel. "I'll see you when I see you. Don't come looking. Don't call."

Lindell waited a moment, staring, before she put the cap back on and climbed into her car. "Fine," she called back over the sound of the engine turning over. "Good riddance."

***

The emptiness of Virginia's apartment was surprisingly unwelcome.

She'd spent the time downstate wishing for silence, for peace, for the blissful relief of an empty room. Standing inside the door, keys still in hand, the creaky solitude weighed on her heavier than the oppression of overwhelmed senses or the stickiness of the heat that remained, lingering at eye level.

The sofa was just as Jolie had left it, blanket folded haphazardly over the back. The damned cat was sat there, purring noisily, stretched out across the cushions.

"How in shadows did you get in here?" Virginia asked, before spying the window, slightly ajar. "I thought I closed that." She pushed it open wider, hungry for a cool breeze that never came.

Virginia trailed her fingers over the cat's soft black fur, bright green eyes staring curiously back at her. Much to her surprise, it began to purr, rolling over to show its belly. "You're awfully trusting," she murmured, petting it gently. "What if I wasn't a cat person?" The cat chirped strangely at her before it ducked beneath her arms to sidle out the open window.

She stared at the cold kettle, craving hot coffee despite the weather, but unable to bring herself to light the stove the mortal way. Jolie's absence was pressingly palpable, the quiet of the living room like a yawning void that would swallow her whole if she wasn't careful. The only sounds were those of the street below, rumbling car engines and the distant bustle from two blocks up, where commuters gathered to wait for the train, newspapers in tow, the headlines boasting Senator J.D.'s latest victory in Congress.

Verdance was getting more dangerous. The whole world was, but Virginia couldn't bring herself to care much for the nameless, faceless hoards that would suffer under the tyranny of a new government power. No, her concerns were much more specific and localized.

Anya had driven Jolie over state lines. The girl was safe, but not for long. No, to ensure she was removed from the mythics register and the conscription rolls, the feds would want something much better than a fire demon.

Something like a seer.

Epilogue

A rattling like beetles, or maybe cockroaches, wrested its way into Virginia's stomach as she pushed open the doors of the federal building on Ninth Avenue. She could still turn back. She could still run, pretend she'd gotten the wrong address, or that she'd arrived there for some work related to a case.

No.

She tugged at the lapels of her jacket, squaring her shoulders. It was time. There was no other viable option, no change for things to work themselves out. "Agent Lindell's office," she said to the receptionist.

"First floor, third door on the left," the woman replied, eyeing Virginia with suspicion.

"Do you have an appointment?"

"Yes," Virginia lied, smiling broadly because it tended to scare most people paired with the scars that hung low over her cheekbones.

The building was artfully built, with marble tiled floors polished to a shine brilliant enough to spot her reflection in before she caught sight of herself and looked away. The pillars shot up towards the high ceilings, the lines carved with perfect perpendicular angles that never once wavered.

She didn't even bother to knock, opening the door with an unnecessary flourish. "Agent Lindell," she said, seating herself across from Shirin. "How nice to see you again."

Shirin looked up from her work, surprised but not quite shocked. "Ms. Vane," she said coldly. "I didn't expect to see you so soon, and especially not barging into my office."

"You know, I hear people barge in less if you're not on the first floor." Virginia offered up a smirk as she crossed one leg over the other in a display of dominance that she hoped would have an impact. "How long before they let you move up to one of the real offices?"

Shirin scowled, snapping the file shut. "How can I help you?"

"I have a proposition for you."

"A proposition?"

"A proposal, if you will." Virginia let the words hang in the air a long, undisturbed moment before she continued. "I don't want Jolie on the conscription rolls, not in two years, not ever."

"I told you, I've already done everything I can to delay that."

Virginia interlaced her fingers, resting them on her knee. "And I understand that, but you and I both know that with the way things are going, it won't be long before that age restriction gets lowered to sixteen, maybe even fifteen for some of the more powerful mythics. You did your part in changing her age to sixteen in her file, thank you very much for that—"

She grimaced, hating the sound of the words, but swallowed back whatever rage and bile had long since collected at the back of her throat. "Thank you for that, but it's not going to make a difference for much longer."

"I can't help you," Shirin said flatly, opening her folder

once again. "Next time, make an appointment."

"What if I offered your superiors a trade?" Virginia asked. "Nothing under the table, a flat trade. But they'd have to agree before I revealed the identity."

"What kind of trade?"

"The Federal Authority for Freedom here agrees to forget Jolie ever existed, and I can point them towards an unregistered seer with one hell of an in with the underworld in Verdance."

Shirin leaned forward across the desk. "Who?"

"Get them to agree, Shirin. In writing, with a contract," Virginia insisted. "And the seer gets immunity for not having been on the rolls in the first place."

Agent Lindell lifted one eyebrow, and then another, but left her office without another word. She was only gone for fifteen minutes before she returned with a stack of papers, each of them paired with a carbon copy beneath it. "Before we agree, we need to know if this seer has ever been a felon."

"No."

"Misdemeanor?"

"Never served time," Virginia answered. "If they want to grant immunity for parking tickets, too, I'm sure the subject in question wouldn't mind."

Shirin rolled her eyes, setting the contracts down in front of her. "Sign and date those three. I hope you realize that by doing this, you know that this seer will be immediately conscripted into federal service."

"I'm aware," Virginia said, signing her full name with a flourish on each page.

"I'm surprised," Shirin said when she'd finished. "I never thought you'd be the kind of mercenary to give up a mythic to the feds." She smiled, leaning back in her chair. "Alright then, Ms. Vane, tell me. Who is this seer, and where can we find them?"

"Oh, she's already in the building," Virginia said casually, relishing how the words melted the grin off of Shirin's face as she put the pieces together. "It's me."

* * *

End of Clocktower Elegy

Keep reading for sneak peeks of other books in The Ruptured Realms Universe: Exiled Advocate, the first Sadie Sinclair Esquire book, and Canon in Death, exhibit C in The Vane Dossier.

Want to get sneak peeks, exclusive sales, and free books? Join the newsletter at Linktr.ee/RyannFletcherWrites

Enter the Ruptured Realms Universe

The Ruptured Realms encompasses three different series, with three different main characters. Read them in linear order:

1. Rhapsody in Flames (The Vane Dossier, exhibit A)
2. Books and Bloodlust (free to read on Patreon)
3. Exiled Advocate (Sadie Sinclair, Esquire: book one)
4. Clocktower Elegy (The Vane Dossier, exhibit B)
5. The Crownless Court (Sadie Sinclair, Esquire: book two)
6. Canon in Death (The Vane Dossier, exhibit C)

The Ruptured Realms will contain novels across these three series! Sign up for the newsletter at Linktr.ee/RyannFletche rWrites for access to beta reader signups, advanced reader copy giveaways, and sneak peeks.

Preview for Books and Bloodlust (read free on Patreon)

Zin stared at the still-smoking hole in the library wall, one hand fastened to her hip, right where the wide belt met the black herringbone wool. "*Filius canis*," she hissed under her breath. *Son of a bitch.* Had she been human, those words would have brought forth a plume of condensation from her lips, ascending into the frigid night air. But her humanity had been long since lost, so the air remained still as an undisturbed grave.

The fire marshall hadn't been joking when he said the damage was "considerable," though if she had been describing it, she may have erred more towards the tone of the searingly dramatic. Half the library would wind up with rot if that gaping maw burned into the building wasn't closed up, and fast. Verdance winters weren't known for their attunement with mild meteorology.

She stepped over a small pile of burned ash, the toe of her black patent leather shoe smudged from the spent embers. "*Merde. Porco miseria.*" She'd always preferred swearing in other languages. English was a strange, cobbled language, even if she'd spent plenty of time speaking it, expletives never felt natural. None, that is, except one. "Goddamn it."

"Ma'am?" the fire chief started, approaching from behind. She'd heard him coming, of course. The man was about as inconspicuous as an elk in mating season. "Fire's out."

"So I see," Zin replied, still staring through the hole at the trees behind the library. "What are the chances that some of your crew could at least board up that hole tonight?"

"Minimal," he said, sidling around her to examine the damage once more with a shrug. "Big city. Lots of fires, you know."

"This is a public institution," she challenged. "Until that is repaired, everything in here is at risk. The archives are of particular concern."

He turned to face her, soot scraped along his left temple. "My job is to put out fires, ma'am. The archives might be your concern, but they're not mine."

"How often do you use the library?" she pressed, wishing she could single-handedly fix the damage herself. Relying on others had never been her purview.

He shrugged again, this time in dismissal. "Honestly, it's the first time I've ever been in here." He tipped his fire helmet and exited through the hole, boots crunching against wood made charcoal.

She shouldn't have been surprised. He didn't seem like much of a reader. There was a time when books were sacred. That time had long passed, but there was good reason for it. She couldn't expect everyone to value the power of the written word. After all, some were more than happy to see it burn.

The fire trucks pulled away from the library, along with the squad unit and Ms. Vane's car. Zin was left alone to fend for the library herself, to assess the damage and to begin writing sternly worded letters to the city council demanding immediate action. It wasn't as though being there late at night was an anomaly—she'd spent a great deal of time reading and working at night. Darkness was a familiar friend, one she'd grown to tolerate over the past three centuries. It was the only friend she still had who'd known her when she was a girl.

Zin ran her fingers along the edges of the hole, the bricks still warm to the touch despite the plummeting, icy temperatures. The only thing that could have done that was a fire demon. Not even inferno witches could sear through brick like that, not without careful consideration and planning. Interesting. It had been at least one-hundred and fifty years since she'd seen a fire demon. They were rare, some of the rarest mythics in the world.

Vampires, witches, and werewolves were a dime a dozen, a fact that had horrified most mortals when the rifts opened and the Rupture marked so many of their neighbors, friends, and spouses. Vampires had taken to hiding until the marks disappeared, a decision that had saved some from detection, but others were dragged into the sunlight or taken for experimentation. Zin supposed that many who knew her suspected what she was, but she was careful to never mention it in polite company. Many people were more squeamish than one might think.

She pulled a book from a nearby shelf, looking for damage. She frowned at the smoke marks, the edges of several pages singed. The moonlight provided plenty of illumination for her work, and she sorted through the shelves one by one until she had sorted every book into three piles. Luckily, the pile representing the undamaged books was twice the size of the one indicating books damaged beyond salvaging. Several in the third pile could be saved, but would need to be fumigated at the very least.

The smell of smoke burned acrid in her nose, too many memories associated with the licking of flames and the devastation at the periphery, be it grief for the loss of knowledge or of life. She sniffed at a black chiffon sleeve and frowned. It would take several washes to remove the smell from her clothes, but the first priority would be to remove it from her hair. She'd never get to sleep with that smell in her space, and if she did, she'd see only nightmares, and too many to count.

What could a fire demon have been looking for in her library? As far as she knew, there was only one title to do with fire demon biology and lineage, and it was checked out to Virginia V. Vane. Strange, how often that woman found herself entangled in trouble. At some point, she may have to admit that she was seeking it out, rather than it being happenstance or bad luck.

The moon began to set, hastening its own demise by laying against the horizon, the glow locked behind the silhouette of the Verdance skyline. Zin set each pile of books on her own desk, not trusting the other librarians enough to know what needed to be done in order to return them to circulation. She wrote several letters, one to the mayor, one to city council, and one to Sheriff Dixon of the Verdance City Police Department, the latter of which had a budget for repairs, but preferred to use it on their own headquarters instead. She had her work cut out for her if she was going to get that hole repaired before spring.

"Good morning, Zin. By blazes, it's frigid in here!"

Zin slid the final letter into an envelope and moistened the edge, sealing it. "Don't look now, Iris, but there's a rather large hole present. I would imagine that's the cause for the drop in temperature." She wrote out the addresses in tiny, cramped florid script, still unaccustomed to the availability of paper and ink after three hundred years.

Iris gasped, the back of her throat emitting a high-pitched squeak. "What *happened?*"

"Inferno witch, so the theories go," she replied. Iris was a respectable enough colleague, but she had an affinity for gossip that might just get her nominated to be the living archive for Verdance's secrets and dirty laundry. She also had a beau that worked as a photographer for one of the local newspapers. "The VCPD only left an hour ago or so."

"What about this hole? The frost damage, the mold, the—"

"Yes, I've already written letters, I just need three stamps. I can drop them in the mail on my way home." Zin leaned over the wooden railing of the second floor, looking down over the catastrophic damage present below. Iris was standing, staring out at the fading night, her bag still clutched firm to her chest. The smooth tan leather shone in what was left of the moonlight, the brass buckles recently polished.

"I thought you weren't on shift last night?" Iris asked, looking up at her and squinting through the darkness of the second-floor stacks.

Zin gestured at the hole, no longer smoldering despite the heavy reek of charcoal. "I wasn't. If I had been, perhaps we wouldn't have found ourselves with a problem to solve."

"Or you'd be *dead*, Zin," Iris said, covering her mouth as she let loose another theatrical gasp. "What if you had been *killed?*"

"Oh, Iris," Zin replied, descending the creaky stairs in such a way that she avoided nearly all of the sounds they'd emit otherwise. "An inferno witch wouldn't be enough to kill me. I'm like a cockroach. I would survive the unsurvivable."

Iris wrinkled her nose, the spell of her hypothetical worse-case scenario broken enough for her to set her bag on the front desk. "You're only mortal, Zin," she said with a light laugh. "So the VCPD called you at home?"

"Yes," Zin lied. She'd smelled the fire from her home half a mile away almost as soon as it happened. Once she'd seen what happened, she knew there wasn't much she could do without waiting for the fire department first, and so clung to the shadows, the same way she had for almost as long as she could remember. "I suppose they wanted to be sure we didn't walk into a nasty surprise this morning."

"Still a rather nasty surprise, if we're being honest," Iris said, swallowing back a heavy sigh. "How long before it's fixed, do you think?"

"I suspect these aren't the only letters I'll have to write, let's put it that way."

"No one values this place like we do."

Zin shook her head in agreement. "No, I suspect not. The ones who do are the ones who will fight for it regardless. Everyone else has to be reminded of the importance of this building, especially the archives." Sensing Iris was about to exclaim in caution, Zin put up her hand to buy herself some time. "The archive doors are still sealed. We'll have to limit access until the wall is fixed, to limit exposure to frost and temperature degradation."

Iris breathed out a sigh of relief. "Thank goodness," she said. "Imagine if all your work had been ruined?"

"Our work," Zin corrected. "The musical archives are almost solely your passion project."

"We'll have to set out guidelines for the other librarians," Iris said, brushing past the compliment. "You and I may have to work a few extra hours on either side of our usual shifts to be sure no one forgets anything."

Zin nodded. "I don't mind, I just—"

"I know, you can't come in earlier than five." Iris moved to take off her coat, an action of habit, but shrugged the pink wool back over her shoulders. "Gosh, it's not going to be nice for our patrons, is it? Some of them come in here to escape the cold, not to be embraced by it."

"Perhaps we can get a temporary solution in place in the next couple of days," Zin suggested. "Boards, perhaps. And we can order in more coal to offset the temperature, at least in the smaller rooms." She bent, making a note on a slip of paper. "We should instruct the others to keep as many doors closed as possible." She frowned at herself, annoyed that she hadn't already thought of it. "I'm sorry, I should have done that already."

"It's not as if you've had much time to think about it," Iris said, looking over her shoulder. "I'll go do that now. What else do we have on this week that we should think about canceling?"

"Archives tours," Zin replied automatically. "From two of the local universities." She hesitated, looking through the wall at the impending dawn. "I'll send a messenger to deliver a note to the heads of departments."

"Best to have it in writing, anyway. You know how professors can be." Iris laughed lightly, no doubt recalling a particular incident from her past. Wood scraped against wood as she closed two doors on the first floor, the latches catching and the hinges squealing in protest. They weren't in the habit of closing things off at the library. A closed door looked foreign there, and didn't settle well in Zin's chest.

"Unfortunately," she agreed. "I'll take care of it."

Iris closed the last of the doors on the ground floor, hands drifting towards her brass coat buttons once more, but stopped. "My oh my, it's going to be awfully uncomfortable to work in an overcoat."

Zin didn't feel the cold much. She hadn't for a very long time.

"Aren't you half frozen?"

"You know, in all the excitement, I wasn't even thinking when I hung it up. Force of habit." Zin manufactured a shiver, pulling the black wool on around her shoulders. "I'll see you tonight," she promised. "Here's hoping someone is already here to fix that crater." She doubted that immensely, but hope was something she'd never been able to entirely extinguish, despite the lumbering inefficiency of the Verdance City council. At times, she wondered if autocracy was a better fit for humanity and mortals. The Medici family never would have allowed their books to mold. "Good night, Iris."

"Good morning, Zin," Iris replied with a smile. "We'll manage this, don't you worry."

Preview for Exiled Advocate (Sadie Sinclair, Esquire, book 1)

She raced down the crystal-paved path towards the lake, face held to the sun as she shrieked with excitement. Stark birch trees rose up out of the earth, their foliage thick and verdant in the warm summer sun. She had everything she could ever wish for, and in that moment, she was the happiest she would ever be.

"Shailagh!" her mother called, smiling broadly with her arms held wide, beckoning her down to the water. "Would you believe that it's the perfect temperature?"

"Coming!" she squealed, tearing past an errant bramble bush. The delicate silk of her silvery dress caught on a thorn, rending apart each shining thread with the quiet yet insistent snap of permanence. Panic began to rise in her chest as she grasped at it, trying to hide the tear in her clutched fist.

"Shailagh!" her father shouted, grabbing her by the hand. "What have I told you about running like that? It's not befitting of a princess. It's not befitting of royal lineage."

"Faarys, she's just a child," her mother chided, standing up. She straightened her own dress, moving to smooth out the wrinkles. "Royal or not, she deserves to have some fun." She approached, resting a hand on his arm. "It's only fabric, dearest."

"The finest fabric in either realm," he replied sternly. "Child or no, she needs to learn how to hold her place in Fae court. She's old

enough to start understanding the consequences of her actions."

She stared up at her parents, flinching away from the growing tension between them. It wasn't the first argument they'd had about her, and it was difficult not to feel responsible. Pulling from his grasp, she broke free and ran to the water, kneeling on the edge to stare into the glassy, mirrored surface.

At first, it was just her face that stared back at her, young and childlike and innocent. Her parents, rushing to catch up with her, one concerned, one furious. The crisp teal water rippled, disturbing the picture before her. The earth shook, and the lake boiled, disappearing into the deep chasm that had appeared at the center. In its place, a viscous purple sludge oozed up from beneath, pushing aside the land as if it were made of spun sugar.

The forest disintegrated one giant tree at a time, their limbs floating and carried away by the current. She tried to run, but she was rooted to the ground. She reached for her mother first, but she was no longer there. She reached for her father, who stared down from his safety on the bank.

Screams echoed through the ruined woods at the exact moment that the crystalline sparkling path erupted, shooting streams of purple magma into the air with unrepentant fervor. Pain, suffering, exposure.

She held her dress in her hands, and when she looked down at the ruined fabric, it, too, began to melt through her fingers, the purple fluid burning her skin and drawing ripe blisters to the surface. When she reached out, there was nothing there.

Birch trees swayed in the chaos, their roots twisting up out of the ground like tentacles, the wood far too brittle to bend. Bark splintered, the echo of annihilation like barbed thunder in her ears as one trunk after another cracked into fragments, the snap, crack, thwack of files against a worn wood table. "Your Honor." Sadie took a breath, and exhaled it quietly. "As much as it pains me to miss the opportunity to spar with the prosecution, we all have to admit that there just isn't enough evidence for them to bring a case against my client."

The prosecution pointed across the table in accusation. His oversized, ill-fitting suit hung off him, nothing more than a mess of navy pinstripes and white pocket squares. "What Ms. Sinclair seems to be forgetting is that the prosecution had plenty of evidence, the cornerstone of which was our eye-witness to her client's crime of insurance fraud!" He sighed angrily, letting his arms flop back to his sides. "Your Honor, I humbly request an audience in chambers to discuss the possibility that Ms. Sinclair engaged in witness tampering."

"Your Honor!" she protested, gasping audibly, the hard intake of breath echoing around the courtroom and settling in the empty gallery seats. "I am appalled that Mr. Link of the prosecution would accuse me of something quite so unethical, not to mention illegal, in open court." She tugged at the hem of her aubergine suit jacket and flipped a dark curl over her shoulder.

The judge picked up his gavel, turning it around in his hands as he considered. "Mr. Link, are you prepared to offer evidence that the defense engaged in witness tampering?" he asked.

"No, Your Honor, we've yet to uncover hard evidence, but given her track record—"

Sadie spat out a laugh. "My track record?" she repeated. "Please, Mr. Link, point me to even one shred of evidence that I've done anything beyond the scope of the law, and I will immediately turn over this case to another attorney."

She glanced at the door, the huge wood panels still closed, even as the minutes ticked by on the clock that hung above them. She cleared her throat and turned back to the judge. "Your Honor, I am simply asking for this case to be dismissed, as the prosecution no longer knows the whereabouts of their eyewitness. That's all."

Edward Link offered her an oily smile over the gap between their tables. "Your Honor, the prosecution asks for a continuance, in order to regroup and issue a subpoena to our errant witness. We are still prepared to question her, even if she has decided to be a hostile witness."

"Ms. Sinclair, I am inclined to side with the prosecution," Judge Haber said, clearing his throat with a wet sound. "They have indicated that there may be more evidence to support their claims, even if their witness declined to show up to court."

Hinges creaked open and Sadie had to resist the urge to spin around, triumphant, instead of waiting until Ella tapped her on the shoulder.

"Ms. Sinclair," Ella said in a loud whisper that could still be heard across the court, "I think you should see this." She looked perfect in a sapphire blue dress that skimmed over her shapely hips, her dark brunette hair shiny even in the dark courtroom, braided into an intricate crown around her head.

"Thank you, Ms. Beaufort," Sadie said, taking the envelope. She opened the flap and looked inside, feeling every eye in the court on her. The page read exactly as she knew it would, having prepared it that morning. Evidence, hidden by the prosecution that implicated another perpetrator that had long since fled the country. She raised an eyebrow, looking across to the prosecution. "How very interesting," she said evenly.

Edward flinched, shuffling through his paperwork noisily. He dropped a page, and it fluttered silently to the floor, coming to a rest under his polished patent leather shoe. "Your Honor, I would like to respectfully request a recess," he announced. "Just a brief one, if you will. The prosecution doesn't wish to waste the court's time."

Judge Haber considered the request before nodding. "Fifteen minutes," he said, smacking the gavel against its platform.

"What do you have?" Edward Link demanded, reaching for the envelope. Sadie snatched it out of his grasp, sitting back down in her chair.

"What do you think I have?" she asked. "Come on, Ed, you can't be serious with this case. You've got nothing, and this envelope proves that your office has been—"

He bent down, his face inches from hers. "Keep your voice down, alright?" he hissed. "Now, what do you want?"

Sadie glanced over at her client, a thin, weedy-looking man hunched over the table, still looking as terrified as a wounded gazelle on the plains, waiting for a hyena to finish him off. "Probation," she said. "Six months."

"A year and he has to pay a fine," Ed challenged. "Come on, Sadie, you know I can't go lower than that or I'll be on the chopping block next week." He pulled at his red silk tie, standing up straight again. "Or, we meet the judge in chambers, and I tell him everything I learned about how you employed the enforcer who scared off our witness."

"Do you have proof of that?" Sadie asked. "Because if not, it's nothing more than conjecture. You're grasping at straws, counselor. You and I both know I did not engage in witness tampering." She smiled up at him, clutching the envelope to her chest. "If you want the fine, then no probation."

"Six months probation and a fine, and that's the best I can do," he said. "And don't think I won't be watching you all the more closely next time we face off in court, Ms. Sinclair." Edward huffed out an angry sigh, irritated that he'd let a sure-thing case slip through his fingers. "Take the deal, you're not going to get a better one. Your client is in dire straits. Neither of us wants this to continue in court."

"Deal," she agreed, extending her hand to shake his. "We're ready to sign." She shuffled through her folders, locating the one with the green tab poking out of the side where Ella had placed it. "Fortunately, I already have it drawn up."

Ed narrowed his eyes. "Oh yes, fortunate," he deadpanned. "What a completely unforeseen scenario." He took a pen from his inside pocket, signing each page and dating it after he skimmed through the wording. "Tell your client to keep his nose clean or we'll be back in this courtroom in six months, and next time I'll make sure that he does time."

"Pleasure doing business with you," Sadie said, leaning back in her chair. "Anything good coming up next on your docket?"

"Why, so you can undermine that case, too?" he retorted. "All you shadows-damned ambulance chasers—"

Sadie interrupted him with a theatrical gasp. "Mr. Link!" she protested, folding her hands atop the table. "I've never once chased an ambulance, nor do I make it my business to scrape cases off the public defender's floor. Working on contingency certainly won't pay the rent, now will it?"

She crossed one leg over the other, sliding the contract to her client along with the pen, already bleeding black ink into the margins of the first page. "We are supposed to be professional peers, not adversaries. After all, we all have to attend the same dry galas, don't we?"

"I happen to enjoy the galas," he said politely, taking the signed contract from her client and closing it into a folder. "As does my wife. It's an opportunity for the women to get out of the house and get gussied up." He shifted, staring a little too hard. "Perhaps I will see you there, if you aren't busy undermining more of my witness prep."

"I'll try to make time for it," Sadie said easily, ignoring the latter half of his statement. "Judge Haber, I think the defense and the prosecution have reached an agreement," she said, standing again. "I believe Mr. Link has the completed contract."

"Excellent," the judge said, taking the folder from Ed. He settled a pair of wire-frame glasses on his nose, reading over the contracts and nodding. "This all looks appropriate," he said, signing his name on the final page. "Ms. Sinclair, your client is free to go, but will need to stop at the probation office on the way out of the building."

"Thank you, Your Honor," Sadie said politely. The jury began to shuffle out, grumbling to one another no doubt about their wasted time and Sadie couldn't blame them. She hated her time to be wasted, too. "Mr. Pender, you will need to be assigned a parole officer, do you understand?"

Her client nodded, wringing his hands in his lap.

"My payment terms are thirty days," she reminded him. "And you will need to pay the court's fine, there's no getting around that." She nodded towards the door, and he silently followed her instruction, disappearing through the doors along with the rest of the jury.

Sadie turned in her chair, leaning over the divider that separated the attorney desks from the court gallery. "Nice timing," she whispered to Ella. "I wondered for a moment if you'd forgotten."

"Who, me?" Ella asked, batting her eyelashes. "Never."

"That last-minute evidence tactic is going to run out of steam now, at least with Ed Link. That man is out to get me. He hates me."

Ella shrugged, playing with the pearl stud in her ear, dainty and polite in its size. "He only hates you because you beat him." She crossed her legs, showing off shapely calves and a pair of blue t-strap heels that matched her dress. "And if that's the problem, I imagine most of the state's attorney's office hates you."

"Yes, it makes these galas rather uncomfortable." Sadie cast a sideways glance at Ella, wondering if it was worth roping her into it. If nothing else, she'd look amazing, just as she always did. "You wouldn't want to come with me, would you?" she offered, looking back towards the door to make sure her client didn't pass up the probation office on his way out. She'd almost been surprised he'd shown up to the court date at all. He'd made it clear that he preferred the idea of following his ex-friend out of the country to exile, but she'd convinced him to stay and clear his name.

"Oh, I can't," Ella apologized, biting her lip. "Ray is taking me to The Saffron Rose tonight."

"Of course," Sadie said, waving her away while internally roiling with poisonous envy. "I forgot. Your anniversary, right?"

Ella nodded. "One year this weekend!" She smoothed her skirt, plucking an errant thread from the hem. "You have that meeting tomorrow," she said, leaning in close. "Astrid Frost."

Sadie stifled a noise of irritation, aware that Ed was still watching her. "My favorite client," she said. "Her account pays the bills, I'm afraid, but it makes up for her perfectly repulsive attitude." She cleared her throat, watching Ed cross the courtroom once more. "What was it she wanted, again?"

"She thinks she has a squealer in her club."

"I can't imagine why she might require my services, then. Ella, do me a favor, call her when you're back at the office, and tell her to call Ms. Vane for this."

Ella nodded, standing up from the worn wooden bench. "Of course." She laid a hand on top of Sadie's, smiling. "I'm awfully sorry I can't come tonight. I hope it's not too terrible on your own."

"I will likely survive it," Sadie said, feeling like she should wave her off, but being completely unable to move her hand from where it was under Ella's. "It serves me right for being so perilously single all the time."

"Oh, Sadie," Ella sighed. "You'll meet that special guy soon enough, I just know it."

"Perhaps," Sadie said, staring, and she was distracted just long enough for Ed Link to snatch the empty envelope from her table. "Excuse me, Ed," she said, standing to snatch it back, "that's confidential."

"Oh really?" he said, holding it out of her reach, utilizing his tall, wiry frame to his advantage. "Something from my own investigation is confidential?"

"My case strategy certainly is," she said. "If you wanted

to know what additional evidence I had, you should have pressed the issue before we signed a deal." She stood, aiming to match his height but falling short by about six inches. She reached for it, breath constricted in her chest, but he stepped backward, pulling at the lip of the envelope.

He held it upside-down and took the page, reading it with bewilderment. Ed looked back at her, fury collecting in the shallow lines on his face. "How did you get this?" he whispered, and the softness of the realization was far more threatening than any raised voice would have been. "You used pitted evidence?" Ed asked, still staring at the envelope. "How many times have you gotten your hands on something like this?" he demanded. "Who do you know in the state's attorney's office?"

"Ed, you and I both know that this never should have happened," Sadie said carefully. She took the envelope, slid it between her other files, and handed it to Ella over the barrier. "Do you mind taking these back to the office?" she asked.

"Of course," Ella said, keeping things short and sweet because she wasn't just one of the most beautiful women in Verdance, she was whip-smart and had saved cases more times than Sadie could count. Before Ed knew what was happening, Ella was out of the courtroom and rushing to flag down a cab from the front of the building.

"I'm taking this to Judge Haber," Ed declared, crowing it loudly, full-voiced as if he had a leg to stand on. "You manipulated this trial, Sadie. That would never have been allowed into evidence."

"Please, I encourage you to take this to him," Sadie replied easily, leaning back against the barrier because it was easier than staring up at Ed's narrow face, cheeks red and blotchy from the barely contained rage. She smiled at him, being sure to show all of her teeth. She'd had the second set of canines filed down years back, but the slight point was sometimes enough to cow people who weren't observant enough to realize why she was as unsettling as she was. "I'm sure the judge would love to hear about how you didn't do your due diligence before presenting a plea bargain."

"You should be disbarred," he growled. "You're an embarrassment to the law."

Sadie straightened herself to her full height, albeit petite in stature. "Mr. Link, I have done nothing that would merit being disbarred. I received new evidence that may or may not have been admitted into the trial, but before you could ascertain the veracity of the documents, you panicked." She tilted her chin upwards, glancing at the mirror just at the edge of her periphery. "You may want to discern why it is that you felt like that was the best option." Standing with every ounce of her tarnished regal expectations, she adjusted the placement of the briefcase handle in her grip. "I hope to see you at the gala later."

Preview for Canon in Death (The Vane Dossier: exhibit C)

A surprisingly crisp breeze rattled the wood blinds and ruffled the loose papers on the desk. Summer would soon begin to fade, leaving the city to slide into winter, one progressively dark morning at a time.

"Virginia, did you hear me?"

"I heard you, Shirin."

"You don't look like you're paying attention."

"I've been pulling all-nighters chasing down leads for you. It's not my fault that I'm half-dead after almost a month of this." Virginia sat upright in the chair, the legs creaking from the motion. "Where did it happen?"

Shirin's mouth pressed into a thin line. "Docks."

"I thought you had surveillance down there."

"Yes, well, I can't control how well the police department does it's job."

Virginia huffed out a sardonic laugh. "That didn't take long, did it? Barely four weeks in the job and you're already blaming problems on your ex-department."

"You signed a contract to —"

"Yeah, yeah, you don't have to remind me. I'm more than aware of the deal I made with the devil."

"We're a federal agency, Virginia, trying to get scum off

the streets," Shirin chided. She already sounded like a fed. But then, maybe she'd always sounded like one, righteous and holier than thou with her incorruptible mortal fortitude. She pressed her meaty forearms into the desk, raising one dark, full eyebrow. "And here I thought you'd find a serial killer more interesting than chasing down mid-level Nether dealers."

"It's all the same to me, one way or another," Virginia lied. There was something about this killer, these cases that felt different. The unsolved mystery sat heavy in her gut, the same way that Juliette had. "What happened down at the docks?"

"Do you remember Frankie Fiske?"

"My fractured eye socket certainly does."

"After he disappeared, there was a void of power. Several of the crews were scattered, there was that whole mess with Astrid—" Shirin stopped short, glaring. "She managed to get herself out of trouble again, thanks to that lawyer of hers, and someone new moved in. We don't know much about him other than the fact that he's been running that heavy Nether out of the docks for almost six months or so."

"Why didn't VCPD scoop him up earlier?"

"Never enough evidence. He's smart."

"Not smart enough." Virginia drummed her fingers against the arms of the unupholstered chair. "You sure it wasn't a rival crew? Someone ready to get back into the game here, looking to level the playing field?"

"Local PD says there are certain abnormalities in the scene."

Virginia huffed out a beleaguered sigh. "Once more, into the breach."

"Are you ready to head out?"

"No. I'll take my own vehicle, thank you."

Shirin's glare softened over the desk, but only slightly. "You don't have to keep avoiding me at all costs, Virginia. I'm not your superior, you're a contractor."

"Yeah, an indentured one." Virginia threw open the office door, rattling the glass in its pane. She'd made the deal with a full understanding of what it would mean, but that didn't make the taste of it go down any easier. "Where at the docks? I'll meet you there."

"I would rather you followed me."

"I'm sure you would."

"It's easier for scene protocol if—"

Virginia started down the stairs, worn wooden steps firm under each step. It was a newer building, and recently refurbished. President Ariano was already bending to pressures about law and order in the country. "Shirin, I'll meet you there. I need to get gas and coffee, I'll be five minutes behind you."

"We have coffee here, you know."

"Yeah, and it tastes like the ashes of every dream that died in here." Virginia continued down the stairs, hitting the landing with loud thud that echoed down into the marble reception area. "Where, Shirin?"

"If you're going to behave like this, then you can address me as Agent Lindell," she retorted, standing at the top of the stairs with her arms folded. "I insist you ride in my vehicle, as that will be easiest for site access and protocol. If I start allowing civilian vehicles on site, then who knows what the press could pick up from a lousy punt in the dark."

"Press won't clock anything, not when the last two were

down state.”

“Virginia, I insist—”

“Alright, alright!” Virginia hissed. “Shadows fucked, woman, isn’t there any other agent they could put me with?”

“I requested to be your liaison.”

“Perfect.” Virginia let Shirin pass her on the stairs, and fell into line behind her, resisting the temptation to allow a growl to escape her throat. She didn’t say a single word until they were in Shirin’s unmarked federal vehicle, black and shined to perfection. “Looks like the budget for transportation got a bump this year.”

“Some of us prefer to keep our spaces tidy.”

“You could be in a competition with Seamus, he’s almost worse than you.” Virginia slumped back in the seat, staring out the window at a freedom she’d probably never taste again. “I need to go to my own office later,” she stated. “I have work to do that is outside of federal jurisdiction, if you haven’t recalled.”

“We’ll see how long this takes,” Shirin answered.

“I’m going regardless. You can’t keep me hostage, I’m not a—”

“Virginia,” Shirin said, weariness dragging at her voice, “you are not a prisoner, nor a hostage, nor an indentured servant. You are a contractor to the federal government, with certain expectations and responsibilities that you agreed to in order to keep that girl off the registry. As we discussed before, multiple times, that was your choice.”

“Not much of a choice though, was it?” Virginia asked. She hadn’t been sleeping well, and the lack of rest was beginning to eat at her sanity. “Sometimes I wonder if you knew all along what I was, and used Jolie to entrap me into doing your bidding anyway."

"I had no idea what you are." Shirin took a breath as though she were about to launch into another lecture, but swallowed the sharp intake of air instead. "You could have told me, though."

"I'd have wound up in exactly the same position."

Shirin didn't say anything after that, driving them both to the riverside docks in silence, even as they approached the scene, laden with police tape and reporters held off by a desperate sergeant.

"No, no!" he shouted. "Absolutely no access, I've told you all before. This is an ongoing investigation, and you, Mr. Jones, are starting to tap dance on my very last nerve."

One of the reporters at the front tipped his wire-rimmed glasses down over his nose, notepad held aloft. "The people of this city have a right to know what's going on, Sergeant. The Verdance City Police Department cannot continue to obfuscate the truth of the matter."

"You'll know the truth when we're damned well ready to tell it!" the sergeant shot back. "Now, get off my scene, until—oh, hello, Agent Lindell!" he mopped his face with a handkerchief, seeming relieved that he was about to get some backup. "Thank you for coming down, if you'll just head past the—"

"Federal agent?" Mr. Jones interrupted. "Is this a federal issue, Sergeant Thomas?"

"I believe you were invited to leave," Shirin said coldly, staring the reporter down. "You will know what we know, when we know it, at the press conference tomorrow afternoon." She continued to glare at him until he started to lose his resolve, crumbling beneath her influence. "Any leaks at this time would jeopardize finding justice for the victim and his family. Do you want to explain to his mother that the killer got away with it due to an issue of jury influence from the press?"

"No," Mr. Jones admitted through gritted teeth.

"Then I'm sure I will see you at tomorrow's press conference."

"Will you release the name of the victim and a list of suspects?"

Shirin stepped closer to him and he staggered backwards. "That is up to the VCPD."

The members of the press grumbled, but began to dissipate when they realized they wouldn't be getting any more information. "Where is the sheriff?" she asked the sergeant. "I can't believe he's not here to contain the scene."

"He's in there already," the sergeant replied. "Waiting on you, as it were." The last words were delivered with a slight steely edge. "I didn't realize that the federal agency took so long to attend the scene of a likely serial killer."

"Our contractors aren't as efficient as we are," Shirin replied without skipping a beat.

"Thanks," Virginia retorted, rolling her eyes. "Real nice, *Agent* Lindell." She stalked past both of them and under the police tape, following the trail of mud that dragged through the half-dead grass towards one of the warehouses. In fact, it was the same one she'd been convinced Jolie was being held in the previous winter.

"Vane," Arthur said, stumbling over her name as though he hadn't known it most of both of their lives. He'd been trying to stray from calling her by her childhood nickname once he knew why it bothered her so much. It was hard to hear it and not think of Juliette saying it, instead. "I'm glad you're here." He glanced around, brow furrowed. "Where's our friend?"

"Lindell is outside, arguing with your sergeant. New promotion?"

"It's been chaos since she left with no notice."

"Still thinking of Kang for her old position?"

He nodded. "I am."

"Good. Kang is a solid choice, he won't let you down." Virginia entered the warehouse, taking in the sight of it all. "It's not the serial killer," she said.

"Commissioner thought it would be best to investigate—"

"Because the commissioner has air between his ears," Virginia interrupted. "Come on, Arthur, you know this is a hit."

A current or possibly previous member of the Krakens sat hunched over a table, numbers scrawled across his face in black marker. Fourteen, thirty-eight, twelve. His tattoo had been carved out of his skin, but not entirely. The tips of two tentacles remained in his forearm, obscured by thick, arterial blood that had spilled over them an onto the ground, soaking into fissures between slabs of concrete.

"The imprecise nature of this doesn't seem like our guy," Virginia said, pointing. "It's a hit from someone he royally pissed off."

"And the numbers?" Arthur prompted.

She shook her head. "Not sure. A combination, maybe?"

"No locks on the premises, but that was my first thought, too." Arthur rubbed his head, the same way he always did when he was worried about a case. His dark, bare skin shone in glare that came from the sole window on the second floor.

"We found some of that heavy Nether in a cache under the floor. The hatch is in back."

Virginia nodded. "I always knew there was something fishy about this place. Did he buy it after Fiske disappeared?"

They both knew he was dead, but it was easier to pretend they didn't. Less paperwork.

"Records office says someone did. Not sure yet if it was him.I don"

"He wasn't one of Fiske's, though." Virginia gestured at the tattoo. "My guess is an old affiliate, that's why they took the ink."

"Can you back all of that up with some sight?" Shirin asked loudly, practically dragging a rookie cop behind her. "Found this one straggling at the edge of the cordon. Thought you might want to give him a talking to."

Arthur blinked, and then sighed. "Officer Abraham, you can head back to the precinct. We'll talk there."

"I'm s-sorry, Sheriff," the young man stammered. "I was checking to make sure the press had l-left the premises, and—"

"It's alright, Officer," Arthur replied with a sigh. "You're dismissed."

"So," Shirin continued, leaning against a wooden support beam. "What do you think then, Virginia?"

"I think that this is no concern of the federal government," Virginia replied. "There seems to have been some Nether distribution, but not enough to merit a terrorism charge, and if you couldn't tell, your main suspect there is dead."

"A vision wouldn't hurt, just to put this all to bed." Shirin waited, a cat-like grin on her face. "Go on, then, see what you can see."

"Fine." Virginia hadn't mastered the art of sight yet, still only seeing inarticulate flashes that sometimes didn't amount to very much. Still, once or twice they'd led to a clue, so her servitude endured.

She should be grateful, really. Without sight, she wouldn't have had any bargaining chips to keep Jolie safe from conscription.

Approaching the body, Virginia breathed deeply, urging her senses to calm. They never did, not really, but it was worth a try regardless.

She brushed against the table, the half-empty bottle of whiskey that sat beside him, and the chair. "Nothing," she reported. He had a neat exit wound at his temple. "If he didn't see it coming, there might not have been much to see from his perspective."

"Coroner says the tattoo may have been taken postmortem," Arthur confirmed.

Virginia brushed against the body, flinching from what there could have been, but there was once again nothing to be seen. "Our serial killer doesn't seem to have that kind of restraint. Whoever did this still had a sense of respect for the victim."

"I don't know a single person who'd have respect for a Nether dealer," a man said from the doorway, dressed to the nines in a pinstriped suit. "You're in my building," he said. "And I am formally asking you to leave."

About the Author

Ryann Fletcher is a writer who lives in Glasgow with too many books and craft supplies. She writes science fiction and fantasy novels because real life is boring without spaceships and magic. She loves to cook and go for long hikes in the wilderness, searching for the meaning of life and probably the keys she lost three days ago.

You can connect with me on:

- https://ryannfletcher.com
- https://facebook.com/RyannFletcherWrites
- https://instagram.com/RyannFletcherWrites
- https://www.tiktok.com/@ryannfletcherwrites
- https://patreon.com/RyannFletcherWrites

Subscribe to my newsletter:

- https://linktr.ee/ryannfletcherwrites

Also by Ryann Fletcher

Books and Bloodlust: read FREE on Patreon

https://www.patreon.com/RyannFletcherWrites

Zinnia Mezzasalma has been searching for a cure for her vampirism for over three centuries, and across two continents. After all, to die as a vampire would mean to lose her soul forever.

When a mysterious Verdance City aristocrat snakes her way into Zin's business, she's left wondering if it was wise to isolate herself from mythic politics.

Will this librarian find the cure she seeks?

Exiled Advocate: Sadie Sinclair, book 1
When Astrid, notorious club owner, siren, and Sadie Sinclair's premier client is targeted, this half-Fae lawyer has more questions than answers.

How to navigate a legal system which is increasingly weaponized? When laws designed to protect become tools to entrap, can any mythic obtain justice? What to do when "Human Rights" no longer apply?

Only one fact is clear. Being different has never been more dangerous.

Canon in Death (The Vane Dossier, exhibit C)
https://books2read.com/CanonInDeath
Virginia's work is feast or famine in Verdance, and with four open cases and counting, she has almost more than she can handle.

A kidnapping with no leads. A serial killer who's still on the loose. Crews that are fighting for control of the Nether trade. Now that she's agreed to work for the Federal Agency for Freedom, she's in even more danger than ever - and so is everyone around her.

www.ingramcontent.com/pod-product-compliance
Lightning Source LLC
Chambersburg PA
CBHW031731180726
48283CB00005B/1459